CASIDDIE WILLIAMS

The Rescuer's Heart

When you're in the dark, just remember, the sun will be on the horizon soon. All in due time.
~Justin "Danger" Finkle

Contents

Foreword

In loving memory of Justin D. Finkle 4/19/78-6/23/14

When I was writing Annie's book and there was a need for a "helper" the first name that came to mind was Justin. Justin was a former boyfriend of mine who served on his local Fire Department and Rescue Squads for over two decades of his life and was also a 911 dispatcher.

As a child, they always tell you in a traumatic situation to "look for the helpers." It felt natural to commemorate his memory as a helper for Annie. As her story went on (I'm a pantser and never know where my characters will take me) Justin appeared for a second time. Then, a third and forth, and by the end of the book, he demanded to tell a story.

With the permission of Justin's family, I used his name as the main male character in this book. None of the events in these pages depict his life. However, the emotions behind his character and Nicole's, the main female lead, are my feelings towards many of the events that happened within our relationship and his life.

Justin dedicated his life to helping others. Through all of his volunteer work and his full-time job, he found his happiness. He struggled daily with migraines, OCD, and PTSD from hearing the fire fighters on 9/11 talk on the radios, while attempting to rescue people…and then the silence when the towers fell.

While my Justin could not overcome his demons, and at the age of 36, took his own life, this fictional Justin and his love interest, Nicole, do get their happily ever after.

You matter and YOU ARE ENOUGH!

Preface

CONTENT WARNING:

Thank you so much for picking up The Rescuer's Heart. I am so honored that you have chosen this contemporary romance as your next read. However, I want to make you aware of a few triggers and heavy topics that run through this book before you dive in.

This is an 18+ contemporary romance. These characters go through a traumatic emotional journey together including dealing with mental health issues, a suicide attempt and character death. This novel in no part is a guide on how you should take care of your mental and physical health. How the characters deal with mental health/trauma in this book may differ from how you or someone you know has dealt with the same trauma.

YOUR MENTAL HEALTH MATTERS and this novel is not here to lessen that fact. I hope you enjoy reading The Rescuer's Heart and the journey they take towards healing.

TW: Pregnancy, attempted suicide, minor child neglect, on

page child death, cockwarning, somnophilia, spanking.

Substance Abuse and Mental Health Services: SAMHSA
(800)662-4357

Acknowledgement

All the love to all my bestest people goes here!

This section feels more challenging to write with every book. The people who take their time to work on each book with me become a piece of my heart with every published work. When I cry, they cry. When I stress over a character, they do.

K. K. Moore and author N. Slater are my ride-or-die, or more like type and cry. I can't thank either of you enough for everything you have done, do daily, and will do in the future for me. I love you to pieces.

My Beta and ARC readers also hold a special place in my heart for giving me their honest thoughts and opinions and making my books better! Thank you!!!

1

Justin

She just slapped me. She threw a cup of water in my face and slapped me. And then...*and fucking then,* she kissed me. The slap I expected. I've seen several people meet the same fate tonight. But that kiss. Fuck. Nicole is already a beautiful woman, which is almost weird to say because she looks like her brother, Cole, with big tits, a petite frame, and long hair.

I had plans today to have coffee with BlakeLynn and catch up with her, but she invited me to Midnight Moonshine, a country line dancing bar, with her boyfriend, Cole, and Cole's sister, Nicole. I'm not typically a social person outside my inner circle. I appreciate my downtime from the hectic life of being a paramedic in a big city like Chicago, but Blake has wiggled her way into my heart, and I find saying no to her very difficult. Besides, I know the hardship they're going through and how a simple night out can be good for anyone's spirit.

I wasn't expecting Cole's sister to be so... her. Nicole is gorgeous in the girl next door way that she has no idea about.

Her eyes are the color of a tropical ocean, crystal clear blue on a cloudless day. It was the first thing I noticed when I went to Blake and Cole's house to prepare for our night out. Well, that and the lack of clothes she was wearing. Tiny red shorts framed her long legs, and a band-printed crop top left little to the imagination. Her sandy blonde curls made my hands ache to be wrapped around them.

When she asked me to help her up onto the bar top, my hands had no choice but to wrap around her bare waist. Her skin was silky and warm from the dancing and drinking we'd already done tonight. And when she leaned down and kissed me after the slap, I restrained myself from touching her. I knew I'd be carrying her out of here over my shoulder if I started.

Nicole slides off the bar in front of me and firmly pokes me in the chest.

"That was fucking hot. Raincheck for later." That wasn't a question. That was a promise. She grabs Blake's hand, and they head off to the bathroom. What a pair the two of them make as they walk away. Two beautiful women in contrast with each other. Nicole is sandy blonde with blue eyes, and BlakeLynn is dark brown with honey-brown eyes.

Cole tries to apologize for his sister's behavior, blaming it on her drunkenness, but my mind is still on the fact that she thought that kiss was as fucking hot as I did.

"It's all good. She doesn't scare me." He arches a brow and shakes his head.

"Famous last words." Blake and Nicole come bouncing back from the bathroom a few minutes later ready to go home. Knowing the girls were planning to drink heavily tonight, Cole and I made arrangements for me to crash with

Nicole at her apartment in his old bedroom. We wanted to make sure the girls had a good night at the club and a safe evening at home after.

"Hey, Justin." Nicole's voice is sing-songy as we take our rideshare back to her apartment, the last few shots taking their toll on her.

"Hey." She twists her body to face me and cuddles into the seat.

"I have dogs. Do you like dogs? They're little sausage dogs. Java and Beans. Like coffee. I like coffee."

"I like dogs, and I like coffee, too. Maybe we can get you some coffee and water before you go to sleep tonight? It might help you feel better in the morning." She reaches over, runs her hand up and down my forearm, and hums. The electricity that radiates from her touch shoots straight to my cock. This woman is going to be trouble.

"Coffee sounds good. I like it iced, with flavoring. Pumpkin flavoring. And spices." She flings her arm and flops back against the seat, huffing. "I like iced pumpkin spice lattes. I'm a basic white bitch." I hear our driver stifle a laugh, and I cover my mouth to hide my own amusement.

"There's nothing wrong with what you like, and it doesn't make you a basic white bitch." She rolls in her seat until she's facing me again.

"Do you know you're beautiful, Justin?"

"I think you must be looking in a mirror, Nicole." Her face lights up.

"You think I'm pretty?" I can't help myself. I move a curl out of her face and tuck it behind her ear, momentarily getting lost in her ocean-blue eyes.

"I didn't say pretty. I said beautiful." She grabs the collar of

3

my shirt and pulls me in for a searing kiss. No one is around this time but the driver, and I give in to my temptations. My hand slides up her neck and dives into her thick curls. They're as soft as I expected, and when I get lost in the kiss, my fist closes a little tighter than I planned, and Nicole pulls away.

"Excuse me, mister. Are you trying to get rough with me in the back seat of our rideshare? Our driver isn't paying us for a show." Is she taunting me? I'm having trouble concentrating on her words when all I want is to suck her pouty lip into my mouth.

"I-I-I don't mind." This poor young twenty-something kid is going to get more than he bargained for if I don't calm Nicole and myself down.

"Okay, Pumpkin. Maybe we should keep our hands to ourselves." She pouts, rubbing my chest, and I adjust in my seat, trying to make room in my pants for my expanding cock. She needs to stop touching me. She's wearing down my resolve with every passing minute.

"Where's the fun in that? You're so pretty to look at…" Her hand trails down the front of my shirt, and just when I'm about to stop her, she lifts the hem of my green button-up and brushes her fingers over my stomach. "And touch." Such a little vixen.

I hold back a moan. It's been far too long since a woman has touched me. As embarrassing as that is to admit, I wasn't kidding about enjoying my solitude. It's helpful that my work partner, Spencer, doesn't require a lot of talking. We work well together in the field and have developed a nonverbal language all of our own. Being a paramedic only requires minimal socialization outside of an emergency situation.

"Nicole, you've been drinking. Let's just get you home and get some food and coffee in you." Her hand wanders farther up my bare chest, brushing through my chest hair. I close my eyes, trying not to look at the heat in hers. My dick continues to grow in my pants from her simple touches.

A throat clears from the front seat, and I catch the driver's sheepish stare in the rearview.

"Sorry to interrupt. We're here." Nicole's hand disappears like it was never there.

"Yay! Home." She claps her hands, and it's so fucking adorable.

"Thanks, man. I'll give you five stars." He nods his thanks, and Nicole gets out. I slide across the seat and follow behind her.

"Home sweet home." She sweeps her hands in the air, motioning towards the generic-looking apartment building. It's a five-story rundown brick structure with balconies.

"Is there an elevator?" I'm not opposed to walking up stairs, but the tipsy beauty in heels standing next to me seems like a disaster waiting to happen. I'm off work tonight, and I'd like to keep it that way.

"Of course there is." She plants both hands on her hips and juts one out. She scowls at me, and even that is adorable. But it doesn't last long when she perks up remembering something. "Oh, we're gonna have to take the doggos out when we get up there. They have tiny bladders. Will you help?" She bats her eyelashes at me like a cartoon character, and I laugh at her ridiculousness.

"You don't even have to ask, Pumpkin."

"Pump-kin. Puuuumpkin. Pum-p-kin. I like it."

"I'm glad you do. Ladies first." I gesture towards the front doors of the building. She hooks her elbow in mine and leads the way.

The building does in fact have an elevator. She lives on the third floor, and I'm not sure how much higher the rickety old thing would have gone. The numbers are mostly worn off of the buttons, and it doesn't smell the greatest.

We step off, and she leads us to the left, following the worn burgundy carpet down the hall. She stops at an ugly green-painted door with a number three and a crooked D above a peephole.

"It's not fancy, but it's home." I hand her the keys from my pocket. She had given them to me before we left for the club, stating they didn't go with her outfit. When she opens the door, the smell of something enticing that I can't quite place hits my senses.

"Hi, babies. Mommy is home." I hear the sound of panting and low whining from further inside the apartment. The inside looks exactly as I would expect from the rest of the building, but you can tell Nicole has done a great job making it her home. "They like to jump. Don't acknowledge them until we get outside, or they'll piddle on the floor. They have excited bladders."

"They do what? What was that word you used?" She cocks her head to the side, digesting my question.

"Um, piddle? It means peeing, but only a little. Piddle. But seriously, wait here, then follow me back downstairs and ignore them."

"Alright. I'll follow your lead." She closes the door behind us, and I wait as she walks in to get the dogs. Moments later, two of the most adorable creatures I've ever seen come charging toward me.

6

"The little white one with the red spots is Java, and Beans is the multi-colored brown one. Will you hand me their leashes behind you?" I hand her the pink retractable leashes, and she clips them to their collars and hands me Java's leash.

They do their business quickly outside, and I finally get to love on them.

"Aren't they the cutest? I love them so much. Even on the toughest days, they can cheer me up." Hard days. I know those all too well.

"Are you ready for some coffee and food?" She's sobered some, but I know if she doesn't hydrate and get some food in her stomach, she's going to feel terrible in the morning.

"I'm ready for *something*." She steps close to me and places her hand on my chest. "I'd really like to cash in on that raincheck." By the look in her eyes, she definitely wants more than just another kiss.

Can I do this? I mean, I *can*, but can I? It's hard for me to develop relationships in my line of work. I always see people at their worst. I'm not saying this is going to lead to a relationship, but a night of fun, meaningless sex isn't something that I ever do.

"Nicole." She steps closer to me.

"Don't say no. You're hot. I'm hot. Let's go have hot sex together. 1+1=2. That's how that works, right?" How can I argue with that logic? I brush my lips against hers, and she fists her hand in my shirt, pulling me closer. Her lips are soft and plush, and as I move my arm to wrap it around her back, I feel resistance.

"Shit. Java." I forgot the leash was around my wrist. "Let's go inside." She takes my non-leashed hand and leads me back upstairs.

Once inside, I finally get a full look at her apartment. Her style is eclectic but minimal. A black leather couch with several colorful throw pillows and an old trunk for a coffee table make up most of the living room. The TV stand looks like an old dresser painted with flowers and butterflies.

I hear the sound of metal and turn to see her scooping food into the dog food bowls. The kitchen is your standard small apartment kitchen with dachshunds everywhere you look. The potholders, tea towels, and what looks like a cookie jar all have dachshunds of every size and color.

"You like your dogs, don't you?"

"They are the best breed ever." She squats down to rub their heads while they eat, then looks up at me, and smiles. I have to look away because seeing her in that position has my cock stirring again. She stands and closes a gate, locking the dogs in the kitchen area. "Now we won't be bothered."

Nicole pushes on my chest until I step back. She continues to do it until the back of my legs hit the couch. One more push, and I fall back onto the cushions. By the look on her face, she has me right where she wants me, and if I'm honest with myself, I'm right where I want to be, too.

2

Nicole

Justin is hot in the nerdy way that screams he's a freak in bed. He's taller than me by at least six inches, even in my heels. His wire-framed glasses sit on a nose so straight, it's obvious it's never seen a fight. And his goatee. I'm not usually attracted to men with facial hair, but all I can imagine is how I want it to scratch me in places I probably shouldn't be thinking about. His face is serious, but his hazel eyes give away his humor. I have no idea what came over me at Midnight Moonshine that made me kiss him, but I'm not regretting it one bit.

He seems a little shy, but I saw the fire in his eyes when he pulled away from our kiss outside. He wants me, but he's battling with himself. Well, my sweet paramedic boy, you're winning this war with me as your prize.

I push him down onto the couch and take a moment to stare into his eyes.

"How badly do you need these?" I tap my fingers on the side of his glasses, and he takes them off, handing them to me. I place them on the side table and smile at my new view.

He took them off for the Kickin' Cowboy shots tonight, but I didn't get to appreciate him there.

Grabbing the hem of my crop top, I lift it over my head and toss it to the side. I notice his breathing increase by the rising and falling of his chest. My hands dip to my shorts to remove them, and he stops me, holding his hands over mine.

"May I?" I smile and pull back, giving him full access. The button pops open, and my breath hitches as his fingers run along the top of my shorts. Torturously slow, he unzips my red daisy dukes. With a little tug, they fall to the floor. His eyes wander over my body, taking in my baby blue bra and thong set.

Justin makes a circular motion in the air with his finger, asking me to spin for him. I hold in a smile, knowing he's about to everything my thong doesn't cover. I hear his growl before he palms my cheeks like basketballs. Nice to see he's coming out of his shell.

"Your ass is incredible, Nicole." I look over my shoulder at him and pout. His brows furrow. "What's wrong?"

"I like Pumpkin." He huffs a laugh and kneads his fingers into my skin.

"Your ass is incredible, *Pumpkin*." I wiggle said ass in appreciation, and I feel a stinging sensation on my left cheek.

"Did you just...bite me?" I spin, leaving his hands dangling in the air, and straddle his lap. Grabbing his wrists, I push them down to the couch. His eyes look apologetic, and I tilt his chin up to look at me. "Don't do that." He moves his hands to my waist.

"I'm sorry. I got carried away." He really is shy, and it's adorable.

"Justin, it surprised me. You've been very timid."

"If only you could see in my mind." He closes his eyes, not believing he just said that out loud. We all drank tonight. Blake and me more than the guys, but that doesn't mean he still isn't affected by the alcohol.

"I'm a big girl, Justin. You don't need to worry about me. I can take a lot." I bend forward into his ear. "And I like a lot." His hips flex under me, and I smile. "Would it make you more comfortable if we had a safeword?"

"Do you...normally use a safeword?" *Fuck.* I'm either going to bring this man out of his shell or ruin him. Either way, it's going to be enjoyable.

"Justin, I'm pretty adventurous when it comes to sex. I like sex, and I like you. I want to make tonight fun." I unbutton the top of his green dress shirt and look into his eyes for any apprehension. All I see is heat. "I want you to feel comfortable." *Pop.* "If having a safeword helps you..." *Pop.* "Then let's have one. Because your teeth on my ass, needs to be repeated." I undo the last two buttons and push his shirt open. His chest heaves, and his hands flex on my hips. I lean down and lick the shell of his ear. "Give me a safeword, Justin, but I promise you I won't use it."

He turns his head and slams his lips into mine. Strong arms wrap around my back, fusing our bodies together. I moan into his mouth when he nips my bottom lip, and I run my hands along the sides of his shaved head, deepening the kiss.

"Banana." The word brushes over my lips.

"What?" Did he say banana?

"Our safeword is banana." I can't contain my laughter. It's such a fun, innocent word. I throw my head back at the thought of using the word banana during sex, and Justin

11

takes the opportunity to run his fingers across the exposed swells of my breasts. They're gentle and exploratory, and as much as I enjoy being rough and manhandled, this is just as seductive.

Justin's touch grazes my breasts, my collarbone, down my arms, and he locks our fingers together, kissing my knuckles one by one. We haven't even done anything yet, and this already feels like more than just a meaningless fuck.

"Take me to your bedroom, Pumpkin. I want to worship you." Holy shit. I almost want to tell him banana. I'm not the type of girl that gets worshiped. I'm the girl you screw on the bathroom sink in a bar. Not because I enjoy one night stands, but I just don't like commitment. There are too many rules and feelings, and I just like to have fun and get my rocks off.

He must see my apprehension because he grabs my cheeks and looks into my eyes.

"The safeword is for both of us. Something just changed, and I don't want you to feel uncomfortable. We can stay out here." I cup my hands over his.

"Justin, you're such a fucking enigma. I want to throw you down on this couch and fuck your brains out, but I also want to burrito us in a plethora of blankets and cuddle. How can you make me feel both of those things at once?"

"When you figure out the answer to that question, let me know because I'm feeling the exact same way." I grab his wrists and bring his hands down to my breasts.

"There's a way we can have both." I reach behind me and unclip my bra, pulling it out from under his hands so he's touching my bare breasts. His hands move to brush his thumbs over my nipples, and I moan. My hips move of their own accord, and I hear him curse under his breath.

12

Justin leans forward and brings one of my nipples into his mouth, swirling his tongue around the peaking bud. I arch back, resting my hands on his knees so he has full access to my chest while I ride him over his jeans.

"God, yes. Harder. You don't have to be soft with me." He nipped my nipple, but I want him to bite it. "Yes. Just like that." He bites harder and eases it with a gentle tongue. It's good to know he takes instructions well.

"Pumpkin, you have to stop grinding on my cock. It feels too fucking good. Let me make you feel good. Lay down." Mmm. I like where this is going. I give him a reprieve and sit forward, taking his lips again. His tongue dips and twists against mine, and I can't wait to feel what he can do with it.

His hands encircle my hips, and he moves me to sit on the couch next to him. A firm hand spreads across the middle of my chest as he pushes me back onto the throw pillows. There's fire in his eyes as his thumbs hook into my thong and slowly glide it down my legs.

"Spread for me." Gladly. Maybe he's not so shy after all. I bring my knees up and let them fall open. His hands roam up and down my inner thighs, making me squirm. Just a few more inches, and he'd be touching me where I want him, but I can tell he's enjoying teasing me. Maybe he's just playing coy?

He kisses from my knee down my inner thigh until he's hovering over my pussy. Cold air blows onto my heated core, and I nearly jump out of my skin.

"Justin, don't tease me. Give me what I want." I can't believe how whiny my voice sounds. I don't beg for anything, least of all a man's attention.

"Shhh, Pumpkin. Is someone a little eager?" Fuck, I really

13

am.

"Nah. Just getting bored." I fake a yawn, and he suctions my clit into his mouth, causing a moan to come out of my throat that sounds more animal than human.

I fucking knew he would have a talented tongue. My fingers twine through his short, dark hair. It's shaved on the sides and a little longer on top, but there's enough for me to get a handful. He moans, and it vibrates my clit, causing me to gasp.

Justin's fingers toy around my entrance, and my hips pump, wanting more. He doesn't leave me waiting long before he slips one inside me. Realizing how wet I am, a second one quickly follows, and he's expertly working me inside and out.

"Fuck, Justin. I'm so close already." His tongue starts twisting in some kind of pattern. Maybe a figure eight? Whatever it is, he has to hold me down with his free arm because I buck uncontrollably as my orgasm takes over my entire body. I come so hard I think I black out from lack of oxygen. When I look down, Justin is licking his fingers, and it makes my clit pulse watching him.

"Holy Jesus fuck, Justin. What the hell was that?" He smiles up at me like the cat that ate the fucking canary.

"It was obviously something you enjoyed."

"Enjoyed? I think I floated out of my body and was re-birthed a new person."

"You better be careful, Pumpkin. You could give a guy a big head." He peppers kisses on my inner thigh, his goatee almost tickling me, and it's both soothing and nerve-wracking as it feels like every touch sends little shocks of electricity straight to my clit.

"Oh, I want your big head. Let's go to the bedroom." He stops kissing my thigh and looks up at me, his hazel eyes full of questions.

"Are you sure? There's no pressure."

"After that orgasm, I'd let you introduce me to your parents." His eyes darken, and I realize I've stepped on a landmine. "Or maybe I'll just let you fuck me in a bed rather than a couch. Besides, I think I was promised cuddles in a blanket fort." There are a few tense moments where I'm not sure if I've successfully turned the conversation around before he nips my inner thigh, causing me to squeal. He stands and offers me his hand.

"Show me to your lair, my Pumpkin Queen." *Phew.* Back to being dorky, and I love it.

3

Justin

I just gave Nicole an orgasm that I know had her flying high, and then she made that offhand comment about my parents, and it almost all went to shit.

She had no idea. I understand what she was getting at when she said it. It was so innocent, yet for me, it was laced with heartbreak and pain. I don't know what she saw because I didn't feel like I moved a muscle, but her quick change of subject pulled me back from the dark places my mind was about to wander.

I follow behind her down a short hallway with three doors.

"Bathroom." She points to the door at the end of the hall. "Guest room is on your right. It's all yours if you want to use it." If the door to the right is the guest room, the one on the left must be hers. She leans against the outside frame of the remaining door and hikes a thumb behind her. "My room." She grabs my belt and pulls me towards her. "Are you choosing what's behind door A or B?" I love this take-charge woman. Her confidence is sexy. Most men probably wouldn't like it, but my goal is happiness and pleasure. I can be whoever she wants me to be as long as we achieve both things.

"Where would the Pumpkin Queen like me to go?"

"Well, seeing as I'm naked,"—her hand trails down my bare chest to the protruding bulge in my pants—"and you're hard, my room seems like the obvious choice." I flex my hips into her hand, making her rub my cock over my pants, and she smiles.

"I think your skills of deduction are spot on. After you, my Queen." I place a chaste kiss on her cheek and step back. Nicole's smile is radiant. As she walks past me to step into the room, her hand holds onto my belt, and she pulls me in like I'm on a leash. Does she want me to crawl for her, too? Because I will. However, I'd love to see her on her knees, crawling for me even more.

She sits on the blue floral bedspread and crosses her legs, leaning back on her hands. Her eyes wander my body, assessing me.

"You're wearing too many clothes for the activities I have planned. I think you should strip." And here is where things go downhill. This is why I don't get around much. I sit down on the bed next to her.

"I want to tell you something before we go any farther." She sits up and turns, giving me her full attention.

"This sounds ominous."

"It's…There's no easy way to say it than to just get it out. And I don't want you panicking that it's something too major."

"I'm listening without judgment." Her face looks sincere, and I believe her.

"I take antidepressants." I see her open her mouth to speak

but put my hand on her leg to stop her. "Sometimes the meds can make it…difficult to ejaculate. Getting hard obviously isn't the problem." I motion to the very prominent hard-on behind my zipper. She takes my hand for comfort.

"Justin, I get it. It's okay." I sigh. Her words are ones I've heard plenty of times before and after.

"It is, until it isn't. I just wanted you to know, so if you decide you still want to go through with this, if I don't come, it's not because of you. It's me, and as much as I hate the most cliche sentence in the world, it's true. It's not you, it's me." Nicole moves to climb on top of me, but I stop her once again. "I'm about to sound like an asshole, but could you please not tell me it's your new mission to make me come." She chuckles, and it lasts so long it turns into a full-blown laugh.

Pushing me onto my back, she straddles my stomach. Her pussy is hot, and I can feel the wetness from her orgasm smearing on me. She has a look of determination in her eyes, which contradicts what I just asked her.

"Listen up, Doc."

"I'm not a doctor, just a paramedic."

"But you're cute enough to play one on TV." She boops me on the nose, and I want to flip her over and fuck her right now, but I also want to hear what she has to say. "So, listen up, Doc. I don't know who hurt you in the past, but fuck'em." She bites her lips together, attempting to hold back a laugh.

"What's wrong?" I don't understand what I'm missing.

"I said 'butt fuck' and I realize it's very juvenile, but it made me want to laugh." I smile as she takes a deep breath, composing herself. "As I was saying. Fuck whoever made you feel self-conscious about yourself. Your tongue was amazing–Wait. Are you so good at that because you're trying to overcompensate for your very real medical issue?" Damn this woman. She's trying to get all of my secrets in one night.

"That's a big part of it. I also like to please my partner, so I learned what I could and figured out the rest. You were easy to please, though." I glide my hands over her legs. "You're very responsive and vocal." She shivers, and it makes her nipples harden. I want to touch them, but we need to finish our conversation.

"Let me ask you this. Do you still enjoy sex even if you don't come?" Straight to the point.

"Yes."

"Then I don't see a problem. We'll just stop when one of us gets bored, or you come. Whichever happens first." She shrugs like it's no big deal, and I really believe it's not.

"You're too perfect, Pumpkin. Marry me." My joke falls flat, and I can tell by the look on her face it's my turn to make a quick turnaround. "Or fuck me. I'll take either option." I reach up and roll her nipples between my fingers with as big of a smile as I can manage. Her body responds before her mind snaps back to me as her nipples harden again and her hips rock on my stomach.

"Pumpkin?" She closes her eyes and explores my chest with her hands. Her fingers run through my chest hair.

"You're still too clothed." She smiles, and I breathe a sigh of relief and roll us over so I can stand and remove my pants. She watches me as I toe off my shoes and socks. Shaking my hips to a song in my head, I pretend to do a little strip tease, and she starts humming her own song for me to dance to. Her smile grows the more layers I take off. I strip down to my boxers, and she clears her throat.

19

"Problem?" I give a knowing smirk as she starts to giggle.

"Those are...interesting?" I look down and already know what she's laughing at. I have a thing for funny underwear. She's currently looking at bright green boxers with cartoon turtles on them.

"These are classic, and I will take no arguments on them."

"Note to self. Underneath all of his hot guyness, Doc likes cartoon undies." I'll let her laugh at me, but I stand by my fun underwear. I live in navy uniforms day in and day out. This gives me something fun in my life despite all of the despair of my job. I drop my boxers, and she stops laughing. She bites her bottom lip, taking me all in.

"So it was fun packaging for a very nice present, I see."

"You could say that."

"You're full of surprises, Doc. Does that do what I think it does?"

"If you're asking if my piercing rubs over your clit while you grind on my cock then the answer is yes." She's staring in awe at my pubic piercing. It's a curved barbell right at the top of my shaft to enhance a woman's pleasure.

"Is that you overcompensating again? Because your tongue skills are expert level. I don't think fancy piercings are necessary."

"I haven't shown you the full extent of my finger skills yet. But, yes, if I'm being honest, I want to make sure my partners are satisfied. It's been known to make some women uncomfortable when I can't complete the act. At least this way, I know they're walking away satisfied." I stroke my cock in my hand, and her eyes follow my every move.

"I...um. Did it just get hotter in here?" I crawl on top of her on the bed. She slides back towards the headboard, and

I follow.

"It's about to be." I lean down and kiss her, molding our naked bodies together. She moans into my mouth, and it's a delicious sound. Her hands roam all over my back, and she parts her legs so I'm grinding against her pussy.

"Fuck, Pumpkin." I bury my head into her neck.

"What's wrong?"

"I had no idea the night would go this way, and I don't have any condoms. Please tell me you have some, or your brother left some here." She chuckles and reaches to the side, opening her nightstand drawer.

"Aren't you supposed to always be prepared? You work in the medical field."

"I think you're thinking about the Boy Scouts." I tear off a wrapper from the string of condoms she pulls out. "Good to know we have plenty of supplies for the evening." Using my teeth to open the condom, I roll it on and line back up between her legs. "If you get bored just–"

"Shut up and fuck me." She pulls my mouth down to her, and I thrust my cock deep into her wanting pussy. A groan escapes us both as the anticipation of the act finally hits its precipice. I hover over her body, our mouths still fused, and I piston my hips into her.

"Holy fuck. You weren't kidding about that piercing. Uhhh." Her neck arches back, and I suck on the pulse point that's newly exposed. Sharp nails glide down my back, spurring me on to move faster. Releasing her neck, I sit back on my knees and lift her legs, testing her flexibility.

"You can bend me in half, Doc. Keep going."

"O-fucking-kay." I push her legs up, burying my cock deeper inside her. The position change makes my piercing

21

grind directly on her clit, and it's not long before she's chanting my name and coming again. Nicole's nails dig into my forearms as her body spasms under me. I pull a nipple into my mouth, prolonging her sensation and putting more pressure on her already sensitive clit. Her moaning turns into screaming as another orgasm rushes through her before the first even has a chance to calm.

"Oh god. I can't. Fuck." She pushes on my chest, and I sit up, allowing her legs to fall. I caress her inner thighs and slow my pace, enjoying her blissed-out expression and her labored breathing. *This* is why sex is enjoyable for me whether I come or not. I did this to her. I made this tiger of a woman fall apart. My dick is hard and happy, but there's no sign of the pressure or tingling sensation signaling an orgasm anytime soon for me.

I fold on top of her and pepper kisses on her cheeks. I'm careful not to thrust in too deep, or my piercing will rub on her again.

"You're gorgeous when you fall apart for me." She smiles, but it's through sleepy exhaustion. "Nicole, have you had enough?" Her eyes open, and she grabs my cheeks.

"No, but you—" I cut her off. This is where things can go downhill fast.

"But you—nothing. I gave you three orgasms. *I* did that. I'm happy to give you more, but you look like you've had enough, and you're ready for sleep."

"You feel so fucking good." Her last word is a whine as she massages her nails through my hair, and my eyes roll back into my head. I thrust harder into her, knowing she can't take another orgasm.

"Oh, god. Okay. You win. I'm done."

I chuckle into her neck. "How about a hot shower and then sleep?" She hums her approval and gasps at the empty feeling when I pull out.

Wrapping my arm around her neck, I slowly pull her toward the edge of the bed. She wraps her legs around my hips like a koala, and I take us to the bathroom.

4

Nicole

Holy Shit. I've never orgasmed like that before in my life. I'm clinging to Justin with every ounce of energy I have left as he walks us to the bathroom. A hot shower sounds fantastic.

We walk into the bathroom, and I brace myself for the cold counter on my bare ass, but he grabs a towel off the rack and spreads it down before setting me on top of it. I'm shocked that he would think of something like that. He reaches into the shower and starts the water. When he's satisfied with the temperature, he turns back to me, and I spread my legs. He takes the invitation and steps into me.

"Are you joining me, Doc?"

"I was hoping you'd ask." He's still hard, and a part of me feels bad, but he knows his body, and I heard his moans mixed with mine. We both enjoyed ourselves.

He kisses me tenderly, and his erection jumps between us. I reach down and stroke his cock from base to tip and watch his eyes close when I do it again. A soft moan escapes and melts on my lips. Justin pulls away and presses our foreheads together. He chuckles and moves his hand behind me.

"I think it's time to get in the shower." I look over my shoulder to see the mirror fogged, and in the corner, he's written "Hi" with a smiley face. He steps back, and I take his offered hand, entering the shower first. When he joins me, he inspects all my bottles as if he's looking for something.

"Ah ha. I knew I smelt mint on you." He picks up my rose and mint-infused shampoo. "May I?"

"If you're asking to wash my hair, I'd love it." I saturate my curls under the water and give him my back so he can lather my hair. When his fingers massage my scalp, my legs turn to jelly.

"You weren't kidding when you said you had magic fingers."

"Turn around." He rinses the shampoo from my hair and repeats the steps with the conditioner. Once he washes the conditioner out, I pick up my wide-tooth comb.

"Would you like to comb it? You just have to start at the bottom and work your way up through the curls." He takes the comb and kisses my shoulder.

"I'd love to." My scalp tingles with the extra attention, and truthfully, so does my entire body. With the same tenderness he used for my hair, he washes my body with a loofah. When it's his turn, he quickly washes his hair, and as he grabs for the body wash, I stop him.

"Let me." I pump a quarter-sized amount in the palm of my hands and lather them together. I place my hands on him and rub over his chest and abs. His neck, shoulders, and arms are next, and I slip my still-soapy hands down to his cock. He's been hard the entire time, rubbing it against my lower back every time I faced the water.

My hands slide up and down, and he braces himself on the wall behind me. His other hand moves between my legs, and his fingers easily slide in my wetness that isn't from the shower.

"Fuck, Nicole. You're so wet." Two fingers slide easily inside me, and I squeeze his cock harder in return, making him moan.

"I'm not the only vocal one here." I gasp as I find my chest pushed up against the cold tile wall and feel a warm body pinning me to it. Justin's hand brushes over my hip, and his fingers find my clit. Fuck. I'm so sensitive from the three orgasms I've already had.

His warm breath fans over my ear. "I want to take you right here, against the cold tile. I want your nipples to harden and rub against the wall as I thrust in and out of you until you're coming on my cock." He bites down on my neck just hard enough to inflict pain and quickly licks it away.

"Do it. Please." He freezes.

"The condoms are in the other room."

"I'm on the pill. Please do it. Besides, I'm sure you'll get bored and stop." I wiggle my ass into his hard cock, teasing him.

"Not before you pass out from exhaustion." I have no doubt he's right about that. He lifts my leg onto the rim of the tub and easily slides inside me. His fingers play with my clit like it's a fiddle he's been strumming on for decades. Our bodies are connected. Our moans echo off the ceiling.

"Oh god. I'm so close."

He growls in my ear, and it's almost my undoing. "I want you to scream my name when you come, Pumpkin. I want your neighbors to know who's fucking you so well." I'm so damn close. SO. Damn. Close. He pinches my clit, and that's it. The dam opens. I see black dots in my eyes.

"Fuck, Justin. Yeeeees." I throw my head back on his shoulder, and I hear a string of curses fly out of his mouth as his hips sputter.

"Fuck, I'm gonna-"

"Keep going. Fuck me, Justin. Don't stop." He latches onto my neck, sucking and biting, and I feel his body go stiff as a long moan that's almost a growl erupts from his chest. His body convulses as he spills into me. As soon as he finishes, he pulls out, and I can feel him pulling away. I quickly spin in his arms and grab his face.

"Hey, stay with me. Don't disappear into your head." The look in his eyes is guilt.

"I'm sorry. I should have—"

"Pulled out? I told you to keep going. You did nothing wrong. God, that was so fucking good. Don't kill my buzz, man." The corner of his lips twitches, and I can see his wall coming back down.

"Your orgasm. Your pussy sucked me in and squeezed me so tight. I barely had time to realize what was happening." I kiss him softly, hoping to ease some of this tension.

"Did it feel good?"

"Fucking phenomenal, Pumpkin. Thank you." He kisses my cheek, nose, forehead, everywhere.

"How long has it been, if you don't mind me asking?" He sighs into my shoulder and runs his nose up the side of my neck.

"How long has it been since I've come without using my hand? Too fucking long." He captures my lips again, and there's passion behind it this time. "I think I was promised cuddles, and you better deliver Pumpkin."

"With pleasure, Doc. Let's go." We quickly finish washing up, and I turn the shower off. Stepping out, I grab us two fluffy yellow bath towels. Justin takes the time to dry me off, only reminding me further that tonight is more than it should be.

5

Justin

What the actual fuck? I haven't been with a woman in a while, simply because I couldn't stand the looks of sympathy and pity when I couldn't finish. I never left unsatisfied, and neither did they, but life has just been easier, throwing myself into work and using my hand when I needed release.

I finished. I fucking came...inside her. That alone goes against everything I stand for. I'm a medical worker. I know the complications of unprotected sex. She's not a complete stranger. Well, she is. We just met tonight, but I have connections with her brother and his girlfriend, or should I say, girl*friends.* I'm not sure at this point. Fuck.

She told me to keep going. I did what she asked. She's a grown woman and knows her body. I need to not beat myself up over this, but god dammit, she made me come. I might be obsessed. *And* she wants to cuddle. I'm taking this night and getting every second out of it that I can.

I take the fluffy yellow towel and dry her off. She adds products to her hair, telling me it helps with the frizz in her curls. I've never washed or brushed a woman's hair before. It was...I don't even know how to describe it. I enjoyed it, and I could tell she did too.

"I need you to promise not to laugh at me." She holds my gaze in the mirror, and I kiss the top of her shoulder.

"Never."

"I wear a silk bonnet to sleep, especially if my hair is still wet. Curly hair is a bitch to maintain." I grab a curl and twist it around my finger.

"So you're telling me you're about to look like a sexy grandma? That's hot." She rolls her eyes at me, and I can't help myself. I spin her around in my arms and kiss her. I try to say so much in a simple kiss. Thank you. You're amazing. This is a night I'll never forget. And so much more that I can't even put into words yet.

Just one night.

I can pretend this kind-hearted, funny, stunning woman is mine for just one night. I can't think about anything beyond that.

She pulls away and takes her pink silk bonnet from the bathroom closet. She looks adorable once she has all of her curls tucked in, and I follow her back to her bedroom. I take a look around her room. I was a little preoccupied when we walked in here the first time. It's as eclectic as the living room and kitchen. No two pieces of furniture match, but the entire room feels like her. Fun, colorful, and a little complicated. She sees me looking around and misunderstands my observations.

"You're welcome to sleep in the guest room or even leave if you'd prefer." I grab her wrist and pull her into me. Sliding my hands under her towel, I palm her ass cheeks.

"I was promised there would be cuddles. A man never gives up cuddling with a gorgeous woman who just rocked his world."

She giggles. "Okay there Casanova. Big spoon or little spoon?"

"Neither. I want to stare into those gorgeous blue eyes as you drift to sleep." Her smile covers her entire face, and I hear her towel hit the floor. She spins and walks to the bed, giving me a view of her fantastic ass.

Joining her, we curl up and intertwine our legs together. She's so soft under my fingers as I trail lines and circles up her back and listen to her hums of appreciation as she drifts off.

I watch her sleep. Listen to her gentle snoring. See the fluttering of her eyes as she dreams. I wonder what she's dreaming about. I envy her ability to drift into a world of peace and tranquility that restores her body.

Without my sleeping pills, which I don't have with me, I can't sleep. It's safer for her anyway if I don't sleep. I don't know what my physical body does when I have nightmares, but I know my mental and emotional state when I wake from one, and I'd hate to put another person through that.

Nicole rolls over, giving me her back, and I curl into her, being the big spoon. She feels heavenly in my arms. She sighs, and her body relaxes even further as I cocoon her into mine. I have to remember to thank Blake for inviting me out tonight. It's a night I won't soon forget.

My alarm goes off only a few short hours after she drifts off to sleep. I'm on day shift this month and need to get home and ready for work. I leave a note on her pillow and kiss her forehead before leaving, petting the dogs before I go.

"Something seems different about you this morning?" I peek my head inside the ambulance at Spencer. We're doing our pre-shift inspection of the rig before we head out for the day. I check the exterior cabinets, and Spencer does the interior. It's been our routine for the last four years that we have been partners.

"Different good or different bad?"

"Why are you smiling so much?" My smile widens at the question. "That. You look ridiculous."

"I got laid."

"Are you aching to give me details? Have you been waiting for me to notice the change in your demeanor?" Spencer knows me all too well, just like I know her. To the outside world, we look like two regular people. When you work with someone as intimately as we do and for as long as we have, you learn your partner's secrets.

Spencer is...Spencer. At first glance, she comes off as abrasive and unapproachable. She isn't a very social person and prefers to do things her way. Despite all the obstacles her life has thrown at her, Spencer's brilliance and adaptability constantly mesmerize me.

We've helped each other a lot as partners. We work as one in the field, and people are constantly in awe of how in sync we can be. The best part of being partners is that neither of us feels the need to fill the silence with talking. We've gone entire shifts only speaking when on a call, and we were perfectly fine with it.

"I was curious to see how long it took you to notice, yes." She shakes her head at me, and her red braids shift over her

32

shoulders. She French braids her hair for every shift. Her blue eyes are bright, but not as bright as Nicole's, and her face is smattered with freckles that most women would hate at her age, but she embraces.

"It's not the first time you've had sex in the last six years, Justin. Why would I notice a difference?" She sounds dismissive, but that's just Spencer. She's always watching and observing. She knows she doesn't have to pretend to be someone she isn't in front of me. Society expects a bubbly, friendly paramedic when on a call, and she can be that when needed. When we have a call that involves a child, she's in the back with the patient every time. Otherwise, she usually drives, and I do patient care. I'm the people person of our duo.

"Because Spencer, this woman rocked my fucking world. She made me come." Spencer pauses and looks at me over her clipboard. We know everything about each other. She's well versed in the side effects of all medication, including antidepressants. She's seen me go through several different variations over the years, trying to find the right ones to keep me regulated. The side effects have varied from sleeplessness to manic episodes, but the difficulty of coming to completion seems to be a constant one for me.

"Did she do something kinky to make it happen?" Of course, she would go there. I laugh, and the corner of her lip lifts.

"It was shower sex. Nothing fancy. I told her about my issue beforehand, and she was fine with it like most women claim to be, but she was actually fine."

"I'm sure the multiple orgasms that you probably provided her were a bonus." Always blunt. Spencer never beats around the bush.

"Of course they did. I'm a people pleaser to the core."

"Finish counting so we can have breakfast. Do you need to stop by Dov Memorial at any point today?"

"No, I can swing by after shift."

"Do you need a nap after your sex-a-thon last night?" I love this woman. She's my best friend. She knows about my nightmares as much as I know about hers. We're a mess but a great team.

"Only if you don't." In between calls, especially when we work night shifts, we'll take turns closing our eyes, trying to catch up on lost sleep from the nights our demons invade our minds. We have very different reasons for our sleeplessness, but when you have no control over what haunts your mind at night, any reprieve you can get is a blessing.

"Well, my lack of sleep wasn't from too much sex, but you look like you need it more than me."

"Gee, thanks. Are you saying you don't like the post-sex look on me?" I scoff and run my hand through my short hair.

"You smell funny. Why?" You can't get anything past this woman.

"I told you, shower sex. She had some rose and mint stuff in her shower. I actually like it. You don't?"

"It's just different." Before I can banter back with her, the pager on my hip sounds. The dispatcher, through my pager, tells us we're responding to a slip and fall, possible broken leg.

"Great, your post-sex slowness means no breakfast for us anytime soon. Get in."

"Lunch is on me."

I love my job. There aren't many things you can control in your life, but your job is one of them. Helping people gives me a rush. Not every person can be helped, and of course, there are hard days, but the good far outweighs the bad.

Today, my mind keeps wandering back to the bonneted beauty I left sleeping this morning. I left my number in the note on her pillow, so the ball is in her court if she wants to see me again.

"Are you going to see her again?" Spencer's question brings me back to the present. We stopped for lunch at a local burger joint, and in true first responder fashion, our fries have already been eaten, and we're halfway through our burgers. Early on, I learned that it's easier to hold a burger while speeding down the streets of downtown Chicago while responding to a call than trying to shove individual fries in your face.

"I left my number, so we'll see."

"How did you meet?" I must have a significant attitude change today for Spencer to be asking for more information.

"Do you remember the MVC we did a while back with the SUV and the overturned car? Two fatalities." She nods. Of course, she remembers. Her mind is a crazy place. "The woman Annie, the one I got in the car with, is in a relationship with a guy named Cole and a woman named Blake. I've run into Blake several times, and we've had coffee. She invited me out last night to join them at Midnight Moonshine, and Cole's sister, who also came with us, is who I went home with last night."

"Oh, so a blind date?"

"No, it was just supposed to be a fun night out, but she slapped me and then kissed me, and I was putty in her hands." Her brows pinch at my explanation, and it's hilarious to almost hear the gears turning in her head.

"Do you enjoy physical violence for pleasure?" That question causes me to almost choke on my burger. She hands me a napkin, and I beat on my chest, attempting to regain my composure.

"Damn, Spencer. You caught me off guard with that one. It's a shot at the bar. It's called a Kickin' Cowboy. You take a shot, and then the other person throws water in your face and slaps you. The kiss was just an added bonus. A very enjoyable bonus."

"Your face just flushed." I touch my cheek, and she's right; it's warm. Warmer than this hot Chicago day. "What were you thinking about?"

"Spencer, a girl doesn't kiss and tell." That one takes her a moment longer to decipher. Sometimes, sarcasm isn't the easiest for her to understand.

"You told me you gave her multiple orgasms, and she made you come for the first time in a long time that wasn't by your hand. But your line in the sand is what made your blood pressure rise right now, causing your face to heat?"

"You're on a roll today, Spence. Honestly, it wasn't even anything sexual. She let me brush her hair in the shower. She has long, curly hair, and it felt like such an intimate act." Just as I take my last bite of burger, our pagers go off again. A car accident with a minor head injury.

"Duty calls."

6

Nicole

Make the ringing stop. I feel around on my nightstand for my phone. It's the third time someone has called me. Either someone died, or it's my brother.

"What?"

"Nice to hear from you too, big sis. Just calling to check on you. Blake isn't doing too great this morning, and I'm pretty sure you drank more than her." Drinking. Ugh. That explains the headache. My hand grazes my bonnet when I place it on my forehead.

"My bonnet?"

"What? What about your goofy bonnet?" I'm wearing my bonnet. Holy shit. "Justin."

"Is he still there? I think he mentioned he had to work today." I feel the bed next to me, and it's cold. On my nightstand, I notice a bottle of water, some pain meds, and I see a note on my pillow.

"He's not here."

"You sound terrible."

"Thanks a lot, Coleman." Picking up the note, there's a simple message that makes me laugh.

Take two of these and call me in the morning. ~Doc

Underneath is his phone number. Does he actually want me to call him, or was he just playing into the funny doctor line?

"How well do you know Justin?"

"Not really well. Blake does, though. And so does Annie. He's helping her. From what I know of him, he's a great guy. I wouldn't have offered him my drunk sister if I didn't think he was."

"Offered him?" Was last night a blind date that I didn't know about?

"Offered to take care of you. I knew you girls would get wasted, and Blake is enough of a handful on her own. There was no way I could have handled both of you. Did he take care of you?" I stretch and feel my sore muscles.

"He sure did." He took care of me on the couch, in my bed, and in the shower.

"I'm glad. Let me get back to Blake. She's thrown up a few times this morning, and I don't want to leave her alone for too long. Love ya, big sis."

"Love you, little bro."

Rolling on my back in bed, I scrub my hands over my face as I recall last night. The dancing, slapping, kissing, and fucking. So many orgasms. How many did I have? Three? Four? I lost count, but I've never been that satisfied in my entire life.

I made him come. I feel proud about that. But should I? Cole said he didn't know him very well. Was that just a line?

He didn't come when he had a condom on, but as soon as I gave him permission not to wear one, he came inside me. The anxiety fills me as I consider that it might have all been an elaborate plan to raw dog me.

Whatever. I'm on the pill. We both got amazing sex out of it. You live, and you learn. I crumple the note in my hand and toss it into the trash can next to my bed. If fate wants our paths to cross again, then it will.

My phone dings with a notification, and I roll my eyes. Being a hairdresser is amazing. I love my job, but it doesn't always pay the bills. Especially since Cole moved in with Blake. I've had to resort to some of the more creative online options. This message is from Tootsie Footsies.

Opening the app, I wonder what color I'll have to paint my toes for this fifty dollars.

Prince_Charming_4U: Hey there, curly. Ever sell anything other than feet?

I'm bored, so I'll play along.

CurlyGirlSnips: Hey Prince. What did you have in mind?

Prince_Charming_4U: Are you looking for a sugar daddy because I need a sugar baby?

CurlyGirlSnips: Tell me more.

I get out of bed and ready for the day as this guy floods my inbox with promises of gifts and a weekly allowance. All he wants in return is to see me spending his money. I reply back with several "Yes, Daddys" and "I'd love to do that for yous."

I'm brushing my teeth when he finally says the words I've been waiting to hear. He tells me he can send me three thousand right now, and I'll have an allowance of fifteen hundred every week after. All he needs from me is a fifty dollar one-time processing fee since we aren't friends on the money app.

The fun is over. I report the conversation to Tootsie Footsie support and block Prince_Charming_4U. I've made some actual money on the site, which is why I stay on, but the creeps still find their way to you. Although they aren't nearly as creepy as the guys on Fancy Pantsies. Does it weird me out to sell used underwear to guys online? Yeah. But when someone sends you two hundred dollars to go for a jog in a thong and mail it to him, a girl's gotta eat. And so do her adorable puppies.

Logging into my work app, I check my schedule for today. I have several appointments this afternoon. I rent a space and work for myself, which is great because I get to create my own schedule. I'm not really a morning person, but I have a few clients who like morning appointments. Most of my clients are professional women who need after-work hours, and I'm happy to accommodate them.

I check the overdue tab in my app and see Annie's name. I wonder if I should reach out to her. I know things are rocky with her and my brother since the accident, but she was my client before she was his employer. I decide it's better to ask Cole first and close my app. Walking into the kitchen, I greet my puppies, who are excited to see me. There's another note on the counter from Justin.

They looked too cute, so I took them out before I left. I hope it helps. ~Justin

He took my dogs out? Wow.

"Do you ladies want to go out again or just snuggle on the couch for a bit?" Java rolls to her back, wagging her tail.

40

"Snuggles it is." I open the gate, and they run to the ramp next to the couch. I grab a bottle of water, some salami from the fridge, and a pack of crackers from the cabinet. Hydration, carbs, and protein will hopefully help me bounce back from the mild hangover I have.

7

Justin

"JJ, go faster! Go faster!"

"I gotta be careful, Ivy. There's mud coming up here. Hold on tight. I've got you, little sister."

"You've got me, big brother."

"There's no blood, Mama. She's okay. She's just sleeping."

"Wake up, Ivy. It's not funny anymore."

"Oh my god. My baby. What have you done, Justin?"

"Go get your father!"

"Mama, she's okay, right? We slid on the mud."

"Why won't she wake up, Daddy?"

"Wake up, baby girl. Wake up for Daddy."

"There's no blood. She's okay."

No blood.

No Blood.

NO BLOOD.

"Ivy!" I flail around in my bed. Legs and arms tangled in the blankets. Sweat soaks my sheets, and my breathing is ragged. I fucking hate my nightmares.

Me: You up?
  Spencer: Nightmare?
  Me: A brutal one. My parents were in it.
  Spencer: I'm sorry for that. Popcorn and Grey's?
  Me: Same episode or did you move on?
  Spencer: I'm not cruel like you.
  Me: Give me 10

Spencer and I both have trouble sleeping. We started watching TV medical dramas together at night, and we text back and forth, making fun of the terrible medical terminology they use.

I make a pot of coffee while the popcorn is popping because there's no chance I'll be getting any more sleep tonight.

Spencer: Ready?
  Me: Three
  Spencer: Two
  Me: Play
  Spencer: Play

We spend the next several hours laughing and making fun of all of the dialogue until the sun rises and it's time to get ready for work.

Spencer: See you in 90.
  Me: Thanks

Today is group therapy session at the Dov Memorial Wing of

43

the Rehabilitation Center. Today's session included Annie, who is Blake and Cole's girlfriend. After a few weeks of hard love, she's finally turned things around, doing her physical therapy and putting in the work. She had a broken leg and shattered her pelvis in a car accident. It was by pure coincidence that she ended up in my wing.

Well, being in my wing was by my doing. Her rehab could have been anywhere, but she chose this facility. I just happen to own the mental health wing and took it upon myself to help her.

"Sorry, Ms. Poulsen, I'm required to deliver all packages to their appropriate room." The nurse looks nervous as she places a bouquet of red roses on the table with the half dozen others sitting there. I had spoken with Blake when Annie was at her lowest, and although Annie wouldn't allow her or Cole to visit, I knew she needed some hope from the outside world. She was drowning in herself. Roses have come every other day since I asked.

"I. Don't. Want. Them. Take them away. Take them *all* away." Annie steps away from her desk, where I assisted her after group therapy. She has yet to walk independently, until now. I watch in fascination as she walks to the table with the roses and rages out.

"Fucking. Reminders." *Smash.* "I did this." *Scream.* "I ruined everything." *Bang.* Glass shatters everywhere around us. The nurse takes a step toward Annie, and I stop her. I whisper into her ear to get a janitor to clean up the mess, and I'll take care of Annie.

"I can't do this anymore." *Scream.* "I don't deserve their blind faith." *Crash.* She collapses to the ground, wracked with sobs, and curls into the fetal position. "I...can't..." *hiccup,* "do…thi-is…anymore."

Grabbing a blanket, I gently place it over her, trying to take as little glass with us as possible. I pick her up bridal-style and we leave the room.

"This is my office, Danika. We're going to wait in here while your room gets cleaned up. Would you like the door open or closed?"

"Closed." I close the door behind me and explain that I'm going to put her down so we can brush off any glass sticking to her.

Annie doesn't remember who I am. The day of her accident, I climbed into the car with her. I stayed while she drifted in and out of consciousness as they used the jaws of life to cut her out of the vehicle. I introduced myself to her as Justin, but here I go by Jay, and I've been calling her by her proper name, Danika. It seems she uses that name when she wants to keep people at a distance.

Her grip falters as we're removing the glass, and I grab her hips to help stabilize her.

"Annie, I've got you. I won't let you fall." She pauses. Something snaps in her brain. I see it on her face. Her eyes widen, and tears brim at the edges. I slipped and called her Annie.

"J-Justin?"

"Hey, Annie. I wondered when you'd put the pieces together in your memory." I smile down at her.

"But how?"

"A story for a story? Are you ready to really talk?" She knows I have a dark secret, and we've been toying with each other, trying to get information. She's upset by my question and lets go of me to walks over to the couch.

45

"You did it again." I can't stop the awe in my voice. She did it again.

"Did what?" She doesn't realize. You can tell by the edge in her voice.

"You just walked away from me without your cane and sat on the couch. In your room, you walked from your desk to the table to smash the roses. Without your cane, Annie. You got out of your head and did what your body has wanted to do all along."

"I did it?"

"I think you're ready, Annie. But first, I want to give you something." I open my desk drawer and then sit next to her on the couch. I flip her palm open and drop the delicate piece of jewelry into her hand.

"How?"

"I needed to remove all your jewelry in the ambulance because I knew you were going directly into surgery. The bracelet had to be cut off, and I must have missed your bag when I was putting it all in. I found it in a corner a few weeks ago when we were deep cleaning the ambulance, but I knew you couldn't handle it yet if I gave it back to you. Blake told me to hold on to it until you were ready." I reached out to Blake when I found it. I assumed it had some kind of sentimental value, and I was correct. Both Blake and Annie wore permanent jewelry bracelets.

"Blake? How do you know Blake?"

"I'm going to tell you my story now, and then you can tell me yours. Deal?"

"A story for a story. Okay. Deal."

Annie and I share our stories. She tells me about her relationship with Cole and Blake and her grief over her

46

driver's death in the accident. I tell Annie about how I killed my sister when I was seven, and she was five.

8

Justin

Farm life is fun, adventurous, and early. So early. The sun isn't even up yet, but I have to milk the cows and collect eggs. Well, collecting the eggs is actually Ivy's job, but she's only five and can't carry as many as I can without breaking some, so I help her. Mama doesn't care as long as I get my chores done, too.

"JJ, can we ride today?" Ivy loves riding on the 4-wheeler with me. She asks almost every day, and most days, I can take her for a short ride, but it's been raining the past few days, and we haven't had a chance.

"We'll try after lunch as long as the weather stays nice. I'll race you to the chicken coop."

"GO!" She wins as usual because I let her. I walk while she runs, her golden hair flowing behind her in the breeze as she giggles her way to the coop. When I reach her, she hands me the apron with all the pockets to collect the eggs, and I tie it

48

securely around her back.

We take turns retrieving the eggs. Ivy lets me collect from under the broody hens because she's afraid to get pecked, and she gathers them from all the friendly hens, which she's given names.

"Chicken Little is my favorite hen, JJ. She's so sweet." She pets the chicken with one hand while removing eggs with the other. When her apron is full, I collect the eggs and put them in a basket, and she continues. Once we've successfully collected all the eggs, or unsuccessfully in my case because I have a scratch from an ornery chicken, we bring them inside to Mama. Ivy stays inside to help with cooking and cleaning, and I head to the barn for my next chore.

We have four dairy cows in our herd. The rest are beef cows we use for breeding to sell or raise for meat. Our cows get milked twice daily, and it's my job to do it. Mama jars up the milk, and we sell them to the neighbors. I get a small amount of the money from each jar sold because I do the milking and deliver the jars. I really want to buy a horse, so I'm saving up.

After lunch, which Ivy was very excited about because she helped flip the grilled cheese, I milk the cows again, with Ivy watching the entire time. Her bright pink shirt stands out in the neutral colors of the barn. She sits on a bail of hay and swings her legs impatiently twirling her blonde braid in her fingers.

"How much longer? I wanna ride."

"I have two more cows to milk. Why don't you go check if there's any more eggs?"

"Fiiiiiine. You're so slow."

"Love you too, Ivy." She stalks off and returns just as I

49

finish the third cow.

"Ready now?" She's so pushy sometimes.

"I have one more. I need about another thirty minutes. Do you want to help?" Her nose scrunches up, and her face turns sour. I know she doesn't like milking the cows.

"JJ, gross. Could you hurry, please? I wanna go." Her whining is adorable. I love my role as a big brother and take it very seriously.

I already know I'll have to beat up some kids next year when she starts school. Boys can be mean.

She wanders off to pet some of the other animals in the barn, and I'm able to finish milking in peace. When I search for her, I find Ivy hanging out on a pile of hay, cuddling one of the barn cats.

"Are you ready, sissy?" She jumps up, startling the cat.

"Yes. Yes. Let's go riding!" We walk over to the barn, where all the big equipment is stored, to my 4-wheeler. It's smaller than the others and easier for me to handle. I climb on and help pull her up behind me. She wraps her arms around me, and I rev the engine, making her giggle.

We drive around the pastures for a while and see Daddy in the field, stopping to say hi.

"Dinner will be done soon. Don't be out too much longer."

"We won't. Ivy wants to go see the pond before we go back." We wave and head toward the back of our property. Just over a hill, there's a pond that we swim and fish in. There are lots of flowers around it this time of year, and it's Ivy's favorite spot on the farm. Since it's rained, the flowers will all be in full bloom, and she's excited to see them.

Ivy waves at the cows as we ride past the pastures.

"JJ, go faster! Go Faster!" She loves when her hair whips

in the wind.

"I gotta be careful, Ivy. There's mud coming up here. Hold on tight. I've got you, little sister."

"You've got me, big brother." She squeezes my waist tighter as I maneuver around the puddles.

We make it to the top of the hill with only a little mud on us, and she squeals when she sees all the flowers.

I sit on the dock I helped Daddy build while Ivy chases butterflies around the flowers. It's a perfect summer afternoon.

"Ivy, we better get back before we're late for dinner."

"But it's so pretty." It really is beautiful here. You can't hear any of the animals or farm equipment, only birds and bugs and the occasional splash of water from a fish or turtle.

"We can come back tomorrow and go swimming after chores." She huffs in defeat. We get back on the 4-wheeler and start to ride back out.

"Can we ride around and see the rest of the flowers?" The pond isn't very large, and it only takes about ten minutes to ride around.

"Only for you, Ivy."

"You're the best, big brother." She laughs and points at the different colored flowers and animals we see.

"We're going back up the hill. Hold on tight." We're on a different path than we came in from. This side is a little steeper, but I know more flowers are lining this one, and it's Ivy's favorite of the two options. Revving the engine to get more speed, we head up. There are still some puddles here, and I have to weave off and on the path to avoid them.

It has been a while since we last used this path because it comes out on the opposite side of the farm, making the trip a little longer. Some parts have started to grow over and I miss a puddle because of it. My tires spin, and we slip backward a bit. I hit the accelerator and turn the wheel, trying to get out of the slick spot. The front wheels push through the mud, and I think we're in the clear, but when the back wheels hit solid ground, I don't release the accelerator quick enough, and the front wheels are still turned. The 4-wheeler tips backward, throwing us both off. Luckily, we weren't going fast and only tumbled a bit.

"Oh man, Ivy. Daddy is going to be upset, and we're gonna have to walk back now. I can't get the 4-wheeler on all fours by myself." I stand up and brush off the dirt and mud from my fall.

"Ivy?" I look around and see her pink shirt a little farther down the hill. She's smaller and must have rolled farther than me. I walk down to her, and her eyes are closed.

"Ivy. Come on, we have a long walk back. We're definitely going to be late now." I grab her arm to help her up, and it's limp. Looking around, I can't see anything she could have hit her head on, but she's knocked out. I quickly look around her body and don't see any blood or injuries, so I pick her up and start the walk back to the house.

"You're sleeping for a long time, Ivy. It would be great if you could wake up and walk yourself. It would make it so much quicker. Daddy is going to be upset that we're late."

It takes about twenty minutes to walk back to the house. When I step into the kitchen, Ivy is still sleeping. Mama hears the back door close and spins to yell at us for being late. Her face is angry but quickly turns to fear. She pulls Ivy from my arms and bursts into tears.

"What happened?"

"We fell off the 4-wheeler and tumbled down the hill." Her

52

hands move all over Ivy, looking for any injuries. I don't understand why she's so upset.

"My baby," she whispers through sobs.

"There's no blood, Mama. She's okay. She's just sleeping." Mama cries harder and falls to the floor. I walk over and shake her shoulder. "Wake up, Ivy. It's not funny anymore."

"Oh my god. My baby. What have you done, Justin?" Me? I didn't do anything. Why is she blaming me for Ivy sleeping so long? She wouldn't wake up for me either. "Go get your father!" Her yelling startles me. Mama never yells. I don't understand the crying and yelling.

I notice that Ivy's color is really light. Her lips don't look pink anymore, either.

"Mama, she's okay, right? We just slid on the mud." She screams my daddy's name, and he comes running from somewhere in the house. He sees Mama and Ivy on the floor and drops to his knees next to them. He takes her from Mama, and she looks like a doll in his arms.

"Why won't she wake up, Daddy?" He doesn't even look at me. Neither of them do.

"Wake up, baby girl. Wake up for Daddy." He's crying now, too. Why are they crying? She's okay, right? She's just sleeping.

"There's no blood. She's okay." She has to be okay. She's my little sister. I'm her big brother. I protect her.

Annie grabs my arm, bringing me back to the present. She hands me the tissue box. I don't talk about Ivy often. Everything in my life changed in that moment.

"It wasn't your fault, Justin." I tell myself that every day but it doesn't help. Even two decades later, I still carry the grief.

It's the reason I need antidepressants.

"She broke her neck when she fell. I understand that I couldn't have prevented that specifically. It took me until I went through paramedic classes to fully understand the mechanics of it. But I drove her up the hill. I missed the puddle."

"You had no idea."

"And neither did you, Annie. You weren't driving the SUV that hit you and killed Josh."

"I distracted him."

"And I drove the 4-wheeler through the puddle." There are a few long minutes of silence while we both wallow in our guilt.

"It's your turn. Tell your story, Annie." I can tell she wants to object, but I won't allow it. "We made a deal, and I know you're a fierce business woman, and don't go back on your deals." She concedes and tells me about Blake, Cole, and Josh.

9

Nicole

Fuck. Fuck. FUCK. What in the actual fuck. This is not my life right now. I'm not this woman. I'm dreaming. I peed the bed. I did not just pee on a stick and currently see the word "Pregnant" staring at me like a grenade without a pin.

How is this even possible? I've been taking birth control for over a decade. I'm diligent most days. I had a period last month. Right? Maybe? I definitely had one the month before because I had to sell a feet pic for tampon money. This last month was a blur. I had an unexpected car repair and had to take on as many clients as possible to make up for the loss of that money. *This is ridiculous.*

Taking my phone out of my pocket, I tap on the compass icon on my phone.

How effective is the birth control pill?

If you use it perfectly, the pill is 99% effective. But people aren't perfect, and it's easy to forget or miss pills — so in reality, the pill is about 93% effective. That means about 7 out of 100 pill users get pregnant each year.

What the hell kind of statistic is that? Seven people? They should warn you more about this. Or maybe I should read the million words on the pamphlet that comes with the pills every month. Reaching into my medicine cabinet, I grab the offending pills and toss them in the trash.

"Guess I won't be needing those anymore, Beans." At the sound of her name, she sits on her hind legs and paws at me. I sit on the floor, and she hops into my lap. "Looks like you're getting a brother or sister." She licks the salty tears as they fall down my cheeks.

My phone rings, and it's Cole. I clear my throat and try to make my voice sound steady.

"Hey, little brother." Please, don't ask how I'm doing because "Knocked up by your friend because of your invitations to Midnight Moonshine" is not something I'm ready to say.

"Big sis. I'm mailing out invitations to our party in a couple of weeks. I wanted to give you a heads up to check the mail since I know how much you hate to do it." The mailboxes are in the main office of the apartment complex, and the guy behind the desk is a creeper who constantly hits on me.

"Why can't you just bring it to me?"

"Because apparently, that's not proper party etiquette. Annie's party planner insists on mailing invitations. But it's puppers friendly, so you can bring the girls." That makes me smile for the first time today.

Annie came to Cole and Blake on a rainy day, and they rekindled their relationship. They still work on it every day, but I've never seen him so happy.

"They miss Candy. They'll love that." Java and Beans fell in love with Annie's crazy Doberman when she stayed with us. I watched her for a while when Annie first got into the accident until Cole and Blake moved in together and took her with them. Candy is a little wild, and my girls are calm, but together, they played so well, and the three of them cuddling still makes my heart swell just remembering it.

"I knew they would. You doing okay? You sound a little off, sis." I'm more than a little off. I haven't been able to keep anything down for a week and thought I picked up a stomach bug. It's the hazard of working with the public and wouldn't be the first time. That is, until this morning when I realized I was taking the last sugar pill in my packet, and I still didn't have my period. I swore I had a period last month, but it was lighter than usual. It happens sometimes being on the pill, so I didn't think anything about it.

"Yeah, little brother. I'm good. Just tired." *And pregnant.* I share everything with Cole, and as much as I want to tell him about this, I can't right now. I have to process. I have to decide if and how to tell Justin. I haven't even talked to him since that night.

"Okay, well, let me know if you need anything. And check your mail in a few days."

"K. Love you."

"Love you." I let the phone slip from my hands and cuddle into Beans harder. I'm going to allow myself today only. Today, I can wallow and cry and scream. Whatever I need to get through this. I'm going to have a baby. I have an apartment that I have to sell feet pics and used panties to afford and a car that's one pothole away from falling apart, but I'm going to be a mother.

I knew it wouldn't be long before Java came pittering in to join the snuggle fest on the floor. Soon, I'm dodging licking tongues to the face as they excitedly jump in my lap.

57

"Okay. Okay, girls. I love you too." They can always cheer me up. "How about we go sit on the couch with some ice cream while I look up on the internet what the next eight or nine months of my life will look like?

Sitting in my car outside the house that has become my brother's residence, I look over the invitation again.

You are cordially invited to a
"No Reason" BBQ.
Your hosts, Annie, Blake & Cole
Welcome you to their home to celebrate
BEING ENOUGH.
Please join them to eat, drink, and
Swim. Bring yourself, your smile, and
A bathing suit. Friendly dogs are welcome.

I know this has nothing to do with Annie and everything to do with Cole and Blake. I step out of my little rundown sedan that I've had since college. Even then, it was a used car. I open the back door with a squeak, and two little heads pop up at the noise.

"You ready, ladies?" Java and Beans, my crazy dachshund sisters, wag their tails as I grab their leashes and my hair bag. Although I'm a guest, Blake and Annie asked if I would come early to do their hair.

"You can do this." I pep myself up. "You're a big girl. A big, *'you make stupid decisions when you're drunk'* girl, but still, you got this." I pat my pants pocket and listen for the crinkle of my wrapped peppermints. They have been my lifesaver lately when I get nauseous.

I'm about to ring the doorbell when it opens. A gentleman in black bathing suit trunks and a Hawaiian shirt stands before me.

"Good afternoon. Name, please?"

"Nicole McGrath."

"Ah, yes. Welcome, Miss McGrath. Your brother is near the living room. The ladies are upstairs in their bedroom. They are expecting you." *Near* the living room. What does that mean?

"Thank you." He gestures to what I assume is "near" when Java and Beans pull on their leashes. I look up to see Candy standing just inside the doorway. Her little tail wags so hard that her entire butt swings in the breeze. Bending down, I release them off their leashes, and craziness ensues. Candy spins and takes off toward the back of the house while my two attempt to chase her as quickly as their little legs allow them.

I can't help but laugh at their antics. I place my bag at the bottom of the stairs. I know their bedroom is upstairs, but I want to say hello to Cole before I go up. I continue further into the house toward the sound of music and stop in my tracks.

"Oh my god, Cole!" My brother is hanging upside down on a stripper pole, wearing barely any clothes. "What the hell are you doing?" He rights himself and slides down the rest of the pole.

"Hey, big sis. You're early." He walks towards me, arms outstretched for a hug.

"Eww, gross. I can see your sweat from here. Stay back."

"Aww, you don't want a hug?" He's wiggling his fingers, taunting me.

"Ugh, I should have gone straight upstairs. This is what I get for wanting to be a nice sister and say hi first. What the hell were you doing? How can you climb the pole like that, and why are you doing it almost naked?" He drops his arms and cocks a brow.

"Which question would you like me to answer first?" His smile beams with his teasing tone.

"How about wha-"

"Hey man, that pool is amazing." I freeze. I haven't heard that voice in almost two months. The voice my sober brain is having trouble connecting with the eager, breathy tone the last time I heard it. Cole senses my change in demeanor and closes the distance between us.

"What's wrong, Nicole?" Before I have a chance to answer him, my name is repeated again by someone else.

"Nicole?" He starts walking in my direction, and I back away.

"I, um. I have to go do the girls' hair. I'll catch you later, Cole. It was good to see you, Justin."

I scramble back towards the stairs and hear their confused mumbles as I pick up my bag and find my way to their bedroom. I hear strange sounds as I walk down the hallway. Is it crying or moaning? After what I already witnessed downstairs, I hope it's not moaning. As I get closer, I can hear part of their conversations.

"How is it possible?"

"I-I have no idea. They said it wasn't completely *impossible, but the chances were extremely slim."*

60

"Baby, this is incredible."

"I'm not sure I believe it."

"Believe it! What made you test?" Test? What are they talking about? I hope Annie isn't sick. *"Why didn't you say anything?"*

Stepping into the doorway, I see them embracing each other in the bathroom.

"It was an impulse buy at the store today. I've felt 'off' in a way I couldn't describe. Someone walked by me, and their perfume was so strong I almost lost my breakfast in the middle of the aisle." That sounds familiar. *Wait, What?*

"I just...I peed on the stick, and there was almost instantly a plus sign. I couldn't believe it, so I tested with all three in the pack and got the same results."

They both jump when my bag slips from my shoulder. My body is trembling, and I have to lean on the door frame to hold myself up. I want that—the enthusiasm and support for a new life.

"Oh my god, Nicole. Are you alright?" Blake gets to me first and helps me walk over to the bed.

"I'm so sorry. I didn't mean to eavesdrop. This was a private moment, and I ruined it." Annie runs a soothing hand along my arm.

"You didn't ruin it. Although, your brother might think differently when he finds out you knew before he did." She laughs at the thought. I'm so happy that they found their way back to each other. He was so lost without her.

"My baby brother is going to be a dad. That's wild to think about."

"And amazing, and exciting, and monumental. You did it, Annie." There's so much love between them.

"How do you think Cole's going to feel about being an uncle?" That's the first thing I've said out loud, acknowledging my situation.

"No, silly, you'll be the Aunt, Cole's the dad." I'm staring at the floor, lost in the flashes of my lonely future.

"Darling, I think Nicole understands that she's the aunt. I don't believe that's what she was referring to, though. Was it Nicole?" I slowly shake my head in response to her question.

"Wait, what? If Cole is our baby's daddy, and Nicole is its aunt, the only way he could be an uncle is if…"

"…I were pregnant." Those three words crush my soul. Pregnant. I'm so stupid and pregnant. "I'm pregnant…" I look over at Blake, "And it's Justin's."

10

Justin

I've never been to Annie's house before. It's nothing like I would expect from a woman of her status. This house looks like a fancier version of every other home in the neighborhood. I received an invitation to their "No Reason" BBQ, and Cole said I could come by early to hang out with him if I wanted.

Knocking on the door, a large man wearing black swim trunks answers.

"Good afternoon. Name, please."

"Justin Webb."

"Welcome, Mr. Webb. The ladies are upstairs getting ready, and Mr. McGrath was in the backyard last I saw him." He steps back and extends his hand inside.

I hear clicking to my left and look to see Candy walking down the stairs. She excitedly walks up to me and sits, waiting for me to pet her.

"It's good to see you, Candy. Where's your daddy? Is he outside?" Her ears turn at the word 'outside,' and she heads towards the back of the house. I follow her since I have no idea where I'm going, putting faith in a dog to lead me to her owner.

We walk between a kitchen and living room with a large sectional. I pause momentarily when I see a dancer's pole constructed near the dining room but continue to a back door. Candy walks through a dog door, and I open it, walking out onto a gorgeous patio ready for an elegant backyard event.

I feel underdressed in my Hawaiian patterned bathing suit trunks until I see Cole standing in front of a large built-in grill wearing...a speedo? Candy walks up to him and nudges his hip. He absentmindedly pets her head, and she ruffs at him to catch his attention. When he turns to her, I clear my throat to make my presence known, and he shifts to look at me.

"Justin. Glad you made it. Come check out this grill. Annie had it built this week for the party. It's a man's wet dream of grills." I walk over to him and see exactly what he's talking about. It's a gas grill with four side burners. There's a pizza oven on one side and a full refrigerator with a freezer on the other.

"Shit, Cole. This is incredible."

"Last week she asked me if I could have my dream grill set up, what would it be. This is it. She made my dream come true. I have my own fairy godmother in a petite, sexy-as-sin blonde." I laugh at the expression on his face. It's worse than a kid in a candy store. I clamp him on the shoulder.

"I'm happy for you, man, but I have to ask. Why are you in a speedo?" He looks down at his lack of attire and laughs.

"I was about to do a set on the pole inside. It's great fucking exercise and relieves stress. You're welcome to come watch, or you can hang out here for about ten minutes and check out the pool.

"I think I'll hang out near the pool and let you do your thing." He smiles and goes inside to do his *workout*. The pool is as spectacular as the BBQ is. There's a slate stone waterfall on one side and a diving board on the other. A tall fence runs the length of the property and disappears into trees. I wander with Candy following me until something catches her attention, and she runs back inside. I feel like I've been outside long enough for Cole to almost be done, and I head back into the house. Candy runs past me with two small, familiar looking blurs following her.

"Hey man, that pool is amazing." I round the corner to where I saw the pole when I came in, and stop in my tracks. It's her—my curly-haired beauty. I haven't seen her since the night we spent together. Despite giving her my number, she never contacted me. I can't believe I didn't think about her being Cole's sister. Of course, she would be here.

Nicole seems equally as shocked to see me and Cole senses the change in her demeanor.

"What's wrong, Nicole?" Cole sounds concerned, but I can't pay him any attention.

"Nicole?" My feet carry me in her direction, but she backs away.

"I, um. I have to go do the girl' hair. I'll catch you later, Cole. It was good to see you, Justin." She runs away towards the stairs like a scared little mouse, grabs a bag at the bottom, and disappears upstairs.

"What was that all about?" Cole turns toward me and looks back at the stairs.

"I'm not entirely sure. I haven't spoken to her since the

night at Midnight Moonshine."

"Well, what the hell happened that night to make her react like that?" That's a good fucking question. It's clear by his reaction that she never told him about our evening. Should I? I have to tell him something. The longer the silence sits in the air, the sharper his jawline gets.

"We slept together. I'm sorry, Cole. We had a great evening, though. At least, I thought we did." My gaze drifts to the stairs, where she literally ran from me. I hang my head, realizing that I might have just ruined my only male friendship.

"Well, fuck. That explains it." There's no longer any anger in his tone.

"What do you mean?" I look at him in confusion.

"You're a great guy, Justin. She usually gets together with assholes. She probably has a girl crush and was shocked to see you."

"You're not pissed at me?" He contemplates that for a moment before he shrugs.

"She's a big girl. As long as you don't hurt her, we're good. Wait. She consented to sleep with you, right?" Talk about whiplash. He went from friendly to icy in one sentence.

"Absolutely, I would never do that to anyone. I spent the night in her bed. I only left before she woke up because I had to go to work. I even walked the dogs and left her with water and pain meds before I left."

"Huh. I don't know, Justin. Women are strange creatures. If it can't be fixed with a coffee, food, or an orgasm, I don't know how to fix it."

"Cole, you just recited my motto when it comes to women. Without a doubt, one of those things will always fix a woman."

He laughs, and I join in with him.

"I'm going to grab a shower before more people arrive. The fridges are stocked inside and out. Make yourself at home." He walks upstairs, and I want to follow to see where Nicole retreated to, but I won't.

What could be so wrong? I wouldn't expect her to welcome me with a kiss, but she ran away scared. Does she regret what happened between us?

11

Nicole

"Wait, what? If Cole is our baby's daddy, and Nicole is its aunt, the only way he could be an uncle is if..."

"...I were pregnant. I'm pregnant... And it's Justin's."

Those words echo in my mind as I sit in a waiting room with Annie and Blake. It's been a week since I saw Justin at their party. I managed to avoid him for most of the night, only catching a few glances. The girls understood my apprehension about telling him, although they insisted he would be supportive of my situation. Ugh. I hate thinking of my baby as a *situation,* but that's exactly what it is right now.

Cole came upstairs to shower right after my confession, and it was hard enough to keep my own secret, let alone Annie's. While he was showering, Annie decided that we shouldn't tell either of them until we both saw a doctor and confirmed everything—one step at a time. First, a doctor, then we would worry about how to tell them. I'm still unsure if I want to tell him at all, but that's an issue for another day.

Today, I get to see the terror bean that's been making me nauseous for weeks. My heart is full sitting in the waiting room with Blake and Annie. Once the shock wore off of my situation, they welcomed me with open arms and rejoiced with me. The longing I felt when I saw them celebrating was gone, replaced with their job of being aunts. Our babies will get to grow up together with an instant cousin. I only hope I can continue to feel the happiness I have and not the worries that come with being a single mother. Even if Justin is in my life, it will still be me and my baby.

"Ms. Poulsen? Ms. McGrath?" A nurse in pink scrubs stands in the doorway, holding our charts. Having money seems to have its perks because Annie got us in to see a doctor within a week, and together. I have no doubt if we didn't get in here so soon, she would have had an entire OB set up in her home office so we could have these appointments.

"Time to see our little babies." Blake jumps up from the chair and offers Annie her hand like she can't get up by herself. I love the contrast between the two of them. Sunshine Blake and grumpy Annie balance each other out. Mix in my sarcastic brother, and the three of them have an envious relationship.

The nurse leads Annie and me to a bathroom where we have to leave our urine samples and then sit in another room while we wait for the doctor to come in. I tried to object when Annie called to tell me, not ask me, that she had set up an appointment for us. She's aware of my financial situation. I've done her hair for years, and while I make good money, it's not a lucrative career. She wouldn't hear anything of it when I told her I couldn't afford to see a fancy OB, and I planned to go to the local free clinic.

Annie and Blake talk quietly while I stew in my thoughts. There's a gentle knock at the door, and a middle-aged man in blue scrubs and a white coat walks into the room, followed by the nurse who brought us back. He's a good-looking man with graying hair at his temples and dark brown eyes hidden behind wire-framed glasses. He smiles at Annie and Blake when he enters.

"Ms. Poulsen. Ms. Rogers. Always good to see you. And I see you've brought another companion with you." He approaches me and offers his hand. "Ms. McGrath, I assume. I'm Dr. Dailey. It's so nice to meet you."

"She's not a companion. She's my companion's sister."

"I'm sorry, Ms. Poulsen. I didn't mean to assume anything." Dr. Daily backpedals at her harsh words.

"Relax, Baby. He didn't mean it like that." Annie visibly relaxes as Blake rubs her arm. I want what they have. The love. The simple companionship.

"Let's see what we have here." He opens both charts in his hand and smiles. "It appears we have two expectant mothers in the room. Congratulations to you both." My shoulders rise as a huge sigh takes over my body. I don't know if it's relief or anxiety

"I'd like to give you both ultrasounds as neither of you is entirely sure of your last periods. I'll also take some blood and get the standard tests run. Ms. Poulsen, you have an extensive medical history that we'll need to discuss, and once we know more, I'll consult with your surgeons to see what our best course of action is going forward. Just glancing over your charts, I want to prepare you that I don't see any other option but a cesarean section. We have plenty of time to discuss that though. Let's go see these babies."

As I lay on the table, I have to keep my hands in fists; I can feel them trembling. It's already confirmed that I'm pregnant, so I don't know why I'm so nervous. Annie said I could go first, and she and Blake are standing next to me while the tech sets everything up. Blake reaches out and grabs my hand, linking our fingers together. She's vibrating with excitement for us both.

Annie didn't think she would be able to have children after her accident. This is truly a miracle for her—for all of them. I'm so excited for my brother. He's going to be a fantastic father.

"Are we ready to see baby?" A sweet young brunette smiles at us. I nod, and she wheels her chair between my legs. Since we don't know when our last periods were, we have to do internal ultrasounds to check the size.

I stare at the black and white screen as a small picture of something resembling a jelly bean appears on the screen.

"Is that?"

"That's your baby. Listen." She outlines something on the screen, and a thumping sound echoes in the room. I hear Blake gasp and squeeze my hand.

"Nicole, that's my niece or nephew. Listen to that heart-beat." I can't help but smile at the excitement in her voice as a tear rolls down my cheek. Annie hands me a tissue and gives me a sweet smile. The tech moves the wand around and takes measurements.

"The heartbeat is nice and strong. Let me print you out some pictures. You're about eight weeks and three days along based on measurements." I exhale all the air from my lungs as she hands me pictures. It's really real. The technician looks to Annie.

71

"Are you ready to see yours?" We shuffle around, and I move back so Blake can be at Annie's side.

"Let's see what we have here." Annie's screen looks different from mine. Her little jelly bean is smaller and looks slightly more round than bean-shaped.

"What's that?" Blake points at the screen, and the tech smiles. Annie looks tense as she stares at the screen, not understanding Blake's question.

"What do you see, *Mijn Diamant?*" I stare at the screen and see what Blake sees.

"Is that…"

"It is." The tech moves the wand to get a better picture. "Congratulations, Mom. There are two sacs in there with little heartbeats. Let's listen." The room is silent as she clicks on one of the flickering spots in the image. The thumping echoes in the room again. She clicks on the screen, and we hear another heartbeat.

"Baby, are you okay?" Annie hasn't said a word, and Blake looks worried.

"Two?" She looks at the tech. "And they both look well?" Her voice is full of disbelief.

"Everything looks good on my end. You're at six weeks and two days. I'll print you out some pictures as well."

"Oh my god, Annie. This is incredible! When do we get to tell Cole? I can't believe we found this out without him. He's going to be so mad at you. I can't wait to see how you get punished." The tech gives Blake the side eyes. Not knowing them and their dynamic, that last sentence doesn't come off the best to a stranger.

"It's completely consensual." I don't know why I felt like I needed to validate their relationship, but the tech visibly relaxes. Blake and Annie are in their own little blissful bubble; they don't even hear my exchange with her.

"I'll leave you two alone for a minute and meet you in the waiting room." I attempt to take a step towards the door but Blake grabs my arm to stop me from leaving.

"What? No. This is amazing news for everyone. We have to celebrate. We have to tell Cole right away. He's going to flip out. You're going to be an aunt to twins. Oh my god, Annie. We are going to be moms to twins." I know she says her excitement is for me as well, and a small part of me believes her, but there's still a feeling of apprehension. It's too late now to worry about it, though. I'll tell Cole about my situation, and we can all work it out together. But not until he finds out he's going to be a dad. He needs to bask in all of the joy and excitement.

They text Cole and tell him to meet us at S'morgasm. It's Blake's favorite coffee shop that sells s'more set-ups that you can make at your table. I've never been, but they both assure me it's as unique as it sounds.

We stop at a pharmacy to fill Annie's prescriptions, and somehow, I walk out with enough prenatal vitamins to get me through at least half of my pregnancy. I hate asking for help, and I hate handouts even more, but I've learned over the last few months that there's no declining anything when it comes from Annie. And honestly, I'm in uncharted waters. I know I'll have a lot of expenses coming up soon, and if a simple gesture of vitamins helps alleviate some of that, I'll accept it.

Annie and Blake picked me up at my apartment, so the rest of my day is at their mercy. Blake is driving a gorgeous brand new car, and I'm envious. It still has the new car smell.

Blake parks us in a parking lot, and we walk into the most heavenly-smelling place I've ever been. Coffee and chocolate invade my senses.

My stomach rumbles from the smell. I was too nervous to eat before the appointment, and it's now protesting. Looking back, I should have eaten since I'm no longer eating for one. But at least I'm not eating for three.

When I get to the counter, I order myself a chai tea, and luckily, they have a few different pastry selections as well. I order a cheese Danish, and before I can pull out my card to pay for my order, Blake tells them to add five mugs to my order and hands her card to the barista. I look over my shoulder at Blake, confused.

"What did you just order me five of?" She tilts her head toward a wall at the front of the store full of hanging mugs.

"Those are prepaid coffees for anyone in need. They just have to bring a mug up, and it gets filled for free. I bought five more cups for the wall." I listen to her explain this incredible program as we move toward a couch where Annie is already sitting when my vision goes blurry. I swipe my hand over my eyes and realize I'm crying.

"Oh, Nicole." Blake rummages through her purse for a tissue. I thank her and wipe away the tears.

"I'm not usually a crier. It must be the hormones." From the other side of the couch, I see Annie go pale. Blake looks panicked.

"What's wrong, Baby?"

"I can't be like that. People can't see me being weak. We have to hide this for as long as possible." I've never seen Annie lose her cool before. It seems the hormones are already affecting her too. Blake takes Annie's hand, and I see her visibly calm. Once again, I'm filled with a feeling of jealousy. There's so much love and support for two little lives who won't be in the world for eight more months.

"Annie, we will talk to your lawyers and your team. This is not a bad thing. Look at me." Whoa. That's interesting. Annie's eyes snap to Blake. That's not their dynamic at all. "This is not a bad thing. Do you understand me?" I'm so enthralled by the scene unfolding in front of me that I'm startled when Cole squats in front of Annie.

"What's wrong, Kitten? What happened?" He must see the stress and panic on her face. She looks at him and stares into his eyes silently. Blake's face lights up with the anticipation of the news they are about to share with Cole.

"Cole." Annie breathes his name out in a sigh.

"What happened? Talk to me." He cups one of her cheeks, caressing it with her thumb.

"I'm…We're…You're…" She closes her eyes and takes a deep breath. "Cole, I'm pregnant." Blake squeals, and Cole freezes. His eyes dart between Blake and Annie, clearly shocked by the information.

"Tell him, Annie. Show him." She reaches into her purse and pulls out the ultrasound pictures. He takes them from her, still not making a sound. This is what they wanted but were told they could never have. Not by Annie at least. Annie's assumed infertility after her accident was a significant catalyst to their almost break up. She thought she wasn't good enough after finding out that news.

"You're pregnant, Kitten? How?"

"Cole, I'm sure I don't have to explain the mechanics of conception to you." And Annie is back. He smiles hearing it, too.

"Don't be fresh, Danika." They lock eyes, having a private moment in a room full of people.

"Pup, look at the pictures." His gaze lingers on Annie for a moment longer before he looks down at his hand. "Look." Her finger moves back and forth between the two dark circles in the pictures.

"What is that, Princess? I think I know, but I need confirmation. Tell me exactly what I'm looking at." Annie grabs his cheeks, and the love radiating between them is infectious.

"It's twins, Coleman. There are two babies." Cole falls to his butt from his crouched position. His hands move to her stomach.

"How is this even possible? It's a miracle. Annie, you're fucking incredible. Two? I'm going to be a dad to twins." His voice trails off as he stares at his hands—tears well in his eyes. "Marry me. Right now, marry me." I hear our names called by the barista and I walk away to get our order. They don't notice, and if I thought I could get away with it, I'd leave and let them celebrate together. I don't know how someone's heart can simultaneously fill and break at the same time, but it's not something I recommend. It hurts.

I place our tray of food on the table behind Cole, and he looks in my direction, finally realizing I'm here.

"Big sister. Did you get to know before me? You realize how very unfair that is, right?" I give him a half-hearted smile, not feeling like teasing him back. Blake grabs my hand and offers me the most genuine smile I've ever seen.

"Nicole. Let's celebrate. *Everyone*." She wants me to tell Cole. She's giving me an opportunity to share in their excitement but not enough information to give it away if I choose not to.

Do I want to? I want every emotion they've felt in the past several moments, even the panic. Because their panic was together and I want a together. Blake nods, encouraging me.

"What's wrong, big sis?" I move around the table and sit on the couch. Cole sits on the coffee table in front of us. I've kept this secret from my brother long enough.

"I'm...pregnant too, Cole." His eyes widen and I know he's thinking who. "It's Justin's. From the night at Midnight Moonshine."

"Nicole, are you sure?" I can't help but go on the defensive. This isn't the elation that he just showed for Annie.

"Yes. I'm sure. Thanks for the confidence." I sit back on the couch, creating distance from him.

"Pup, we all just came from the OB's office together. Nicole is about two weeks ahead of Annie."

"Nicole."

"Don't, Coleman. I get it. It's not nearly as exciting as your news, and I barely even know Justin. Don't think I haven't had these same thoughts running through my head for the last couple of weeks. Your screw-up sister strikes again. She can't even use birth control right and gets drunk and knocked up. I'll deal with it. I'll figure it out. Don't worry." I stand up, grab my coffee cup, and walk towards the door.

"Nicole, wait." It hurts to even hear his voice right now, so I don't stop. I hear Annie tell him to let me go. Maybe I really am on my own.

12

Justin

Weekly therapy sessions at Dov Memorial are for me as much as they are for the people in them. The death of my sister isn't the only demon that I hold inside of me. Talking with Annie a few months back has brought memories to the surface that I try hard to keep contained, but I had to share for her to help heal. I'm always happy to share a piece of me if it means someone else can have a breakthrough. I went into the medical field because of the events of my sister's death.

"There's no blood, Mama. She's okay. She's just sleeping."

My seven year old brain couldn't understand that just because she wasn't bleeding didn't mean she couldn't be dead. The mental torture that occurred when I realized I had carried my sister's lifeless body the twenty minutes back to our house from the pond has left me with decades of nightmares and heartbreak.

My parents lost two children that day, and I lost my parents. They were never the same towards me, haunted by the knowledge that their son's actions killed their daughter. I spent the next eleven years in a trance of working on the farm, going to school, and sleeping.

When I turned eighteen, and they had no legal responsibility towards me, I was handed an envelope and a suitcase. In it was paperwork for a bank account that contained more zeros than an average adolescent mind would have comprehended. My parents had a life insurance policy on each of us due to living on a farm.

"It's time for you to go, Justin. Your mother and I can't handle another day without Ivy with you here. This is blood money to us, and we want nothing to do with it. It's been in a savings account since we received it, and it's yours to do with it however you want. We're sorry, but we have to let you go, too. We hope you have a fulfilling life, son." I tried to walk further into the house, and he put a hand to my chest. *"Don't."*

"But, Mama?"

"She doesn't want to see you. Please don't make this any harder than it already is. We made peace with it a long time ago. We were only fulfilling our obligation to raise you. We've done that, and it's time for you to go. We love you. Goodbye, Justin." He offers me his hand to shake, and I slap it away.

"Jay?" I look up to see one of my nurses looking at me, concerned. A glance around the room shows I'm alone. Did the session end?

"You've been zoned out for a while. I thought you might have needed some alone time, so I had everyone leave quietly." I haven't been that lost in thought in a really long time. I smile at her politely. Her kind eyes brim with sadness behind her wide-rimmed glasses.

"Thank you. Is everyone alright?"

"Of course. There's still twenty minutes left in the session if you'd like me to bring them back?" I feel emotionally wrung out after that flashback. I shake my head.

"If everyone seemed fine, I'd rather just end the session for the day. Please apologize to them for me."

"There's no need. They all understand. They've been there, Jay. Maybe you need to talk to someone. You've been wandering off a lot lately. Some of us are worried about you." She's right. I've been having flashbacks, and they aren't good for me. I don't need to be pulled back to where I was a few years ago.

"Thank you for everything. I appreciate you."

"And we appreciate you. Take care of yourself just like you take care of everyone else." Just like I didn't take care of my sister. *Fuck. Don't do that, asshole.*

I give her a half smile and nod, and she leaves. I need to get my head on straight before I fall into old habits I can't crawl myself out of.

Me: Drink? Mini golf? *Uno?*

Spencer: Pick one.

Me: Beers and *Uno.* I'll be there in thirty.

Spencer: I'll unlock the door.

Spencer and I don't hang out often outside of work, so when I ask, she knows I've reached my mental limit and need to decompress. I stop at the gas station near her house and pick up two six-packs and some chips. When I get to Spencer's I knock and walk in, the door unlocked as promised.

"Honey, I'm home." Spencer's house is the antithesis of

Nicole's. There's minimal color. Everything is black, white, and gray. The lines are all clean and crisp. I love annoying her by leaving things slightly out of place. It's a game we play that she both loves and hates. I do it in the ambulance, too. She understands that she can't always have the things in her life as perfect as she wants them, and it's something that helps keep her mind aware of that.

Walking into the house, I place my keys into the dish on the small entry table. I move it a few inches to the right, smiling. Just that simple, ridiculous act makes me feel a tiny bit better. As I take my shoes off and put them on the shoe rack, I stare at the beautiful black and white picture of a wooden dock looking over a lake that hangs in the foyer.

Spencer walks around the corner wearing black leggings and a sports bra. She hates clothes, and the ones she wears have to be tight on her body. Her uniform took some getting used to for her. She usually wears snug clothes under them to help alleviate her sensory issues.

"How bad?"

"One of my nurses cleared the room, and I didn't even know it."

"Sister?"

"Parents." Her face sours. Neither event is better than the other. They're both traumas of my past that hold equal weight. "I brought beer and snacks."

"*Uno* is already on the coffee table."

The next several hours are spent mostly in silence, and my mind has time to heal and relax without being bombarded by outside forces. This is what Spencer and I do best: sit in companionable silence. Sometimes, we watch TV; sometimes, we play cards, like today. Some days, we simply play on our phones or listen to music. We are each other's safe space from our traumas. If I wanted to talk, she would listen, and vice versa.

"Is it because of Annie?" I know what she means. I told her I had confessed my past to Annie. Well, not all of it, but enough that she felt she could trust me enough to tell hers.

"Not fully. The nightmares have started gradually coming back. My conversation with her just accelerated things." She nods in understanding, and our silent game play continues.

My phone rings, startling me from the silence that permeates the room.

"Hey, Cole, how's it—"

"You mother fucker. What the fuck?"

"Cole, what's wrong?"

"What's wrong? Don't play fucking dumb with me, Justin. You better plan to make this right. I swear to fucking god, if you walk out on my sister, I'll break both of your goddamn legs so you won't think about doing it ever again."

"Cole?"

"How long have you fucking known? I know we aren't close, but she's my fucking sister. Don't you dare fuck her over. This is your responsibility, and I expect you to step the fuck up. How long, Justin? How fucking long?"

Spencer mouths "what" to me. I can only imagine the expression on my face because I have no idea what I did to make Cole this irate. I shrug back at her and shake my head. Placing my phone on the couch between us, I hit the speaker button.

"Cole. I promise you whatever it is, I'd never intentionally hurt Nicole, but I honestly don't know what I did." There's silence on the line, and I check to make sure he hasn't hung up.

"You don't know what I'm talking about?" His anger is gone, replaced with something else. Guilt?

"No, I'm clueless. Is she alright? I haven't seen or talked to her since the BBQ, so I can't imagine I've done anything that could hurt her since then.

"Fuck. Justin, when I hang up this phone, you better call my goddamn sister and talk to her. I'll text you her number. And if she doesn't answer, you call her until she does. Do you understand?"

"Yeah. I get it. I still have no idea what's going on, but it sounds important. I'll call right now."

"We'll finish this conversation after you talk to her, but everything I've said still stands." He hangs up, and I have never been so confused in my life.

"What did you do, Justin?"

"Other than sleeping with his sister, which he was fine with when he found out, nothing. She ignored me the last time I saw her." My phone vibrates as Nicole's number appears in a text on my screen.

"You should call her. Cole sounded serious." The phone call rings through to voicemail. I try several more times to no avail. Either she's ignoring me, or she isn't near her phone.

13

Nicole

I can't believe my brother would question me like that.
"Are you sure?" Yes, I'm fucking sure. I'm not a goddamn
slut. I haven't even slept with anyone since Justin. I
don't know if that's what he was asking, but none of the
other options make me feel any better either.

Are you sure you're pregnant?

Are you sure it's Justin's?

Are you sure you want to have a baby?

Yes. Yes. No, but there's no other alternative for me.

My phone dings in my pocket, and it's a text from Blake.

Blake: Cole is going to take Annie home. Can I give you a
ride?

Fuck. I walked out of S'morgasm and just started walking
aimlessly. I knew I'd eventually have to call for a rideshare,
but I don't really have the money to spend since we're about
thirty minutes from home.

Me: Please. I'll send you a pin of my location.

Another text comes in, and this one is from Cole.

Cole: I'm sorry big sister, I fucked up.
  Me: Yes, you did.
  Cole: Get home safely, and I'll talk to you later. Love you.

Before I can answer Cole, my phone rings, and an unknown number pops up on the screen. I owe too many creditors, so I never answer a number that I haven't programmed in. I let it ring out to voicemail because I've learned if you disconnect early, they just call right back, except they call right back anyway. In fact, they call four times before they stop.

Blake pulls up, and I quickly tuck my phone into my pocket. Whoever it was will have to bother someone else.

"Hey, Nicole. I'm really sorry." She smiles as I get in the front seat.

"Don't apologize for my brother being an ass."

"He's excited for you. He unfortunately didn't express it the greatest at first."

"I'm in as much shock as everyone else. Can I confess something to you, Blake?" She reaches over and grabs my hand.

"Of course. Anything, anytime. We're kind of related now." Her perky attitude is lifting my mood. I hate admitting my weakness as much as asking for help.

"I'm jealous of what the three of you have. I want the excitement over my baby. The joy and happiness. Cole's question squashed any positive feeling I had at that moment."

"Nicole, we are all so happy for you and Annie. I'm so sorry if we didn't make you feel included in our joy for today."

"I felt included at the OB, but the reality of my situation screamed at me when you told Cole. My brother is going to be an amazing father."

"Are you going to tell Justin?" Yes. No. I have no fucking clue. "He's a great guy, Nicole. I had no idea you two had gotten intimate, but you should give him a chance." Smiling at her use of the word "intimate," I sigh. I know she's right.

"My mind tells me no, but my heart tells me yes." I know what the *right* thing to do is, but it doesn't mean it isn't hard. "Do you think you could give me his number?" Pulling out my phone, I see I have a missed text. "Nevermind. It appears I already have it. What did Cole do?"

Unknown: Nicole, it's Justin. Cole gave me your number and said I needed to talk to you immediately. Please call or text me back. He made it sound important.

"Did Cole talk to Justin?" Blake shakes her head.

"Not that I'm aware of, but I came to get you, so I don't know what he did after I left. "What's wrong?" I stare at the message on my phone, feeling like it's burning a hole in my head.

"I have a text from Justin. He says Cole told him we needed to talk."

"Oh shit. Do you think he said something to Justin? I don't think Cole would be that malicious. He was pretty upset when I left, though."

"Fucking Cole. He can't just let me do things at my own pace."

86

Me: Hi, Justin. Could you come over tonight to talk?
  Justin: Tell me when, and I'll be there.
  Me: How about 6?
  Justin: I'll be there. I hope everything is okay.

I can't respond to that because it's really not.

Blake drops me off in front of my apartment and makes sure I take my copious amount of prenatal vitamins. It's absurd how many Annie bought me.

I take the dogs out before straightening up my apartment. I have two hours before Justin gets here, and I'm exhausted. I've read that the first trimester can be tiring, but this seems excessive. I can't imagine how Annie is going to feel growing two babies.

I sit on the couch for a moment and lean my head back on the top cushion to relax when I hear a loud knock on the door. I sigh heavily. I got so comfortable in the few minutes off my feet. Walking to the door, the dogs are practically tripping me with excitement, and I have no idea why.

I look through the peephole and see Justin standing in the hallway. What is he doing here so early? I told him six.

"Hey, you're early." He looks at his watch and looks back at me in confusion.

"It's five minutes after six. I've been knocking for a few minutes." I lean back and look at the clock on the microwave.

"Holy shit. I sat down on the couch and must have passed out without realizing it. Wow. Come in." I step back so he can walk in, and he kisses me on the cheek before he continues by.

"Nicole, I have no idea what's happening, but Cole called me, cursing me out." I haven't even shut the door yet, and we're already getting started.

I turn around and spot the bag of vitamins on the kitchen counter right next to where he's standing.

"Could we sit on the couch and talk?" He looks behind him before turning around and walking over to the living room. Java and Beans follow Justin excitedly and run up the ramp when he sits. They fight for his lap and affection, and I watch for a moment as he pets them and dodges face kisses.

"Ladies, there's plenty of me to go around." I laugh, and it relieves some of the stress of the moment.

"Come on, girls. Let's eat." I open the cabinet where I keep their food, and they run down the ramp into the kitchen and wait by their bowls. I give them food and fresh water, and when I have no other reason to stall, I close the kitchen gate behind me and join Justin.

Sitting on the edge of the couch, I grab a throw pillow and hold it in my lap. It feels too raw to be sitting next to him, and I need a barrier.

"I want to first apologize for the way I treated you at the BBQ. You didn't deserve to be ignored. I was...dealing with some things." He reaches out and touches my elbow.

"It's okay, Pumpkin." I close my eyes at the warmth that spreads down my arm at his touch and his little pet name for me. "We all go through things. Will you relax and talk to me?" Relax? That's not going to happen anytime soon. I slide back until I hit the cushion and exhale a shaky breath.

"Did you get the note I left you?"

"Yeah, I got both of them. It was sweet of you. All of it. It explains why the pups were so excited to see you when you were knocking."

"Yeah. They're pretty cute." His hand rubs the back of his

88

neck like he's uneasy. "I thought you might have called. You don't owe me any explanation, of course. I just thought we had a good time." I had a fucking incredible time.

"Justin."

"No. It's okay. My ego can take the rejection."

"It was a great night, Justin." He puffs out his chest in an attempt to look macho, but it just makes me laugh.

"I aim to please." His eyes soften, and he touches my arm again. "I really want to kiss you right now." Damn. Please do, but don't.

"As much as the idea of getting lost in your kisses right now sounds perfect, we have to talk first. You might reconsider that thought once we do."

"Doubtful." His smile kills me. It's warm and gentle and inviting and so fucking sinful because I know what that mouth can do. His smile widens when he catches me lingering on his lips.

"What did Cole tell you?" I need a baseline.

"Cole didn't *tell* me anything. There was a lot of yelling, and me being clueless as to what I was getting yelled at about. All I know is it has something to do with you and him threatening to break my legs." I roll my eyes and huff a laugh.

"Yeah, that sounds like my little brother." My hands begin to tremble at the realization that I have to tell him, and I have to tell him now.

"Nicole, I'm going to ask a bold question because you look nervous as hell. Would you like me to hold you while you work out whatever it is that you need to say?" Fuck. Who dropped this man from fucking heaven. Or maybe it's hell. My own personal hell, where I make shitty mistakes, and this kind soul of a man doesn't hold me accountable for them.

And really, who the fuck would say no to his offer. Not me. I nod, and he opens his arms.

"Next to me or in my lap. Whatever you feel comfortable with." I fight the inner demons in me telling me not to do it. I shouldn't be seeking comfort in the man who is literally offering me his open arms.

"Lap." He slouches down a bit and opens his legs wider. My petite frame fits perfectly in his large arms. He feels like a comforting blanket as he guides my cheek to rest on his chest. One arm comes around my lower back, and a thumb slips under my shirt to caress my bare skin. His other hand weaves its way through my curls to massage the base of my scalp. Forget my confession. I want to stay in the bubble and never leave.

"That's better, Pumpkin. I don't like seeing you stressed." He smells clean, like fresh laundry that's hung outside to dry in the sun. I burrow further into his neck, and a moan escapes me. His magic fingers massage the base of my neck where my shoulders meet.

"You're killing me. Between your moans and subtle hip shifts, I know you can feel what you're doing to me." He's right. I can feel his cock hardening underneath me. He's not here for sex, but god, does it sound amazing right now. His hand slides from my neck into my hair, and he flexes his hand, tugging at my curls.

I look into his hazel eyes, getting lost in the depth of the green mixed with swirls of brown.

"I really want to fucking kiss you. Please say yes, Pumpkin." I lick my lips, knowing there's no denying him right now, and nod.

"Please." I arch my head to meet his lips, and he pulls me

closer. The feeling of being cocooned in a blanket increases as he tightens around me. His tongue dances tenderly over mine, and I melt into his. All feelings of stress disappear from my body. How does he do this? Pulling away, he rests his forehead on mine.

"I'm sorry. I had to do that. I just couldn't stand not kissing you for another moment. You wanted to talk. I'm all ears."

"Fuck talking". I reposition myself to straddle him and cage his head between my arms and the couch. I crash my mouth back into him, and he responds without hesitation. He grabs my hips, grinding them over his jeans. The soft cotton shorts I changed into when I got home make a minimal barrier between my needy pussy and his hardening cock. I don't even have underwear on. I planned to change before he arrived, and my body decided I needed a nap.

I pull away to catch my breath, and he attacks my neck, sucking and pulling at the skin as we continue to dry hump on the couch.

"I need you, Justin. Please. I need you inside me, Doc." These pregnancy hormones are no fucking joke. He grabs my breasts, giving them a firm squeeze, and I slap his hands away. "Maybe I didn't say it clearly enough. Pull out your magical pierced cock and fuck my dripping pussy. Right. Now. I want you like a fucking bull at the rodeo."

"Yes, Ma'am." He pretends to tip a cowboy hat and slides me down his legs so he can access his pants. As his fingers undo his belt, I remove what little clothes I'm wearing. I tug at his navy shirt, and he lifts his hands to let me remove it. His hips lift under me to push down his jeans, and his cock springs free.

"What are they today?" Large hands knead my breast as he

smirks at me.

"I thought I had to fuck you right now, but you want to pause to know what kind of boxers I'm wearing?" I shift forward to rub myself along his length.

"Fuck, Pumpkin." His eyes squeeze tight, and so do his fingers on my nipples.

"Oh, god. Tell me. I want to know." I don't know who's being more tortured by my teasing, him or me.

"B-bacon. They have bacon on them." I giggle and look down, pulling at a small piece of bright blue fabric to reveal a brown, squiggly piece of bacon.

Grabbing his shaft, I line him up and sit, all the way down. I'm so turned on and wet his cock slides in without resistance.

"Fuck me." His words hiss out through gritted teeth.

"Oh, I'm about to, Doc. Hold the fuck on." I grab the back of the couch, tuck my knees under me, and bounce. I bounce and bounce, watching his eyes turn black with lust. Feeling his piercing pound against my clit with every jolt of his hips meeting mine.

"Fuck, Nicole. A condom." His hands squeeze on my hips to get me to stop, but I can't.

"It's okay. It's okay." I'm pregnant, and it doesn't fucking matter. "Your cock is electric inside me. Keep going. Fuck, please don't stop." He hesitated for a split second before thrusting harder into me.

"Are you going to come for me? Are my piercing and cock going to make your clit sing? I want you to come all over my cock, Pumpkin." He pulls a nipple into his mouth and bites the tip while licking with his tongue. It's a heady sensation of pleasure and pain.

"I want....I want you to come. What can I do?"

"Keep doing everything you're doing. I'm going to come for you. You said I have a magical pierced cock; well, you have a magical orgasm-inducing pussy. I could get obsessed with it." His words spur me on. I don't know where this energy is coming from. Maybe my power nap gave me the boost I needed.

"Oh, fuck. Pinch them harder. Yes. Fuck. Fuck. Come with me." I run my nails down his chest, and a guttural moan invades my ear.

"Fuuuuuck, fuck." We both fall glorious over the edge of ecstasy. My orgasm crests and my moans turn into high-pitched screams. The dogs howl from the sound, and our moans turn into laughter as we try to catch our breath.

Justin leans his head on my chest and puffs out a breath of air. "I don't know how the fuck you do that, Pumpkin. You seriously have a magical pussy."

"You might not think that in a minute," I mumble. Unfortunately, I didn't mumble low enough.

"Why would you say that?" He chuckles. "I guess we skipped the talking part. Tell me what's wrong." He sweeps a curl out of my face and tucks it behind my ear.

"I want you to remember that I have a magical pussy that you're currently still buried in. Can you do that?"

He flexes his hips and smiles. "It's hard to forget. Sure."

"Justin—" Two fingers push my chin up that I had tucked to my chest.

"Don't do that. Don't feel any shame for whatever you're about to say." He's hyping me up for his letdown.

"Justin, I'm…"

14

Justin

Nicole went from looking like a fierce woman to a meek little mouse. I can't let her hang her head.

"Don't do that. Don't feel any shame for whatever you're about to say." She looks so stunning right now. Her forehead glistens with a few stray curls stuck to it, her hair slightly messed from my fingers running through it—rosy cheeks from her orgasm.

"Justin, I'm...pregnant." She's my wet dream.

What? I don't dare move a muscle or take a breath. Did she say *pregnant?*

"Say something, Doc."

"Repeat yourself."

"I'm pregnant, and it's yours. I haven't been with anyone since you and for a while before you." I need my rapidly shriveling dick put away to deal with this.

"Can we put some clothes on for this conversation, please?"

"Um, yeah. Sure. Let me just…" She lifts off me, and before she's fully standing, I have myself tucked away. She's looking around on the floor for her clothes. I see my shirt and hand it to her. She'll swim in it, but it will cover everything I need to have this talk.

"Thanks." She pulls it over her head and sits on the couch beside me, tucking her legs under her. I watch as she grabs another throw pillow, pulling it close to herself for support.

"Okay. I'm pretty sure you told me you're pregnant... after we just had sex. Now, I understand biology well, and it doesn't happen that fast, so I need a little more of an explanation, Pumpkin."

"I've known for about three weeks."

"Three. Three weeks?" I scrub my hand over my face, doing the math. "So you're about eight weeks pregnant?"

"And three days." Her voice shakes as she speaks. "Eight weeks and three days. I have pictures if you'd like to see them." See pictures. Of a baby. A baby, that's mine. My. Baby.

"No." My abrupt answer startles her and I try again, calmer. "Not yet. Let me process it first, please."

"I don't expect anything from you. I know we barely know each other and—"

"We are absolutely not going to do that. I understand now everything that Cole was saying. I'm not an asshole deadbeat. If that baby is half mine, then I will be the other half of its parents. Plural."

"It is. I swear." I put out my hand in offering, allowing her to accept or reject it. I can see her battling within herself as she stares at it. She finally reaches out and lets me take hers.

In the softest tone I can muster, I look into her eyes. "I believe you, Nicole." I squeeze her hand, and she flings herself across the couch into me. I cradle her in my arms as her body quakes with tears. "Shhh. What can I do?"

"You're doing it. The fact that you believe me is all I need right now." I have no reason not to believe her, but I have every reason to be scared out of my fucking mind.

Pregnant. Nicole, a woman I have no real connection to, is pregnant. I know the guy at the gas station on my route to work better than this fragile woman in my arms. I only know her last name because of another woman she isn't even related to. Cole's information is in Annie's file. Fuck. Keep it together man.

I can't be a father. I have no example of being a good father. My own kicked me to the curb the first chance he had. I killed my sister. How can I keep a baby alive? I don't have a schedule conducive to raising a baby.

"Doc? Are you okay? Your whole body just went rigid." Because I'm having a fucking mental breakdown. Warm hands grab my cheek, and I find myself looking into ocean-blue eyes.

"Come back to me, Justin. Hey. Where did you go?" I didn't realize I had gone anywhere. I knew I was spiraling, but I didn't think I was that deep.

"I'm here." I run my hands up and down her bare thighs to try and ground myself.

"We don't have to have all the answers right now. Hell, we don't have to have *any* answers right now. We have at least thirty weeks or more to figure things out." Thirty weeks. A lot can happen in thirty weeks. We can get to know each other. This blue-eyed beauty will be in my life for the rest of my existence. An existence that's shaky on the best days.

What if she has a girl? It has to be a boy. She can't have a girl. It could look like Ivy, and I couldn't handle that.

"Who's Ivy? Is that a name that you like for a girl? It's

pretty. We have plenty of time to put it on a list—"

"No." I've startled her again with another sharp remark. I need to get better control of myself. "It's no one. I don't want to use that name."

"Okay." The look on her face is even more proof she knows nothing about me. I never speak her name out loud, although I must have if she heard it.

"Nicole…" I have no idea what I intended to say, but whatever it was has slipped from my mind.

"Pumpkin. Call me Pumpkin. Something is going on behind those eyes, and I'm sure whatever it is, we can figure it out." She has no clue. I've been trying to figure it out for over two decades. Therapy hasn't fixed it. Medications haven't fixed it. My brain got rewired that day at the pond, and I fight every day to stay above water.

I take a shaky breath and lean in to kiss her. I need a distraction—something to ground me and keep me in the present.

Metal crashes as the heavy doors hit the walls. Bright white lights burn into my barely open eyes. There's beeping and shouting all around me. I'm going too fast. My body is lifted and dropped down onto another soft surface.

"What did he take?" Who took something? Is someone stealing? The bright lights dim, and the room goes quiet. Peace.

"Clear." I'm zapped by lightning. Why is it so cold? I can't… there's something in my throat. My vision is hazy. Blinking doesn't help. Are my glasses on?

"Sir, can you hear me? What's his name?" Someone far away

says my name. "Justin." The voice sounds angelic. "What did he take?"

"This is everything we found around him." My angel hands over several orange blurs, making rattling sounds."

"Fuck, these are all antidepressants. All by different doctors." The bright lights start to dim again. I'm glad because they hurt my eyes.

"He's crashing again. Clear."

I jolt awake, gasping for air. Something heavy is on my chest. I can't breathe. Get it off me. Get it off me.

"Justin. Justin. Hey. Wake up. " I am fucking awake, and I can't breathe. I can't take a deep breath.

"Open your eyes." The weight lifts, and I can inhale a big gulp of air. And another. I open my eyes, but it's still blurry. My hand goes to my face, feeling around.

"Here. I took them off you when you fell asleep." This isn't the voice of my angel, but my glasses are put in my hands. "Doc?" Doc. I open my eyes more, blinking rapidly once my glasses are on. My eyes dart around the room. It's warm and colorful. Not cold and white.

"Where am I?" Something touches my leg, and I pull it back.

"It's Nicole. You're at my house. You fell asleep on my couch, and I laid with you and fell asleep on your chest. I'm sorry." I take a few cleansing breaths and run her words through my mind like rocks in a rock tumbler. Nicole. Her house. Fell asleep. My chest.

"Pumpkin."

"Hey, Doc. Are you back with me?" Her voice is soothing. I lean forward and pull her back down on top of me, clinging to her as my lifeline.

"Pumpkin. I'm sorry." She nestles into me closer. I still have no shirt on, and her hand caresses my chest.

"Don't be. Was it a nightmare?" It was reality. A reality I lived about six years ago.

"Yeah." Her fingers leave goosebumps on my skin.

"Do you want to talk about it?" I force myself to take a breath before I answer. I don't want to overreact again and startle her with another abrupt answer.

"No." I smooth a hand down her back. She's still in my shirt.

"I'm a great listener if you change your mind." *You don't want to hear about my demons.*

"I'll keep it in mind."

"Do we want to move this to my bedroom?" I have no idea what time it is, but I don't trust myself to fall asleep again, not that I think there will be any more sleeping for me.

"I should go." Her face falls.

"Oh. Okay." She moves to shift off of me, and I hold her closer.

"I can lay with you until you fall asleep. I don't think I'll get back to sleep by myself, and I don't want to keep you up any more than I already have." She gives me a half smile, and I know she is considering if she should object. Please don't.

"I understand. I'd like that." I reach under her thighs and hold on as I swing us to the edge of the couch.

"I can walk." She giggles, and it's a soothing balm to my soul.

"And I can carry you. Let me." I stand us up and walk down the hall. Kneeling on the bed, I crawl to the middle and carefully lay her down below me.

"I'll stay until you fall asleep. I don't want you waking up in the morning thinking I've abandoned you because of what you told me. I only want you to have a good night's rest. Okay?"

"Okay."

"Good." I kiss her forehead before laying next to her. "Did you save my number today?" She nods into the pillow, and I pull her closer. I inhale her rose and mint shampoo and feel the warmth of her back against my chest.

"You're lucky it's summer. Otherwise, I'd look strange walking out of here in the middle of the night without a shirt." She tries to shift under me, and I hold her tighter. "It's okay. Keep it."

"Are you sure? I can take it off."

"As much as I'd love to lay here naked with you, it will only make leaving even harder." Her ass wiggles against my hips.

"I can make it even harder." I grasp her hip, stopping her wiggles.

"Don't be a brat, Pumpkin."

"What if I wan—" I stop her words with a hand over her mouth.

"Be a good girl and do as you're told. Would you like me to help you fall asleep?" She nods her head under my hand. I slide my other hand from her hip, moving it under her thigh. Pushing forward, I hike her leg up, giving me better access to her pussy. My hand moves down her thigh, grazing her entrance before finding her clit. My Pumpkin gasps as I use gentle pressure in a circular motion to wind her up.

Her hips rotate in time with my fingers, rocking into my cock, and I groan.

"Be still and enjoy yourself." Her hips push back farther.

"I am enjoying myself." She grabs my hand from under her head and sucks my thumb into her mouth, swirling her tongue around the tip of my pad.

"Pumpkin," I growl in her ear. She nips the tip of my finger making my cock jump. "What are you trying to do, fresh girl?"

"As nice as an orgasm sounds, I'm trying to get you to fuck me before you leave." She sucks my thumb into her mouth and moans around it. Any resolve I had—which isn't much around her—dissipates.

"All you had to do was ask." I slide my hand over her ass, squeezing it before I reach to undo my pants again. For some reason, my anxiety gets the best of me. "Please don't have any expectations for me this time. I'll make sure you get your orgasm, though." I push a kiss into the back of her head through her mess of curls.

"You meet all my expectations, Justin. Now, quit stalling and fuck me to sleep."

"That I can do." I finish undoing my pants and push them off. I position myself behind her, opening her up with my hands, and gently slide myself in. Inch by inch, I pump inside her until my hips meet her ass. A soft moan escapes her, and it sounds like a release of stress.

"Honestly, if you did nothing else but stay right here, lying inside me, I'd be a satisfied woman." I chuckled into her soft curls.

"Did I just unlock a new kink?"

"What?" She cranes her neck to look at me over her shoulder.

"It's called cockwarming. When you penetrate your partner for the simple act of being inside them and nothing

101

more."

"Cockwarming." She rolls the word around a few times. I gently pump my hips for the sheer purpose of needing some friction. "I really like that idea. Would it make you stay? If you could just lay here behind me and warm your cock." She giggles, and I feel the pressure squeeze my cock inside her.

"Pumpkin, you need your sleep."

"Have you ever done it before? Done cockwarming with someone overnight?" It takes a bold person to ask about a partner's previous relationships so early into meeting them.

"I haven't."

"Would you try? You never know until you try. If it doesn't work, then you know for next time. I won't even require an orgasm. Just sleep."

"Require, huh?"

"I'm just making sure you're aware of all your options."

"I really should go, Pumpkin."

"Or you really could stay, Doc." I could. It feels so fucking good to be inside her. Could I try it? *Should* I try it is more the question. I've never had more than one nightmare in a night. I want to.

15

Nicole

If his thoughts had an audiobook, I would be able to hear Justin's back-and-forth conversation with himself. I can tell he's debating my request solely based on his breathing.

"Doc, it's okay to tell me no. But it's also okay to tell yourself yes." Every few seconds, his hips shift, moving his cock slightly inside me. It's a delicious feeling of being full that I've never felt before. Who knew in my mid-twenties, I could still learn sex terms?

"Pumpkin, I'll try. I'll stay right here with you and try." His arm bands around my waist, pulling me closer to him. "I usually take sleeping pills. They help keep the nightmares away." My heart breaks a little to hear he has trauma that invades his dreams. I wonder what he's gone through to have them so regularly as an adult.

"Hey, Doc?" He hmms his response. "How old are you?" He chuckles. We really don't know much about each other.

"I'm thirty-four. How old are you, Pumpkin?"

"I'm twenty-five."

"You're just a baby." The word baby coming from his lips makes him stop breathing. His hand tentatively moves from around my chest, creeping down my body. It comes to rest on top of my pubic bone. His medical knowledge would tell him exactly where the baby, our baby, would be located in my body right now. He's about as close as he can get. His hand splays flat, warming my body. When he speaks, it's in a reverent whisper, sending a chill down my spine.

"I have a past that scares me for the future. I'll share with you as much as I can, when I can. Just please be patient with me. I promise to try. Every damn day I'll try for you and for the life we created."

"Thank you." I feel his kiss on my shoulder and hear his inhale into my messy locks. I drift off with a smile on my face and a cock warming inside me.

I wake up to a tongue licking my face, but it's not human. I crack an eye to a blur of white.

"Morning, Java. Where'd you come from?" I roll onto my back, stretching before my memory reminds me that I didn't fall asleep alone. The bed next to me is unfortunately empty. I roll back to my side, scooping up my sausage dog, and pull her into my chest for a cuddle. "Did Doc take you out again before he escaped this morning?" Java licks my face, and I close my eyes for the assault. The smell of pumpkin spice permeates the air, and another bundle of fur attacks my ear. "Morning to you too, Beans." I hear the deep timber of a laugh and look up.

"Fuck."

"What's wrong?" His brows knit in confusion.

"I can't decide what's sexier, your smile, your bare chest, or the cup of coffee you're holding for me." The corner of his lip tilts up.

"How do you know the coffee is for you?" I sit up, scooting my back to the headboard, and extend my hands, wiggling my fingers in the 'gimme' motion.

"Because this basic white bitch could smell pumpkin spice a mile away." He laughs as he hands me the coffee. The color is perfect. I keep pumpkin spice creamer in my refrigerator as much of the year as possible. I even buy in bulk when I'm able and freeze it. "You're still here."

"I'm still here." He sits on the bed beside me, and I move my legs to give him more room. Reaching my hand out, I rub his upper thigh.

"Thank you. Did you get any sleep?"

"Actually, I did. And it was peaceful. Thank you for the little push." His eyes look genuine as they stare back at me.

"They like you." He turns to see my two crazy ladies burrowing under the blankets.

"Why wouldn't they?"

"Because when you're here at night, they don't get to sleep in the bed with me. Weenie dogs can hold grudges like people do." He lays next to me, resting his head against my stomach, and my heart melts into a puddle.

"I happen to know you're a top-notch cuddler, so I can understand why they would get upset." My hand moves on its own accord, caressing his short hair. His eyes close at my gentle touch. "Can I take you out?"

"Out?"

"Yeah, like on a date. We may have done things a little out of order, but I want to get to know you properly."

"You want to go on a date? With me?"

"You say that like it's a foreign concept."

105

"I don't usually *date* men." And I just made myself sound like a slut. I slap my forehead, and he laughs. "I didn't mean it like that. It's not like I sleep around or anything. I just don't usually have interest in anything serious." His hand caresses my lower belly.

"We've passed serious, Pumpkin." Isn't that the truth. "I have lunch plans with my partner, Spencer, but I'm free tonight. How about you?" I lean over, grab my phone off the nightstand, and check my schedule. I notice I have several missed texts from Cole. I'll save those for later.

"I'm free after about sixish."

"Perfect. I'll come by around seven. Does that work for you?" I nod, and he sits up.

"I have to get going." He kisses my forehead, and I pause to ogle his bare chest again.

"Oh shit." I quickly grab the hem of his shirt I'm still wearing and pull it over my head, extending it to him. He stares at me as he mindlessly grabs the shirt, pulling it up to his nose. He takes a deep inhale, and his eyes flutter close.

"If this shirt didn't smell so fucking much like you right now, I'd insist you keep it. But damn, Pumpkin, I want to use it to jerk off with." He tucks it into his back pocket and smiles.

"That's weirdly erotic and endearing and equally creepy all at the same time." He kisses my forehead and walks toward the door.

"I aim to please. I'll see you at seven."

What have I gotten myself into?

16

Justin

"Please repeat yourself." Spencer's hand is stopped mid-air with her sub between her fingers. An Italian sub with spicy mustard and everything else on the side: lettuce, onions, tomatoes, salt, pepper, oil, and vinegar. Oh, and I can't forget the Italian cheese bread. I know her orders everywhere we go, like the back of my hand.

I stopped and picked up lunch before coming to her house. She's comfortable here, and I'm always happy to do what makes her the most at ease. She's dressed strangely today. She's in her usual sports bra with a pair of spandex shorts, but the design is a pink cheetah print, and that's not usually her type of thing.

"I know you heard me and don't actually need me to repeat myself. Don't use your trained people processing skills on me, woman." Sometimes, her mind processes things a little slower, and rather than make people feel awkward while she takes it all in, she's taught herself to ask them to repeat what they said to give her a few extra seconds. It's genius, really.

"Humor me. It's not that I didn't hear you; it's just a bit

unbelievable. You seem too calm for the severity of your sentence." Huffing, I put my sandwich down. Mine mirrors hers, except all my condiments are on mine sans the onions."

"Spencer, Nicole is pregnant, and I'm the father."

"Again, you are unbelievably calm for an unplanned pregnancy with a woman you barely know." Leave it to Spencer to give it to me straight.

"Those are both accurate observations."

"And you're feeling?" What *am* I feeling?

"I slept last night. Well, I slept after a nightmare. But I was able to fall back asleep without pills."

"That's wonderful. Did you do something new?" I chuckle. She's going to find this one interesting.

"Well, I spent the night at Nicole's house…cockwarming." She picks up her phone to look up what I just said. She doesn't like things she doesn't understand, and the internet is her best friend for new information. I put my hand over her screen.

"You probably don't want to look that one up. I'm happy to explain it." She looks at me expectantly, and I explain it to her like I did for Nicole.

"So I understand correctly, there was no sex. Just penetration? Didn't you fall out? Roll in your sleep? Were you hard the entire time?" I love her inquisitive nature and her unabashed way of asking what she wants to know. She thrives on knowledge.

"No sex. I woke up several hours later to the sun, and we were both still in the same position with me inside her, and I still had a semi." Her face processes all of the information I've just given her.

"Final question. Why?"

"Why? Well, it started off as sex, but once I was inside her, it just felt like that's where I wanted to be. She asked me to stay and give it a chance. I considered my options and realized I had no real reason not to try."

"So now we have cockwarming and babies. I'm not sure I know who you are anymore, Justin." My entire demeanor changes as I remember the dream that started my evening.

"It was you."

"What was me?"

"My nightmare. It was you. Six years ago." I know she doesn't need any more information. She found me. She saved me. I'm a paramedic because of her.

"Do you want to talk about it?"

"Do I *want* to? Never. But I know talking helps bring the real issues to the surface." There are several minutes of silence as we finish our sandwiches. When the sound of the paper crinkling cuts the air, it's time to talk. Wiping my mouth with a napkin, I slump back into my chair and throw the wadded-up ball onto the table.

"It was the few moments I remember in the hospital before…"

"Before you died, Justin. You have to say it."

"Before I flatlined, and they had to use a defibrillator to restart my heart."

"No. Say it. Not the medical term. Say the layman's term. You died."

"I did."

"Justin."

"Fuck, you were there. Why do I have to say it?" I lean forward, bracing my head in my hands.

"And I watched you die. Twice, for that matter. After

busting my fucking ass in the ambulance to keep you alive, you died in that Emergency Department. Twice." Shit. She rarely curses. She wants me to confess this truth out loud.

"Fuck. I...I died. I died the day we met."

"Twice."

"Twice, okay. I fucking died twice. Damn, you're a pushy bitch."

"Thank you."

Despair.

Useless.

Lonely.

Hopeless.

Sitting on the couch in my living room, I stare at the almost dozen orange pill bottles in front of me. I've been an EMT long enough to know what they do and how they all interact together, and the ones I wasn't sure about, I looked up.

I have no friends, no family that wants to claim me. When I don't show up for work in a few days, someone might come check on me. I hate that whoever it is will have to find me and live with the sight of my lifeless body. I live every day with the guilt of my sister's death, and the carousel of pills in front of me proves that nothing helps.

I dispense the proper amount of each pill onto a paper plate like I'm fixing myself a dinner. I don't need to devour entire bottles to do the job I need them to do. All I need is the right combination to stop my heart after the sleeping pills kick in. The perfect amount so I can fade away into an endless dark oblivion where I don't hurt anymore.

It's not a physical pain; although some days it hurts so bad, it seems like it is. It's not even a mental pain. The medication would fix that if it was. It's a pain that encapsulates every cell that flows through my body. A black sludge that pulls each layer of my being deeper into a hole until everything I do feels like I'm drowning, and no amount of kicking or flailing gets me any closer to the surface.

No one understands. Therapists prescribe pills or exercise for endorphins. Doctors prescribe therapy or pills. It's a vicious rotating cycle of endless unknowns. Something has to stop the cycle, and it has to be me.

I grab the bottle of water off the table, getting ready to take my first pills, when there's a knock at the door. I try to ignore it, but I know she won't go away. She sees my truck outside and knows I'm home.

Standing up, I toss a throw blanket over the coffee table, covering my impending date with destiny, and walk to the door. I open it to my smiling seven year old neighbor with her dark hair in pigtails, dressed in a red and pink polka dot dress. Sadly, she's probably my best and only friend.

"Hi, Mr. Jay. Wanna play?" By play, she means the piano. I have a keyboard we play together, and she enjoys making parodies of popular songs with me.

"Not today, Katy. I'm tired and need to take a nap." She plants her hand on her hips, looking up at me with her light brown eyes.

"Aren't you too old to nap?" She's a little spitfire.

"Nah. Old people need naps too. Our bodies are falling apart." She purses her lips, trying to decide if I'm telling the truth. Her hands fall to her sides, and her face softens.

"Okay. Enjoy your nap, Mr. Jay. I'll try again later."

"Tomorrow, Katy. I'm really tired and will probably take a long nap."

"Okay." She skips off just as I hear a crash behind me. I turn to

see the blanket I had placed over the table has fallen off, taking several things with it. I sigh and pick up all the pill bottles strewn on the floor. Stacking them neatly on the table, I double-check all of the legal paperwork I've left for whoever needs it—papers including bank account information, passwords, and my Will and life insurance policy. I don't want to make this hard on anyone.

I relax back on the couch, taking one more look around and ensuring everything is in order. The first time I tried this, I was nineteen. I had no one and nothing, much like I do now, but I was young and dumb then. That day, I drank a bottle of cheap liquor that tasted like rubbing alcohol and took a bunch of over-the-counter sleeping pills. The next afternoon, when I missed my checkout, the motel housekeeper found me passed out and called an ambulance. All I got was a long, well-rested nap, my stomach pumped, and a seventy-two-hour psych hold.

After that, I took an EMT class and vowed to myself that when I knew what I was doing, I'd do it right. It took almost a decade of trying every alternative I could find to not feel the weight of my guilt, but things got worse, not better, as evident by the situation I find myself currently in.

The sleeping pills go down as easily as they do every night. It's the only way for me to sleep without constant nightmares. I still have them occasionally, but at least I can get a few days of fake peace. I palm the rest of the pills that I've carefully combined like some mad scientist and roll them around in my hands. There are a few capsules, some half-blue, others half-red, and several white pills of various lengths and sizes.

"Whoever objects to this life ending, speak now or forever hold your peace..." I laugh because there's silence. Nothing but silence like there always is—just blank nothingness.

"Bottoms up, bitches." I can feel the sleeping pills taking effect,

and I tilt my palm into my mouth, swallowing all the remaining pills at once.

I pick up my phone and open the notes app in case some last-minute philosophical words need to be written before I no longer exist. Nothing comes to mind, only darkness. Darkness as the sleep takes me over, and I feel myself floating, feeling light for the first time since I was seven, and watched Ivy dance in the flowers around the pond.

"You saved me, Spencer."

"No, the annoying, screaming little girl who walked into your unlocked apartment and found you asleep and couldn't wake you up, saved you. Her screaming alerted another neighbor who called 9-1-1. I transported your almost lifeless body to the hospital when I responded to the call." I hate how she downplays her role in my life.

"But you listened when I spoke to you." I don't remember speaking until I was in the hospital, but afterward, Spencer told me I said three words to her in my apartment. Three words that somehow bonded two random strangers together and made her stay in the hospital with me until they committed me once again to the psychiatric ward. "I'm not ready."

I voluntarily committed myself to a ninety-day rehab center. Spencer showed up one day with books for a paramedic certification. She was crass and blunt and had zero issues telling me to cut my shit. I fell in love in a very platonic way with her.

At the end of the ninety days, she put me in her office/guest room, which is where I stayed until I finished my paramedic training. As a graduation present, she promptly kicked me out, telling me all baby birds needed to leave the nest. As I walked out the door, she handed me an application and told me I had an interview in three days. We've been partners ever since.

17

Nicole

I dodged my brother's calls and texts all day while meeting with my clients until now. Blake text me asking if I'm okay. I feel guilty and call Cole.

"Glad to know you're not dead, big sister. Unless this is her ghost calling me back."

"Har-har. That was so funny I forgot to laugh."

"Except you said 'har-har,' which is a form of laughter, so…"

"Ugh, Coleman. Why are you so frustrating?"

"Why haven't you returned any of my calls or texts all day? Why did my girlfriend have to contact you before you called me? Why did I stop by your house last night and see Justin's truck in your parking lot?"

"You did what? Why did you come by here?"

"Because, big sister, I made an ass of myself yesterday, and I felt like complete shit. I was coming by to apologize because I wanted to do it in person, but when I saw his truck, I figured you were busy." I was definitely busy. "How did it go? Do I need to kick some ass?"

"No ass-kicking needed. Although I heard you threatened

to break his legs?" I can hear the nonchalant shrug through the phone.

"I had to make sure he knew his place. Does he? What did you two decide?" Did we actually decide anything? I don't think we did.

"Um, I'm honestly not sure. I told him, I cried, and he stayed the night. This morning, he took the dogs out and brought me coffee in bed. He'll be here in about forty-five minutes. He's taking me on a date."

"Good." His tone is so matter-of-fact it makes me laugh.

"Why is that good?"

"Because I told him to man up and take care of you. It sounds like he listened."

"Coleman, I don't need anyone to take care of me."

"Like hell you don't. You've always taken care of me. Let him take care of you. He helped make half of that bean growing inside of you. He can help you take care of it whether it's inside or outside." I understand what he's saying, but it's not in my nature. It goes against everything in me.

"Nicole." Ugh.

"Yeah. Okay. Fine. I have to go so I can get ready."

"Make him take you somewhere fancy so you can dress up, and he can pay."

"I'm not going to make him waste his money. He's just a paramedic. He works hard for what he has. I'm happy going for fast food."

"Oh, big sister. *Just* a paramedic? You don't know him at all, do you? Make sure to ask him lots of questions about himself tonight." What is he talking about? He's not a paramedic? That's what he told me at Midnight Moonshine. He crawled in Annie's car when she rolled in the accident. He's definitely

116

a paramedic. Right?

"Hey, little brother?"

"Yeah?"

"I didn't get a chance to ask how *you* were doing. The last I really remember of your conversation is you asking Annie to marry you. How'd that turn out?" He laughs.

"She turned me down, rightly so. I'd hate myself forever if she had accepted that lame proposal, but it's coming. You'll have two new sisters soon enough. And as for the babies… babies with a fucking S, I'm over the damn moon, Nicole." His smile is wide enough that I can hear it over the phone.

"I can't wait. Tell them I said hi."

We hang up, and I search my closet for something to wear. Having no idea what we're doing, I decide on a simple sundress and sandals. If I need to change my shoes, it's an easy switch.

At about ten minutes to seven, I sit on the couch to relax before Justin arrives. The dogs have been walked and fed. I changed my bed sheets in case he stays the night, and now I'm exhausted. Promptly at seven, there's a knock at the door. I open it with a smile that's quickly short-lived. I cup my hands over my mouth, and my stomach rolls.

There's a smell of something in the hallway that my senses don't appreciate. Chinese, Indian, Italian? I have no clue, but there's a spiciness to the smell. I pull Justin inside and slam the door as I run toward the bathroom, praying I make it to the toilet.

"Pumpkin?" There's panic and concern in his voice as he follows me down the hall. I make it to the toilet, barely. Justin is instantly behind me, holding back my hair as I empty the small contents of my stomach into the freshly cleaned toilet.

117

I'm singing my praises to past Nicole, who scrubbed the toilet clean because she was having a guest over.

Justin must find a hair tie on the counter because my hair gets pulled into a ponytail at the base of my neck, and he's stepped next to me, wetting a washcloth.

"I'm sorry." My voice is hoarse. I try to stand up, but his hand caresses my back and he crouches beside me.

"Don't apologize, and just relax for a moment." He pushes my ponytail aside, and I feel the coolness of the washcloth drape across my neck. "Any idea what set you off? I'm assuming this is baby-related."

"There was a smell in the hallway." I lean over and dry heave into the toilet just thinking about it.

"A takeout guy got in the elevator when I got off. I think it was Indian food."

"The spice..." I try not to think about it again, but my stomach still rolls. He flips the washcloth around the other side, cooling my skin again.

"You didn't throw up much. Have you eaten today?" Uh oh. I'm being triaged, and he's about to get upset.

"Coffee, yogurt, protein bar." I list off the few things I've consumed.

"And? Pumpkin, please tell me that's not all you ate today?"

"Prenatal vitamins."

"Nicole." He sighs my name and pulls out his phone. "What do you feel like eating? Do you have any aversions yet?" I arch a brow at him and glance back at the toilet. "Other than curry."

I shake my head. "Not that I know of."

"Any cravings yet?" He must see my face light up because he chuckles. "What is it?"

"Well, I didn't even think about it until you just asked, but the pizzeria a few blocks over sells a macaroni and cheese pizza, and it sounds fantastic right now." My stomach growls in joy at the thought of the cheese melting on my tongue.

"Mac n Cheese on a pizza? That's a new one. Garlic knots?"

"Oh god, yes." I moan at the buttery goodness of their garlic knots.

"Last question. Are we going out, ordering in, or I can pick it up?"

"Don't leave me. Eww. That was horrible and so needy sounding. Ignore me. I can't go out in that hallway anytime soon. Pickup or deliver. It's your choice."

"Pumpkin, if you don't want me to leave, I won't. And please don't ever be afraid to tell me how you feel. I'm here for you."

He taps away on his phone, pulls out his card to pay for the order, and smiles at me once the order is placed. "It will be here in about thirty minutes. How do you feel? Do you want to move to the couch?" I nod, and he helps me up.

He gets me settled on the couch and walks into my kitchen, searching through the cabinets, refrigerator, and freezer.

"Can I help you find something?" I know what he's going to say before he speaks, and I'm already on the defensive.

"Pumpkin, where's all your food?"

"I've been busy and haven't been to the store lately. I'll go soon." I buy what I need. A ten-dollar pizza can last me a week. I always have stuff for PB&J and microwavable noodle cups.

He's tapping on his phone again when he sits beside me, lifting my legs and placing them on his lap. "What do you like? And don't tell me nothing. Otherwise, I'll order one of

119

everything the store has, and that seems pretty wasteful."

"Justin."

"Nicole." He sees me wince and smiles. "You don't like it any more than I do, Pumpkin. I'm ordering you a grocery delivery. You need food to grow our baby. Tell me what you like." He said *our* baby. Our. He's willing to take responsibility and do this with me. It seems silly to think he wouldn't since he's here, but he said it out loud.

"Pumpkin?" He startles me from my daydream.

"Sorry." He smiles and extends the phone out to me.

"Please order whatever you want." I shake my head at him.

"I can take care of it tomorrow. Don't spend any more of your money on me." He growls in frustration.

"Money means nothing." He moves my legs and crawls on top of me. "Your health and this baby mean everything to me. Please let me feed you both." He rests his head on my stomach. "Please." How do you say no to a man that's begging to take care of you?

"Okay. Hand it over. But you don't get to make fun of my cereal choices, and I won't make fun of your boxers."

"Deal. And thank you." He nestles back into my stomach. "I told you there are things in my past that scare me. I can't control something that has already happened, but I can take care of you to the best of my ability right now."

18

Justin

Morning sickness can be a bitch. I've transported enough dehydrated pregnant mothers to know how to help take care of Nicole. She needs to keep letting me in.

We stay on the couch until there's a knock at the door. I look up over her breasts into her eyes.

"Do you want to hide in your bedroom in case the smell still lingers in the hall?' She shakes her head and grabs a pillow to cover her face. I stand and rub a hand through her hair as I pass her to get the pizza. Luckily, the smell seems to have dissipated, and the aroma of garlic overpowers anything that lingers.

When I turn from the door, Nicole is standing right behind me, and she swipes the bag of garlic knots.

"Oh my fucking god. These smell better than sex."

"I should probably be insulted, but I'm inclined to agree with you. They smell amazing." Her hand reaches into the bag, and when she pulls it out, buttery, garlic goodness covers her knuckles. I grab her wrist, and she growls at me. It's the cutest fucking thing.

"Don't get between a pregnant woman and food. You could lose a finger."

"I wouldn't dream of it." I guide her hand to her mouth, and she opens it, taking a bite of her garlic knots. I dart my tongue out to lick the knuckle on her pinky finger, and we both moan at the delicious bread.

"I want more, Pumpkin." She takes another bite, and I lick across the top of her hand, cleaning more garlic off her. She takes the last bite, and I turn her hand to me, sucking each fingertip into my mouth until there's pure fire staring back at me. She grabs my neck and pulls me into her. The fusion of garlic and butter lingers on our tongues as they twist together, making me deepen the kiss. I pull away, panting, and she tries to bring me back.

"Pumpkin, you need to eat." Her lips attach to my neck, and my cock wants to take her, but my primal need to take care *of* her wins. I walk backward with the pizza in hand to the coffee table, almost sitting on Java as I sit down.

"Come. Sit. Eat." I pat the cushion next to me, urging her to obey. I can take care of her *and* take care of her. She's wearing a dress, and I'm about to make good use of it. Nicole calls the dogs to the kitchen and locks the gate. Opening the pizza box I see a strange but intriguing sight. It's actually macaroni and cheese on a pizza crust. "You were serious? I don't know what I was expecting, but definitely not cheesy noodles on a pizza."

"I'm serious about my pizza. I never joke." I stand, and she gives me a look. "That's going to require plates." She nods in understanding.

Carefully putting a triangle of cheesy goodness on a plate

for her, I watch with too much attention as she lifts it to her mouth. Her eyes shut, and she moans as her lips close onto the crust, and she pulls the slice away from her mouth. It shouldn't be so fucking seductive to watch someone eat pizza.

"Sit back." Her jaw bobs as she chews, and her tongue darts out to lick a stray piece of cheese. I want to be that cheese right now. *Stay on task.*

When her back leans against the couch, I drop to my knees on the floor and pull her hips to the edge. She gasps and giggles at the sudden movement.

"What are you doing, Doc?"

"I'm going to eat while you eat. Take another bite." Her eyes watch my hands trail up her bare thighs, lifting her dress as I go. Her hips shift to get comfortable, and she spreads her legs in offering. My hands reach the apex of her thighs while I watch her take another bite. I extend my pointer fingers to hook into her panties and watch her smile grow as her head moves slowly left to right and back again.

"Were you planning to go out like this?" She shrugs and takes another bite.

"I was going to ask what the plan was first. Dinner? Sure. Horseback riding? Probably not." She's so blase about sitting in front of me with nothing covering her pussy. She takes yet another bite, and I shove her thighs apart and dive into her.

"Don't you stop eating that fucking pizza, or I'll stop eating you."

"Understood loud and clear, Doc."

"Good girl. Now eat." I lick her lips, parting her with my fingers. I'm going to make this slow and torturous. Her lack of panties was a direct tease for me. She needs to eat, and I fully intend to edge her until she's eaten at least another slice and a few more garlic knots.

Nicole's gentle moans and whimpers are music to my ears as she adds another slice to her plate. I wait until she's swallowed to slide two fingers into her eager pussy. She's ready for me. She wants me as badly as I want to take her right now. Her head rolls on the back of the couch as she chews and feels my tongue flick over her clit once, twice, then I back away again.

"Please, Doc. Please. I want to come. I need to come so fucking bad." I pull away completely, and her moan is feral at the lack of stimulation. "I fucking hate you."

"Good. That's exactly the way I want you." Teasingly I run my finger up and down her wet pussy. "Finish your pizza, and I'll finish you. Be my good girl. Feed our baby bean." She smiles the sweetest smile at the mention of our baby. My fingers stutter at that thought. It's still surreal. Nicole takes a bite, and I slip my fingers inside her gently so she doesn't get too excited and choke. I want her to finish her pizza so I can make her come and then bury myself in her. Scissoring my fingers I suck her clit into my mouth. Her breathing increases and I know she can't take much more. She's ready to explode with a simple look.

"Two more bites, Pumpkin. You can do it." She whimpers her way through the last pieces and moans a loud, open-mouth moan, showing me she's finished. "Good fucking girl. Now come all over my fingers." Tonguing her clit in the figure eight that drives her wild, I stroke her g-spot, and she bucks into my mouth. She's a fucking goner when I reach up and pinch her nipple through the top of her dress. Her body convulses forward as she comes so hard it's dripping down my fingers.

"Turn the fuck over." I drop my pants to the floor as she turns and bends over the back of the couch. She lifts the back of her dress, exposing her perfect pussy and round ass to me, and I rub circles over the globes and squeeze.

"Pumpkin, have you ever been spanked?"

"God, yes. I thought you'd never ask." She wiggles her ass under my hands, and I dole out her first smack. The sound she makes is one of pure pleasure.

"Again. Harder." She arches her back more, pushing her ass farther into my hands. I give two swift smacks, one to each ass cheek ,before I line up and thrust my aching cock into her. She's wet and slick from her orgasm and need.

"I want to live in this fucking pussy, Pumpkin. I want to warm my cock inside you every fucking night."

"Oh fuck. Yes. Please. Every fucking night." She's meeting me thrust for thrust. Every time I smack her ass, her pussy clamps down harder on my cock. I want her to come again, but my release is building.

"Play with your clit. Make yourself come again." Grabbing both hips, I continue my punishing pace. Curses fly from our mouths. She's teasing the base of my cock with her fingers as she strums her clit. I'm so fucking hard and ready to explode.

"Stop teasing me, Pumpkin. Let me hear you scream my name. Make your neighbors jealous." Her inner walls start to flutter, and I dip my hips a little lower for a different angle.

"Fuck. Fuck, Justin."

"There's my name on those pretty little lips. Fuck, Pumpkin, you're fucking perfect." One more hard slap to her ass as our orgasms erupt around us, and we collapse to the couch, all wild limbs and heavy breathing.

"You're ridiculous, you know that, right?" She giggles and it's my favorite sound.

"I know we need a shower and some sleep."

Her eyes look up at me, hopeful. "You're staying?"

"I brought my pills. And I think someone just promised me she'll warm my cock every night." I playfully pop her still-exposed ass. Her face turns serious.

"Doc, you can always talk to me about anything. You know that, right?" She sits up on the couch, pulling me with her. I take her hands, needing to touch her—to continue our connection. "I know we don't know each other well. And despite what kind of a future you and I may or may not have, we are tied to each other." She pulls my hands to her belly. The image of it swollen, with my child inside, makes me want to wrap her in a bubble and never let go.

"I know, and I'm happy to share things with you slowly."

"How about one question a day? Any question, and you must answer it no matter how painful. No follow-up questions, but it's up to you how much information you choose to share. If you need more information, you wait for the next day." That sounds entirely reasonable.

"Okay. You ask first." I can tell she already has a brimming question. She adjusts herself on the cushion and makes a serious face.

"Cole made an offhand comment when I said I didn't want you spending excessive money on me because you're a paramedic and work hard for what you have. He told me I should ask you what you really do. So, Doc, other than being a paramedic, what is your job?" Of all the questions she could have asked, she dives right into this one.

126

"We're starting right for the jugular, I see." I run a hand over my goatee, thinking. I only have to give her a straightforward answer today. She can't ask anymore. Here goes.

"I own the Dov Memorial Mental Health Wing where Annie stayed after her accident."

Her jaw drops.

"This isn't a second question, just a confirmation. You said own? As in, it *belongs* to you. Like, you sign people's paychecks."

"Well, a machine signs my signature, but yes. It is mine in totality."

"That's a rehab center. A huge, very prominent mental health rehabilitation center." I don't have to, but I nod, answering her non-questions. "I eat ramen. I sell pictures of my feet. I drive a car that's held together by utility tape, a hope, and a prayer, and you probably have a toilet made of gold." I watch the panic build as she looks around at her apartment. We will have to discuss the car and the feet pictures, but I can't let her emotions run away with her right now. I already know what she's thinking. She thinks she isn't good enough for me.

19

Nicole

Own. Own. OWN. That's a multi-million, probably even billion-dollar facility, or wing, or whatever you want to call it. Justin owns it. He owns it. My Doc owns it. Oh no, he's not mine. I can't even believe he's here. He looks so humble. He works as a paramedic. He works. Why?

Justin reaches over and grabs my cheeks, pausing my very rapid downward spiral.

"Nicole. Whatever you're thinking, stop."

"I guess I should have started with something simpler like your favorite color."

"Green."

"Is it?"

"Is my favorite color green? Yeah." He winks. "I'll give you that one as a freebie." I give him a half-hearted smile because that's all I can manage at the moment.

"You're right. That probably would have been an easier one to start with. Instead, you just jumped right into the fact that there are more zeroes in your bank account than numbers in my phone number. But it wasn't your question, it was mine. I asked and should have been prepared, but I wasn't. I couldn't have even predicted that."

"We aren't going to do this, Pumpkin. I won't allow you to look at me differently. I'm the same man I was five minutes ago. What may or may not be in my bank account doesn't change the explosive orgasm that you just had." I almost snort at his ridiculous statement, but it helps ease the panic a small fraction.

"I'm not sure how I can pretend I don't know this information." I look around my apartment again. "This place must be a dump to you."

"I love this apartment. It's so much you. Do you think I'd come over here if I didn't? I already told you money doesn't mean anything to me and it wasn't because I'm swimming in it. It's because I understand that no matter how many zeroes are in your bank account, it can't buy happiness, and it can't buy the life you breathe every day." That sounds heavy and like a statement that comes from experience. A shadow crosses his face, and I hate it.

"It's your turn." He looks at me, confused. "It's your turn to ask a question?"

"Oh, right? Let's see if I can lighten the mood. What's your favorite color?" I laugh.

"Blue, but you can do better than that, Doc. I'll give you that one as a freebie too."

"Okay, okay. Fine." He's smiling now, and that makes my heart happy again. His hand comes up and twirls a lock of my curls between his fingers. "Did you always want to be a hairdresser?"

"I see we're sticking with a theme tonight?" Will my answer

change things? I didn't realize our worlds collide so much. "No, I didn't always want to be a hairdresser. You may not know this, but Cole became an exotic dancer to help put me through college. The pole was apparently his specialty, as I just recently witnessed. But while I was in college full time, I also went to hair school at night for the first year to help him pay the tuition. I actually have a diploma in Psychology. I wanted to be a psychologist, but a master's degree wasn't in the cards for me."

"You...wait. You have a Psychology degree? That's—wow. Small world."

"Why do you look worried?" He relaxes his face, the worry lines between his brows smoothing out.

"You're concerned about my money, and now I'm concerned you're constantly over analyzing me. But I guess it makes sense now."

"What makes sense?"

"Your acceptance of my issues." I look into his eyes and see so many emotions swirling in them. Pulling his arms apart, I crawl up his body, straddling him.

"You don't seem to have any issues with me, Doc." I lean in and kiss him hungrily. Fucking pregnancy hormones. "Oh!" I pop up from our kiss, startling him. Jumping off his lap, I grab my purse from the kitchen and take out the ultrasound pictures. As I walk back to him, his face morphs from confusion to awe as he realizes what's in my hand.

"Would you like to see our bean?"

"I want nothing more." I hand him the pictures, and his eyes soften even further. Tears form in the corner, and I wipe away the first one as it falls. "I'm sorry."

"Doc, it's okay to cry. I don't care how unmacho people

think it is for men. Please feel comfortable with me to not even think about it." He grabs my wrist and pulls me into his lap. We sit for a few minutes, staring at the pictures.

"I'm going to be good for you both. I promise." There's more behind that statement that I don't understand yet. A finger pokes into my side as my earlobe gets nipped. "I'm ready to get my cock warmed now, ma'am." He hands me back the pictures and stands, placing me on my feet. "Let's clean up and go to bed."

"It's only nine. I'm not even tired."

"That sounds like a challenge. Let's clean up, and I'll orgasm you into exhaustion." I laugh because the life I'm currently living is nothing like it was a few months back. A man just told me he was going to exhaust me with orgasms. Sign me up.

A girl could get used to waking up to the smell of coffee from her bed. I can hear footsteps coming down the hall, and I close my eyes and cover the smile on my face with the blanket.

"You're a terrible faker, Pumpkin. I can see your eyes smiling."

"That's not a thing."

"It's definitely a thing." I hear him place a mug on the nightstand, and I feel his finger trail a circle around my eyes. "The corner of your eyes lift when you smile." He pulls down the blanket and traces the outline of my lips. I suck them into my mouth, using my teeth to itch my lips.

"That tickles. Why is it so early? Did you sleep?" A warm

smile lifts his face.

"I slept. Very well, actually. No bad dreams. Only sweet pussy flutters on my dick." I never thought a statement like that would warm my heart, but it makes me feel like I have a magic pussy that staves off all the evil nighttime monsters.

"That's me. The pussy monster eliminator. No, that doesn't sound right. The monster pussy eliminator? The monster eliminator pussy? Whatever. You get my point."

"Exactly. But to answer your original question, I have to get to work. Do you want your coffee now, or should I put it in the microwave?"

"Always coffee now. And then again later." His face tells me something that his mouth isn't sure it wants to say. "What is it?'

"You might want to consider switching to decaf if you drink that much coffee regularly." I sit up in bed, allowing the blanket to fall to my lap, exposing my naked breasts. It's the only defense I have right now. Distraction.

"Are you going to go all Alpha male on me? Last night, it was 'you must eat,' and today, you're going to tell me to decrease my caffeine intake. What's next? You don't need to work. I'll lavish you with grapes and fan you with large leaves while you lounge around naked all day growing our baby?"

"As long as the leaf fanners are female, I can make that happen in the next three hours."

"You're the worst, Doc. Go to work and save women and children."

"It's more like middle-aged men and homeless people, but I get your point."

"And occasionally beautiful billionaires. You can't forget

about Annie."

"I can never forget about Annie." He leans down and kisses my forehead, making my stomach flutter. "Are you working today?"

"Nope. I plan to stay in bed and read while snuggling my puppers. Will you let them out of the kitchen before you go?"

"Of course. Your groceries will be delivered around eleven." Oh yeah. I had completely forgotten about that. I suddenly don't feel so bad letting him stock my kitchen with food.

"Thank you."

"Always. Call me if you need anything." I smile and sink back into the warmth of my blankets.

20

Justin

"I normally don't complain about the silence, but you've been sitting in that passenger seat for hours clicking away on your cell phone. What are you doing?" I can't blame her for the question. Spencer and I don't usually talk, but I'll usually sleep or read. My scrolling and typing are probably distracting.

"Buying a car. A small SUV, actually."

"I think if you had said you were watching porn, it might have been less surprising. Why are you buying a small SUV?"

"Because I saw Nicole's car when I left her house this morning, and it's a death trap. She needs something safe and reliable for herself and the baby when it gets here." I straighten up in my seat and puff out my chest. "I saw the ultrasound pictures last night."

"Justin. Let me unpack all of those words. First, you slept over again. How did it go?"

"It's her, Spencer. Or her pussy that I slept inside again. My mind is peaceful when she's in my arms."

"Justin. Please be careful. The spike of endorphins you're

getting from these new experiences can fizzle out or even make you crash. I don't want you to come to depend on them. We don't need to discuss it. Just maintain everything you've been doing prior to Nicole. Second, does she know you're buying her a new vehicle?" Her words have an impact that I hadn't thought about. I'm aware of the manic stages that extra endorphins can cause.

"Will you be my eyes? Tell me if you notice anything. And if I don't listen, push me like you always do. You know I trust you, Spencer." She glances at me and nods. That's all the reassurance I need from her because I know she'll do everything I just asked of her. She's my power of attorney for all of my assets. Spencer insisted I needed an actual Will after seeing the cheap seventy-five dollar one I downloaded online. My finances were a mess. She doesn't believe she saved my life that day, but she has every day since.

"And no, she doesn't know I'm buying it." Spencer is silent, which causes me to think about my actions. She's like a sniper. Her silence speaks louder than her words. "I need to talk to her about it, don't I?"

"Do you think she'll let you buy her a new vehicle?"

"Not at all. Nicole's very independent to her own detri-ment. Fuck, Spencer. She told me last night she sells feet pictures and eats ramen. I want more for her and for our baby."

"Buy it and take whatever consequences. If it's something she needs to better her life and you can do it for her, do it. She'll come to understand."

"I have an idea."

Me: I have an idea. Can you call me when you get a chance,

135

please?

A few minutes later, my phone rings.

"Hey, Cole. How's it going?"

"You tell me. How's my sister? Do I need to break any legs yet?" I'm glad Nicole has a brother who's as protective over her as I feel.

"That's actually why I wanted to talk to you. I had groceries delivered to Nicole's house about an hour ago, so she's stocked up and eating more than ramen and protein bars."

"Good. She never eats enough. I don't know why I never considered having groceries delivered to her."

"Well, it wasn't easy. I had to threaten to order one of everything the store has if she didn't make me a list." He chuckles, knowing his sister well. "But that's not the reason for my call. I was hoping you could help me by taking the fall for something. Actually, maybe this is something I should ask Annie or Blake for?"

"Spit it out, Webb."

"I bought her a small SUV to replace her falling apart junker. My partner has pointed out that she might not be very receptive to a handout like that, even though it's not my intention. Safety and reliability for her are my top priority."

"So you want it to be from one of us instead of you? You think she might take it easier as a gift from me?" I'm glad he understands where I'm coming from.

"Or one of the girls? It seems like a very Annie thing to do."

"It's exactly an Annie thing. She did it to Blake and me. I appreciate you thinking about her like this, Justin. We'll do it. Let me talk to them and come up with a game plan. When do you want to give it to her?"

"I don't have a plan yet. I thought one day I might slip it into her parking spot without saying anything."

"She's going to be so mad at us. I think you're right about Annie being our best bet. I'll talk to her and get back to you soon. Don't do anything crazy. Well, crazier than replacing her vehicle without her permission."

Hanging up with Cole, I continue my online purchase. At least I have a game plan now.

"Last point, Justin. You saw the pictures?" I forgot Spencer had a list of questions.

"I did. She's only eight weeks, so there wasn't much to see, but there was a little bean there." *My* little bean.

"You sound happy. Have you thought about what happens next?"

"Next?"

"Next, Justin. That little bean will turn into a baby and need things. Lots of things. Have you discussed any of that?" She's always my voice of reason. I haven't thought about that, and I'm usually a planner. "Get your head on straight, Justin. Don't backpedal."

"Fuck, Spencer. Some days, I don't know what I would do without you. Thank you. I'll be more vigilant. But I'm still buying her a new car."

"You need to do that. I'm not sure I agree with you lying to her, but it's your relationship."

Today's shift was long and tedious. The only perk to a slow day when there aren't many calls is not having to restock too many things at shift change. I'm reviewing the checklist while Spencer grabs supplies from the supply closet when I hear the doors open behind me.

"Stupid fucking thing. I don't know how I get roped into this every damn year." I peek out the ambulance's back doors to see a disgruntled Lincoln stalking by.

"You okay, Linc?" Lincoln is a Chicago Police officer who, unfortunately, due to a bullet he took to the leg, has been restricted to light duty behind the dispatch desk for the foreseeable future.

"Webb, hey. No. I'm not fucking okay. Have you seen the memo yet? No, of course not. You just got in." He looks at his watch to check the time. "I thought since I'm not officially on the force at the moment, I'd get out of the stupid Christmas fundraiser calendar. Apparently, not this fucking year. They decided they want everyone in it." He reaches in and slaps my shoulder. "Even you Para-monkeys. If I have to wear a Santa hat, topless with suspenders this year, so do you." He walks away, laughing.

"Who were you talking to?" Spencer walks over with an armful of supplies. We didn't use nearly that much, but she sometimes overcompensates, liking to be prepared for the worst-case situation.

"One of the new dispatchers, Lincoln." Am I seeing this correctly? Did she just blush?

"Spencer?" She quickly turns around and gives me her back. "Don't run away from me. Are you keeping a secret from your best friend?"

"There's no secret." Her voice is monotone. She's assessing her feelings in this situation. "He has a nice voice on the radio, and I enjoy listening to it."

138

"A voice enjoyable enough to make you blush. Very interesting."

"Coble, Webb. Get in here." Our Chief's voice booms through the ambulance bay, saving Spencer from any further interrogation.

"What's up, Chief?" Chief Wetli is a small man with a big attitude. No one here messes with him. His bite is as big as his bark, and despite his bald head and short stature, he's all muscle.

"Not sure if you've seen or heard, but you're included in this year's Christmas calendar. Pictures are next week. It's not optional. Spencer, will this be a problem?"

"I'd prefer not to participate, but you said it's not optional, so I'll be there. As long as I get to wear clothes."

"Of course, Spencer. Actually, you're a woman. We need someone for hair and makeup. Do you know anyone?" Spencer looks at me with a knowing glance.

"Yeah, I think I can give you a name."

"Great. Just get me that information soon so we can take care of it."

"Yes, Sir." As we leave the office, I elbow Spencer in the arm.

"You know someone, huh, Spence?"

"You said Nicole doesn't like handouts. This isn't a handout. She does hair. Chief needs someone to do hair. Ask her."

"Thank you."

21

Nicole

I've never done anything like this before. Justin asked me if I could do hair for fifty people. There are only about a dozen of them that need actual hair done; the rest need a little touch-up. I also agreed to do the makeup since it's mostly just some foundation and highlight. These days, photo editing does most of the work.

I was skeptical when he asked, thinking he was only trying to pad my pockets, but he gave me his chief's information, and his offer was legitimate. It's an all-day event, and I hope I can make it through without having any morning sickness. Smells are becoming more sensitive, and I'm unsure how much Justin has shared with his coworkers about me or my situation.

"Are you almost ready, Pumpkin?" I look up from the bathroom mirror to see Justin leaning against the door frame, watching me get ready.

I was greeted early this morning with my usual cup of coffee and a smile. However, I was also gifted with scrambled eggs, sausage, toast, and an orgasm. Justin has made it his

140

mission to feed me as often as possible and continues his threatening game of I eat food, he eats me. A girl could seriously get used to it. Nope. Scratch that. This girl is already used to it. Food doesn't taste the same on my tongue if there isn't a tongue between my legs. He's spoiling me, and I hope he knows he's created a monster that he'll have to satiate.

Between the food orgasms and the cockwarning every night, I'm ready to let this man keep me knocked up for the rest of my life. *Holy shit.* Let's not go there, you needy bitch. Let's have this baby first and make sure he stays around.

Warmth spreads down my body as Justin presses himself to my back and caresses my arms.

"Are you alright, Pumpkin? Are you feeling okay?" His hands continue down my arms and trails over my stomach, stopping over my lower belly. He rests his chin on my shoulder, and I watch as his line of sight takes me in, starting at my eyes and stopping at his hands.

"I'm feeling good. I'm nervous, but it's an excited nervousness. Once I start, I'll get in my groove and be fine. I get to meet your partner today, right?" His smile is genuine.

"You do. Spencer is about as good as they come."

"You've been partners for four years?"

"It's been almost five, but we've known each other for six."

"You must have a great friendship and working relationship."

"There's no one quite like Spencer."

I'm nervous about meeting the only person that he seems to have in his life. I haven't heard him mention any siblings or his parents. We still ask our daily questions, but after the shocking first day, the questions have been more fun and playful. Things like our favorite restaurants, which he asked me every detail about as if memorizing my orders. We've talked about our hobbies, favorite movies, and music. All of the typical things you learn about a person before you decide to procreate with them. We're just doing it backward.

Justin kisses a line up the side of my neck, making it extremely difficult to finish my makeup. "You know, no one will take me seriously if I walk in with smudged makeup and messed up hair." His hand brushes the nape of my neck and closes, fisting my hair. He pulls it to one side to gain better access to my neck. I sigh in contentment, knowing I've already lost the battle and the war from the simple brush of his lips.

"We're going to be late, Doc." He hums in my neck, and I rub my butt over his growing bulge.

"Not fair, Pumpkin. Let's go. A surprise was delivered for you." I lock eyes with him in the mirror, looking for a clue, but he shows nothing. "No hints. Let's go." He pats my butt and walks away. I double-check my makeup in the mirror and second-guess my outfit. My belly is all bloat, not baby, but my shorts are already getting tight. I chose to wear black leggings and a flowy baby blue sleeveless top. Comfortable yet stylish.

"We're going to be late, Pumpkin."

"I'm coming. I'm coming."

"Not yet, but you could be." Justin's head pops around the corner from the hallway with a devilish grin.

"Stop it. Let's go." I grab my purse and push his shoulder as I walk past him. "Where's my surprise?" I look around the living room and kitchen areas and don't see anything out of the ordinary.

"It's outside." What kind of surprise could be outside? He smiles and motions toward the door. I reluctantly walk to the door, and he follows. Once outside, I glance in the direction of my car, not wanting him to see what I actually drive by following my gaze.

"What the fuck." I search the parking lot looking for my shit brown sedan with the nearly bald tires that I park in the exact space every time I drive, but the spot is empty. I grab Justin's forearm, and my stomach roils. "It's gone. Doc, my car is gone. Someone stole it, or it got towed or...or..." Justin dangles a keyring in front of my face. My eyes cross and unfocus, and I lean back to try and see his hand.

"What are these?" He pushes a button, and I hear a beep just to my left. The lights flash on a small blue SUV parked at the curb. Justin lifts my hand and places the key inside them.

"Go look inside." My head whips back and forth between the SUV and Justin. He presses a light hand to the small of my back and urges me forward. I know I'm moving, but my body is in too much shock to register it. When we reach the door, he opens it for me, and I'm rushed with the unique smell only a brand new car can have. The interior is black, and there's a stark white piece of paper folded up on the center console. "Get in." I hesitate for another moment before sliding into the buttery, soft leather seats. I grab the piece of paper and unfold it.

We all want what's best for you. ~Annie

"She didn't." I run my hands over the steering wheel in awe. Everything is shiny and clean.

"Do you like it?" My head whips to the side to stare at

Justin.

"You knew about this?"

"I had a hand in picking it out."

"Why? Why would you do that? Why would she do this?" I step out of the car and take my phone from my purse, quickly scrolling through my recent calls.

"Nicole—" I cut Annie off.

"Why did you buy me a new car?"

"Hello to you too, Nicole. I didn't buy you a new car." I scoff.

"That's not the impression from the note."

"The note expresses the sentiment it was supposed to. We all want what's best for you. No need to read into it."

"But..." I start to pace the length of the SUV. It's beautiful and perfect. Everything I could want and need for my business and a new baby on the way. "Where's my stuff? Where's my old car?"

"Pumpkin, your things are in a box in the trunk. Your car was taken for scrap. You'll have a check in a few days in the mail." Justin reaches inside the vehicle and pushes a button. The trunk opens automatically, and I see a brown box with my jumper cables, fuzzy dice, my knock-off water bottle, and lots of other random stuff that's honestly just junk.

"Make sure to thank everyone, Nicole. This was a group effort." The line goes dead as it always does with Annie, who doesn't believe in goodbyes.

"Pumpkin?" I spin on my heels and face Justin, then smack him across the arm.

"Annie said this was a group effort, and I should thank everyone. So, thank you, but I'm mad at you. Get in the car. I'm driving." I hear him laughing as he walks around to the

144

passenger side of my shiny new SUV. He gets in and looks in the back seat.

"Won't it look amazing with a car seat back there?" I can't help but melt at the love and awe in his eyes for our unborn child. But then I remember I'm upset with him.

"Yes, but I'm not talking to you, so stop trying to toy with my hormones. I'm defenseless to anything baby-related, and it's rude to play so unfairly." He sits back and buckles his seatbelt with a smug smile.

Driving this car is like floating on a cloud. I barely feel any bumps, and it's as if the outside world doesn't exist because it's so quiet. Justin offered to program the radio stations for me, and as much as I wanted to be stubborn and tell him no, I hate having to figure those things out. I simply gave him the stations I wanted and told him thank you.

I am fully aware I'm being unreasonable. I was given a brand new, scott-free vehicle. Annie won't let me even try to repay her a penny, but I'm not going to back down now and let him win. I'll die on this hill until I get bored or convinced by orgasms. Yes, orgasms will have to be the apology I need for fooling me.

"At the risk of making you more mad, there's one more thing that comes with the vehicle." I give him the evilest side eye I can while still watching the road. He opens the glove compartment and pulls out a tiny envelope. "I'm aware that this is probably going to piss you off more, but it's my gift to you and baby bean." He opens the envelope and tips it into his hand. A black credit card falls out. Not just any black credit card, an *American Express Black* card, and at a quick glance, I don't see a J or a W on the card.

"Justin?" I almost growl at the realization of what it is. "Is my name on that card?"

"This is a card for gas and vehicle emergencies. This vehicle will take twice as much gas as your little sedan, and I don't want that to be a burden. You'll have doctor's appointments you'll need to go to, and I hope today will open doors for you, and you'll get more clients."

"Justin." My jaw clenches as I say his name. He quietly puts the card back in the envelope and places it in the glove compartment. The click that it makes when it closes sounds deafeningly loud.

I'm being such a bitch. I'm going to blame it on the hormones and the baby. I'm allowed to be irrationally upset for people pouring their hearts into my health and well-being. It's a perfectly sane way for a pregnant lady to be acting.

We pull into the fire department, and Justin directs me where to park. I let him step out of the car, and he opens the back seat, getting out my work bag. He comes around to my door, and I hold up a finger. I need to compose myself before I'm around people. Thankfully, he steps back, and I'm able to take a deep breath. I should probably count backward from ten or sheep or something, but I feel like everything I try will make me angrier.

Whipping open the car door, Justin jumps back, startled by the quick movement. I grabbed a handful of his shirt and pulled him close to me.

"I'm irritated, I'm pissed off, and I'm horny. There's only one of those that you can fix right now, so find us a quiet place and put your magic fingers to work."

"Yes, ma'am." I give him a death stare, and he grabs the wrist attached to his shirt. Carefully, he pulls my hand away and nods towards the building. He weaves his fingers through mine, and I let him. These are his coworkers, and I won't embarrass him despite my current disposition.

We walk through the building, and he greets people as we walk past them. He stops us at a door in the back with a touchpad lock marked with a red and yellow sign that says MEDICAL SUPPLIES. He looks around, checks his watch, and punches in a code. The door opens with a click, and he shuffles us in, dropping my supply bag next to the door.

Metal shelves filled with containers of medical supplies line the walls. I assume they restock the ambulances from here.

I momentarily lose my breath when Justin pushes me up against the door, boxing me in. His eyes are wild and lust-filled.

"Do you want my fingers or my tongue, Pumpkin?"

"Your fingers. This is for me, not you. You don't get to tongue fuck me and enjoy yourself."

"As you wish." He leans down to kiss me, and I cover his mouth. "I have to get you ready somehow. I can't go in without a little prep."

"You can have my neck. Remember, it's my pleasure only. You're talking too much. Hurry up. We're already running late." His lips drag kisses over my jaw and down the pulse line of my neck. "And you better not leave any marks."

I feel his smile on my neck. "I wouldn't dream of it." I've never been more grateful for leggings when he slips his hand into them without any resistance. I'm already panting in anticipation and feel as fragile as a guitar string strung too tight. I need the release that only Justin can give me.

His fingers separate my pussy lips, and he runs a circle around my entrance. I feel the growl in his chest before I hear it. "You're already wet for me."

"Make me come, Doc. Quit teasing and get the job done, or I'll do it myself." He pulls away from my neck.

"Is that an option?"

"Justin."

"Sorry. Right, sorry." He dips his finger in, gathering my arousal, and swirls it around my clit. I gasp, and my head bangs on the door.

"Shh. We don't want to get caught. I could get fired."

"Uhhh...you could just...fuck, your fingers...buy the entire department. Oh god, Justin. Fuck yes." He kisses me to swallow my moans, and I let him.

"You're going to come for me. All over my fingers. Then, I'll lick them clean, but I won't wash my hands. I'm going to walk around this firehouse and shake the hands of every man here, knowing that I have something they can never have."

"Holy fuck." That's so possessively hot, and I shouldn't like the sound of it as much as I do, but holy hell, it's working.

"Come on, Pumpkin. Give it up to me." God, his words. The tips of my fingers begin to tingle, and I know this orgasm is going to be intense. My pussy begins to contract around nothing, and there's no way I can be quiet. Burying my face as far into Justin's chest as I can, I scream. He wraps his arm around my waist as my knees try to give out.

"Holy fucking shit. Fuck. Fuck." I know he can't hear what I'm saying, but I can't stop the curses as they pour from my mouth. I take deep breaths as the orgasm finally subsides. When my body jolts at his light flicks, he removes his hands and does exactly what he said he'd do.

Slowly he stares into my eyes, and he sucks my orgasm off his fingers. I want to bend over and let him fuck me against this door, but I remember I'm mad at him. With two flat hands, I push him away and reach down to grab my bag.

"I've got it." Justin leans down, attempting to pick up the bag for me.

"Don't you have handshaking to do?"

"Yes, and I've got your bag. I'll bring you to the chow hall, where they've set things up for you."

"Fine." He grabs my chin and tilts it towards him.

"I can see that orgasm didn't change your attitude towards me, but are you okay to be around everyone today?" It's an entirely valid question, but my annoyance towards him is still simmering.

"Don't worry, Doc. I won't ruin your precious reputation. I'll be on my best behavior." I reach up and pat him on the head. "Let's go." I open the door and walk out without checking if anyone was in the area. I hope nobody saw me.

22

Justin

Well, I guess I can add angry orgasm to the list of things I never thought I'd do, but oh god, did she fall apart beautifully.

Rubbing my fingers together, I can't help but smile, thinking of the words I said to her about what I'm planning to do. She loves it when I talk dirty, and her body's reaction told me today was no different than any other, despite her annoyance.

Annie's words were perfect, both in the note and on the phone. She took no direct responsibility and didn't point fingers at anyone else. I'll take the brunt of Nicole's anger because I know she's safer on the road now.

Nicole stopped in the middle of the bay, waiting for me. I walk up next to her and offer her my hand. She hesitates for a moment before taking it but reluctantly does. We walk into the chow hall, and guys hoop and holler. Her hand tightens in mine, and I lean in to whisper.

"This reaction is because I've never brought a girl here in the five years they've known me. They're just being asses."

"Are you sure?" I hate how insecure she looks right now.

"Positive." A cadette steps up next to us and points to the corner.

"This fancy setup over here is for your pretty lady, Webb."

"Webb?" She looks at me, confused. Has she never heard my last name?

"A lot of the guys here go by their last names. There's another Justin, so it's easier just to go by Webb."

"Oh. I um... I didn't know your last name, and after what we just did in the closet, I feel a little slutty."

"Pumpkin, if I didn't already know it would embarrass you, I'd kiss the fuck out of you in front of this room full of men and stake my claim. What we just did wasn't slutty, it was fucking sexy, and if I have to do it again to remind you of that, I will."

"Okay." I can't help but smirk at the far-off look that's glazed over her eyes.

"Are you saying okay to the kiss, the orgasm, or the lack of embarrassment?" Her eyes snap to mine.

"Don't push your luck, *Webb*. If you embarrass me, your cock will be awfully cold tonight."

I gasp in mock shock. "You wouldn't?"

"Try me." I extend my arm to the corner set up and place her bag on the table.

"Is there anything you need from me right now?"

"I don't think so. Thank you, but also, I'm still upset with you."

"As you should be. I'm going to find Spencer. I'll be back to introduce you." I kiss her on the forehead quickly so she can't object. Before I leave the room, I stand on a chair and stick two fingers under my tongue, blowing out a high-pitched whistle to quiet the room.

"Listen up, assholes. Nicole is here to do hair and makeup. If you give her a hard time, I'm not even going to threaten you because she'll have your balls before I get to you. Be kind, be respectful, and tip your server." I dramatically jump off the chair as the noisy ruckus ensues.

I wander around the building until I find Spencer sitting on the back of our rig.

"Hey Lady. Did you get your month yet?"

"January. I have to wear a puffy fur-lined jacket, but I'm allowed to show as much cleavage as I'm comfortable with, says the Chief." I start to holler. Laughter bursts through so loud it echoes off the tall ceilings.

"Do they know you'd prefer to be naked?" She shrugs.

"I'm debating if I should wear my sports bra under the jacket or just go naked."

"Please go naked. Please. Holy shit, their faces. You have to make sure I'm there so I can video their reactions." She's deep in thought, considering which option she wants to do. I hope she wears only the jacket.

"Oh, Nicole is here. Did you want to get your hair and makeup done?"

"No. I like the braids, and makeup doesn't feel good on my skin." I pull on the bottom of one braided pigtail, and she smiles at me. I'm the only one allowed to touch her like this, and it's only because of our years of being together.

"I like them too. Did you want to come up and meet Nicole?"

"January models, we need you in bay one." The Chief's prominent voice echoes his orders over the loudspeaker.

"Guess that's me. I'll meet her while she's here." I debate if

I should go upstairs to see how Nicole is doing or watch the shock that Spencer is about to cause. Whether she chooses a sports bra or no sports bra, she will still show them more skin than they'll know what to do with. Chief probably expects her to keep it zipped up to her neck. Hell, if they allowed her, she'd probably wear nothing *but* the jacket. Decision made. I'm going to watch her shoot.

I check the list of months and assignments posted on the bay window before walking over to the January set. I'm doing August with Miller, a firefighter; Westin, a new police recruit; and Lincoln, our dispatcher. This should be fun.

"July models, back of bay two." I guess they are doing two shoots at once. That will make the day go by quicker. Nicole cleaned up my hair last night, so I was one less person she had to worry about today. I can watch Spencer's shoot until it's my time.

"Everyone in January, come lineup so we can check costumes." A young, dark-haired woman wearing all black with a camera around her neck and thick red-rimmed glasses directs them all to file in front of her. Some of the guys are wearing snow pants and no tops. One is ironically in swim trunks with polar bears. The photographer goes down the line, checking everyone. She gets to Spencer and asks how she would like to wear the jacket.

"Unzipped."

"Okay, hun. Let's figure out how low." Spencer's hand grabs the tab on the silver zipper and, in a silky smooth move, pulls it completely down. My smile grows as the room gasps. She chose no sports bra. The puffy jacket gapes open about four inches, exposing a naked line from neck to navel. Even her snow bottoms are open, and the top of her yellow

153

underwear peeks out.

"Coble, what the hell. I... You...What..." The chief sputtering might be the best thing I've ever seen in my life. "Where are your clothes?"

"I was told I could wear what I was comfortable with. I'm comfortable. Isn't the point of the calendar to sell sex? Is this not sexy?" Chief stares at her face, unable to look anywhere else or answer her question. I let him suffer for a few moments before I whoop and catcall Spencer.

"Hey there, sexy lady. Can I get your number?" The tension eases in the room as everyone laughs at my question. Chief looks at me with appreciation in his eyes. I nod, and he turns back to Spencer.

"And you're comfortable wearing just this in a calendar that we're selling for the intentions of the buyers drooling over the people in the pictures?"

"I'll ask again, is this not sexy?" I hope he fucking answers her because I dare him to lie. She's a knockout. If our instant connection hadn't been brother and sister, I would have tried to date her years ago. She's slim but not skinny. The jacket is hiding them, but she has muscular arms. She lifts with the guys in the gym here, and they are constantly impressed.

"Your outfit will work fine, Spencer." He called her Spencer and not Coble. He's running away with his tail tucked between his legs. Mark today on your calendar, folks. The day that Spencer brought down Chief with a zipper and some cleavage.

A hand clasps my shoulder. "Damn, Webb. Have you taken that ass yet?"

"Seriously, Miller?"

"Yeah, man. Who knew all that was hiding under there?"

JUSTIN

"You did, asshole. It's not like you've never seen Spencer in her gym clothes before." She wears her usual sports bra and leggings or shorts when she works out. This shouldn't be surprising for him or any of the other guys here, except the Chief. He doesn't use the gym here with us.

"Either way. She's gorgeous. I want to pull those pigtails that she always wears while I rail her from—"

"You realize that's my best friend you're objectifying right now, right dickhead?"

"Yeah, yeah. I saw your girl upstairs. She's something sweet." I look up towards the Eagle's Nest, the balcony that overlooks the bays just outside the Chow Hall where Nicole is set up, and see her leaning against the railing. I smile and wave at her, but the returning glare is murderous. Shit. She's truly mad about the car.

"Okay, I'm just going to put this out there, Miller, and then we'll stop talking about it. For all intents and purposes, both of these women belong to me—hands off. Look with your eyes and not with your hands. Did your mother ever tell you that?" I clasp his shoulder, he elbows my side, and I know we're good.

He makes a strange face while looking at my hand. I see his nose scrunch up.

"Dude, why do you smell like pussy?" I squeeze his shoulder, and he looks at my hand and steps back.

"Shit, Webb. I'm happy for you, but can you keep that to yourself, unless you want to share." He wiggles his eyebrows at me, and I glare back. "Just fucking with you. Nicole seems like she's good for you. You look happy."

"I am."

"Now, can you give me Spencer's number?"

155

"If you want her number, you'll have to get it yourself. I'm not playing middleman. If you're too afraid to ask, then you don't deserve her."

"Damn, man. Alright. Do you think I have a chance?"

"You have about as much of a chance as you do getting hit by a car while riding in an airplane." I slap his shoulder and turn to walk away but stop dead in my tracks. Nicole is standing a few feet away, and if looks could kill, I'd be incinerated.

"Pumpkin?" Miller turns with a smile to greet her and freezes.

"Oh, shit. Good luck man." He quickly walks away.

23

Nicole

I know I didn't just hear him whistle and yell for someone's phone number. We're in a firehouse. There aren't many women here, and even if there were, he wouldn't act like that with me around. Right?

I finish spraying down a few flyaways from a young blonde firefighter and ask where the bathroom is. He points to the door and tells me the women's room is off the Eagle's Nest, which I assume is the name of the balcony we came in from.

The view from up here spans the entire four double bay area. The rescue vehicles can come in from the back or front of the station. The two bays to my left are where the photo shoots are happening.

I look over the railing and see Justin standing beside a man taller than him with tanned skin and dark shaggy hair. Both Justin and the dark-haired man are staring and pointing toward the people who are currently getting their pictures taken.

Following their line of sight, there's only one thing, or person, their attention could be focused on. A gorgeous woman with jealous-worthy dark strawberry blonde French braids is seductively brooding at the camera. Her very non-sexy puffy jacket is open several inches with nothing under it. He sees me looking and waves, but I can't move to wave back. My blood boils.

Is that who he whistled for? It can't be. He wouldn't do that to me. My feet move me down the stairs before my brain connects with my actions. I stop a few feet behind Justin and his coworker.

"Now, can you give me Spencer's number?" Spencer? Unless the man he's speaking to is into guys, only two women are in their line of sight. One is the photographer, and the other is the half-naked goddess in the puffy jacket.

I want to interrupt their conversation. I want to get clarification because there's no way Justin's "partner" is a female. Thinking as hard as I can with my hormone-rage-filled, baby dumb memory, I can't think of a single time Justin has said he or she in reference to Spencer. It's always been the name, Spencer or my partner. Has he been hiding the fact that he has a female partner?

"Pumpkin?" My nickname pulls away some of the red haze of my anger, but my face must still show my distaste because the dark-haired guy quickly retreats. Justin walks towards me cautiously as if I'm a feral animal he's too afraid to approach. Smart man. "Is everything okay?"

"Who were you looking at?" He looks over his shoulder at the shoot and back at me.

"Um, my partner?"

"There it is. 'My partner.'" I use air quotes to accentuate my annoyance with his term. "Who's your partner, Justin?"

"Spencer? But you know that. I'm confused why you're

158

so angry." He steps towards me, and I put a hand up to stop him, taking a step back. He looks around us, checking to see if anyone is watching our interaction.

"Would Spencer be the buff blond wearing board shorts or the one in the furry snow pants? Oh no, wait. Spencer isn't either of them." He's looking at me like I've lost my mind. He hasn't realized what I'm annoyed about yet, but he's about to find out. "Spencer isn't even a *he*. Spencer is that insanely gorgeous woman that's walking around with her tits half hanging out, isn't she." His head tilts to the side, trying to register all of my words.

"Pumpkin." He looks behind him at Spencer and back at me. "Did you not know Spencer was a woman?"

"No, *Justin*." He flinches when I hiss his name. "You failed to mention that your partner, whom you spend many, many hours a day with, is a woman. A woman that looks like *that* when I'm over here wearing leggings because I'm bloated. Not once have you mentioned her. I know plenty about the Spencer that you stay up late with playing cards and crash on their couch. A whole heaps about the Spencer, who is your best friend and knows all about *me*. Hell, I even know the Spencer who likes their Italian sandwiches a specific way. I could probably even tell you how *that* Spencer likes said sandwich." Despite my best efforts, tears fall, and my voice rises. I'm causing a scene.

Justin looks both apologetic and horrified, but I don't know if it's because he's realized his mistake or because of the embarrassment I'm causing him.

"Has anyone seen the baby oil? These guys need to be lubed up." I turn my head to see the photographer for another month looking around. I see the oil he's looking for and walk past Justin, cross the bay, and pick it up.

"How can I help? Who needs to be oiled?" The older man with salt and pepper hair, wearing all black, cautiously raises his finger, pointing.

"Um? Okay. All four of them need it. I'm sure they can do it themselv—"

"I've got it." I squirt a generous amount of oil into my hand and approach the first guy he pointed to. "Arms up." This poor guy clearly realizes he's in no position to argue with the woman having a mental breakdown.

I feel his presence, but he doesn't say a word. When all four men are generously glistening like a teenage vampire, I walk away, heading upstairs to the bathroom so I can wash my hands.

"Pumpkin. Nicole. Please wait." Ignoring him, I walk into the women's bathroom and try to turn the sink on without getting everything oily. The door opens behind me, and Justin walks in.

"Seriously. This is the women's room, Justin."

"Please talk to me." I pump soap into my hands and start scrubbing. I look into the mirror, catch his eyes watching me, and quickly look away. "I never meant to be deceiving. I'm actually baffled myself that I never mentioned she was a woman." He rubs the back of his neck and stares down at the floor.

I pump more soap into my hand. Dammit, why won't this stupid oil come off my hands? I feel Justin step up behind me and wrap his arms around mine.

"Can I help?" He locks eyes with me in the mirror, waiting for approval.

"Fine, but you need to talk while you do it." He turns the

cold water down and blasts the hot. Pumping soap into his own hands, he lathers them up before taking mine in his.

"Oil and water don't mix. Especially cold water." His soapy fingers gently massage each of mine, making sure to scrub in between and at my nail beds where the oil is the thickest. It's calming my frazzled nerves, unraveling them with each finger.

"Can I take a guess at what you're feeling right now, Pumpkin?"

"Sure. This should be interesting."

"You're in shock at the image you had in your head,"—I clear my throat so he'll correct his statement—"The image that I painted for you of my work partner is wildly different. So different that you were under the impression my partner was a male."

"Yes. That's the impression you gave me." He's massaging my left wrist, and my fingers are tingling with the stimulation of blood flow. Justin leans back, and I follow him, pressing my back to his chest.

"What you think you just saw, and maybe even heard, was me talking to my best friend. There is nothing, nor has there ever been anything sexual between us. At all." I want to continue being mad, but my body is turning to mush. He switches wrists, and the tingling starts in my right hand. His voice when he speaks is calm and soothing.

"She's gorgeous. Why not?" She's so stunning *I* want to ask her for her number.

"Beauty and attraction aren't always about looks, Pumpkin."

"So you're saying you don't find her attractive?"

"I won't lie to you and tell you that. I'm well aware of

Spencer's physical attributes."

"So, she's basically a runway goddess, but what? She has an ugly personality?"

"Pumpkin, Spencer is the best person I know next to you, but there's nothing sexual between us." I want to believe him, but his magic fingers appear to extend farther than orgasms. Why my clit is throbbing from hand washing is so fucking beyond me. A whisper of a moan escapes me as my head rolls around on his chest. He begins to rub the web muscles between my thumb and index finger, and I have to bite my lip.

Our hands are still slick from the baby oil and soap. He leans us down, and I hiss at the water temperature.

"It's not as hot as it feels. Your hands are just overstimulated and sensitive right now." He rubs each finger from knuckle to tip, removing the soap and oil. I can feel them coming clean. Justin's hands massage, pull, and rub, and I'm panting from the attention.

"Doc." He leans in and kisses my neck.

"Shh, Pumpkin. I'm not taking you in the fire department bathroom. I have more respect for you than that."

"Can you not be chivalrous right now?" He huffs a laugh on my neck.

"Believe me, if it were just about chivalry, you'd already be naked with me balls deep in your pussy. This is about not being sanitary. I know the guys that clean these bathrooms." A slightly hysterical laugh builds inside me. Justin reaches for the paper towels, pulling several out of the dispenser and drying our hands off while I laugh more.

"Pumpkin, are we okay?"

"Not yet. And not about the car. But I want to talk to

Spencer before I make my final decision."

"I understand, but you might want to know a few things first."

"I can talk to her, Justin." I jump at the intruding voice. "Let me talk to Nicole. Woman to woman." Spencer stands at the door. She's changed into a form-fitting tank top and leggings in an olive green color that looks stunning against her sandy red braids.

Justin looks at me silently, asking if I'm okay with him leaving. My eyes flick between the two, and I nod at Justin.

"Nicole, would you like to have a conversation outside of this bathroom with me?" I take a look around.

"Yeah. Anywhere but here." Justin looks worried as I follow Spencer out of the bathroom to another room off the Eagle's Nest. Inside are several couches, a bookshelf full of various books and magazines, and an obscenely large TV.

"This is the lounge. We can talk freely." I see a recliner in the corner that looks like it's perfectly worn in and plop my tired ass in the chair.

"Pregnancy is exhausting. I do not recommend. Zero stars. I'm either nauseous, tired, hungry, or horny. Sometimes, all of them at once."

"Have you eaten or hydrated recently?" I squint my eyes at her.

"You sound like Justin. I ate breakfast at seven." She picks up her phone and taps at the screen before coming to sit next to me.

"Hi, I'm Spencer. Justin's female partner. What have you heard about me?"

"An hour ago, I would have said plenty. Now you're a woman, and I'm second-guessing everything I thought I knew." She nods, seemingly in understanding.

"Does it bother you that I'm not a man?" Yes.

"No."

"False. Does it bother you that you thought Justin's partner was male?" Extremely.

"Not at all."

"False. Are you being irrational because you thought Justin's partner was a male, only to find out that I'm really female and your first sight of me was with my cleavage and underwear showing?"

"That was a hell of a lot more than just cleavage," I mumble under my breath.

"Finally, a true statement from you." I snap my eyes to hers. How the hell did she hear me? "Your mumbling is terrible. That was more of a stage whisper. Should I repeat my question, or will you answer it honestly?"

"How do you know I'm lying?"

"You have a tell. I'm very perceptive to micro-movements of people's faces."

"What's my tell?"

"We aren't friends. I won't share secrets with you." Wow. Okay. "Has Justin told you nothing of substance about me?"

"I know how you like your subs." She shakes her head.

"Nicole, I'm on the spectrum. Verbal cues aren't my personal strong suit, which is why I've adapted and trained myself to be so good at reading facial expressions." On the spectrum? Autism? Justin didn't tell me anything about her. "Yes, I'm also upset he didn't tell you about me." It's so weird how she can do that.

"You've been partners for five years?"

"Correct. But we've known each other for six years."

"Oh, did you go to training together?"

"No." Feel free not to elaborate. "How we met is not my story to tell. You will have to ask him." There's a knock at the door, and Spencer tells them to come in. Justin opens the door with a bottle of water and a plate of food, most likely from the catering tables downstairs.

"Hey, Pumpkin." He smiles at me timidly as he puts the food and water on a TV table and brings it to me. "Spencer told me you hadn't eaten since breakfast, so I made you a plate." I turn to Spencer and glare at her.

"And here I thought we were becoming friends, but you narced on me."

"It's important for the baby that you eat properly and stay hydrated." Ugh. I know she's right. They're both right.

"Awesome. Now there really is two of you."

"Do you need anything else, Pumpkin?"

"To get back out there and finish the job I'm being paid for. And what are you wearing?" He's wearing neon green board shorts, flip flops and a backwards ball cap. If I'm being honest, he looks sexy as fuck. He smirks and I'm sure he can tell where my mind drifts.

"I'm August. It's beach-themed. Do you like it?" He does a slow spin, and I have to bite my lip to prevent my jaw from dropping.

"Horny." I blink several times and look at Spencer.

"What?"

"You told me you're always nauseous, hungry, tired or horny. This face is horny." I bury my horny face in my hands to hide from my embarrassment, and Justin laughs. Hands pull at my wrists, and Justin's smiling face looks back at me.

"Hiding from her doesn't work. She's that good." He

extends his hand to me, and I stare at it momentarily before I accept it and stand. "Nicole, I'd like you to meet my best friend and work partner, Spencer. She's the light of my life, the apple of my eye, and the hemorrhoid on my asshole." I snort a laugh and quickly cover my mouth. I'm just embarrassing myself left and right today.

"That was adorable." Justin kisses my temple, and I no longer have the energy to be mad. I lean into his chest, and he wraps his arms around me. Turning my head to see Spencer, I offer her a sweet smile.

"Hi, Spencer. It's so nice to meet you finally. I'm sorry I'm an exhausted, hungry, hormonal mess." Justin's hands caress my back, and I know if I don't get back to work soon, I'm going to need a nap. "Can someone get me a coffee so I can return to work?"

"You shouldn't be drinking too much coffee."

"Too much caffeine isn't good for a growing fetus." Justin and Spencer step on each other's words, and I groan.

"I'll find it myself." I hear Justin inhale as he kisses the top of my head and breathes in my shampoo.

"Come on, Pumpkin. You eat, and I'll go find you some coffee and meet you back at your little work area. Will French vanilla creamer work? I know we have some in the Chow Hall, but I doubt there's pumpkin spice anywhere.

"My inner basic bitch is clutching her pearls." A laugh that doesn't leave Spencer's throat sound next to us.

"She's funny. I like her."

"Spencer, are you cheating on me? I'm the funny one in this relationship."

"No, I'm pretty sure you're the puppy about to fetch some coffee. French vanilla is fine for me." Spencer offers me her elbow, and I pick up my plate of food and hook mine with hers.

"I'll accept French vanilla if that's my only option, Doc." We walk towards the door, leaving Justin behind.

"Doc? You know he's only a paramedic. You're going to inflate his ego."

"It's too late for him, but I must know if you color your hair. I'm jealous of how incredible it looks."

24

Justin

"How about there?" I point at a picnic table under a shady oak tree up ahead.

"Looks perfect. I'm so hungry I could eat a horse, and that smells delicious."

"Cole, are you having sympathetic pregnancy symptoms?" He swings his leg over the wooden bench seat and his forehead crinkles. I sit on the opposite side of the table and put the large brown bag in the middle.

"What's that?" I reach into the bag and pull out several foil-wrapped street tacos. Cole's eyes have hearts in them as he unwraps his first one.

"It's when the partner of a pregnant woman craves things even though they aren't the ones pregnant." He tilts his head at almost ninety degrees and takes an obscenely large bite.

"Oh, maybe." He's barely audible through his mouthful of food. "Annie has been trying to eat super healthy. She's currently addicted to these peanut butter smoothies. I don't know what she puts in them, but it must be drugs. They taste like heaven. I swear Blake has an orgasm every morning when she takes the first sip." He perks up. "Hmm, that sounds like an idea." I shake my head at his quick topic change and take a modest bite of my taco.

"Thanks for covering with the car. I really appreciate it."

"Is she still mad at you?"

"No, she's given in about it because she loves it. She firmly believes it's from Annie, but she refuses to use my card to get gas, so I've been taking it to fill up myself. Your sister is stubborn."

"As hell. How's she feeling? Annie has had terrible morning sickness. I wish I could take it from her and be the one hugging the porcelain throne." The image of someone as powerful as Annie curled up around a toilet is almost unimaginable.

If I hadn't seen it myself recently, I probably wouldn't believe it. Luckily, Nicole only seems triggered by specific smells like curry from the Indian restaurant. We found out the other night that burnt popcorn turns her stomach. I got a little frisky while she was popping some in the microwave, and the timer went for the entire time, resulting in burnt popcorn that I had to air out the apartment from while Nicole took a shower to avoid the smell. I felt terrible.

"She's doing pretty good. Only two more weeks until she's out of the first trimester; hopefully, her morning sickness will subside. Four weeks for you guys. I bet you're excited."

"I'm excited about the increased horniness and the little baby bump that's forming. The girls are talking about doing a gender something-or-another to find out the sex of the twins. It sounds like they want to try and rope Nicole into it, too."

"A gender reveal sounds like fun. I bet Nicole would be

interested in doing it with them."

"I'm going to let the girls figure it out, and you'd probably be smart to as well. The littlest things make Annie cry, and I do everything in my power not to upset her. With my luck, I'd suggest having pigs in a blanket for hors d'oeuvres, and she'll suddenly become a vegan. I can't take that chance."

"Hey Cole? Are you even chewing?" He's currently devouring his third taco. He's stress-eating. "Talk to me. What's going on?"

"I'm…She's…Shit man, I'm gonna be a dad. My sister is gonna be a mom. Annie is growing two babies. TWO BABIES." Cole's eyes are wild with panic as he shoves the entire taco in his mouth. I grab the bag off the table before he can stick his hand in for another.

"Cole, it's two babies and three parents. Three wonderful, loving parents. I thought this was what you wanted?"

"I do. So fucking much. Then last week, we went in for an ultrasound, and I saw their little black and white bodies moving and floating around. They are people. Annie has tiny humans just growing in her stomach. My sister has one, too." I grab his forearm, trying to ground him from his rambling.

"First, is everything okay? Why did she have an ultrasound? It's too early for any needed scans."

"She's wonderful and just as nervous. She paid for a scan. I think if Blake didn't talk her out of it, she would buy her own ultrasound machine and pay to have a tech on call 24/7." That sounds like an Annie thing to do. "How do you seem so calm?"

"I have the medicine on my side."

"Okay? But that will only get you as far as the birth. There's car seats, bottles, breastfeeding, breast pumps, cribs, baby monitors; it's an endless list that has nothing to do with medicine." Fuck. He's right. Nicole and I haven't talked about any of that. There's still plenty of time, though, right? She's only twelve weeks along.

"Justin." I blink and find Cole snapping in my face. "Now you look like I feel. I didn't mean to freak you out."

"I have to buy us a house. A house with a big backyard and a swing set for when he or she gets bigger. I'll have to babyproof the house. You can hire someone to do that now, did you know that? I should probably trade in my truck for a more sensible SUV—something with an excellent crash rating.

"Okay there, super dad. Calm down. Think about the science, man. Deep breath, Justin." I pick my phone up off the table and call Nicole. It rings through to voicemail, and I remember she's at work.

"Pumpkin. We need to buy a house. Call me back with the things you want in it, and I'll call my realtor."

"Whoa, Justin. Relax. You're going to freak my sister out." A million things are swirling in my head as I inhale the tacos I took away from Cole.

"I guess we could live in my house temporarily, but I want Nicole to decorate with her eclectic style. It's so weird, and I love it."

"JUSTIN!" Cole slams his fist on the table to get my attention. "Hand me your phone." I squint my eyes at him, wondering why he wants my phone. "Phone. Now." He shoves his hand out. It's right on the table between us, and he could grab it, but he's waiting for some permission from me by handing it to him.

"Why?"

"Unlock your phone and give it to me." I finally give in, type my code and hand it to him. I watch him pull up my call log. He just saw me call his sister, so I'm not sure what he's looking for. Cole taps on a contact I can't see and puts the phone to his ear.

"Hi, no. This is Nicole's brother, Cole... Yes, my parents were lame... It's actually Coleman and Nicole." Who the hell is he talking to?

"Justin needs you... He seems to be spiraling, and it's my fault."

"I'm not spiraling. I'm just thinking of all the things that need to get done."

"We're at McKinley Park. I'll send you a pin of our exact location."

"Cole. Who are you talking to?" I can only stare at him while he ignores me and talks to this mystery person on the phone.

"Fifteen minutes? We'll be here." He hangs up and puts my phone on the table in front of me.

"Who did you call?" Cole stares me down with infuriating silence. "Who did you call, Cole?"

"You have your phone. You can either look or wait fifteen minutes and find out who shows up." I want to look, but I don't want to give him the satisfaction. There's nothing wrong with me. It's perfectly reasonable to want to provide for your child. I rest my chin in my palm and watch a couple play catch with their dog. We could get a dog with our big backyard.

"Justin?" A hand shakes my arm. I know that voice. "Justin, wake up." Spencer? I open my eyes to double braids staring back at me. I look across the table, and Cole is gone.

"What are you doing here? Where's Cole?"

"Cole called me to come to you. When I got here, you were asleep. I sent him home."

"Sleeping. No way. I didn't even close my eyes." I check the time on my phone. "Holy shit."

"I've been here for about fifteen minutes. Cole said you passed out shortly after his call, so you slept nearly half an hour. How are you feeling?"

"Completely fine. Why?"

"Justin, Cole told me about everything you were saying. He said you were panicking and obsessing. Have you been taking your meds?"

"Yes, of course."

"On time, every day?" Fuck. Why does she have to ask such specific questions? "Come on, let's go."

"Where are we going?" She grabs my forearm and tugs for me to stand.

"To the clinic. To talk to your doctor."

"Spencer, I'm fine, and I don't have an appointment for two more months."

"And you own the place and don't need an appointment. You're disregarding your meds and showing signs of spiraling." Spencer drives a sensible hybrid vehicle in sleek black that is meticulously clean, the way she prefers things in her life.

"Spencer." She stops and looks at me with concern in her eyes that only I can tell from years of friendship. She's saying a monologue's worth of words with just a single look. I nod. I trust her. She knows me probably better than I know myself.

"Okay. Let's go. Can we keep this quiet from Nicole? I don't want her to worry."

"I won't interrupt your relationship unless I have to intervene."

"Thank you, Spencer."

"Justin, don't make me have to intervene." I hear her threat, and I will heed it. She's not someone you want to get on the wrong side of.

Spencer places her hand on the knee of my crossed leg. She's done it several times as I can't seem to get it to stop shaking. She side-eyes me, and I huff.

"I know. I know. You don't have to yell so loud." The door opens in front of us, and I stand.

"Justin."

"Garret." He extends his hand, and we shake. He steps back so I can enter his office, and I look back at Spencer. "Spencer, are you coming?"

"Do you want me to?" Is she serious? She's the reason I'm here.

"Get your ass out of that chair." Garret laughs as I walk past him and shakes Spencer's hand when she does the same.

I look around his office and can't understand how someone can work in this kind of environment. His bookcases are full of texts, and there are stacks of more piled in front of them. His diplomas hang on the wall, but the top one doesn't quite align with the one below it, and it's crooked. It's been crooked since I've been coming to him.

"Thank you for staying late, Garret."

He chuckles. "Spencer didn't give me much of a choice. Not that I minded for you, Justin." Even though it's still early afternoon, Dr. Garret Fox keeps a strict golf schedule but also knows who signs his checks.

Garret is an older man with mostly gray hair, and his cheeks are always flushed slightly pink. When he fully smiles, he reminds me of someone who could play a mall Santa. But despite his appearance, he's been my doctor for the last five years, and Spencer has been to enough appointments that he respects her and her judgment of my mental health.

"Thank you all the same."

"So I hear you've been having increased episodes of anxiety, and today's caused you fatigue. You fell asleep on a park bench?"

"It was a picnic table, and I haven't been anxious. If you haven't heard, my—" My what? What is Nicole? Are we dating? Is she my girlfriend? She's going to be the mother of my child, but other than that, we haven't put any label or title on anything. Is she seeing anyone else?

"Your what, Justin?"

"This is what I was telling you about, Garret. He's been zoning out, panicking." Have I?

"Nicole." My Nicole. The woman I'm sleeping with, living with. My baby mama? Jesus. None of that sounds right.

"Justin, who is Nicole?" I take a deep cleansing breath. It's such a simple question. I see Garret and Spencer exchange a look. *Fuck.*

"Nicole is the woman who is having my baby. We're also sleeping together."

"Do you spend the night at her house?" I nod. "Are you taking your sleeping pill?"

"Most nights, yes. I can sleep through the night without nightmares when I'm there, especially when there's extracurriculars before bed."

"And how's that aspect going?"

"That's going great. My issue seems to have resolved itself with Nicole's help." Garret nods and looks to Spencer again. He sits back in his rolling chair and crosses his arms over his chest.

"I'm not missing my T-time for great sex and good sleep. What's going on, Justin?" You're a patient right now. Be a patient, Justin.

"I've been zoning out."

"Zoning out like daydreaming or getting lost in your head?" Long moments pass, and I don't want to say the words out loud because I know this is how my episodes start. I adjust my glasses, trying to buy myself a few more seconds.

"He's been zoning out. I should have said something sooner." I hang my head at her words.

"Spencer, I'm a grown man. I'm not your responsibility."

"You're my family, Justin. That trumps responsibility."

"Spencer—" She stops me with a look.

"Family, Justin."

"Alright, Justin. Everyone here has your best interest at heart. How do we fix this?" I know what I need. He knows I know. It's been essential for me to have a crucial role in every part of my mental health journey.

"Daily meetings and med check-ins."

"Garret, I can help with the check-ins, and we're about to start afternoon shifts, so meetings won't be an issue." She really is my angel. I don't know what I did in another life to deserve her.

"Thank you, Spencer. That would be helpful. Justin, is there anything more you need for support to get back on track?"

"He needs to tell Nicole." That's not going to happen right now.

"No. I can't do that." I move to the edge of my seat and face her. My heart gallops in my chest. Nicole doesn't know me well enough to know my crazy yet. "You promised you wouldn't intervene, Spencer. We aren't there yet."

"You're right, we aren't, but I can't be around you 24/7, Justin, and you need all the support you can get. You spend the majority of your time with Nicole."

"Justin, why don't you want her to know?" Garret doesn't understand. She can't know how broken I've been in the past. She won't want me.

"She has enough on her plate. I don't want to feel like a burden to her. This is just a minor blip. Nothing to worry her about." Garret leans his elbows on his desk and looks at me.

"Justin, if you think you can get things back to normal, I won't push. You've always been your best advocate for your mental health, but you need to also trust Spencer. You gave her partial responsibility because you trust her judgment as much as your own." I smile at my best friend, who nods back at me.

"I hear you. I hear you both. I promise I'll get back on track."

"Good. Now, let's get out of here. I can still catch up with my group on the back nine." He reaches over his cluttered desk and shakes our hands. I feel jittery inside. I know if Spencer hadn't intervened today, things would have declined rapidly. I owe Cole a thanks for calling her. It feels good to have people in my corner, but it's also scary as fuck. It's more people to disappoint if things go sideways.

25

Nicole

I'm so excited to have a lunch date with Blake. It's been weeks since I've had some good girl's talk. We're meeting at S'morgasm, and she said she has a surprise for me. I hope it's some ooey, gooey goodness of s'mores because a sweet marshmallow dipped in warm chocolate with salted peanuts sounds heavenly right now.

"There's my favorite baby mama." I walk in the door, and Blake has already found a seat in a corner and has a s'mores set up on her table with two steaming mugs.

Walking over to her, we greet each other with a hug, and I smell it.

"Blake?"

"Yeah?" Her smile tells me she knows that I noticed the smell.

"Why do I smell heaven in the middle of the summer?" Sitting down, I raise the mug in front of the empty seat, and my mouth waters when pumpkin, nutmeg, and cinnamon waft over me.

"Because we are big supporters of this little establishment, and Annie made a call. The owners stocked everything needed to make your basic white girl drink whenever you come here." I'm sure she can see the hearts in my eyes when I take my first sip and moan. I don't care who heard it or how embarrassing it might be.

"Okay, but you have to get it right. I'm a basic white *bitch*. But also, please be aware I will probably tongue kiss your girlfriend next time I see her for this."

"And I'll probably allow it. Not sure how your brother will feel about that?" I scrunch my face, thinking hard about it.

"Eh, he'll get over it." She laughs, and then I remember something she said.

"Speaking of Annie, shouldn't *she* be your favorite baby mama?"

"You can share the title. How's my little niece or nephew doing? How are you feeling?"

"Bloated, hungry, horny, tired, in love." I rub my hand over my tiny belly. I'm finally starting to show a little more than just looking like I've eaten too many donuts.

"So basically, all things pregnant." I laugh because she's entirely accurate.

"Was this my surprise because I'm about ready to tongue kiss *you* for this." I look over my mug and wink.

"No, I have a better surprise, but not until after we're done here." She stabs a marshmallow and makes a concoction with Oreos and sprinkles, and I want to simultaneously throw up and inhale one myself. Pregnancy is so strange.

"Blake, can I ask you a question?"

"Anything."

"You've known Justin longer than I have. Does he seem a little off lately?" She ponders the question before shaking her head.

"I don't think so. What have you noticed?"

"Nothing specific, I don't think. I don't know. He was super obsessed with the pregnancy at first, but lately he's been…distant isn't the right word. He's been texting a lot. He says it's Spencer, and it's not that I don't believe him; it's just been more the last few weeks.

"More?"

"Yeah. Every morning and then right before we go to bed. Justin's been coming over later since they're working afternoons, and he's still texting her after being with her all shift."

"Hmm. I can see that being a little weird. Are you worried about them?" I have to laugh at the thought.

"Justin and Spencer? God, no. We had a good talk during the calendar photoshoot. I'm not the least bit insecure about anything more than friendship between them. I just have a nagging feeling something is going on, and instead of talking to me about it, he's talking to her."

"Have you asked him? Or her, for that matter. I'm sure she would be forthcoming with you about it." I never thought to ask Spencer. I know how close they are. I wonder if she would tell me if there was something to worry about?

"Not yet." I take another sip of my heavenly deliciousness and remember something. "Holy crap. Did I tell you he wants to buy a house?" Her lips purse deep in thought.

"Okay, I have mixed feelings about that."

I sit back and relax in the deep-cushioned chair. "Me, too. He left me a random voicemail while I was at work a few weeks back. We played phone tag the rest of the day, and when he came over that night, he didn't bring it up again, so neither did I." She pauses mid-air with her dipped marshmallow and cups her hand under the treat, catching some falling sprinkles.

"Wait. Justin threw you that bomb over voicemail and then ignored it?" Blake looks concerned.

"Yeah." I draw out the vowels because her face is worrying me. "Why?"

"That's just very unlike the Justin I know. He does things with purpose and heart. Him wanting to buy a house for his family to live and grow in sounds a little out there, but it's the kind of calculated thing he would do. He's a planner. But the way he did it—that's unusual." Awesome. Now I'm paranoid about what that could mean.

She waves her hands in the air as if she's shooing a fly. "I have an actual fun surprise for you. Are we done?" I nod, take the last sip of my pumpkin spice latte, and watch the foam remnants slide down the cup's inside wall. This is definitely my new favorite coffee shop.

"Blake! This is my new favorite fucking coffee shop. How could you keep this a secret? I had no idea this was back here." I feel like a kid in a candy store. When we returned to the coffee line, and Blake asked me for my ID, I was confused. Then she walked us back to an inconspicuous-looking blue door and the wonders it was hiding...OMG. Sex toys are everywhere. Ropes. Bindings. Lingerie. Butt plugs that Blake looked a little too longingly at. "This place is magical!"

"I somehow thought you'd like it." I can only imagine what I look like because I feel like I have stars in my eyes.

"I want...Everything." Blake chuckles next to me.

"Well, I don't know about *everything*, but Annie said our shopping trip is on her."

"She. Did. Not. I love you Blake, but Annie's my new favorite soon-to-be sister-in-law. Does this place have shopping carts?"

"Whoa there, killer. Your apartment only has so many outlets for chargers." I shrug and smile.

"I'll just have Justin buy me a house with more outlets." She's silent, and I wonder if I've said the wrong thing. "Too soon?" A few more seconds of just staring before she bursts into laughter.

"No, that's hilarious. I just wanted to keep you hanging. Shall we start in bondage or skimpy clothes?" I look down at the dress I'm wearing because it's comfy and doesn't hug my ever-growing waistline and rub my belly.

We look at each other and simultaneously say, "bondage." I get a nauseating play-by-play of the toys they already have in their bedroom and try not to think about the fact my brother is part of their bedroom life. Especially when she points out a chastity belt and mentions that Cole refers to them as a cock cage. She must see the pure horror on my face because she backpedals and tells me how the three of them officially met at one of Annie's infamous parties. It sounds incredible. An evening of tacos, margaritas, men in cock cages and shibari.

I rub a piece of red silk tie between my fingers and wonder if Justin is even into any of these types of things. Blake walks up next to me and slides her fingers along a piece of black silk.

"These work well as blindfolds."

"Oh. I take it you have one?" She shakes her head.

"Not one. Several." She saunters off back towards the butt plugs, and I really don't want to think about who she plans to use them on.

I grab the red piece of silk and text Justin a picture with it woven between my fingers.

Me: How do you feel about being blindfolded?

Almost immediately, I see the three dancing dots.

Justin: That's not fair. Why do you get to have all the fun?
    Me: Trust me. It will be fun for you.
    Justin: Buy a dozen. I'll pay.
    Me: My shopping trip is on Annie's dime. Any requests?
    Justin: Anything YOU want, I'll like. And get something sexy to wear that shows off your adorable bump.

"Blake." She turns around with a green camo butt plug in her hand. "Justin says I need something sexy to wear.

"I thought you'd never ask." She places the butt plug in a basket on her arm, which I have no idea when she acquired it, but there are several boxes in it. We walk to the lingerie section when she reaches me, and I let Blake do her thing.

By the end of our shopping trip, we're walking out the back door, each with two full bags in one hand and to go coffees in the other. Because the toy store is only one way in and one way out, the cashier had to take our coffee orders, which were then delivered to the blue door for us. It felt like we were doing something naughty. Well, naughtier than what we were already doing.

I periodically sent Justin pictures of what I was trying on, but never an entire picture. Little teases here and there of my hip, a shoulder with the top of the triangle of a bra. My favorite was the back of a sheer lace bodysuit Blake had me

184

try on. It was challenging to get on, and I didn't buy it, but I could practically hear Justin cursing me through his texts at what I was doing to him.

By the time I get home from our day of shopping and pumpkin spice lattes, I'm exhausted. I decide I need a nap but set the alarm since I want to prepare before Justin arrives after work.

When my alarm goes off, I groggily get up, wondering if I could have just five more minutes. I give myself a pep talk because I'm excited for what I have planned tonight, and five more minutes will only delay the inevitable. I need to get up and shower.

As I curl my hair into barrel curls after my shower, I smile at myself in the mirror. I know doing my hair and makeup is pointless, but I want to look and feel sexy. I keep my makeup neutral but paint on a bright red lip stain so it can stay on as long as possible without leaving red smudges all over Justin's body. I chose the lipstick because it matches the red silk I bought along with a red outfit.

Justin wanted something that showed off my baby bump, as small as it still is. The babydoll top Blake picked has a sheer lace triangle top barely held up by spaghetti straps. The red material flows from the cups and sits just below my ass cheeks. But what makes it provocative is the entire piece is held together only by a clip between my cleavage. I have no idea what kind of magic this clip is doing, but it's managing to not only hold my breasts in place but also lift them.

"You're one sexy bitch, Nicole." Beans yips her approval at my feet, and I leave the bathroom to set up my evening. Along with the red silk for the blindfold, I also bought Velcro handcuffs, a vibrator, and a cream that's supposed to make my clit tingle and be more sensitive. It's raspberry flavored, and I bought the companion cream for my nipples as well. Tonight should be a fun evening.

I hear the door open, and excitement floods through me. Justin has had a key for a while. I've become a deep sleeper since getting pregnant, and there were a few nights when he had to knock and call me several times to wake me up.

Java and Beans' nails clack on the floor as he greets them. His clothes rustle while he takes his shoes off at the door, and I hear the rhythmic sound of his bare feet coming down the hall.

I already applied the raspberry balm to my nipples and clit, and holy shit, am I ready to go. My nipples are hard, and my pussy is humming with anticipation. When Justin walks into the room expecting me to be asleep, he freezes. I'm lounging on the end of the bed, leaning back on my hands, legs spread. This outfit came with a thong, but I chose to be bare under it tonight.

Justin's jaw drops. Not in a metaphorical way. His mouth is literally hanging open as his eyes scan every inch of me.

"Fuuuuuck, Pumpkin." In two quick strides, he's on his knees in front of me, fingers splayed on my inner thighs, holding me open even further. His hands slide up my thighs, grazing the outside of my lips before continuing under the mesh of my top. When the fabric falls apart to reveal my baby bump, he groans and cups my belly.

"Do you have any idea how feral it makes me to know that you are growing my baby inside of you?" His hands massage my bump tenderly. "It makes me want to bury deep inside you and get you pregnant again." A giggle escapes me from his absurd words.

186

"I'm not quite sure that's how biology works, Doc."

"It doesn't hurt to try." His hands dip under my arms, and he throws me further onto the bed. He leans down to kiss me and sees the other accessories on the bed. "What else did you get, naughty girl?"

He straddles my legs and picks up the piece of red silk. "What is this for?"

"A blindfold." He twirls it between his fingers. "To use on you."

"On me?" He's intrigued. His fingers loop into one of the cuffs. "Are these for me too?" I nod slowly. "Well, aren't you just full of surprises? Is there any more?" I nod one more time, and he arches a brow, waiting for me to tell him. I pull the vibrator out from under my shoulder, where I landed on it when he tossed me.

"What the hell is this contraption?" He slides off my legs so I can sit up. I understand his confusion. It's black and shaped like a J with two rings on the bottom.

"Sooooo. You slide yourself in through the rings, and one goes in front and the other behind your balls. Then the length sits on top of your dick, and this part stimulates me. It's a dual vibrator." He turns it around in his hands, trying to picture what I just described.

"Blake corrupted you today, didn't she? Is there any more?" I hold up my index finger. "One more? Jesus, Pumpkin. Okay. Tell me, or show me."

"I'm, um…flavored." He closes his eyes and shakes his head. His forehead scrunches as he's trying to figure out exactly what I said.

"I'm going to need more details than that because my mind is wandering to some interesting things right now."

"I'm flavored on all the fun parts." A low growl escapes his throat.

"Tell me where."

"Why don't you find out yourself." Justin places a flat hand in the center of my chest and pushes me down to the bed. He climbs on top of me on all fours and gets close to my face.

"Are you ready for every inch of your body to be tasted?" His tongue runs the line of the pulse point on my neck. "Because if you don't give me a hint, I'll just have to lick and suck every part of you."

"Oh, the travesty. Please don't ravish my body, causing multiple orgasms. Uuugh." Teeth sink into the top of my breast.

"Don't get sassy with me, Pumpkin." His tongue licks at the spot he just bit, and he peppers kisses towards my cleavage. He pauses, and I see his nostrils flair. Does he smell it? He continues to kiss and lick lower between my breasts. "Is this a clip?" My smile grows as he inspects it.

"Easy access." He gives me a devilish smile and pulls the clip apart. My breasts spill out, and my nipples are hard enough to cut glass. His mouth surrounds one, and he hums when he tastes the balm.

"Is that...raspberry? And my tongue feels tingly." Giggling, I flick my opposite nipple as he watches me. "That's mine." He noses my finger away and licks a circle around the peak. "Definitely raspberry. And you said you're flavored in all of the fun places?" He takes a look between our bodies and slides between my legs. He gets within an inch of my needy pussy and inhales deeply. With a long stroke of his tongue, he licks me from entrance to clit, and I arch off the bed with the intensity.

188

"Fuck, Doc." My hands fly to his hair and grab at what little I can as he laps at my pussy.

"I love when you call me Doc. It makes me want to be a better man."

"You can be whatever you want as long as you continue to eat my pussy like it's your last meal."

"Gladly." He pushes his face further into me and sucks in my clit.

"Holy shit. It's too much." Of course he doesn't listen, and his hand slides down my inner thigh and circles my entrance before he slips two fingers into my needy pussy. I'm already so wet from the balm and his mouth that my pussy sucks him in, and I'm overwhelmed. My body feels like it's vibrating with the need to come. The roller coaster is riding up the tracks. Tick. Tick. Tick. Justin's fingers explore my inner walls, looking for the sweet spot.

"Fuck. Oh my fuck. I can't. What are you, fuuuuuck." The strangest sensation washes over my body—pure pleasure and bliss. My orgasm feels never ending. Black spots dance in my vision. I feel his hand palm my belly to try and stop me from jerking around, but it's no use. At the intensity, I feel like I'm floating on a cloud.

"Fuck, Pumpkin. Have you ever done that before?" I prop up on my elbows and look at his glistening face.

"Done what?" I just had an incredible orgasm. Probably the most intense one I've ever had in my life.

"Pumpkin, you just drenched the bed. You squirted all over me."

"I did what? I've never done that before. That's why it felt the way it did." I plop back on the bed and stare at the ceiling. I'm still a little out of breath—thank you, pregnancy—and take a few deep inhales to calm myself down.

"So, about this blindfold you bought. What exactly is your plan?" The smile that washes over my face is nothing short of devious.

"Would you like to find out?"

"Yes the fuck, I would."

"Good." Sitting up again, I adjust my position and direct Justin to lay in the middle of the bed, slightly up against the headboard.

"Do you remember our safeword?"

He nods. "Banana."

I caress his cheek, and his eyes flutter closed. "Good boy." His eyes pop back open, and he's laser-focused on me. I can't tell if his reaction is good or bad. "Too much?" He pulls me in for a deep, passionate kiss. Our tongues tangle, and I can still taste a hint of the raspberry on them. The tingling sensation he shares with me feels like I have popping candy in my mouth.

"Not enough. I'll happily be your good boy if you want me to. I'll crawl on my hands and knees and beg for you if I need to." I stroke his cheek, and he leans his head into my hand.

"Not tonight, Doc. We can take a raincheck on that thought, though. And you know how I love my rainchecks." I reach next to us and grab the silk. "Are you ready?"

"More than ready." I reach for his face and remove his glasses, placing them on the nightstand.

"Hmm. We should probably get you naked first. It will be easier for me." He quickly strips and haphazardly throws his clothes over my shoulders. "I'd like to blindfold and cuff you. Are you okay with that?"

"You want to take away two of my five senses? So I'll only

get to smell and hear you. And possibly taste if you allow it?"

"Correct." I laugh as he closes his eyes and sticks his hands out between us.

"I'm going to take that as a yes." I wrap one wrist with the Velcro strap and look at my work. "Is it too tight?" He flexes his hand a few times.

"It's perfect." I lift his wrist, and he looks at me, puzzled. "What are you doing?"

"Using the handcuffs." I bring the cuff over my slatted headboard and secure his other wrist. "Did you think I would make it easy for you and leave your hands in the front? No touchy, Doc. Still good?" His fingers wiggle, and he nods. "Blindfold time." I loop it around his eyes and secure the back with a basic shoe-tying knot.

"Last check-in. Everything feel fine?" I run a pink manicured finger down his sternum, stopping at his pubic piercing.

"Last before the action starts? I'm completely at your mercy, Pumpkin, and I love it." I open his legs wider, bend his knees, and move in close. Drawing circles on his chest with my finger, I watch his skin form goosebumps from my touch. His hard cock bobs between us. I see pre-cum beading on his tip, and I want to lick it off, but I want to torture him some more first.

Circling his nipple with my nail, I flick it, and he jerks forward. I pop my finger in my mouth to get it wet and rub it on his nipple, blowing cold air onto it. He hisses through his teeth. When I smack his cock he grunts.

"Are you being a bad boy and trying to keep your noises from me? Those moans are mine, and I want them." He squirms in his hold.

191

"Fuck, yes. They're all yours, Pumpkin. I'm so sorry. You can have all my moans."

26

Justin

I have no idea where this badass confident woman came from, but god damn, I'm here for all of it. This is the woman from the first night we were together but without the alcohol. Confident, sexy, and take charge. I fucking love it.

She graces me with a long, pressure-filled stroke of my cock. When she gets to my tip, she avoids it and removes her hand. My moan of pleasure turns into a groan of need. The pressure on the bed moves, and her lips brush against mine, so tender and slow. I try to deepen the kiss, wanting more contact than she's allowing, but she moves back, and I can only go so far with my arms cuffed to the bed.

"Pumpkin. Touch me. You're driving me crazy." Soft, plush lips nip the apex of my shoulder. With barely any movement, she's licking a nipple. A finger grazes my upper thigh. A nail trails across the plains of my abs, and it feels like she's everywhere all at once. I can't do anything but sit here and feel.

A feather-like touch whispers over my balls, but the

returning stroke is all nails—such a contrast of feelings. Slight pressure runs along the seam of my balls, and I moan loudly like my Pumpkin wants.

"There's my good boy." My cock twitches and it bumps her baby bump.

"Hi, baby nugget." The bed shifts again, and I jerk at my handcuffs when Nicole's tongue slides through the slit at my tip, lapping up my pre-cum and quickly disappears.

"Jesus, Pumpkin." My other senses heighten without my sight. Nicole's nail follows the thick vein on the bottom of my cock. It's a hint of a sting mixed with pure desire and lust. She lays something soft over my desperate cock. I hear a click, and fuck if American trade secrets aren't pouring from my mouth. Who killed Kennedy. Area 51 is real and so are aliens. Clinton got his dick sucked by his intern in the oval office.

I can only assume that Nicole laid the vibrator over my length and turned it on. She turns it off just as quickly, but I can still feel the faint hum vibrating through my body. The anticipation of what she'll do next has my adrenaline spiking.

She shifts on me again, and I hear the nightstand drawer open. Is she grabbing a condom? We've never used one except the first night we hooked up.

Her hand strokes my cock a few times, and I feel the silicone of the vibrator slip over my length. It feels uncomfortable when she places the back ring over my balls. I hear a click—the telltale sign of a lube bottle. Any man that has ever jacked off knows what that sound is. Now I know what she pulled out of the drawer.

Nicole rubs the cool gel over my cock and the vibrator, and my body is buzzing, much like the vibrator did a few minutes ago.

"You'll be bigger with the vibrator. I thought we could use an assist."

"I want to touch you. Please Pumpkin, uncuff me." I'm whining. I know it, and I don't care. I sit and wait in silence. Long, drawn-out silence. All I can hear is my labored breathing. This is sweet torture, and she knows exactly what she's doing to me. "Puuuumpkin. Do you want me to beg? I'll beg." She giggles as she moves up my body, and it smooths my frazzled edges.

"I'll uncuff you, but the blindfold stays on. Although begging does sound like fun." Her fingers run along my inner forearm, causing me to jolt.

"Pumpkin, you're the most stunning woman in the world. I want to touch and worship you. Please uncuff me. Please let me, please." I can feel her body heat leaning over me, and I take a chance with an open mouth and tilt forward, catching the top of her breast in my mouth. Sucking in the flesh, she moans, and the sound goes straight to my straining cock. My balls tingle from the rings I had momentarily forgotten were on me.

"Naughty boys shouldn't get rewards, but I happen to like your dirty mouth." She uncuffs one wrist, and I slip my hands from the headboard. I don't care that my other wrist is still cuffed. I wrap my hands around her waist and flip us over so I'm hovering on top of her. It's an interesting sensation still being blindfolded, but that was her criteria.

"I'm at a disadvantage here. I want inside you, but I can't see. Line me up, and let's take this vibrator for a test drive."

"A little eager, Doc."

"Abso-fucking-lutely. You've teased me enough. Either

line me up, or I'm taking this blindfold off and doing it myself." I feel the pressure on my temple when she touches the blindfold.

"Leave it on." Her hips shift under me, and I hear her groan.

"Are you alright?"

"The bump is in the way. I have to reach at a different angle." I huff a laugh and she swats at my arm. "Don't laugh at the pregnant woman. She cries easily."

"Oh, Pumpkin. I hope to make you cry, but it won't be tears of sadness. You'll be crying out my name when you come all over my cock. Now, be a good girl, line me up and let me fuck you." Her hand wraps around me, and I feel my tip hit her heated core. "Fuck yes."

Rocking my hips, I slowly push into her. The lube she applied allows me to sink in without much resistance. When I reach the top of the vibrator, I have to adjust my position to allow full access.

"That feels...different. But don't stop. You feel so good." I have no intention of stopping. Her walls are tighter with the added thickness, and I'm a little nervous about what this vibrator can do. When I bottom out inside of her, I pause to let us both adjust.

"So tell me how this thing works?" My hips wiggle left to right, feeling the attachment.

"There's a remote and a phone app."

"An app? No shit." I slowly rock in and out while I feel her reach towards her nightstand. Pausing, I rub my hand down her arm.

"Is everything alright?"

"Yeah, sorry. Grabbing my phone from the table." Her screen makes the unlocking sound, and my anticipation spikes again.

"Are you planning to make a porn of our sex to watch later, Pumpkin? I'm not opposed to the idea."

"Hmm, not a bad idea, but no."

"Holy fuck." I slam into her as my body convulses from the vibration.

"Shit. That feels...oh god, I can't even describe it." Nicole's nails dig into my shoulders as my hips slam into hers in a steady rhythm that I have no control over. I feel like a marionette being tugged by its strings. The vibrations reverberate through our bodies, feeling like constant explosions. "Fuck, Pumpkin. Turn it off. It's so much." She giggles, and the buzzing stops. My body jolts at the loss of the added stimulation, and I lose my breath.

"I like that." Her voice comes out like a purr.

I stare down at her presence. This blindfold is doing insane things to my other senses.

"I was two seconds from coming. I'm not ready to leave you yet." A delicate finger touches my nose and sweeps across my cheek. It feels like a path of fire is left behind.

"Everything you're doing feels so intense. All you did was blindfold me, but holy hell. I want to kiss you, but I don't want to bash your face in." She snorts, and then I hear a muffled giggle. She must have covered her mouth in embarrassment. "That was adorable, Pumpkin. No need to hide it from me. But I really want to kiss you."

"Roll over. Let me get on top." *Fuck yes.* "But wait—" Swinging my leg over her hip, expecting my ass to land on the mattress and my head to lay on the pillow, I flop back... onto nothingness. There's only a moment of panic before my tailbone bangs on the floor, and my head bounces off the nightstand.

"Fuck." I fell off the bed. Now who's embarrassed? I had no idea where we were in relation to the edge because of my lack of sight, and I just busted my ass. Nicole is trying her hardest not to laugh but failing miserably.

"I'm...so...sorry." Her words come out in huffs between laughter.

I rip off the blindfold and take the other cuff off my wrist. "You don't sound very sorry, Pumpkin." Standing, I look down at my dick. It's red and angry from the beating the vibrator put it through. "Playtime is over." I carefully remove the rings from my balls and throw the offending toy to the floor.

Reaching across the bed, I grab her ankle and pull her towards me. She's laughing as I pull her to the edge and clap her thigh.

"Roll over and get your ass in the air."

"Yes, Sir." I watch as she slowly rolls to her belly, putting her feet on the floor, and pauses. "This position might not work. The terror bean is going to get smushed." She wiggles her ass in the air, tempting me despite her protest. My hands migrate to her ass, and I grab handfuls of their roundness and squeeze.

"Up on the bed on all fours. I want to stare at this ass while I pound into your pussy." I give her another light slap, and she crawls on like she was told.

Mounting the bed, I wince at my already sore hip from the fall but ignore it, positioning myself behind her.

"You're an absolute vision, Pumpkin. Fucking stunning. I feel honored to call you mine." I push into her and groan, getting lost in the feel of her hips in my hands. This is my happy place.

"Am I yours?" My hips pause mid-thrust, and I give hers a squeeze.

"Do you have doubts?"

"Let's fuck first and talk second, Doc. I shouldn't have said anything."

I rub a soothing hand up her spine, tracing each bump. "Pumpkin, you're mine." I reach under her, wrapping an arm around her chest, and pull her up flush to me. Brushing her hair to one side, I press my lips to the soft spot below her ear. "You. Are. Mine." I punctuate each word with a hard thrust. "Don't you dare doubt that. I've thought of no one else but you since that night at the club. No one has ever made me feel the things you make me feel. You've awakened my body in ways I never knew existed."

"Keep talking." She leans her head back on my shoulder, giving me better access to her neck. "Keep talking." Her words are barely a whisper between her panting and moaning.

"You're the most frustratingly beautiful person I've ever met." Palming her tiny baby bump, I whisper more praises into her ear. "This baby may not have been planned, but I don't regret it. I love knowing that half of me is growing inside you. Your body is housing and growing a piece of my heart. You are mine. I'm sorry if I've made you feel anything less than." Her hand slides between her legs, and I can feel when her fingers touch her clit. My cock feels like it's in a vice grip with the way her inner walls are closing in on it.

"The question is, Pumpkin, are you mine?" I don't know if it's the question or the corresponding bite I give her neck, but she comes and comes hard. My arm around her tightens as her body convulses and takes me over the edge with her. I spill into her as my name pours from her lips in a prayer.

When our orgasms subside, I pull out, not wanting to leave but knowing we need to clean up ourselves and the sheets.

"You did it."

"Did what?" What did I do? She turns to face me as she sits on her bed, and I see the tears in her eyes.

"You told me you'd make me cry and look at me. I'm such a hormonal mess sometimes."

I scoop her into my lap, pulling her in close. "You are, but it's okay because you're *my* hormonal mess." She laughs and nestles into my chest.

"You're sitting in the wet spot, Doc. How about you start the shower, and I'll change the sheets?"

"Sounds perfect."

27

Nicole

"Annie, have I told you lately that you're not my favorite? Having to wait until twenty weeks was hard enough but making me wait an extra week to find out the sex of my baby has been torture. You only had to wait a day."

"Yes, but I have double the anticipation." She's not wrong.

A young man in a tailored suit with a pink and blue tie walks past me with a tray of mini quiche in his hand, and I grab a few.

"This party is beautiful. Your decorator does a phenomenal job."

"She's paid to do her job well."

"Annie," Blake scoffs. "Elise does her job well despite what you pay her. Give her some credit." Blake is right. The entire house is ornately decorated in blues and pinks. Balloons, streamers, and tulle decorate every corner. The hors d'oeuvres are all miniature versions of the actual food.

I look outside to the staging area for the reveal and laugh. "I can't believe you convinced the guys to do a paint balloon reveal. It's going to be hilarious and epic." Outside is a stage draped in a white backdrop and a single chair in the center. The daddy in question will sit in the chair, and the mama or mamas will take turns throwing black balloons at them on stage. In the basket of balloons, one is filled with the paint color of the baby, and the rest contain white paint.

Blake's smile is bright with her excitement. "It was Cole's idea. He had to convince Justin, though. He was a little skeptical."

"I bet he was." I look down at my watch and huff. "Do we have to wait twenty more minutes? It's killing me." I'm whining, and I know it. Warm hands wrap around me from the back, and I smell his clean scent.

"Patience, Pumpkin. It's almost time." I spin in his arms and lose my breath.

"You look...wow." Justin is wearing all white, from his dress shoes to his tailored button-up. He takes a step back and does a slow spin.

"I clean up nice."

"I think I might enjoy taking this off of you later, Doc."

"Oh, Pumpkin. Don't tempt me. We can go find a room right now and—"

"It's almost time. I've waited long enough to find out what this little kickboxer in my belly is. I'm not waiting a minute longer. If we didn't have to stick to Annie's timeline, I'd have you up on the stage right now throwing balloons at you." A devilish grin forms on his face and he takes my hand and walks towards the back door. I follow because I have no choice. His grip is firm, and he walks with a purpose.

Justin releases my hand at the base of the stage and steps up. Finding a microphone, he clicks a button, and a loud screeching sound pierces the air.

"Sorry about that. Can I get everyone's attention, please?" He pauses to let the crowd gather around, and I stifle my laugh behind my hands. "Thank you all for coming to Annie and Nicole's gender reveal. If you can't tell by my outfit, I am one of the proud soon-to-be daddies." Annie had all guests wear black and, at the door, had them pick out a ribbon color to wear based on their gender guesses. The five of us are wearing white. "Annie, I know you have a schedule in mind, but my girl and I are impatient and don't want to wait any longer."

Annie walks up to the stage with her hands on her hips and a scowl on her face. Elise stands next to her, trying to cover a smile. Cole saunters up next to Annie and kisses her temple, whispering in her ear. Annie drops her hands to her sides and leans into Cole.

"You've got some big balls, Justin. Elise will grab your balloons for you." Justin fist-bumps the air and sits down in the chair, eagerly waiting.

"He's going to be a great dad." I turn my head toward the voice and see Blake smiling at me. She looks stunning in a white pantsuit with a deep V in the front of the jacket and nothing under it. "And you're going to make an amazing mom. Are you ready to find out what you're having?"

"More than ready. Are you?" Her smile beams.

"I'm so ready. Look at her. She is stunning." Annie is curled into Cole's arms. Her baby bump is more prominent than mine since she's carrying two babies, and her empire-waisted dress flows beautifully over her bump and straight down to the floor.

"She is. I'm so glad I get to do this with you all." Two men place a basket of black balloons at the front of the stage.

"Let's find out the sex of our baby!" I've never seen Justin so happy.

"Go put him out of his misery. I can't listen to him rant about this anymore." I look over my shoulder and see Spencer wearing a tight, black, sleeveless dress that hugs her muscular frame. "I know, I look to die for. Justin has already told me. Get up there." The crowd chants my name as I move to the front of the stage, and Justin extends his hand to help me.

Once on the stage, Justin pulls me in for a kiss inappropriate for the crowd of people we're standing in front of. Most everyone here is for Annie, but they are just as excited for us. Justin pulls away and looks into my eyes.

"I love you, Pumpkin. Now let's find out what baby nugget is." He walks away and sits back in the chair, not caring that he just told me he loved me for the first time.

A black-suited man hands me my first balloon, and I stare at it. The crowd starts chanting again. This time, it's the word 'throw.'

Justin sits about six feet in front of me, smiling and chanting. I pull my arm back and throw. It nicks his shoulder and splatters white paint on the floor beside him. The crowd gasps as it explodes.

"I know you can aim better than that, Pumpkin." The gentleman hands me another balloon, and this one lands on his chest. Everyone whoops at the white streaks on his face. I rush over and grab his glasses from him.

"Guess I'm going blind for the rest of these." I hand his glasses off to Cole and pick up another balloon. And another. And another. Eight balloons later, and there are only four left.

"Justin, pick a number. One through four."

"Three." I take the third balloon and throw it—still white paint. Justin is covered from head to toe. "I'm impatient. Throw them all at once. I need to know what this baby is." I maneuver all three balloons in my hands and step up close to him.

"Are you ready, Doc?"

"More than ready, Pumpkin." Raising my hand over his lap, the crowd starts a countdown.

"Three...Two...One." The scene plays out in slow motion. All three balloons hit his legs and bounce in different directions. One bounces back at me and sprays pink paint, and the other two hit the ground and spray white. I'm covered in paint, only made worse when Justin jumps up from the chair and hugs me in an air-restricting vice grip.

"It's a girl, Pumpkin. We're having a girl." We turn around to face the group and show off my pink splattered dress when I slip in the paint, crashing into Justin. We both fall to the floor in a fit of giggles. We slide our butts to the end of the stage so we don't accidentally fall again, and Annie's staff whisks us away to change our clothes.

Identical outfits in pink and blue await our choice in a guest room, and I can't help but laugh at Annie's preparedness.

"Guess we're putting on pink. At least I get to wear gray pants. Those white ones made me nervous." We quickly change and head back out to see the stage already cleared. Cole is waiting in the chair for our return.

"They're back. Congrats big sister, on your upcoming baby girl. I can't wait to meet my niece. Now let's find out what I'm having. Paint me like one of your French models, ladies." The crowd laughs at his cheesy reference.

205

Annie and Blake are smiling with black balloons in their hands. They look at each other, exchange a chaste kiss, and launch the balloons at Cole. White paint splatters across him and the stage. Unlike me, the girls rapid-fire the balloons, and it doesn't take long before a splatter of blue paints Cole's chest. He jumps up screaming and quickly sits when he almost slips. Annie and Blake are hugging and squealing.

"I got a boy!" I've never seen my brother so excited. They already know the twins aren't identical, so the second baby could be either gender. Spencer walks over to us to say congratulations and asks if she can speak to Justin. Spencer looks concerned but assures me everything is fine when I express my worry.

"I'll be right back, Pumpkin." He kisses my cheek and walks to the back of the group. I turn my attention back to the reveal and watch as more white balloons burst on Cole. Finally, after several more throws, a pop produces a pink splatter across his knees. They're having a boy and a girl; I couldn't be happier.

The girls learn from my mistake and wait for Cole to exit the stage before celebrating with him. They're whisked away to change as we were. I wonder what color they'll be wearing?

While the crowd disperses and the staff cleans up the stage area, I find Justin and Spencer in a corner, looking like they're having a heated discussion.

I can only imagine it must be serious because Spencer is always calm and collected, except right now, she looks distressed. Justin looks like he's seen a ghost. As much as I want to go over and intervene whatever is happening, I know their relationship runs deep, and I don't want to interrupt. They walk off down a hallway and before I can wonder where they're going, commotion takes over the room.

I hear everyone cheering and turn to the stairs as the power trio walks down. Blake's pantsuit has changed to pink; Cole is wearing a baby blue top and gray bottoms like Justin. Annie looks immaculate in a dress with a pink top and a flowy blue skirt. It seems like she was prepared for any outcome. Walking over, I meet them at the bottom of the stairs. They're all beaming with pride, and their happiness radiates off them like rays of the sun. It's infectious.

I approach Annie and open my arms to embrace her. While we hug she whispers in my ear, "I need to speak with you." I reply with okay, and we release each other so she can receive her congratulations from everyone else.

She sounded ominous. I already have so much to be grateful for when it comes to Annie. She's paying for all my medical expenses for this pregnancy. She didn't want me to feel burdened, and state insurance can take months once you apply. She insisted she pay for Cole's flesh and blood, and I'm not in a position to argue. Justin offered to do the same, but Annie was already taking care of it.

As the party comes to an end, I see Annie speaking with Elise and mingle in their direction. Justin has been suspiciously absent since his discussion with Spencer, and it's hard not to feel his lack of presence.

Annie sees me approach and excuses herself from her conversation. She smiles and nods towards the stairs. We stop in front of her office, and she enters her code into the lock pad before we walk in. I'm too anxious to sit, so I walk to the window and look at her beautiful backyard.

"Is everything alright, Annie? I'll admit I'm nervous you wanted to talk to me."

"Will you have a seat?" She gestures to the burnt orange couch in her beautifully decorated office.

"I—Sure." I want to object, but there's no point. This conversation is going to happen whether I'm standing or sitting. Annie sits beside me, and the slight twitch to her lip tells me she's nervous—an expression I've never seen on her before.

"I'm going to tip-toe around this conversation the best I can without breaching any confidence that Justin has entrusted in me." Annie doesn't tip-toe around anything.

"Okay. That doesn't make me feel any better about what you have to say."

"I know. I apologize, but you deserve to be informed." My nerves pull me upright, and I start pacing.

"Nicole—"

"Annie, please tell me whatever you brought me here to say." My elation from earlier is gone, replaced with frazzled nerves.

"What has Justin told you about his past?" Spinning on my heels, I turn towards her. What does she know and why?

"Not a lot. He doesn't seem to like to talk about it."

She sighs. "I was afraid of that. Has Justin shared any of his medical issues?"

"Medical issues? I know he's on antidepressants and takes sleeping pills because of his nightmares."

"Okay, that's a good start."

"Start?" I need to move and begin pacing again. Why does Annie know more about him than I do? I'm having a baby with this man, and she's making him feel like a stranger. Has he been keeping significant secrets from me? "Annie, what do you know?" She runs a hand through her long blonde hair. It's unnerving to see her so unsettled.

"When I was in the hospital, at my lowest point, Justin shared pieces of himself with me that I'm not at liberty to share. It's not my story, but it should be part of yours. If you're going to share your life with him, you need to know all of his."

"Annie, you're scaring me." I flop down into a wing back chair across from her.

"It's not my intention to scare you. I know sharing trauma can be difficult."

"Trauma?" How much of himself is Justin hiding from me? I never thought of asking him why he takes antidepressants.

"You need to speak with him about it. I'm sorry. Let me get to the point."

"Please do." Acid builds up in my stomach, and I might be sick.

"I need you to be cautious and aware of Justin over the next few weeks. Blake told me you expressed concerns over his behavior recently, and I can assure you nothing nefarious is happening."

"Nothing nefar—Annie, I need more information than that." Rising again, I approach the window and look down at the mingling guests. I don't want to ask the question swimming in my mind, but I have to. Turning, I look at Annie with as much strength as I can muster while hugging my belly. "Do I need to walk away?" She stands and walks to me. Taking my hands, she smiles a genuine smile.

"No, you don't need to walk away. Justin is an amazing man. He saved me from myself. He brought me back to Blake and Cole. I'm saying that you need to talk to him. He needs to open up to you. If I thought for a second that his involvement with you or this baby was anything but wonderful, I'd pay for you to get away, whatever you needed. You're family now, Nicole. I take care of my family. Please know that." She releases my hands and pulls me in for a hug. Annie has become more sentimental while pregnant, and I'll soak up every chance I get.

"He's a good man?"

"Without a doubt. Please, talk to him." She pulls away and holds my shoulders at arm's length. I see the war in her eyes as she battles to speak whatever is running through her mind. Her resolve changes when she's come to a decision. "Has he...Has he mentioned his sister?"

"No. I had no idea Justin has a sister." How did I not know this?

"Had."

"Had? So she's?" Annie shakes her head. My shaky hand rises to cover my gaping mouth as my hormones take over, and a sob escapes me. "Had. Oh god, Justin."

"Nicole. I shouldn't have shared that much, but you need to know him to understand him. I only know a small portion of Justin's history. You can talk to Spencer or go directly to him. But as I came here to tell you, please be gentle with him. I had hoped you were having a boy to make things easier, but nature has other thoughts." With the weight of this new information, all I can do is nod. "Do you want me to send him here to talk to you?"

"No. I haven't actually seen him since the reveal. Spencer wanted to talk to him, and he disappeared."

"I'm sure she has the same concern as I do. I'll let you have the office, and you can come down when you're ready. Just close the door behind you. It will automatically lock."

"Okay, thank you."

"Please, remember, the three of us are here for you no matter what decision you make, Nicole." I nod, and she leaves me alone.

28

Justin

I've never been so mad at Spencer before. She took one of the happiest days of my life and turned it around to focus on my mental health. She couldn't have given me the day to enjoy finding out I'm having a little girl?

The past week has been strange. Something happened at the party with Nicole, but she hasn't said anything specific to me about it. She's treating me differently, and I don't like it. She's too agreeable, and I want my spitfire back.

Whenever I bring up the baby and my excitement for our daughter, I can see a door close in her mind. I know neither of us had a gender preference, but could she have secretly been hoping for a boy, and she's disappointed? I know Annie and Nicole left the party briefly, and Annie returned without her.

I can't be upset since Spencer hauled me off to a room and gave me the riot act.

"We need to discuss this, Justin." Spencer closes the door behind her, and I look around the downstairs guest room. Annie stayed

in here when she first came home from the hospital because the stairs were initially too hard on her pelvic surgery. It seems she's redecorated since then. I understand her not wanting to associate the previously decorated room with her post-recovery life. It's changed from the neutral white and creams to a brighter and more colorful palette. I would take a guess she let Blake decorate it.

"Spencer. Don't kill my buzz. It's a girl. I'm having a daughter. Can you be excited for me?" She gives me a deadpan stare.

"Have you thought about what you're saying? What the potential ramifications are of having a daughter?"

"The ramifications of having a daughter? Yes. There is lots of pink and glitter in my future." I'm trying my hardest to keep the smile plastered on my face, but she's making it difficult.

"Justin, I'm calling Garret." I stop her hand as she raises her phone.

"Spencer. You're being ridiculous. Why can't I just be happy?"

"Ivy. Ivy is why, Justin. You're having a girl. It might not have hit that side of your brain yet, but it will, and I can't allow you to crash."

Her concern for me is unnerving sometimes, and I'm still upset. Once she sets her mind on something, it takes a natural disaster to change it. I love the woman, but she's infuriating. She called Garret, and the next morning, I was in his office, and I have been every day since. He's not a psychologist, but I talk, and he listens and changes my meds if he needs to.

Spencer has felt more like a babysitter than a best friend lately. I missed a nightly text to update her on taking my sleeping pill and Nicole woke me when my phone was ringing off the hook. Based on her accompanying texts, she was only minutes from banging down Nicole's door.

Why are the women in my life going bonkers? At least Nicole has the baby and hormones as an excuse. Spencer is acting like an overbearing mother.

"How long will the silent treatment go on for, Justin?"

"I don't know, Warden. When does my prison sentence end?" Spencer catches my sarcasm and huffs.

"I haven't moved you into my spare bedroom to do hourly med checks yet. Be happy you still have your freedom." Her blow hits home. We've been in that exact position before. I've always been an ideal patient, and she's always been a militant keeper. I don't fault her for helping me. But I wish she wasn't so concerned.

"Touché."

"Have you talked to Nicole?" She's been asking me this question daily. I don't want her to look at me differently. Nicole needs to know about my past, but it's not my future. We're having a daughter together. It's a time to celebrate, not mourn my sister. I've done plenty of that. New life is exciting.

"No." I no longer want to talk about it, and she registers my tone.

"You going to finish your fries, Spencer?" She pushes the box towards me.

"No. They're all yours." As I dig my fingers into the salty goodness, the radio in the ambulance sounds.

"Dammit." I shove a handful into my mouth and put my seatbelt on as Spencer does the same.

"Unit 25. Please respond to an MVC with rollover at the intersection of South Ashland and Roosevelt. Confirmed two cars with injuries. Fire Department is en route."

"10-4 dispatch. Unit 25 en route." Spencer replaces the radio handset, turns on the sirens and throws the rig in drive.

"It's showtime."

Approaching the accident, Spencer and I exchange a look and a nod. She runs to the SUV on scene, and I take off toward the car on its side.

"Webb, there's a DOA over there, and someone is still in the car." As I approach the sedan leaning on its side against another car, Miller steps beside me.

"Get that damn horn turned off." The SUV's horn is blasting in the background. Miller looks over his shoulder and takes off towards the fire truck. The scene is mayhem. I look down at the ground covered in shattered glass and see rose petals scattered everywhere.

I can't get inside this way, so I run around, stopping when I reach the driver of the little red sports car that stopped the sedan from rolling any farther. Checking on the man leaning halfway out of his door, he looks to only be in shock.

"Are you okay, sir?" The gray-haired gentleman looks at me, his hood, and back at me again.

"Y-yeah. I'm good. There's someone in there." He points a shaky finger at the sedan.

"That's why I'm here."

Miller rounds the corner, and I realize the horn has stopped. I can hear muffled yelling coming from inside the sideways vehicle.

"What can I do, Webb?"

"The other driver?" Miller shakes his head with the tiniest

215

movement. *Fuck.* "Check on him, I'm going in." He grabs my arm to stop me.

"It's not stable yet. My guys are setting up the cribbing now."

"Miller, I'm going in, so you better hurry. Someone is surviving this fucking crash." I step onto the hood of the red sports car and drop my medical bag inside. The side windows shattered, allowing me easy access to climb into the front seat.

Inside, I see an unconscious female with a mess of bloody blonde hair. Her leg looks to be pinned under the metal A-frame of the vehicle. I hear a faint voice yelling and look around. It's not coming from the victim. I check for a pulse and heave a relieved sigh when I find one. Putting a finger under her nose, I feel her breathing and quickly grab a C-Collar. Holding her head stable while looking for the voice, I see a phone with an open line wedged into the seat. I carefully reach it, putting the phone on speaker.

"Annie. Please be okay. Talk to me, Baby."

"Hello, ma'am?"

"Oh my god. Who's this? What happened? What's going on?"

"Ma'am, my name is Justin. I'm a paramedic with the Chicago Fire Department. Is Annie a blonde driving a black sedan?"

"Yes, but she's a passenger. Is she okay?" This poor woman is frantic on the phone.

"What's your name?"

"BlakeLynn. Blake. My name is Blake."

"Okay, Blake. I'm Justin. Annie has been in an accident, and I'm going to take good care of her."

216

"Where are you? I'm coming."

"She'll be transported to Dov Memorial. You can go there and wait for us."

"Okay. Okay. I'm on my way. Thank you." I hang up as Annie starts to stir in my arms and instantly screams. I'm glad I disconnected the call when I did.

"Justin?" My eyes snap up to the husky voice that doesn't belong to Annie or Blake. Dr. Linnsy, a linebacker-looking man with straw-colored hair, looks back at me. "You paused. Is everything okay?" I almost forgot I was in a therapy session. The pictures of that day are so vivid. Annie's screaming. The torture in Blake's voice.

"Sorry, I must have gotten carried away by the memory."

"It's fine. Do you want to continue?" No, I don't, but I know I need to.

"Um, sure."

"Why do you think you remember this crash so well? Why did you develop a relationship with these patients?" Ivy. The simple answer is Ivy. My sister had blonde hair, just like Annie, but that's where the similarities end. Annie was covered in blood, and Ivy had none. Annie screamed, and Ivy was silent. I didn't think I had to save Ivy; she was quiet and asleep. I had to save Annie. She was bloody and broken, and I couldn't make the same mistake twice. I wouldn't.

"Um. I—" I'm too chicken shit to say it out loud. Annie reminded me of my sister. If I couldn't save Ivy, I was determined to save Annie. And I did.

"It's alright. Continue with your recollection of the accident."

"Once extricated from the car, we transported her to Dov Memorial. I had removed all her jewelry and placed them in

217

a bag, but I must have missed it because I found her bracelet the next time we did a deep clean of the rig."

"How did you remember it was hers? You must see dozens of patients in a week." That's something I never thought about. How *did* I know it was hers?

"I'm not sure. I just knew." At that point, I was already in connection with Blake and let her know I had found it. She told me to keep it and give it to Annie when she was ready. She explained what it represented to them and that I'd know when it was time to give it to her. And she was right. I knew.

"What happened when you dropped her off?"

"They took her straight back to surgery."

"And?" I wish that were the end.

"And I asked the nurse to keep me updated." Dr. Linnsy sighs and rubs his forehead with his hand.

"Justin, we both know that's not the end of the story. You can't keep ignoring it."

29

Spencer

Seven months earlier

CRACKLE: Dispatch we're en route to Dov Memorial.

"10-4. You good, Webb?"

"Yeah, I'm good, thanks."

Justin responds to Lincoln on the radio as I jump in the front seat and turn on the sirens. I check my surroundings and speed off towards the hospital. As if the situation wasn't bad enough for the victims involved, this accident will take its toll on Justin.

I switch the siren tone as I approach a red light to warn surrounding traffic. There was a time when the shift in siren tones would have been a trigger for me, but my father wouldn't let my autism diagnosis stop me from living. Slowly, he taught me to center myself around the noise and eventually drown it out. This is why I am the driver of our two-man crew. If I control the noises, I can predict them and prepare myself.

My eyes split between the road and Justin, preparing the patient for the hospital. He's communicated her injuries to the ED, and they are preparing an operating room for her. He removes her jewelry and places it in a bag along with a cell phone. I watch his hand hover over her head like he wants to stroke her hair. Instead, he pulls away and grabs gauze to clean up some of her scrapes.

She looks like a grown-up Ivy: blonde hair and light brown eyes. I need to keep a close eye on him because I can see this being a trigger.

I pull up to the ambulance bay and jump out. Several Emergency Department personnel run out to meet us. Justin must have informed them we were pulling in. We pull the stretcher out of the rig and rush her straight through the ED and into an elevator. The nurses switch out our equipment for theirs as we ride the elevator to the operating floor. Once there, we transfer the patient to a hospital bed, and our responsibility is complete.

"Justin?" He's pacing the hallway, hands on his head. His breathing is erratic, and his eyes are glossy.

"Fuck." He backs onto the wall and slides to the floor, burying his head into his knees.

"Do you want me to call Garret?"

"No. Yes. I don't fucking know. I just need a minute to get my head on straight."

"Okay. I'll go to the linen closet and stock up." Guiding the stretcher towards the elevator, I push the button and wait. As the doors open, a hand grabs my elbow.

"Thank you, Spence."

"Do I need to call Garret?"

"No, I'm good. Like I said, I just needed a minute. Let's go restock." Justin hits the button to bring us back down to the Emergency Room, and I know he needs to talk to someone but is unwilling to talk right now.

The doors open and we turn left toward the closet designated for the ambulances to launder and restock linens. We open the door to find two people in scrubs manhandling each other.

"Excuse us." They pull apart, and the brunette's eyes widen as she attempts to straighten her top and wipe the smeared lipstick off her face. She quickly rushes past us, staring at the ground, and a husky chuckle fills the room.

"Axel, this is a supply closet, not your personal brothel."

"Sorry, Tails. I just needed a minute to destress. Since you scared off my lady, would you like to take the open position?" *Tails*. I hate this nickname he's given me. I keep my hair braided in Dutch braids for ease while I work. He insists on calling me tails because all he sees is pigtails.

"I'd rather not. I prefer my men to be disease-free." Axel clutches his chest.

"You wound me, woman. My fragile heart can't handle your harsh words." I understand he's being sarcastic, but it doesn't have the effect he expects it to have. I wear my mask around him just as I do everyone in the hospital.

"Could you please move so we can restock our linens since this is a linen closet?" Justin stands next to me, smiling at our interaction. This is a common occurrence between Axel and me. It's also not the first time we've caught him using this closet for a makeout session. "Actually, what are you doing here? You're usually on the night shift." Axel steps close to me.

"Keeping track of my schedule, Tails?" He's trying to fluster me, and as usual, it's not working.

"Come on, Axel." Justin steps up and grabs his shoulder. "We have to get back to our shift, and I'm sure you have patients who need their bedpans emptied."

"Asshole." He shrugs Justin's hands off, and they clasp hands. "Did you guys just bring in that MVC with extrication?" I watch as Justin's eyes dim. I just got him out of his head, and one question brought him back to that place.

"Yeah, man. We did. Hey, could you actually do me a favor?" What kind of favor could Justin need from Axel?

"Yeah, sure. What's up?"

"You have my number, right?" Axel nods. "Could you keep me updated on her progress?"

"Justin." I don't want him doing this. He'll obsess.

"Yeah, no problem." Damn you, Axel.

"Justin."

"Spencer, I'm fine. Axel, if you get any information, please let me know. I just want to make sure she pulls through." I'm going to let it go for now. He can access her file anytime he wants because of his position with the Mental Health wing. At least he's going through a middleman. But I need to keep a close eye on him to make sure it doesn't go any further.

"I got you. She's in surgery, right? Remind me of her name."

"Danika Poulsen. She's currently in OR 4. I appreciate your help." They shake hands, and Axel leaves. I watch Justin wearily as he dumps our soiled linens into the basket and grabs new ones off the shelves. "He likes you."

"What?" I look around the small closet. Is he talking to me?

"Axel. He likes you."

"Is that sarcasm? I can usually tell with you, but I'm not

sure at the moment." He looks at me and smirks.

"Not being sarcastic at all. Axel always has a gleam in his eyes when he sees you."

"I'm sure it's the post-hand job glow he has from whatever nurse he pulls into this closet."

"Say what you want, Spence, but I see it."

"Like I told him, I like my men disease-free. He doesn't seem like he'd meet that criteria." Thankfully, he drops the subject. I'm not immune to Axel's charm. He's big and built with broad shoulders, brown eyes, and a mop of light brown curls on his head paired with a smile that could melt an iceberg. But I've also seen him with his tongue down the throat of every nurse here. No thank you.

"What are you doing, Justin?" Peering over Justin's shoulders, I see Danika's file pulled up on his computer. He quickly shuts the lid, but I've already been standing there for a minute and seen more than he realizes.

"Nothing. Just checking on some paperwork for work."

"Technically, that wasn't a lie, but we both know it wasn't the truth." I walk around the couch in the lounge of the Eagle's Nest and sit next to him. "Let's try this again. What are you doing, Justin?" The guilt is written all over his face.

"She's not doing great."

"She?" He knows I don't need to hear her name to know who "she" refers to, but I want him to say her name out loud.

"Danika. Annie. She's refusing her physical therapy. She's been in their wing for over a month. It was only supposed to be two weeks.""

"Okay. And that's your concern why?" His eyes rise to look into mine and quickly move away. "The correct answer is, 'It's not my concern, Spencer.' I'm interested to hear what you come up with, though." He sighs and closes his eyes, flopping onto the back of the couch. "Justin."

"I'm not obsessing. I swear. Blake has asked me for updates. I'm just checking in."

"Blake, as in her girlfriend? You're still in contact with her?"

"I'm fine, Spencer. I can hear you judging me with my eyes closed."

"What were you doing, Justin." He doesn't answer, opening his eyes to stare at the ceiling. "Justin." He sits up on the couch and huffs.

"Fine. I was putting in a request to transfer Annie to my wing. If she isn't doing PT, she clearly needs mental health. I thought she might do better with my staff."

"That's not your call. She needs a psych evaluation before that's approved."

"She's paying for everything out of pocket. Insurance isn't an issue." There's a look in his eyes that only I can read.

"But even if she weren't, you'd pay for it. That's what you're thinking, isn't it?"

"I hate that you can read me so well. It's unfair."

"What's unfair is the special treatment you're giving her. She not—"

"I know she's not. I know. But can't I just help someone who needs it?"

"Justin, she doesn't need your help. She has a girlfriend." He stands and walks over to lean his elbows on the railing, looking down into the bays.

"She's pushed everyone away. She's hurting. She has no one. I know what it feels like to have no one. If she gets transferred to my wing, I can help. She'll be required to go to group therapy or be forced to leave despite how deep her pockets are." He's in deep. Too deep.

"And if she refuses? Are you going to be the one to kick her out?" He turns to face me, crossing his arms and leaning back on the railing.

"I already run a group. I'll add Annie to mine." It's worse than I thought.

"Have you talked to Garret? Or Dr. Linnsy? Does anyone know what you're planning to do? You spoke to her in the car. What is she going to say if she sees you in her forced group therapy?"

"I'm just a blip on her radar. Maybe seeing me will help her understand that she still has people. I helped her in that car and want to help her heal now."

"I don't approve, and I worry about you. What you're doing is bordering on unethical. She's not Ivy, Justin. It's not your job to help her."

"Dammit Spencer, I know." He throws himself off the railing, scoops up his laptop, and storms down the stairs. I watch him, worried for my best friend.

"You okay, Spencer?" I jump at the hand on my shoulder, and Miller pulls it away as if I zapped him. "Sorry. I forgot you don't like to be touched."

"I don't like to be surprised, Miller. Being touched doesn't necessarily bother me. Those are two very different things."

"True. I'm still sorry I startled you. Is Webb okay? He seemed a little pissed off." I stare down the stairs, wondering the same question.

225

"He'll be okay. I'll make sure of it."

"Let me know if you need any help. Justin's a good guy."

"He's the best."

Justin: What do I wear to a Country bar, club thingy?

Me: How would I know? Why do you ask?

Justin: Going tonight with Blake, Cole, and his sister. Midnight Moonshine. Ever been?

Me: Why would I have gone there? Wear jeans and a dress shirt. Is it a double date?

"Hey, you didn't want to text anymore, so you called?" Justin sounds happy and light as he questions the change in the mode of our conversation.

"I want to address the company you're keeping this evening."

"Ugh. Here we go again, Spencer." Yes, here we go again.

"Shall I remind you that two weeks ago, you were in Garret's office increasing your meds because of your obsession with this particular group of people?" I forced him to see Garret after finding him doing extensive research into Danika's injuries and alternative ways for physical and mental health to heal.

"Spencer, I love you. Thank you for everything. I needed that push. I—Things were getting out of hand. When I realized Annie had no idea who I was, I did get obsessed. My mental health is a daily struggle, and I'd be lost without you and your loving yet annoying care for me. Don't stop worrying about me because sometimes I don't worry enough.

"Thank you. I think."

"Going out tonight is for me. Blake and Cole's sister wanted a night out and us guys are going to chaperone them. I promise if I need you, I'll call. Love you. Now let me go find a nice button-up shirt like you suggested."

"Be safe. Love you."

30

Nicole

Navigating any new relationship is complicated. Jumping into one when a tiny human grows between you makes it even harder. Annie's words about Justin's sister echo in my head daily.

He *had* a sister. Had. Meaning he no longer does. He hasn't once mentioned her. Is his depression related to the loss of his sister? How did she die? Was she older or younger? I have so many questions and don't know how to ask him. I don't know if I have a right to ask him.

It's been weeks of trying to act normal around him, but I know he can tell something is off. He hasn't asked either, though. We can't keep this silence between us. He's excited about having a daughter, but I tiptoe around the subject whenever it comes up. We promised to communicate, and we need to, or something will break between us.

Justin is currently on night shifts, and I feel like I haven't seen much of him, which isn't helping the situation.

Me: Can we find some time to talk?

Justin: Always. We can talk in the morning when I get in if you're free. Is everything okay?

Me: I'm off so that works. I just miss you. I'll make breakfast.

It's not a lie. I do miss him. I never realized my bed was lonely until he wasn't with me. I'm not sure I'll be able to sleep. Usually, Justin comes here after his shift. He crawls into bed just before eight a.m., and we sleep for a few hours before I have to get up.

Justin: I'll get there as soon as I can. Breakfast sounds wonderful, and I miss you too.

Rummaging through the kitchen, I see I have all the ingredients to make overnight French toast. I actually have the ingredients to make quite a few things since Justin keeps my cabinets and refrigerator full. I now get a weekly grocery delivery with my favorites and some of his.

I put the casserole together and place it in the refrigerator. I'm not the least bit tired, but I know I need to sleep, so I change my clothes and lay in bed with my e-reader. Java and Beans walk up the ramp and burrow under my blanket. Checking my phone to confirm I've set an alarm for the morning, I roll over and open to the latest book on my TBR.

Music fills the room as my alarm sounds on my phone. I hate buzzing alarms, and setting a music tone wakes me without a startled start. I carefully pull myself out of bed, trying not to disturb the puppies, but I have no luck.

"I'm coming right back. It's not time to get up yet." They

don't listen and follow me into the kitchen. I preheat the oven and take the French toast out of the refrigerator. The puppers dance at my feet, and I sigh.

"I guess I can take you out while the oven heats and the glass dish comes to room temperature." I look down to assess my outfit: an oversize t-shirt, no bra, and biker shorts. It'll do. I'm just taking the dogs out. Slipping on a pair of flip-flops near the front door and clipping their leashes, we head outside.

I'm blankly staring at the ground in my half-asleep state while trying to calculate how much more sleep I can get before I have to take the casserole out of the oven when I'm startled by another voice.

"Pumpkin, are you okay?"

"Justin?" I look down at my wrist to check the time, but I'm not wearing a watch. "What time is it?" I pat around my nonexistent pockets to realize I've left my phone upstairs.

"I'm early. We had a messy call and had to bring the rig back to base to clean, and we got to leave as soon as the next crew came in?"

"Messy?" Can I do anything but ask questions? I'm not entirely sure I'm not dreaming. I feel exhausted, but I know I slept.

"Oh no, not like that. We had a drunk, and the guy threw up and peed himself in the ambulance. It wasn't pretty. Are you alright? You look pale?" He takes the leashes from me and wraps his arm around my waist.

"I'm just tired. I was up late reading."

"Let's get you upstairs. I don't like the way you look. You know what? Let me grab my jumpbag from my truck first. Will you be okay for a minute?"

"Yeah, yeah. I'm fine. Go." Justin jogs to the parking lot with the dogs. It's so cute to see their little legs run with him. I watch the headlights flash when he unlocks his truck, and I squint my eyes. Why are they so bright?

Suddenly, it feels like the world around me is dimming like the slow motion of a camera shutter. I wobble on my feet and realize something is wrong.

"Justin." He's coming back towards me when he breaks into a run.

"Nicole!" He sounds like he's yelling in a tunnel. I know he's running, but the shutter is closing, and he seems to be getting farther away.

Ugh. I want off this bumpy ride. It's hurting my head and making me feel nauseous. Really nauseous. I'm going to throw up.

My eyes pop open, and my hands fly to my mouth. Justin quickly reaches above me and hands me a small blue bag. I empty what little food I had in my stomach, but its still protesting.

"Shhh. It's okay." Justin runs a soothing hand down my arm.

"Where am I?" My voice is rough from the vomiting. We hit another bump and I realize I'm in a vehicle. Not just any vehicle, an ambulance. "What happened?"

"You passed out and hit your head pretty hard. You're going to need stitches. I called an ambulance, and we're on our way to the hospital." I nod because everything he's saying makes sense. I was tired, but I also remember feeling dizzy. I wobbled just as Justin started running to me with...

"The dogs...and the oven."

"I took care of it. I got them safely inside and turned the

oven off. How are you feeling?" Good question.

"What happened?"

"Your sugar was too low. I gave you some oral glucose, and your number came back up. How are you feeling?"

"Crappy. Tired. My head hurts."

"All things to be expected. We're almost at the hospital. I already called your OB, and he's aware of the situation."

"Wait. You called my OB? How?"

"I called Annie, and she gave me the number. I checked your phone, but you don't have anything specifically saved for the doctor, so I tried the next best person." Okay, that all seems rational.

"So, dogs are good; oven is off. My casserole?"

"Back in the refrigerator. Why don't you relax, stop worrying about everything, and focus on yourself and our little girl." Justin picks up a radio handset and tells the Emergency Department we're two minutes away.

When we pull up, the back doors open, and I see faces I recognize from the photoshoot.

"How's she doing, Webb?"

"I'm right here. I'm awake, and I have a name. It's Nicole. You can ask me, not him?"

"Snarky. Glad to see you awake. I'm Miller." Justin and Miller pull the stretcher out of the ambulance as smoothly as possible.

"I thought you were a firefighter?" I look behind me. "Did you just drive the ambulance?"

"I called the station directly." I turn to Justin, and he gives me a sheepish smile. "Since I was already there, Miller brought the off-duty rig."

"Completely against protocol, but when Webb asks for the

rules to be broken, we break them and respond."

"I called in a favor. I knew it would be quicker."

"Justin?" Spencer walks up behind him, and I groan.

"Is there anyone you didn't call?" The answer is no, and I can see it on his face. He called Annie, so Cole knows. Spencer is here, and Justin called in a favor to drive me to the hospital.

Spencer walks next to the stretcher as I'm wheeled inside, and she gives me a look that I think is supposed to be sympathy. I don't buy it. After our talk at the firehouse I pay more attention to her facial expressions. She's making her concerned face, but it's not directed towards me. Justin? She keeps glancing his way. She's his best friend, so it makes sense that he would call her.

They roll me to the nurse's desk, and a giant man walks over and gives everyone a manly handshake. His navy scrubs hug all of his dips and curves. He has the most perfect light brown curls. As a hairdresser, I have absolute respect for the routine I know he must go through to get them like that. The hunky man looks at me and smiles a panty-dropping smile.

"Wonderful. The gangs all here." I feel like a circus freak.

"Sorry. Pumpkin. Hazard of the job." He kisses the top of my head. "This is Axel. Axel, this is my girlfriend, Nicole. She had a syncopal episode due to hypoglycemia. L.O.C for about ten minutes. Two-inch LAC behind her left ear." What? Reaching behind my ear, I feel a bandage. That explains the headache.

"Could we please speak English?" Big man Axel smiles at me.

"Sorry about him, Nicole. What he was telling me is you passed out because your blood sugar was low, and you have a cut behind your ear. Has this ever happened before? Passing out? Do you commonly have low blood sugar? While pregnant or not?" Holy rapid-fire questions.

"No. None of that is common." I look up at Justin, shocked. How could he possibly know the answers to any of that?

"Justin."

"Sorry, Pumpkin." I look at Axel and confirm Justin's answers.

"No. I don't usually have blood sugar issues that I know of, and I've never passed out before. Ever." Justin nods to Axel as if my answers need his approval. What's up with him?

"Okay, Nicole. Let's wheel you to room six and get you looked over." I notice Spencer tap Justin on the shoulder, and he shakes his head at her. Why is everyone acting weird?

Once in the room, I stop them from trying to lift me onto the hospital bed.

"I'm not an invalid. I feel fine. I can scoot over myself."

"But—"

"Justin, I'm okay." I get settled on the bed with all eyes on me, and it's unnerving. I feel like a goldfish in a fishbowl.

"Alright, Tails, you can take the stretcher back. Your job here is done." Tails? Who is Axel talking to? Surely not Miller.

"I didn't drive them here, Miller did. I'm off the clock." Spencer? Is she...blushing? I wouldn't blame her if she were. He's a hunk. My eyes dart back and forth between the two as there's a mini stare-off.

"Hmm. A social call? How interesting." Axel breaks their eye contact first, and I hear a tiny breath of relief from Spencer. I'm startled when Justin snaps his fingers.

"Back to the patient. Stop flirting."

234

"Justin." Spencer and I both chastise him at once.

"I'm gonna get the rig back to the station before we all get in trouble." Miller slings a thumb over his shoulder towards the door, and Spencer grabs the end of the stretcher.

"I'll help you make sure everything is restocked before you leave." There's a twinkle in Miller's eyes as he follows her out the door.

"Interesting."

"Very." Shit. I look at Axel, whose eyes also follow them out the door. I guess I spoke out loud.

"Do we need to get someone else in here, or can you get your head out of your ass, Axel?" I grab Justin's arm as Axel turns his attention to me, ignoring Justin.

"We'll get some bloodwork done and see where your levels are at. An A1C will tell us how your sugar levels have been for the last three months, and we'll be able to tell if this was an isolated incident or something we need to watch out for. You haven't had your glucose test yet, have you?" I want to be a strong, independent woman and answer his question, but I'll admit I've reverted back to Justin for a lot of the medical stuff when it comes to the pregnancy. When I don't immediately answer, Justin does it for me.

"Not yet. It's supposed to be next week, but let's do it while Nicole's here. And an ultrasound since she fell." Axel looks at me, and I nod.

"Alright, we can do both of those things. I'll send in a nurse to take some blood—"

"You, Axel. You're the best stick, and we both know it. I want you to take her blood." He nods and squeezes my calf.

"Okay, Nicole. I'll be back in a few minutes to take your blood. And I'll see about getting a portable ultrasound machine and tech down here. If not, I'll make an appointment with radiology. If you need anything before then, which I doubt you will with this overbearing baby daddy, just hit the call button." I give Axel a small smile, and he leaves.

"Justin, what's up with you?" His eyes dart around the room like a caged animal. "Come sit with me." I move my legs over and pat the bed. He hesitates and then lets out a big sigh before settling down at the end of the bed.

"How are you feeling?"

I take his hand and place it on my belly. "I'm okay. Our baby girl is okay. We're good. I promise. How are *you* feeling? You're acting a little squirrely."

"I'm fine." His curt answer tells me he's anything but. "I should get Axel back here to look at your head. Maybe we should get you a CT scan?" I hold tight to his hands on my belly as he tries to pull away.

"Please relax. I'm here in the hospital, and it sounds like you have the best people working on me. We're going to see our little girl. Can you be excited about that?" I see the light start to brighten in his eyes. His fingers flex on my stomach, and he smiles sweetly.

"Our little girl. It's been over a month since we've seen her." He's coming back to me. His tone is soft and reverent. There's a knock at the door, and Spencer has returned.

"Am I interrupting?"

"Not at all. Come in." She smiles, and it feels genuine, but her eyes shift to Justin, and I see concern masked on her face. "We were just talking about seeing the baby again. Justin asked for an ultrasound." She nods at him.

"That's a good idea since you took a fall. How's your head?" Oh no. I hope there aren't going to be two of them now fussing over me.

"I have a minor headache, but otherwise, fine." I feel Justin tense at the mention of me being in any pain. "Hey," I whisper to him. "I'm okay."

"Did Axel look at your wound yet?"

"No," Justin practically growls. "And I should request a CT scan."

"Idiot," she mumbles. "Let's not panic yet, Justin. Would you let me look at it, Nicole?" Spencer walks to the doorway where boxes of Nitrile surgical gloves hang on the wall. She pauses, waiting for my response, and I sit up, giving her my nonverbal answer. Justin raises the bed so I can sit up more easily.

Spencer comes over and gently pushes my hair aside. She looks at Justin in their silent, conversational way, and he takes my hair and holds it back for her.

"I need to remove the gauze, and it might hurt a bit. It's stuck in your hair in a few places." It's interesting to see her mask fully on.

"I'm sorry, Pumpkin. I was in a rush. I should have been more careful."

"It's okay. I was a little unconscious at the time." I laugh to lighten the mood, but it doesn't help. Spencer keeps looking at Justin expectantly. Although I have no idea what she's waiting for. I wince at the sting as a few strands of hair stick to the tape.

"Sorry, Nicole. I'm almost done."

"It's okay." I close my eyes in an attempt to not make any more faces while the rest of the tape is removed. Her fingers gingerly touch around the wound, and I inhale deeply at the pain.

"If you can be careful, I believe we can get away with glue. It's not as bad as it looks. Head wounds bleed a lot, and we can sometimes overreact." Spencer's voice is soft and tender. It's a stark contrast to the blunt, matter-of-fact personality that I'm used to. I can see why she's so successful in her career.

"Are you sure that's the best course of action, Spencer? It's on her head."

"And at her hairline. Her hair will cover any scarring. It's already stopped bleeding."

"But—"

"Justin, do you need to take a lap?" I'm always fascinated by their relationship. They talk without talking. They're like an old couple or a well-oiled machine. I have no idea what's going on, but Spencer sees something happening within Justin. I wish I understood him. We were supposed to talk this morning, but instead, I find myself lying in a hospital bed, watching this strange and fascinating scenario happening around me.

"I'm good." He readjusts his hold on my hair and takes my hand.

"The decision is yours, Pumpkin. We can have a plastic surgeon come down and look to help minimize scarring if you'd like?" Do I care? I am a hairdresser, and Spencer said it's on my hairline. It might be helpful not to have a big ugly scar.

"Don't dudes dig chicks with scars?" He chuckles and kisses my forehead.

"Yeah, yeah, we do."

"It sounds like glue is the final answer, then?" Spencer gives me a small smile.

"Make me your art project, Spencer." Justin almost snorts, but Spencer clearly doesn't understand the joke.

I try to be the perfect patient as Spencer and Axel take care of my head wound. Justin watches everything they do like a hawk. When Axel takes my blood, and I flinch at the needle prick, he growls, and I have to put my hand on his chest to keep him in his seat.

"Did you find a portable ultrasound machine?" There's an edge to Justin's voice, and I'm not sure I like it.

"We are next on the list to use it. It's probably ready by now." Axel smiles at me, and Justin grunts.

"What are you waiting for? Go get it." His edge has turned to irritation.

"Justi—" Axel raises his hand, cutting Spencer off from chastising him again.

"I've got this, Tails. Justin, take a walk. You aren't here as anyone other than the loved one of a patient, and I can have security take you out of here if I need to." The men stare at each other for several heartbeats before Justin looks away.

"You're serious right now, Axel?"

"Dead serious. You can calm down and let us, *let me,* do my job, or you can leave. Choice is yours." Justin sighs, and it's long and defeated.

"Fuck. I'm sorry. I'm still running on adrenaline. I'm worried about Nicole and our daughter."

"We're all good as long as you remember your place, Justin. And congrats on having a girl." Axel removes the gloves from his hands and tosses them in the trash. He looks at me and smiles tenderly. "I'm going to go get the ultrasound machine so we can make sure your little girl is still snug as a bug in there." He pats my hand and eyes Justin one more time before leaving.

A silent conversation happens between Spencer and Justin, and as always, I'm in awe. She says nothing, but he nods and picks up his phone.

"I need to make a few calls. Will you be okay if I step out and leave you with Spencer?"

"Of course. Take your time. I'll call you if Axel gets back before you." He kisses the top of my head and glances at Spencer one more time before he leaves the room.

31

Justin

What a fucking morning. Watching Nicole hit the ground before I could catch her was unbearable. My natural medical instincts kicked in, and I had my phone in hand, calling the station before I got to her. I dropped to my knees at Nicole's head before Miller picked up the phone.

"Station 34, Miller speaking."

"Miller, it's Webb. I need a rig at Bridgewater Apartments. Nicole went down. Assessing her now, but she has a head LAC."

"Shit, I'll grab the spare rig. What apartment?"

"Outside building four. We were walking the dogs. She's still unconscious. Lights and sirens all the way here."

"On my way."

By the time Miller showed up, I had Nicole's head bandaged. When we had her settled in the rig, I ran the dogs upstairs to find the apartment overheated from the oven with a casserole waiting to go in. I quickly settled the dogs, cleaned up, and grabbed Nicole's purse.

Miller had just finished taking Nicole's vitals when I got back, but she was still unconscious. He quickly jumped into the front seat, and we took off to the hospital. Spencer was my first call because, despite my training, when she still wasn't awake, I was internally freaking out and needed her to talk me off the proverbial ledge.

My phone call to Annie to get the doctor's information didn't calm my nerves, as listening to her play twenty questions about Nicole's health when all I wanted was a phone number was unnerving. After she has her twins, I hope she returns to the grumpy businesswoman I became fond of.

My last call before Nicole finally woke up was to Axel. I knew he was getting off shift soon, and I wanted him to stay, even offering to pay him personally if we would work over to take care of her. I trust him the most, and of course, he offered to stay without funds from my personal checkbook.

At that point, I had already taken a finger prick and knew Nicole's sugar levels were low, causing her fall. All of the knowledge in the world can't prepare you when a loved one is the patient of a medical emergency. After administering the glucose and knowing how long it should and could take for her levels to rise back up, I was still a wreck. I don't think I took a deep breath until I saw her eyes pop open, and her face turned green, needing to vomit.

Spencer watched me like a hawk from the second she arrived, and each time she chastised me, I knew I deserved it. My snap at Axel was the last straw, and her look told me what I needed to do. I needed to call Garret or Dr. Linnsy. Do I want talk therapy or medication therapy? We've been *talking* about increasing my anxiety medication, something we haven't had to do in a while. But with each passing day of this pregnancy, I may need it. I send a text to Garret. He can call it in for me without any further discussion.

Axel walks down the hallway, and I rush to catch up.

"Hey, Axel. Wait up." He hesitates a moment and stops, turning around to look at me.

"I'm getting it now, Justin."

"I'm sorry. I appreciate you more than you know. Let me make it up to you. Come over for dinner. When are you free?"

"Justin, you don't have to. I understand." He looks exhausted, and I know he expected to be going home an hour ago, but he is doing me this huge favor.

"Please. I was a dickhead. Let me feed and booze you. I'll invite Miller and Spencer, too. It will be an appreciation dinner. Please." He sighs and runs his hand through his hair; somehow, his curls bounce back into place.

"Yeah, sure. I'm off this weekend. If that doesn't work, I'll have to look at my schedule." I smile at him and hope he understands how much this means to me.

"Do you think she needs a CT scan? She hit her head and was unconscious for a while."

"Do you, Justin? You were there. You know her blood sugar levels were the cause. How badly did she hit her head? I know you'll obviously be checking her for concussion protocols."

I nod my head at everything he's listing off. He knows the answer, but he's letting me roll all the facts around and come to my own conclusion.

"Okay. No CT. Of course I'll be monitoring her. I'll meet you back in the room." I pull him in for a manly back slap

243

hug, and he holds me a second longer.

"She's going to be okay, and so are you. Take care of yourself too, Webb." He smiles at me before turning around and continuing down the hall. My phone buzzes in my hands, and I reluctantly answer.

"Is she okay? Is the baby okay?" I don't even get a word in before Cole is yelling in my ear.

"She's good. Her blood sugar was low, and she fell. We're about to get an ultrasound to check on baby girl, but there's no reason to think anything is wrong."

"Jesus fuck, Justin. Annie was hysterical, and it took me this long to get enough coherent information out of her. She's a sobbing mess. Fucking hormones." I sympathize with him on the "fucking hormones" comment. "Do you need us to come down there? Is she being admitted?"

"We're good. Waiting on blood tests and the ultrasound, but I don't see a reason Nicole would stay. I can let you know if something changes."

"Okay, good. Could you have Nicole Facetime Annie? I think she needs proof of life or some shit." I can't help but laugh because this is so un-Annie-like.

"Yeah, I stepped away, but I'll have her call in a few minutes." I pull the phone away from my ear to end the call but hear Cole's voice again.

"Hey, man? Are you good?" I hate that he saw me that day in the park. It wasn't my finest moment, but now he knows.

"I'm good. Gotta get back to our girl." I plaster on a fake smile, hoping he can hear it through the phone.

"Thanks, Justin. I'm glad you were there and that she's okay."

"I'll always be there for her, Cole."

We hang up, and another wave of panic sets in. What if I wasn't there? We were outside for ten minutes, and no one stopped to ask if she was okay or if I needed help. I came back earlier than she expected. Would she have been lying out there for an hour if I hadn't? What if she made it back inside and then passed out with the oven on, and there had been a fire? If she decided to take a shower before I came over and lost consciousness in the tub and split her head open on the faucet, or worse?

"You ready, Daddy?" Axel's hand on my shoulder stops my downward spiral. I blink several times before I can manage the words to respond.

"Yeah." I follow him back into the room, where Nicole and Spencer laugh together. Seeing my best friend and the woman I love getting along warms my heart.

Woman I love. That's a new one. I need to process that some more. Is that how I feel about Nicole? That thought hasn't even crossed my mind until just now.

"Justin?" Why is there a question in Nicole's tone? Did I miss something?

"Yeah?"

"Spencer asked if you wanted her to leave. It's okay with me if she stays, but it's your decision, too." Stay for what? I look around the room, and everyone looks at me, waiting for an answer. Spencer knows everything, so whatever it is, the answer is yes.

"She can stay." Nicole's smile is bright as she lifts her shirt. Axel rolls a drape over her lower half and squirts the lubricant over her belly bump.

Oh. Stay for the ultrasound. The answer is still yes, Spencer can stay.

"Alright, Mom and Dad...and Auntie, let's check out this little lady." Axel winks at Spencer when he calls her Auntie.

We all stare at the little black and white screen as the silhouette of a baby appears. Nicole reaches for my hand and laces her fingers with mine as tears roll down her cheeks.

"There she is. She's gotten so big." I want to be in awe and wonderment like Nicole, but my mind is still panicking. "Can we get pictures?

"Unfortunately, not with the portable machine. But do you want to hear her heartbeat?"

"Yes, oh please. Yes." I close my eyes, and a moment later, I hear the fast-paced rhythm of a heartbeat. My daughter's heartbeat. MY. DAUGHTER'S. HEARTBEAT.

There's a knock at the door, and a nurse hands Axel paperwork. He puts the ultrasound wand away and wipes off Nicole's stomach while looking over whatever the nurse handed him.

"Okay. It looks like we have some good news and some... bad news isn't the right word." I want to growl at him again, but I see Spencer look my way out of my peripheral. I don't want to cause her any more alarm, so I use every ounce of patience I have left to be calm.

"Axel, what's wrong?" There's a slight tremble in Nicole's voice, and I squeeze her hand in reassurance.

"All your blood work came back great except your blood sugars and A1C. It looks like your sugar levels have been high, and you most likely have gestational diabetes. I'll make sure to send these results over to your OB. They'll probably want to give you the glucose test to make sure and then have you speak with a dietitian." I can feel Nicole's hand tremble in mine.

"Is that bad? Gestational Diabetes?" She looks between Spencer and me. Spencer shakes her head and rests a hand on Nicole's shoulder, putting on her paramedic mask.

"It's not that bad. Most can be treated with diet—"

"You'll move in with me." Perfect solution. I can monitor her more closely at my house than hers.

"What?"

"Justin." Why do these two women seem to always be on my case?

"It's a perfect solution. I can help monitor your sugar levels and help you with meals. I don't have any stairs or janky elevators."

"I don't even know if I have it yet. Right, Axel?" She looks to him in hopes he'll back her up. She doesn't know that it's not something he can diagnose. All he can do is read the paper.

"I can't say either way. Sorry, Nicole. What I can tell you is your numbers are high, so it's most likely. You need to confirm with your OB. But I can also tell you that you would be in the best hands at Justin's house. He isn't wrong. If untreated, gestational diabetes can have a lot of negative effects on the baby."

"But I—" I stop her protest before she can start. I lean down onto the bed and take her cheeks in my hands.

"Pumpkin, you had a really close call today. It scared the fuck out of me. What if I hadn't been there?"

"But you were."

"But what if I wasn't? What if I had been on time instead of early?" I move one hand onto her bump. "Let me take care of you both. It wouldn't be just for you. I know *you* hate accepting help. Let me help her. Let me help our daughter."

- THE RESCUER'S HEART

I know what I said is a low blow, leaving her in a challenging position to say no, which is why I can already see in her eyes she's going to say yes.

"But Java and Beans?"

"Will love it at my house. I have a fenced-in backyard, and I can put in a doggie door if you'd like me to. I know we haven't talked about it yet, but doesn't it seem silly to have two separate homes anyway?"

"I'm not giving up my apartment. I've worked hard to live on my own, Justin."

"Then don't give it up." I cup her cheek in my hand. "But still, come stay with me. Let me provide for you." Her resolve is cracking. "Did I mention no stairs or elevator?" She chuckles, and I know I've got her.

"You might have mentioned that." She sighs and closes her eyes. "Okay. But only if you promise me you have a really good hot water tank because the idea of taking a twenty-minute shower and having hot water the entire time sounds amazing."

"If it doesn't meet your approval, I'll have a better one installed." I'll buy an entirely new house if she doesn't like the one I'm currently living in.

"You wouldn't—yeah. Yeah, you would. I'm sure it will surpass my needs." I'm surprised she can still see with how bright my smile is. It must be blinding. Suddenly, her face falls.

"What's wrong?"

"I've never been to your house. Why have I never been to your house." She looks at Spencer. "Please tell me you've been to his house. There aren't torture chambers in his basement, right?" Spencer, Axel and I are all doing a terrible job trying not to laugh at her little freak-out moment. "Justin, this isn't funny. Why have I never been to your house?"

"Relax, Nicole." Spencer places a comforting hand on her shoulder, and a quick look at her face shows no mask. This is genuine comfort. She's getting comfortable with Nicole, and that warms my heart. "I promise there are no torture chambers in his basement. He doesn't even have a basement."

"Now the attic…"

"Shut up, Axel." *Oh.* Overprotective Spencer is new. "You aren't helping. Don't you have a bedpan to empty or something?" His smile widens at her question.

"Nope." He pops the P and tugs on the end of one of her braids. "I'm technically off the clock and on Justin's dime. Nicole is my only patient." *Fuck.* I can feel her scowl without even looking. She's assessing me. Overanalyzing me. Spencer's been doing it for a while now, and I'm not even surprised. I've given her plenty of reasons to.

"That's so nice of you, Axel." Nicole's sweet charm breaks the tension between Spencer and me. She turns to me and smiles. "As you can see, and you've told me, the baby and I are both good. Can I go home now?"

"Let me take care of all the paperwork, and I'll be right back. Justin, I look forward to that dinner this weekend." He winks at me and leaves the room. *Double fuck.*

"Dinner? What dinner?" Nicole looks at me like I have two heads.

"I thought it would be nice to invite everyone over to thank them for today. You won't have to do a thing. I can also be like a little housewarming for you as well."

"I guess that sounds nice." She seems apprehensive, but she's just been given a lot of new information all at once. I'm

249

sure her head is swimming. I know mine is.

"It will be, I promise." I finally turn to look at Spencer. She's not happy with me. "Since you're the only one here with a vehicle, could we get a ride to Nicole's apartment?"

"Of course. I'll go bring my car around and wait outside for you." Spencer smiles at Nicole and glares at me before she leaves the room.

32

Nicole

Something is going on between Spencer and Justin. I feel the tension between them, but I don't know what could be causing it. My phone buzzes in my hand, and I look at it to see a text from Annie.

Annie: You have an OB appointment scheduled for eight a.m. tomorrow with Dr. Dailey. It's fasting. No food or drink after midnight.

"How? Did you talk to Annie again?" Justin looks back at me, confused.

"No. Why? What's wrong?" I show him my phone, and he reads the text. "Oh. I've spoken to Cole since I've been here. He must have told Annie about your low blood sugar. You need to Facetime her. Cole said she was a hysterical mess worrying over you."

"Annie? A hysterical mess?"

"My thoughts exactly, Pumpkin. Hormones are heavy over at their house." I can understand that. I know how I feel like a hormonal mess lately, and she has double the babies.

"Should I call her now?" Justin opens his mouth to answer as there's a knock at the door, and Axel walks in.

"You're all set to go, momma. Just need your signature on a few pages, and you can leave." He rolls the small table to me and places the papers and a pen down. His eyes wander around the small room.

"She went to pull the car around for us" Justin smirks at Axel.

"Oh I wasn't—"

"Okay. Sure. You weren't looking for Spencer. Don't try to fool a fool, Axel. She'll be at dinner this weekend. You can try and lie some more then."

I think I almost see a slight blush form on Axel's cheeks. Does he have a crush on Spencer? He clears his throat and flips over some of the pages.

"I'll just need you to sign right here, Nicole, and then again on the last page, and you can get out of here." He's definitely blushing, but I won't call him out on it. I sign my name where he tells me to as he pulls in a wheelchair from the hall.

"I'll see you both Saturday. Let me know what time and what I can bring. I'm looking forward to it." His smile is devious as he walks out the door.

"What was that all about?"

Justin extends his hand to help me off the bed. "He likes Spencer. It's like hanging around elementary school kids. He teases her, and she gets annoyed with him. Wash, rinse, repeat."

"She likes him too." I sit in the wheelchair and make myself comfortable. I'd argue about it but I know it's protocol.

Justin gives me a quizzical look. "What makes you say

that?" We wave at Axel as we walk past him, collecting his things to head home.

"A girl can tell." I'm not exactly sure how to explain it to him. I sense there's a mutual attraction between them. Maybe it was the blush that they both shared at different times. Maybe he's right, and it was the childish teasing. Either way, she definitely likes him back.

Great. Now, I sound like an elementary school girl. Maybe I should ask Spencer if she wants me to write her a note and pass it to him in homeroom. *Do you like Spencer? Check yes or no.*

"Alright, Pumpkin. Let's get you home so we can pack up, and I can take you to my house."

"Your house with the good hot water heater?"

Justin chuckles. "Yes, my house with the good hot water heater. And any other amenity that you might need or want. If I don't have it, I'll get it. My home is now your home, Pumpkin. I want you to have everything you need and want." He kisses my forehead as we step outside to Spencer's awaiting car.

I'm not surprised to see that it's a small, black, sensible SUV. I bet it gets excellent gas mileage, too. It seems absolutely like something Spencer would drive.

"Our chariot awaits, my love." Justin opens the back door, seemingly unbothered by the term 'my love' that he just dropped. Does he love me? He told me loved me at our gender reveal party but he hasn't said it again since. Do I love him? My feelings have been growing for him. It's hard not to when half of him is growing inside me.

Justin is an amazing man. He's a wonderful provider. I could easily see why falling in love with him would be so simple. But have I?

"I assume I'm taking you to Nicole's house?" Spencer's voice brings me back to the present.

"Yes, please. I'll have to pack before we go to Justin's house."

"If you get us there quickly, I'll give you a five-star rating." Spencer flashes Justin an unamused look in the rearview mirror, and I try hard to contain my laughter, but a little one slips out.

"Don't encourage him, please."

"Yes, ma'am." I hear her groan, and Justin and I both laugh this time.

"How many stars do I get if I kick you out?"

"Negative five." Justin has given up trying to contain his laughter.

"I might take my chances. Maybe you should get a ride with Axel."

"I don't think I want my pregnant girlfriend riding on the back of a motorcycle. Especially with Axel driving."

"Fair point. Control yourselves back there." Another glare from Spencer through the rearview, and we're on our way to my apartment.

When we arrive in front of my building, my stomach drops at the dark spot visible on the pavement from where I bled. I shudder at the memory of the last several hours and how everything could have gone so differently if Justin hadn't arrived early. He's right. I need the help, and if he's willing to give it to me, I shouldn't complain. Not everyone gets a trained professional to watch over their health and the health of their unborn child.

"Would you like some help packing things up?"

"Spencer, you must be exhausted. I'm sure you'd rather go

home and get some sleep. You both have to work tonight. Justin, maybe we should move everything tomorrow when you don't have to work the evening shift. You've done so much for me already. Both of you." I'm met with grumbling protest. Spencer tells me she only needs a little sleep, and Justin insists we get most of my things moved today.

"Well, if you both insist, let's get it over with. Many hands make lighter work. Or, however that saying goes. But either way, this pregnant lady needs to eat. I'm starving."

"I can grab some food at the dinner up the street while you pack what you need, and I'll meet you back here. Does that sound good?"

"Oh, Spencer, you don't have to do that. I have a french toast casserole we can heat up while I pack." Justin runs his hand over my messy, curly hair.

"Pumpkin, you can't eat that anymore. Let Spencer get you something low-carb from the diner. Maybe some eggs, bacon, and whole wheat toast?"

"What do you mean I can't eat that? What's wrong with it?" A look passes between Spencer and Justin, and I feel like a small child whose parents are silently making fun of their kid's ridiculousness.

"French toast casserole is all carbs and sugar. That's not good if you have gestational diabetes. You need to regulate your sugar intake." Oh yeah. I guess I was being ridiculous then.

"I have a lot to learn, don't I?" God, I know nothing about gestational diabetes. With my budget, eating healthy has never really been on my radar. My diet consisted of Ramen noodles, cereal, hot dogs, and store-brand pizza before Justin started sending me weekly groceries.

Justin kisses me on the forehead, and I close my eyes and take a deep breath. "Don't worry, Pumpkin. I'll teach you." *Pumpkin.* Oh no. I turn in my seat and grab his arm.

"Justin, please tell me I don't have to give up my pumpkin creamer. That's the only luxury I ever allowed myself. Please don't take it away from me." Spencer laughs in the front seat, and Justin pushes a fallen curl behind my ear.

"I'll teach you. Everything in moderation. Okay? Don't panic. I wouldn't even think of taking your pumpkin away. How would you identify yourself if not for being a basic white bitch?" My internal panic calms. I know it's such a silly thing, but even when I was scraping by with bills, I needed something for myself to help me keep going. My pumpkin creamer has always been that thing.

"So breakfast?" Spencer questions from the front seat.

"I trust you can get Nicole a good protein-filled meal, Spence. Just get me the same thing, please." She nods, and Justin and I step out of the SUV. "Thanks." He reaches into his back pocket to grab his wallet, and Spencer glares at him.

"Don't insult me, Justin." His hands fly into the air in surrender.

"Okay. Sorry. Won't happen again. I had to try." Justin and I meet on the sidewalk and wave at Spencer as she drives away. "Let's get you and the pups all packed up." He laces his fingers with mine, and we walk towards my building.

Thirty minutes later and one packed suitcase, Spencer arrives with our food. It smells incredible, and my rumbling stomach agrees. Opening the white foam container reveals an omelet with peppers, onions, spinach, and cheese. Next to it is a generous helping of home fries cooked to crispy perfection.

"Hand it over, Pumpkin." I turn to Justin and give him my best puppy dog eyes and pouty lips.

"But, but…home fries." I reluctantly hand over my box and poke out my lower lip. I watch as he scoops half of the potatoes into his container.

"Everything in moderation. Your carbs should be no bigger than the palm of your hands as long as you're balancing it with protein." I upturn my hand and outline my palm with my opposite finger. I'm a small person, and my palm seems even smaller, thinking of the portions I can and can't have.

"Nicole, it may not look like a lot of food now, but you'll need to eat six times a day. Three regular meals and three snacks." Spencer said six. That's a lot of food. Maybe my palm sized amount of potatoes doesn't seem so small after all. And the omelet is massive. Justin hands me back my to-go container, and I stare at the food.

"Pumpkin, I'm here to help and teach you. There are plenty of apps out now that can help you count carbs and track your meals. It's not as complicated as it sounds." *Counting.* I pick up my fork and stab at one of the potato chunks. I wonder how many carbs are in this small square? My mind starts swirling with numbers when a hand touches my wrist. My eyes snap to Justin.

"It's okay. Just eat. I'm here for you." Justin gives me a warm smile, and I nod as I place the fried potato in my mouth, trying not to think about how many numbers are associated with each bite I take.

We finish breakfast, and Spencer, Justin, and I pack more clothes and all the dog accessories needed.

"They're cute, but I don't think they like me." Spencer stares down at the heap of white fur, wagging her tail furiously. I bend down and pick up Java.

"They love you, or they would be yapping their heads off. This is Java, and her sister is Beans." Java tries to desperately lick my face as I pass her off to Spencer. "She just wants to say hi, and she'll be your best friend. Look." Spencer awkwardly takes Java, and she immediately starts licking her face. A laugh escapes Spencer that sounds like pure joy at the pup's assault.

"Why Spencer? Is that the sound of your icy heart melting that I hear?" She gives him the glare that I'm realizing is specific for him.

"Don't be a dickhead, Justin. I like animals, obviously. They tend not to like me." I pick up Beans, and Spencer and I switch dogs. Beans is just as enthusiastic to lick Spencer's face, and she laughs again.

"Pumpkin, you better take the dogs away. If Spencer keeps laughing like that, the glaciers will melt too much and cause flooding." He thinks he's funny, but now I agree that he's being a dickhead.

"Quit picking on Spencer, or I'm cutting you off." His face feigns shock and horror. Spencer turns her back to us, and I hear her laughing again as she walks away with Beans. Java trails close behind her.

Justin moves close to me and puts his arms around my back as much as my growing belly allows.

"You wouldn't do such a cruel thing as to cut me off from your sweet, sweet pussy, would you? That would be torture." His lips graze the pulse point on my neck, and I tilt to the side, giving him better access.

"Not if you stop picking on Spencer. I like her. You should be nicer." His soft lips feel like feathers on my skin.

"She likes you too." His kisses trail to the other side of my neck, and I move to accommodate him. "You know, light exercise is good for you and your sugar levels. Sex can be a good workout." He thinks he's trying to get some with Spencer in the house?

"Well then, you better hurry and finish getting me packed and loaded." I rub my belly between us. "I can't carry any of those heavy things down." Justin drops to his knees and rests his head on my stomach and his hands over mine.

"Hey, beautiful girl. Daddy can't wait to meet you." He kisses my bump, and I feel the tears burning my eyes.

"Thank you."

Justin looks up at me from my belly. "For what, Pumpkin?" He slowly rises, holding my gaze as he does. A hand comes to wipe the tears that fall down my cheeks. "What's all this for?"

"Sometimes you seem too good to be true. I've never had anyone want to take care of me this much. Cole has always been good to me but his is out of familial obligation. But you. You're just..." Warm lips kiss my forehead.

"I'm just falling hard for the woman carrying my future, and I want to make sure both my girls have the best life possible." I wipe at the endless tears now falling.

"See. You say shit like that, and my hormones kick into overdrive. Let's get out of here before I leak everywhere." I step back from him, and he's smiling his golden smile.

"Between Spencer's melting heart and your leaking eyes, your apartment is at desperate risk of flooding."

"I heard that dickhead." We laugh as Spencer walks back into the room. I look down at her feet to find both dogs following her.

"See, I told you they liked you. They were waiting for their invitation."

33

Justin

Nicole is coming to my house. She's coming to live with me. We are going to cohabitate as she grows my baby inside her. I feel like all of my greatest wishes are coming true. My mind swirls with everything I need to do to make her comfortable. I want her to stay. I want us to be a little family and raise our daughter together.

I wish we could have driven together, but Nicole needs her car, so it only made sense for her to follow me to my house. To *our* house. I know she won't think of it like that for a while, but I already have an appointment with my lawyer next week. I'm updating my will and all of my important documents to include Nicole and our daughter. I want to make sure that no matter what, they will always be taken care of.

I haven't mentioned that bit of information to Spencer because I know she won't approve. I feel like she doesn't approve of many of my decisions lately, but I'm doing what's best for my family. She doesn't need to approve.

I pull up to my driveway and take the spot on the left side, leaving the right for her. It's closer to the door and less space she'll have to walk. I need to get her a garage door opener so she won't ever have to get out in the weather. I'm adding that to my mental to-do list, along with groceries and maybe some new sheets for the bed if what I have isn't to her liking. I want someone out here to check the hot water heater, too.

Nicole opens her car door and I jump out of my truck to meet her and take the dogs.

"Justin, it's beautiful." I bought an old farm-style house and renovated it. I have a simple taste and enjoy the older features that this house offers.

"Wait until you see inside. You're welcome to make any additions that you'd like. I know your style tends to be more eclectic, and I love it." We walk up the path to the front door. Blooming flowers line the walkway that my landscapers keep expertly manicured. I've never been into yard work, but I love a manicured lawn, so I splurge on the expense of a professional. Java and Beans make several stops to smell the foliage.

My front door is a deep hunter-green, and I step up to the keypad to unlock it. Punching in my code, the door unlocks. I open it, and we take off our shoes inside the foyer.

"Once we're all settled, I can program a code into the door just for you so you have a number you can easily remember." I'm not sure she even heard me. Her eyes are as wide as saucers, and her head is on a slow swivel. I try to take in the room for the first time through her eyes, but I've lived here long enough that it all feels natural to me. I walk to the back door as she continues to look around and let Java and Beans outside. I think I'll get a dog door installed. The girls will love the freedom to explore—another item to add to my mental to-do list.

"Justin." My name is breathy and full of awe. Nicole's gaze trails up the stone fireplace to the twelve-foot ceilings and the exposed wood beams. The house is decorated simply in natural wood and stone textures from the floors to the counter tops, and throughout the entire house. The furniture is neutral colors with navy blue "pops of color," as my decorator told me.

"I know it's bland compared to your taste. Please add any colors that you'd like. I want you to feel at home here." She turns to face me once she's in the middle of the room. The open floor plan allows her to see the kitchen, living, and dining rooms.

"It's stunning. I wouldn't change a thing. Except maybe..." Her finger taps her lip as she looks around.

"Except?" She steps closer to me and smiles. Reaching down, she grabs the hem of her shirt and pulls it over her head.

"Except we have too many clothes on." *Oh.* I can agree with that.

"Are we making a no clothing rule in the house? Because I can agree with that if so." I remove my glasses, reach behind my head and pull off my shirt, then return my glasses to my face. I watch as the heat flashes in her eyes.

"Clothing will always be optional. The less, the better." Her hands grab my belt buckle before I get a chance, and her smile grows as she slowly opens it.

"If you're going to undress me, I might choose to start the day with clothes on so that I can watch you do this every morning." She pops the button on my jeans and painfully slowly unzips my zipper. I swear I can hear each tooth of the zipper click as it opens. She tugs on my jeans until I'm standing in nothing but my boxers with my pants pooled at my ankles. I step aside and kick them out of the way.

"Well, now what are you going to do with me, Pumpkin? You've got me mostly naked in our living room."

"These are adorable." Nicole runs her hand along the band of my *Superman* boxers. I spread my legs shoulder width apart, plant my hands on my hips, and stick out my chest.

"If the world is too big, make it small." She giggles.

"Did you just quote *Superman*?"

"I did, and now I'm going to quote myself. What are you going to do with me now that you have me half-naked in our living room?" She taps her pink manicured nail on her lip.

"You got a bedroom around this place?"

"I do. A bedroom with a huge shower, which I could use after the hospital and the moving."

"A shower sounds wonderful. Especially if it has the long-lasting hot water I've been promised." Her obsession with hot water is humorous to me. I have to get someone out here to check on my tank soon. Maybe upgrade to a tankless water heater. I'll have to do my research.

"I'll tell you where it is if you remove your shorts."

"Why don't you take them off of me yourself? I can't do all the work."

"Are you being sassy, brat?" I step forward, and she steps back. We do this several times until she finds herself backed against a wall and squeaks when she realizes she's trapped. "Well?"

"Just stating a fact. I undressed you. No sass, just facts."

"Hmm." I trace a line from the middle of her forehead down the bridge of her nose. My finger outlines her lips, and she smiles. I continue over her chin, down to her collarbone, and between her breasts. My finger swirls around her belly button before dipping into the hem of the soft shorts she put on at her apartment. Hooking my other hand into the hem, I tug them off her hips. A growl escapes me when I see she's wearing a matching navy blue bra and thong set. The swell of her belly turns me on more than anything else. "You're so fucking gorgeous. I would worship you every minute of every day if I could."

"A girl has to eat and sleep."

"Why should that stop me?"

She closes her eyes and chuckles. "Isn't sleep sex some kind of kink?"

"It is. It's called somnophilia." I cup her breasts in my hands, swiping thumbs over her nipples. Her body arches into me.

"I-I don't want to know why you know that." Her nipples harden under my touch, and her body sways from the pleasure.

"Sure you do. And I bet you're curious to try. Your mind is wondering what it would feel like to wake up in the morning and feel sore without any memory of why. To see marks on your body where I sucked your flesh. Still feel the slickness between your legs." She moans, and I feel the vibration in her neck under my lips when I kiss her.

"That sounds…"

"Like you're curious? It takes training. Your body needs to learn that it's alright to stay asleep. To receive the pleasure without waking. Do you want me to train your body to be used for my pleasure? In a way, we've already started. Falling asleep with my cock inside you is a step in the right direction."

I can tell she wants to say yes. Her body is vibrating with the idea of the thrill. "How about that shower?"

"Shower sounds nice." I pull my lips away and take her hand. Her body sinks from the loss of my touch, and I can't help but smile at how easily her body reacts to mine. "Let's go, Pumpkin."

We take our time in the shower, ensuring we're clean, but I don't let my hands linger too long. I want to worship her, but I can't do that here. I need this woman in my bed.

Once we've finished, I turn the water off, which is still hot, and grab a towel from the rack, wrapping it around her chest before grabbing one for myself.

"I'll have to get you some larger towels." This one barely wraps around her swollen bump and won't cover her much longer. "How was the hot water?" When I look at her face, tears are welling in her eyes. "What's wrong?" Her arms wrap around her midsection.

"I'm going to be as big as a whale. You'll need to buy me a beach blanket to get around this belly."

"Pumpkin, no." I cup my hands on either side of her beautiful bump. "I wouldn't care if I needed to buy the entire towel factory to cover you. You're growing my baby inside your body, and big or small, I'll still love the way you look." Now, the drops fall freely down her cheeks.

"I'm not sure if that made me feel better or worse." Her tear-stained cheeks perk up into a smile.

"Honestly, neither am I. Just know I'll love your body and our little girl no matter what." *And you.* It's true. I love her. I love Nicole. But I don't think she's ready to hear it. She never mentioned my slip up at the gender reveal but I've known since that day it was true. Turning Nicole's shoulders, I push her toward my king-size bed.

"If I get in the bed with you right now, and we do all of the dirty things that are running through my head, you're going to have to live with the tangled lion's mane that will become my hair."

"I'll take my chances. Lay back on the bed now, woman." She sits on the edge of the bed and scoots back until she's in the middle, leaning against the headboard. She looks radiant with her blond hair against my dark gray duvet cover." I put a knee up on the bed, and she smiles.

"Crawl to me."

"What?"

"Crawl to me, Justin. You once told me you'd crawl for me if I wanted you to. I want." A smile that I know rivals the Cheshire cat spreads across my face. I'll give her anything she wants. Leaning onto the bed, I get on all fours and crawl, losing my towel after the first shift of my legs.

"Anything for my Lioness Queen."

"God, you're sexy like that." I crawl up her body until I'm hovering over her, my cock, semi-hard, swinging between us. I connect my lips with her shoulder and feel her hand wrap around my cock.

"Fuck, Pumpkin." Without permission, my hips rock in time with her hand. Nicole suddenly giggles, and I pull away, wondering what could be funny.

"Care to share with the class what you find so humorous?" She releases me, and her hands cover her mouth, trying to contain the laughter.

"It's silly and ridiculous. I'd rather not kill the mood." Sitting back on my feet, I look at the giggling beauty in front of me.

"Tell me." She shakes her head. "Tell me." I tickle the sides of her bump, and she laughs harder trying to squirm away, but I'm sitting on her legs, and she's at my mercy.

"Justin...I'm gonna...pee your bed...if you don't... stop." I love the sound of her laughter, but I stop the torture because I'd hate for her to have an accident. I know how a baby can affect the bladder. I'll take a different approach. Leaning down, I take her nipple into my mouth, swirling my tongue and nipping at the peak.

"Tell me, Pumpkin. What was so funny?" I switch nipples, teasing it until it hardens in my mouth like the other one.

"Okay, okay." She pulls my head away from her chest, popping me off her nipple. "But I warned you it's ridiculous, so you can't make fun of me."

"I would never." This must be good for her to be making such a big deal.

"So, you were on all fours, and I grabbed you."

"And it felt amazing. I'm failing to see what's so funny." Her cheeks pinken from embarrassment. "Go on."

"Well, for some reason, I got a mental picture of...milking a cow as if I was pulling an udder and expecting milk. Except your dick wouldn't produce milk, it would be come."

"Pumpkin. If you want to milk my cock until I come, I'm all for it." I can't help myself, and I dive into her neck and moo, causing another fit of giggling. "I'll tell you a secret if you promise not to laugh at me." She nods and I brace myself to share a tiny piece of my past. "I know how to milk a cow." She opens her mouth to ask questions but I kiss her before she can. I'm not ready to share more yet. "While I love the sounds of your laughter, I'd much rather hear you moan right now." I shift my legs and push my way between her thighs. Kissing down her body, I hear the sweet moans of pleasure that I asked for.

When I reach her core, she's all moans. I kiss up her inner thighs, teasing myself as much as her. I can smell her arousal, and it's turning me on more. Finally, I allow myself to indulge in her sweet pussy, and we groan with appreciation. Her's from my touch and mine from her taste.

Everything about Nicole drives me to the edge of insanity. I can never get enough of this woman. Her lips are swollen from the added blood flow of her pregnancy. I love what it's done to her body. Knowing that my seed growing inside her had caused all of these changes makes me feral.

I easily slip in one finger, then two. I want to be inside her, but I want her to have an orgasm first. My hips involuntarily grind my cock into the bed seeking my own relief while my tongue licks and flicks every inch of her pussy. Her eyes roll back into her head, and I know she's close.

"Look at me, Pumpkin. I want to watch you fall apart. Eyes on me." Her eyes open, and her elevation on the pillows allows her to meet mine over her bump.

"Fuck, Justin. Oh fucking god. Right there." I speed up the motion of my fingers, knowing that's what she's enjoying most. Her thighs close over my head, and her hips grind into my face. Her body convulses under me, and the most delicious moans pour from her mouth. We stare at each other as I bring her pleasure to its peak. She's incredible looking when she comes for me.

I know she's finished when the vice grip on my head releases. I pull my fingers out and lick them clean while sitting up.

"I want to think that's gross, but I also find it really hot."

"Do you want to taste?"

"Taste myself? That's weird, right?"

"Not in the slightest, Pumpkin." Dipping my fingers back inside her, I swirl them around, and she gasps. I crawl up her body and paint her lips with her arousal. "Lick." When her tongue darts out, I give her a moment before I suck it into my mouth. We kiss and taste her together.

"That was interesting." There's a shy smile on her face. "Have you ever tasted yourself?"

"Only on your tongue." Her mouth forms an O shape when realization dawns on her what I'm referring to. "And I don't mind it one bit." I pepper her neck and upper chest with kisses, never getting enough of her.

"Justin?"

"Hmm?" She turns her head to the side to allow me more access.

"As nice as this is, I'm hungry, and we left the dogs outside. Either we need to get this show on the road, or we need to get dressed." I pop up on my knees and glare at her.

"Alright, Miss Impatient. Flip over, and I'll *get this show on the road.*" I mock her tone, and she flips onto all fours. Grabbing handfuls of her ass cheeks, I give them a firm squeeze. "This ass is amazing." My palm lands flat across her left cheek, and she gasps in pleasurable pain.

"Justin." Her voice is a melodic whine. I watch my perfect print bloom on her cheek and smack the other, giving myself a matching pair.

"So fucking perfect." I grip her hips and notch the head of my cock to her entrance. I can feel the heat radiating from her pussy and groan as I slide in easily with just a little bit of rocking. Nicole's chest drops to the bed, giving me more of an angle to go deeper, and I slide even further into her.

"Hard and fast, Justin. I want it hard and fast." Music to my ears.

"Anything…you…want." I punctuate each word with a quick thrust, and she matches my rhythm, bucking her hips back to meet mine. It seems we both needed this quick and dirty connection. After I reach around and play with Nicole's clit, it doesn't take long before we're both moaning out our orgasms. As if the dogs hear her screaming, they bark outside my bedroom window, and we both fall onto our sides laughing.

"I guess they want to ensure you're okay after all that moaning and screaming." I lean over and kiss her forehead before rolling out of bed. Extending a hand to help her, we walk to the bathroom to clean ourselves again.

"I'll figure out food, and you can take care of the pups? We might need to order something. I haven't been shopping in a while."

"Sounds good. I'll grab the bag of dog accessories from my car and feed them as well." We finish getting dressed and go our separate ways to do our tasks. I'm rummaging through the refrigerator and freezer when I feel wet tongues on my feet.

"Hey, ladies. Did you have fun outside?" I squat to pet them and look out the back window. Add finding a dog poop service to my long, growing to-do list. I hear a knock and remember my front door automatically locks, and Nicole had gone outside to get the dog's things.

Jogging to the door, I quickly open it and grab the bag from Nicole. "I'm so sorry. I forgot to tell you about the automatic locks."

"It's alright. I'll need that code soon, though."

"I just need a four or five-digit number, and I'll program it for you and give you the spare garage door opener. Your code will unlock all the doors. The front, back, and garage all have keypads."

"Wow, you're thorough. Um, how about four-seven-five-one-two."

"Four-seven-five-one-two? Care to tell me the significance?" She gives me a deadpan stare as if I should know. I roll the five numbers around in my head until I realize the one and two could also be twelve. Five-twelve is Nicole's birthday. "Okay, your birthday and..."

"April seventh is Cole's birthday." I nod in understanding. "I get it now. Sorry, the one-two was throwing me off. I wasn't registering it as a twelve. Of course, I know your birthday, Pumpkin." Opening my arms, she steps into them, and I kiss her forehead. "Let me set up these locks for you, and I'll make some quesadillas and asparagus. How does that sound?" Nicole's stomach growls in response. "On second thought, food first, locks after."

34

Nicole

I've always been a creature of habit, but having someone take care of me for the past few days has been amazing. My glucose test and appointment with my OB confirmed I have gestational diabetes. After an extensive meeting with a dietitian and the most expensive grocery shopping trip I've ever done, I have more knowledge and food than I ever thought I'd have.

When Justin offered to hire someone to make meals for me, I politely declined. I'm perfectly capable of making my own food. Now math? Still not my strong suit. I've downloaded an app to scan labels and add my food to help me keep track. I have to do that for two weeks, as well as prick my finger before and after meals to monitor my sugar levels. I swear I feel like I need a Ph.D. to understand all of this stuff.

Justin: Pumpkin, have you eaten yet this morning?

Crap. I keep forgetting that the app I downloaded also connects to Justin's phone. He can see everything that I input or not input in this instance. I haven't eaten yet. Sometimes, it's so exhausting having to think of what to eat that it feels easier not to.

Me: No (hides face in shame) Don't you want to come home and make me breakfast?

Justin: Eat breakfast, and I'll make you a gourmet lunch before you go to work. I'll be home in about two hours.

It's Justin's last night of nightshift, and then he's back on days next week. Our dinner party is tomorrow night, and I look forward to spending the evening with friends. We also invited Cole, Annie, and Blake, so it will be a great night.

Justin: I made egg muffin cups yesterday, remember? Have two of those with some fruit and a piece of whole wheat toast with peanut butter.

Me: You're the best <kissy face>

I completely forgot about the egg muffin cups. They are these cute little things made in a muffin tin. It's a slice of ham with an egg and chopped-up veggies. I don't have to think about numbers with those. Justin has done all of that for me. If I had my way, I'd figure out what I could eat within my diet and eat that every day for the rest of this pregnancy. Counting carbs and sugars is s o confusing. It makes my head hurt.

Ten minutes later I'm sending Justin a picture of my beautiful full plate of food that I didn't have to think about other than measuring my cup of strawberries and tablespoon of peanut butter.

Justin: Good girl, Pumpkin. Don't forget to log your food in the app.

Those two words do tingly things to my insides. I quickly open the tracking app on my phone and click add for each food on my plate. Sometimes, this feels like a game; other times, it's a chore. My phone buzzes in my hand with a new text message.

Cole: Need us to bring anything tomorrow, big sis?
  Me: Just your beautiful ladies.
  Cole: I'm not beautiful? :(
  Me: No, but I'll allow your ugly mug to come too.
  Cole: Don't forget we look alike. LOL
  Me: Don't remind me. <eye roll emoji> See you tomorrow at 6.

After I eat my lazy breakfast, I decide to curl up on the couch with my puppers and read. Justin's house is so cozy, making me feel like I'm on vacation whenever I sit in front of the massive fireplace and relax.

"Pumpkin, wake up."

"What?" I sit up quickly and almost knock Justin in the nose.

"Hey, relax. It's just me. It looks like you fell asleep reading." Blinking my eyes rapidly, Justin comes into focus. I'm on the couch, curled up in the blankets.

"What time is it?" I pat the couch around me, looking for my phone. He sits next to me and runs a soothing hand over my shoulder.

"It's a little after nine. Did you get a chance to test your sugar before you fell asleep?" Sugar. Nine. Man, I must have knocked out.

"N-no." I rub a hand over my face, trying to wake up from my sleepy haze. I feel a little woozy, almost like I've been drinking. Justin walks across the room and comes back with my glucose monitor.

"Give me your hand."

"I can—"

"I've got you, Pumpkin." I give him my hand palm up, and he gently wipes my middle finger with an alcohol wipe. I watch as he loads a new needle and a test strip into the glucometer. He looks at me silently, asking permission to prick my finger, and I nod. My shoulders jump when the pen clicks, and the needle quickly pricks my finger.

"Sorry." He gives me a shy smile. The click always gets me, no matter how often I have to do it.

I feel exhausted even though I just woke up from a nap. I see Justin's eyes narrow as he looks at the monitor.

"How are you feeling?" He looks concerned. "Did you eat all of your breakfast?"

"I ate the egg cups and a bite of toast, then I was full. I also had my coffee. I'm feeling tired and maybe a little dizzy." He shows me the screen, and it reads 64.

"Is that low?"

"Yeah, that's low. You should be between ninety and one-twenty after eating, but you didn't eat enough. Let me get you some orange juice." I nod, trying to take in all the information in my hazy state. Justin comes back with a glass and a beef stick.

"If you log in your food but don't finish it all, that's cheating the system. You need to know exactly what your intake is for accuracy." He pulls his phone out of his pocket and taps a few things on his screen before turning it around. My breakfast carbs read fifteen on his screen.

"Oh."

"Without the toast, peanut butter, and strawberries, you were well below the total you needed for your meal." I lean my head back on the couch and close my eyes.

"This is so confusing." I feel Justin's hand caress my baby bump, making me smile.

"It's okay. There's a learning curve. That's why you're here with me. I'm happy to prepare meals for you to make it easier." This isn't the first, second, or even fifth time he's offered this. It makes me feel like a child thinking about having meals prepared for me. I'm an adult and should be able to make myself food and accurately log what I've eaten into an app.

"I can do it myself. I'll be better at making sure I log my food correctly." I drink more of the orange juice he handed me, and I'm already feeling better.

"Okay. What can I make you for lunch?"

I point to the beef stick in his hand. "Is that my appetizer?"

He chuckles and hands it over. "Sure, we can call it that."

After a healthy lunch of a beautifully made chicken salad and fresh roasted vegetables, I shower and head to work. Justin sent me off with a kiss and a lunch box full of snacks, promising my dinner would be delivered. Each snack has a post-it note and the number of carbs written on it.

Blake and Annie have scheduled appointments with me this afternoon, so I know the rest of my day will be fun...or emotional with two pregnant ladies together.

When I arrive at work, I unlock the door to my rented

space. Being my own boss has its perks. I can work whatever hours work best for me and my clients. Most of the time, I cut in the afternoons and evenings, and with my pregnancy exhaustion, that's been great for me.

A few minutes after I finish putting all my snacks away, there's a knock at my door, and I open it to a very bubbly brunette.

"My favorite sister-in-law!" Blake throws her arms around my shoulder, arching around my bump. Annie stands behind her, rolling her eyes.

"Technically, she isn't anyone's sister-in-law." Annie smiles at me. "No offense, Nicole."

"None taken." I return her smile. She isn't wrong.

"*Yet.* Yet Annie. You know Cole hasn't asked either of us because he wants to ask both of us and we can't legally both marry him."

"Trust me. If my little brother could, he would. He loves the crap out of both of you." Blake releases me from her death grip, and I step aside to wrap my arms around Annie's belly and address my niece and nephew. "And he loves the crap out of both of you too."

Annie looks down at her stomach, beaming with pride. I'm the only one outside of Blake and Cole who's allowed to touch her belly. I made sure to discuss it with her, wanting to stay within her boundaries.

"Hello, Nicole."

"Hi, Annie."

"How is your gestational diabetes doing? Are you getting the hang of the numbers and diet?" I step back and open my refrigerator and the cabinet above it to reveal the snacks and corresponding Post-its. Annie nods, and Blake laughs.

"That seems very much like Justin." Annie and Justin have a special relationship based in their trauma that they've shared with each other. I remember the warning she gave me during the baby shower and the fact that I never got to have the talk with him that I wanted.

"What are we doing today, ladies? You're all I have this afternoon, so we can be as wild as you like." I gesture for one of them to sit down, and Annie takes the seat.

"Just the usual trim for me."

"Baby, are you sure? You've been talking about wanting to cut it shorter before the babies come." I grab a brush to comb out Annie's long golden hair. It reaches the middle of her back, and I have to pump my chair up a few extra pumps to reach her ends.

"I don't want to make a rash decision. What if I hate having shorter hair? What if the babies don't recognize me because I've cut my hair?" Blake covers her mouth with her hand, attempting to contain the smile I'm failing to hide myself. Blake leans over to look in Annie's eyes.

"You're beautiful with any length of hair. Our babies will still love and recognize you even if you shave your head. They will know your voice and smell." Blake caresses Annie's cheek, and I see her shoulders rise and fall as she sighs.

"I've been thinking of cutting my hair about shoulder length to make it more manageable once the babies come. But I still need to be able to pull it out of my face." Blake beams at Annie, and I can't help but smile at her infectiousness.

"How about a longer asymmetrical bob? Near shoulder length in the back and longer in the front with plenty of hair to pull back." Annie rotates her head back and forth a few times, rolling the idea around in her head.

"I believe I like the sound of that." Blake kisses her on the forehead and steps back so I can get to work.

I'm just starting to brush out Blake's hair when there's a knock at my door. I open it to find two very handsome men smiling at me.

"To what do I owe this surprise?" Cole kisses me on the cheek and slides past me, leaving a smiling Justin, who holds up two large paper bags.

"I said you'd have dinner delivered to you." Justin kisses me on the forehead, and I step back to let him in.

"Kitten, you're gorgeous." I find Cole running his fingers through Annie's new haircut. "I love it." I see Annie's eyes glaze over before she buries her head in Cole's chest. Blake must see my expression of Annie's extreme reaction, and she mouths 'hormones' to me in the mirror. I smile and nod in understanding.

"What did you bring us? I'm going to assume since Cole is here, there's enough for everyone." Justin reaches into a bag and hands me a large takeout bowl followed by a smaller one.

"You are having taco salad with chili." It looks and smells delicious. He continues to hand out everyone's food, and the five of us eat and chat for the next thirty minutes. Justin pulls out his phone, and I see him typing away. When he's finished, he walks over to me and wraps his arms around my back. I think he's going to kiss me, but instead, he pulls my phone out of my back pocket.

"Tease." He opens my phone with my face and taps away.

"Your dinner has been logged. You need to check your sugar in ninety minutes. Should I set an alarm?" I roll my eyes at him.

"No, *Dad*. I can keep track of the time. Thank you." I stick out my tongue and snatch my phone. I see he has the nutrition app open, and he's logged my dinner for me. I wiggle my phone in his face and smile. "Thanks for this."

"Always, Pumpkin. Ninety minutes, okay?" I hear giggling behind me and turn to see Cole going back and forth between his girls with kisses.

"Get a room, you three." My brother winks at me and gives them each one more kiss before heading towards the door.

"Good to see you, big sis. Thanks for taking good care of my girls." He kisses me on the cheek before stepping outside the door.

"Cole and I are going shopping for the dinner party tomorrow night. Call or text me if there's anything special you want. We were thinking steaks and chicken on the grill with some veggies and a salad on the side."

"That sounds wonderful, Justin. I'll see you back at home." He pulls me in for a kiss, and it ends far sooner than my hormones want it to.

"Ninety minutes, Pumpkin, and log it into the app." He sticks a joking finger in my face, and I pretend to try to bite it. Closing the door behind him, I turn back to Blake, who's sitting in the chair.

"What are we doing today?"

"How about highlights with some peek-a-boo pieces of blue and pink for the babies." I hear Annie clear her throat, and when I look, her eyes are glistening. Blake sees me watching again and smiles at me.

"I think that sounds perfect."

I'm deep into foiling Blake's hair when my phone starts

buzzing on the counter. I ignore it, and a minute later, it buzzes again. I glance to see Justin calling.

"Do you need to get that?" Blake meets my eyes in the mirror, and I shake my head.

"It's Justin. I'm almost done, and I'll call him back." My phone rings three more times over the next ten minutes while I finish Blake's hair. I see Annie reach for her purse and pull out her phone.

"Nicole, it's Justin. Would you like me to answer?" I roll my eyes at his insistence.

"No. He can wait a few more minutes." I know why he's calling. I'm almost an hour past my ninety minutes when I should have checked my sugar. I feel fine and want to finish Blake's foils so she processes correctly.

As I set my timer for Blake's hair and grab Annie a water from my mini fridge, my door swings open without a knock. The three of us jump in shock.

"Justin." His body slams into mine in a tight hug.

"None of you answered. I thought something was wrong." I look behind him, waiting for Cole to appear, but he doesn't.

"I'm fine. I was finishing with Blake. Where's Cole?" He pulls away and looks at me, his eyes wild and bouncing between mine. Quickly, he reaches down and grabs my purse from the shelf, pulling out my glucometer.

"Have you checked your sugar?"

"No, but I feel fi—"

"It's been two and a half hours. You needed to check at ninety minutes. Let me do it." He reaches for my hand, and I pull away.

"I can do it." I attempt to take away the small canvas bag with my supplies, and he moves his arm. I glare at him for a long moment before he hands it to me.

"You said you didn't need me to set an alarm."

"I also told you I didn't need a dad." My response is sharp, and I have a tinge of regret, knowing he's only looking out for my best interest, but I feel fine, unlike this morning.

I approach the sink and wash my hands before pulling out the monitor. Justin watches me like a hawk as I replace the needle and enter a new test strip. I force myself not to react to the clicking of the needle prick. I don't want to give him any more of a reason to be overbearing.

When the monitor beeps, I show him the screen that reads one hundred-two and give him a smug smile. It's pretty damn close to ninety, which is a good level.

"That's not a good number. You were over an hour late to check, which probably means that reading would have been elevated if you took it when you were supposed to. Hopefully, it wasn't too much over one-twenty." Dammit, he's right. My shoulders fall in defeat, knowing I have no reason to be upset by his overreactions.

Justin approaches me and rubs his hands up and down my arms. "It's okay, Pumpkin. We want to try and control your GD with diet and exercise, but if you don't monitor it correctly, it'll be hard to tell if it's working." I hate that I feel like a child right now. It's not Justin's tone or even his words; it's the fact that he's right, and I need to stop trying to do it all and let him help. I should have set an alarm. I knew my time had passed. It wouldn't have taken me more than two minutes to check my levels and log them so they would be accurate and Justin wouldn't worry.

"I'm sorry." He pulls me into him again and wraps his arms around me, inhaling deeply.

"I was so worried when you didn't answer. I knew you were here with Annie and Blake, but when Annie didn't answer, I flashed back to you hitting the ground in front of your apartment." A lead brick of guilt hits my stomach.

"Fuck. I'm so sorry. I told her not to answer. I don't ever want to put you through that again. I'll set alarms from now on." All I've done today is fight him when he's just trying to care for me.

"How much longer do you have here?" I turn to see Annie and Blake trying to mind their own business and give us some privacy.

"Ironically, probably about ninety minutes." He chuckles and shakes his head at me.

"Okay. Will you call me before you leave? And make sure to have a snack soon. You don't want that number to get too much lower."

"I promise. Blake has ten more minutes to process, so I'll eat something now." He kisses my forehead, and I relish his touch.

"Thank you, Pumpkin. I'll see you at home. I have to get back to Cole."

"Where is he, by the way?" He smirks and looks at the girls.

35

Justin

I don't know if I should be more mad that she didn't answer, or relieved that she's completely fine. Either way, my anxiety is at its peak, and my adrenaline is finally coming down.

Where is Cole? I practically sprinted out of the grocery store when all my calls went unanswered. I wasn't being sent to voicemail, which would have at least let me know I was intentionally being ignored. Call after call rang through to her voicemail. Finally, I called Annie, expecting her to answer, but she didn't pick up either. I made the split decision to toss the shopping list I had made at Cole, and I told him I'd be right back to get him.

I feared the worst. Flashes of Nicole falling to the ground and Annie being crushed in her driver's car kept running through my mind as I sped back to the shopping center, damning all of the traffic laws.

"I left him at the grocery store with the shopping list when Annie didn't answer. I thought about having him call one of you, but I didn't want to waste a single second of time if there was an actual emergency." I hear giggling and see Annie and Blake typing on their phones. "Sorry, ladies. Desperate times and all."

"It's completely fine...and hysterical." Blake continues to text through her laughter. I can only assume she's texting Cole. I'm going to owe him a six-pack after this. Hopefully, he finished the shopping list.

"Eat and text me when you're done. Please."

"I promise." She leans on her tippy toes, and I meet her halfway for a kiss. Relief washes through me when our lips touch. She's my calm after a storm. I pull away before things get too out of control. My protective instincts are on overdrive, and I want to take her right here, now that I know she's not in any harm.

"Sorry again, ladies. Let me go retrieve your man." One more kiss to the top of Nicole's head, and I leave. I hear the girls laughing as I walk down the hall out of the office suites of her salon.

Me: Sorry, Cole. The girls are all fine. Be back in a few.

Cole: You're a dick. I finished the shopping. Get here quickly because I'm not paying for your dinner party. Or the twelve-pack of lager added to the list.

Me: Fair enough. Be there in a few.

At least he shopped, and it's one less thing to get done before tomorrow. *Fuck.* I barely remember the drive across town. I went into paramedic mode, and everything became singularly focused. Assess and help. Treat and transport.

"Nicole is fine." I let my words hang in the air as I try to convince my elevated heart rate to slow down. It's still racing like I'm in the middle of a 5K, and no amount of focused breathing is helping. "Nicole. Is. Fine." I slam my fist onto the steering wheel. I can't seem to get my mind to understand that reality.

I pull up to the fire lane in front of the grocery store and grab my wallet from my back pocket.

Me: I'm out front. Come grab my card.
Cole: Lazy ass :)

Cole comes walking out with a massive grin on his face; I'm sure he's prepared to give me some shit. My hands shake as I try and pull my card out of my wallet to give to him.

"The ice cream is melti—dude, are you okay?" He flings my door open and jumps in the passenger seat. "Justin, talk to me. Breathe man. What's going on? Are the girls okay?" I grip my chest and try to take a deep breath that isn't coming.

"They…are…fine." My breaths are shallow and labored.

"Fuck, Justin. What can I do?" Closing my eyes tight, I try to breathe and start chanting the coping mechanism they taught me in therapy. 5-4-3-2-1. 5-4-3-2-1. I must be mumbling out loud because I hear Cole repeating the numbers with me.

Five. Look at five separate objects. Opening my eyes, I look at the first thing I see. The steering wheel. *One.* I look to my right and see a half-empty bottle of water. *Two.* Looking up, I see a sign for a sale on watermelon. *Three.* To the left, there's a black SUV. *Four.* Back down again, I see the tire pressure gauge I keep in my door pocket. *Five.* Five separate objects.

Four. Four distinct sounds. Closing my eyes again, I listen.

287

A cart passes by my door with a rattling wheel. *One*. The automatic doors open with a whoosh. *Two*. A car door slams in the parking lot. *Three*. Cole is still mumbling numbers next to me. *Four*. Four sounds.

Three. Touch three objects. I raise my hands to the steering wheel and feel the leather of the cover. *One*. Dropping my hands to my legs, the denim of my jeans is rough. *Two*. I fist the hem of my t-shirt and rub the soft cotton between my fingers. *Three*. Three different feelings.

Two. Identify two smells. I can tell this is working because I can finally take more than just a shallow breath. With my eyes still closed, I hit the button on my window and lean my head towards the door as the smells from outside permeate the air. Gas. A car drives by that needs a tune-up. *One*. Cigarette smoke. Some must be close by smoking. *Two*. Two gross smells, but two nonetheless.

One. Taste something. I open my eyes and reach into the cup holder, where I have a container of gum. Opening it, I pop one, and the taste of sweet mint explodes in my mouth. *One*. Tasting the gum. I take a deep breath, and the cold chill of the gum makes me cough, but I'm happy for the free air to breathe.

5-4-3-2-1.

"Are you back with me, Justin?" I look at a very confused and worried Cole and nod as I continue to chew my gum.

"I'm sorry. I—It was the start of a panic attack, but I got it under control."

"The counting?" He's trying to understand what I just went through. I can't imagine what all of that looked like to an outsider.

"It's more of a process of events. I'll explain it to you at a later date. You said something about melting ice cream?" I look around and find my wallet on the floor by my feet. I hand over my card to Cole, and he looks at me apprehensively before leaving to go back inside for the groceries.

I leave my space in front of the store and wait to see Cole exit. A few minutes later I see him coming out the doors and meet him back at the front. I jump out to help load everything, and when we're done and leaving the parking lot, I can feel him staring at the side of my head.

"Talk to me, Justin. What happened back there?" I hate that this is the second time Cole has seen me in a not-so-great state of mind.

"I told you. It was the beginning of a panic attack. No one answered my calls, and Nicole hadn't logged anything into her nutrition app. I just got worried." Out of the corner of my eye, I see Cole nod. "Between the pregnancy and her health issue, I'm a little on edge about things."

"I can understand that. Annie isn't quite Annie at the moment. The tears freak me out a bit. No. They freak me out a fucking lot." I laugh, and he joins me.

"Being the guy in these pregnancies is weird, isn't it?" I'm not sure how comfortable he is with me talking about his sister, but he never seems to mind. Cole sighs and runs his hands through his dirty blonde hair. It's the same color as Nicole's, just like his blue eyes.

"It's completely unhinged. I want to help, but some days, I can't even look at Annie without her producing tears or rage. Other days she's so up my ass, it seems like if she could, she'd crawl into my skin."

"Nicole isn't nearly as hormonal as Annie, from what I can tell. I don't envy you, Cole."

"Gee, thanks. Are you good now? Everything under control?" Am I good for now, yeah. I hope so.

"I'm good. Can we keep this between you and me? I don't want Nicole worrying." I can see the unease on his face as he decides his answer.

"You're sure you're okay? I'm here if you need anything."

"I'm good. I promise. I'll let you know if I need anything. Spencer helps to keep me in line most of the time." He chuckles.

"That woman scares me. She's intimidating, and I'm dating a powerful CEO, so that should say something."

"Spencer is harmless."

"As harmless as a feral raccoon."

"Oh, Cole. You better not let her hear you say anything like that, especially in front of Axel and Miller." *Shit.* I shouldn't have said anything.

"Hold up. Wait. Spencer has two men?" Dammit.

"Spencer has *no* men. But she does have two very eager admirers. She doesn't see it, but I don't think they fully see her yet, either."

"Interesting. And all three of them will be there tomorrow, right?"

"Yes," I groan. "Are you going to be a gossip? I'm warning you. Spencer will have your head if you step out of line and into her potential love life. I don't even go there as her best friend."

"I'll be good. Or discreet." I can smell the gears turning in his head. Tomorrow night should be interesting.

When we get back to my house, Cole stays long enough to help put the groceries away and have a beer. When Nicole texts me to say she's on her way home, he heads out to meet

Blake and Annie at their house.

I can't wait to see Nicole after my episode earlier. The feelings still linger inside me, and all I want to do is hold her and know she's okay. I haven't had or even come close to having a panic attack in years, but I've never been more thankful for the coping skills that I learned than I am today.

I hear the garage door open and stand to meet Nicole at the interior door. She parks and steps out, and I want to run to her and scoop her up, but I wait patiently. Leaning against the door, I watch as she grabs her purse from the back seat and locks the doors heading my way. When she looks up, I see the heat flash in her eyes.

"Well, aren't you a sight to see?"

"What do you mean, Pumpkin?"

"You. Looking all sexy with your arms folded across your chest, holding up the door frame." I look down at my body, trying to see what she sees, but I don't find anything impressive. I shrug.

"Now *you're* a sight to see. Your swollen belly creating and growing my daughter makes me want to lock you up and throw away the key." She approaches me, and I glide my hands over her baby bump and kiss her forehead. "How was the rest of your appointment with Blake?" Removing my hands, I step inside so she can come in. The fall air is chilly, and I'm glad she's parking in the garage.

"What's this?"

"A snack?"

"Justin, this isn't a snack. It's an entire charcuterie board." Laid out on the table are cheeses, pickles, olives, various crackers, and fruits.

"I don't expect you to eat it all. I thought we could do a

little tasting." I wrap my arms around her back and rub her belly, resting my chin on her shoulder.

"It looks beautiful, and I'm sure it all tastes wonderful."

"Go take a seat on the couch, and I'll bring the food over." As she walks towards the living room, I open the gate and let Java and Beans out to greet Nicole excitedly. The giggle that floats through the room as they bounce and lick her, grounds my frayed nerves from earlier.

"Hi, babies. Did you miss me?" Watching her play with them always tugs at my heartstrings. I already knew she would make a fantastic mother, but how she cares for Java and Beans solidifies it.

We created a doggy corner of the room that's gated off so they have their own little playpen for when we aren't home. It's three times the size of the space they had in Nicole's kitchen, and they love it.

"Yeah, I think they missed you." Nicole pulls a throw from the top of the couch and spreads it over her legs. Java and Beans quickly burrow themselves under the blanket on either side of her. "Poof. No more puppies."

"Exactly." I never realized how much dachshunds like to burrow. Give them a warm place to cuddle, and they'll be happy for hours. I walk over, set the food tray on the coffee table, and sit on the floor at Nicole's feet.

"What are you doing?" Leaning behind me, I stick a tiny pickle with a toothpick and hand it to her.

"I'm taking care of you. Eat." A sly smile crosses her face as she takes the pickle. If she's remembering the last time we played a game like this, she's correct. From my seated position, I grab her foot and peel her sock off. When I rub a firm thumb over the arch of her foot, she moans loudly.

"Oh god, keep doing that." Her moans continue as I rub her foot. When I stand, she groans, thinking I'm going to stop.

"Relax, Pumpkin. I'm just bringing the food to you." I place the tray of food on the sofa table behind her head. "You eat, and I'll rub. I want you to tell me how it tastes. And let's lose these pants."

"You want me to do what?" I chuckle as I sit and remove her other sock and help her shimmy her leggings off.

"Tell me. Describe to me the flavors. I have some surprises on there." Another thumb to her arch, and she flops her head back on the couch.

"You have magic fingers." I smile, knowing she means that in more ways than one.

"Eat, Pumpkin." She picks up an olive and pops it in her mouth, and I continue massaging.

"Whoa. This is...wow."

"Describe it to me." Her brows scrunch, and her jaw moves as she tries to determine the combination of flavors. I move up from her foot and massage her ankle and calf while she chews.

"It's sweet and spicy. Maybe citrusy?"

"Good. Keep going." She grabs another olive. I'm glad she likes them. Her eyes close as she concentrates, and I switch to the other calf.

"It's so good, but I can't quite place it. I can feel the heat from the chili, but the other flavor..." She opens her eyes as my hands reach her knees and slowly push them open.

"Continue." She helps me open her legs since the dogs are caging her in on either side.

"I-I can't figure it out."

293

"Tangerine and chili." Her head nods, and she rolls the flavors around. "Try the cheese ball."

"Is it safe? I know I can't have soft cheeses."

"Pumpkin, would I put anything on there you can't have?" She shifts down on the couch as my hands massage her thigh, and I can't help but smile.

"No, you wouldn't." Picking up a toothpick, she pokes the ball and stares at me as she seductively puts it in her mouth. My fingers reach the top of her thigh, and I can see she's waiting for me to move slightly inward, but I switch legs and start back at her knee. Her body deflates on the couch, but she moans when the flavor of the cheese bursts on her tongue.

"Roasted garlic mozzarella, with something else. This is incredible. What is that other flavor?" Her body sinks farther on the couch, and the dogs stir from her movement.

"Be careful, or you'll disturb the pups."

"Mmm. Tell me. This is heavenly." My hands reach the top of her thigh again, but this time, I swipe a finger over her lacy-covered core.

"Sun ripened tomatoes. Do you like?" My finger swipes gently atop her clit. Just enough to tease.

"I like." I wonder if she's answering for the cheese or my finger. Either way, I'll take it.

"Try something else." I feel the top of her body twist, but I don't see what she grabs because I flip the blanket over my head and kiss up her thigh.

Her moans make my cock stir, and I open my pants to give it more room while I suck and nip at her legs. I nudge my nose over her clit with more pressure than I was using with my finger, and her hips buck.

"Don't wake the dogs, Pumpkin." She whimpers, knowing she'll have to stay as still as possible. I'm going to enjoy torturing her. I push forward, placing my mouth on her pussy through her panties.

"Touch me. Please."

"I am." I suck her into my mouth through the fabric, and she gasps.

"Please," she whines. With as much gentleness as I can to not disturb the dogs, I loop my fingers into her waistband and pull down her panties. Slowly, I kiss back up her leg, and I can tell she's eager by her rapid breathing. Her pregnancy has made her extra sensitive and extremely horny, and I've loved every second of it.

Just before I dive in to take her, I give her one last warning. "Eat, Pumpkin." I hear the crunch of a cracker as I lick a line from her entrance to her clit, and her moan of pleasure drives me forward. I devour her pussy like a starving man getting his first meal. I can never get enough of her. I reach one hand up to rest on her bump and bring the other to bury my fingers deep inside her. One finger, then two pumps into her weeping core.

It doesn't take long for her moans to increase, and I feel the fluttering of her internal walls. I love all the sounds she makes. Her words start to sound more like syllables, and I know she's about to tip over. Suctioning my mouth to her clit, her hips rise off the couch, and her pussy clamps onto my fingers like a vice grip.

"Yes, yes, yeeeeeees. Fuck. Oh god." I hang for as long as possible, but she's woken up the dogs, and I get licked from both sides. I release her clit and can't help but laugh. Nicole swats at my head under the blanket before she uncovers me and realizes why I'm laughing.

"Okay, that was unfair to you. I'm sorry I bopped you." She places a hand on either dog, pulling them away from their licking assault on my face before bursting into hysterical laughter.

"What's so funny?" I have a feeling I already know.

"Your glasses are…foggy." I forgot to take them off before burying myself under the blanket and between her legs.

"Hazards of a job well done." I rise on my knees and place my head on her belly, giving it gentle kisses. My hand caresses up and down her roundness, and I feel a thump.

"Pumpkin?"

"Did you feel her?" Holy shit, I felt her. I felt my daughter.

"I did. Do it again, baby girl. Can you kick Daddy?" I lift Nicole's shirt and pepper kisses across her belly, hoping to feel more movement. I feel another thump under my palm, and my eyes prickle with tears. "Hey, little one. Daddy loves you." My voice cracks, and Nicole rubs her hand over my head soothingly.

"She loves you too, Daddy." A protective feralness takes over my body when she calls me Daddy. I can't help myself, and I stand, dropping the blanket to the floor, and pull Nicole up into my chest. I take her lips into mine possessively. I need to be inside her now. She's already pregnant, but I have this primal need to make her mine even more.

She giggles and squirms into our kiss, and I pull back.

"They're licking my butt. Justin, help." I look over her shoulder to see Java and Beans bouncing on the couch, licking her naked ass as they jump.

Faking a growl at them, I spin her around. "Mine." I grab the food from the sofa table with one hand and Nicole's hand with my other as we walk towards the kitchen.

"I'll put the food away, and you put the dogs away. We're taking this to the bedroom."

"Yes, Sir." I throw a glare in her direction, and she smiles and winks.

36

Nicole

"Yes, Sir." I knew that would get a reaction out of him. I love this protective Alpha male attitude he has going on right now. If it wasn't for the butt-licking, I bet he would have taken me right there on the couch.

"Come on girls, Mommy and Daddy have plans to get frisky." I think I hear Justin growl from across the room as I close the gate to their little play area. I like the sound of Mommy and Daddy, and it seems Justin might also like it.

My task is quicker than his, so I pick up my discarded clothes from the floor and walk to the bedroom, taking off the rest until I find myself naked, sprawled out in the middle of the bed, waiting.

I wonder what position we should try? Navigating my ever-growing belly has been both exciting and adventurous.

"You're fucking stunning, Pumpkin."

"Shit. You startled me." I didn't even hear him coming down the hall. "Don't be so stealthy." He smirks, and I practically drool as he removes his glasses and does the one-handed shirt removal move. Placing his glasses on the nightstand, he tosses his shirt towards the laundry basket and misses.

"Close enough." His hand goes to his belt, and I stop him. "Let me."

"It's all yours." He raises his hands as I crawl across the bed to reach him. "And anytime you want to crawl like that for me, I'm fucking ready for it." I roll my eyes at him, and I undo his belt and pants. With a light shove, they fall to the floor. He's already hard for me, and I can see the outline of his enticing cock through his comical boxers.

"I'm not the only stunning thing in this room. *Stitch*?" I arch a brow as I run my palm over his growing erection, and his eyes flutter closed. His hips shift towards my hand, searching for friction that I'm happy to give.

"*Ohana means family.*" Yes, it does.

Looping a finger through his waistband, I slide his boxers over his hips, freeing his cock. He steps out of his clothes and kicks them out of his way before returning to me.

"What do you plan on doing now that you have me naked?" I smile up at him, remembering this same question not long ago, before grabbing the base of his cock and taking as much of him in my mouth as I can.

"Fuck, Nicole." He grabs a handful of my hair, and the slight pain makes me hum onto his cock. He used my real name. He rarely calls me Nicole, and the fact that he was so caught up in the feel of my mouth on him that it slipped out makes me swell with pride. I love making him feel good.

"I love your fucking mouth. You suck me like a fucking goddess." His hips rock slowly, and I let him control my movement with the hand he has in my hair. I know some women find blow jobs degrading, but I crave the power it gives me. I'm in charge of his pleasure despite his hand in my hair. I could easily take over control again.

His hips pull back, and his cock comes out with a pop of suction. Warm lips replace his cock, and he pushes me onto the bed.

"I want you to ride my face. Let me make you come again." He crawls around me to the middle of the bed and lays on his back.

"Justin, I can't."

"You can, and you fucking will. Get your ass over here." He reaches for my arm, and as I get closer, he grabs my thigh and drags it over his body. "Up. Now."

"Justin—"

"I swear, woman, if you try to give me some bullshit excuse that you're pregnant and too big, I'll pull you over my knee and then make you sit on my face." He must see something in my expression because he drags a hand across his face and sighs. Propping up on his elbows, he looks into my eyes.

"Fucking hell. Is that what you want? Do you want me to spank you first, naughty girl?" I nod. "Shit you do." I feel the growl in his chest between my legs. "Get on your hands and knees then." I quickly comply, my heart already racing in anticipation. Warm hands rub over my ass cheeks, and I hear Justin hum in appreciation.

"Oh, Pumpkin. I'd love to put you over my knee, but our daughter might protest at being squished." I feel his lips graze over my left cheek, and a sting of pain radiates through me as he bites my ass. I hiss at the sting and purr as his tongue licks away the pain.

"Fuck, Justin."

"Mmm, not yet, but I'll get there. Your pussy will be

mine tonight." Thick fingers rub through my lips until they reach my swollen clit. "First, I'll spank this ass. Then you're going to sit on my face without protest. And when I'm done drowning in your come, I will have you however I want."

"How?" I'm panting with anticipation and the expert caress of his finger.

"I haven't decided yet. You'll have to wait to find out." Fingers dance on my clit and caress the globes of my ass cheeks, and I'm buzzing with need and wondering when the first spike of pleasurable pain will happen.

Smack. I barely have time to realize his hand moved before the first surge of pain hits. Comforting circles drag across my cheek before another smack rains down.

"My hand prints look fucking sexy on your ass." I can feel my orgasm building. "How many do you want, Pumpkin?" How many? I can't even think right now. I'm out of my mind with pleasure. I lean down onto my chest and wiggle until I find a comfortable position around my belly. He removes his hand from my clit as I do.

"How about six?"

"Six total or six more?" Fuck, I have no idea.

"Yes." He chuckles, taking handfuls of my ass cheeks. His grip is just hard enough that if I concentrated, I could probably count each of his fingers.

"Six more it is." I can hear the smile in his voice just as his hand cracks down. "Count."

"One." He's never made me count before, but I'm not a stranger to spankings. *Smack.* "Two." Two more rapid smacks come down. "Three and four." I'm panting like a feral dog in heat.

"Shhh. Breathe, Pumpkin. Can you take two more, or do

you need me to stop?" His hand runs up my spine soothingly. I lean back, pushing my butt closer to him.

"More." I hear him growl.

"You." *Smack.* "Are." *Smack.* "Fucking." *Kiss.* "Perfect." *Kiss.* His lips on my cheeks are a warm caress to the final blows.

"Fuck me. Please."

"As you wish." He lines up and teases my entrance with a few swipes before slamming into me. It's pure pleasure. Bliss. Heaven.

"Yes. Keep going." I can feel the orgasm that was building earlier coming back in full force. "Fuck. Don't stop." His punishing thrusts hit all the right spots. Doggy style is my favorite and, lucky enough, also the most comfortable to accommodate my belly.

Suddenly, Justin pulls out, and I groan at the emptiness. He moves away, and I can't help but whine. I was so close.

"Come back."

"Come here." I turn to see him lying on his back, patting his chin. Rolling my eyes, I turn and crawl up his body.

"You really want me to sit on your face?" There isn't a doubt on his lips when he responds.

"I really want to drown in your come. I didn't lie the first time I said it, and now I want you even more. Bring me your pussy and sit." Ugh. I guess there's no getting out of this. When I get close enough, I grab the headboard and use it for support to spread my thighs over Justin's face.

"Keep coming down, Pumpkin. Sit on me." His hands encircle my thighs and pull me towards him. After a moment of hesitation I relax and lower myself.

"Justin?" He hums his response, already licking me. "Tap my leg three times if you need me to get up, okay?" His answer is another hum, and his hands squeeze my thighs. I relax my muscles and descend the rest of the way onto his face. His tongue spears inside me, and I gasp at the sensation. Leaning my head on the headboard, I get lost in the feeling of his mouth. It feels like he's everywhere all at once. My orgasm comes quick and fierce, already being so ramped up. His hands don't allow me to move until I'm begging for him to stop. I'm so sensitive.

As I try to lift my leg off his face, he shakes his head. "Down."

"What?" He slides me down his body, slicking his chest and stomach with the remnants of my orgasm.

"Line us up and sink onto me. I want you on top, unless you want to turn around and I'll be happy to stare at your ass riding me." Oh, decisions, decisions. As fun as reverse cowgirl sounds, my ass is twice the size that it usually is, and it's currently not my favorite asset. Pun intended.

I reach my hand between my legs and line Justin's cock up to my entrance. As I slowly sink to torture us, he moans long and deep.

"God, you feel incredible, Pumpkin." Planting my palms on his chest, I lean forward and prepare to do my favorite party trick that drives him wild.

"My name or yours?" His smile grows, and he's so fucking handsome.

"Mine." I swivel my hips into the shape of a letter J, then U. I continue to spell out this name with my hips, and when I finish with his, I spell mine. Justin's fingers dig deeper and deeper into my hips as he enjoys himself and I tease my already sensitive clit on his piercing.

"Dammit." He growls and flips us over. Hovering over me,

he steals my breath away with his kiss. When he reenters me, the new angle has his piercing bumping directly into my clit. His thrusts are punishing, and my overly sensitive nub comes back to life. I can't possibly orgasm again, but my body thinks otherwise. The tingling builds inside me.

"Fuck. Nicole Alivia McGrath. I love you." Did he...

"Justin."

"You don't have to say it back. I just need you to know. The thought of losing you today when you didn't answer my call made me realize how true it is. I love you. I can't live without you." His thrusts continue through his confession without skipping a beat. "You're more than just the mother of my baby. I love you. It's okay if you can't say it back yet. I just need you to know. I love you, Pumpkin." His words overflow with passion, and I wish I could return them, but I'm not there yet.

I'm not quite ready to say I love you, but I am ready to orgasm again. At least my body is. Justin leans down and takes a nipple in his mouth, and that's all my body was waiting for. I explode around his cock with a scream. The orgasm spreads through my body, making my fingers and toes tingle.

I expect him to follow me, but he doesn't. He continues to pump in and out of me while his body leans over mine. Beads of sweat form at his hairline as he continues. I rub a gentle hand over his cheek, and he lifts his eyes to meet mine.

"Are you okay?" His brows are knit together, and he looks as if he's concentrating hard. I press my thumb between his brows in an attempt to relax them. His forehead comes to mine, and he stops moving inside me.

"I'm sorry." He sighs heavily.

"What are you sorry for?" He pulls out of me and relaxes his body against the side of mine. He peppers kisses on my shoulder and apologizes again. I turn to face him and run a hand down his arm.

"What's wrong?"

"I must be too much in my head. I can't finish. Do you want another orgasm?" His eyes look so sad and hopeful.

"Baby, I'm good. I've had more than I need. Is there anything I can do to help you?" He warned me about this problem the first time we got together, but we haven't had any issues since then. Has he had any med changes or any added stress for this to be an issue?

"No. It's just something that happens. I'm good. I promise."

"Are you sure?" I glance down and see that he's still hard. "How about if I roll over, and we can go to sleep your favorite way." He smiles and nods. I give him a timid kiss on his lips and roll over, sticking my butt out and wiggling. I hear him smile, and that makes me feel a bit better. His hand caresses my ass before pulling my cheeks apart and lining himself up to slide into me.

"Thank you for understanding." His words are half-mumbled as he kisses my shoulder.

He told me he loved me, and I didn't say anything back. Could that have gotten in his head? I hope I didn't contribute to his issue.

37

Justin

Fuck. I haven't had performance issues with Nicole our entire relationship. I'm still so turned on. My cock was so hard it easily slipped inside her. Unfortunately, I know my body, and there wasn't going to be any completion tonight.

Between worrying about her earlier, the panic attack, and my confession of love that she didn't reciprocate, but I didn't expect her to, my body told me to fuck off.

At least I can lay here, buried in her pussy, and cuddle her soft body into mine. My anxiety has been at an all-time high, and I'm sure that was a significant factor as well. I filled the prescription but haven't increased my meds yet. I should sit down and talk about my almost panic attack with Dr. Linnsy, but it was just one, and I was able to get it under control, so maybe it wasn't bad enough to warrant a therapy appointment.

Nicole feels incredible in my arms. I close the few inches of space between our bodies and lean up flush against her back. My hand moves from her hip to cup her stomach, the protective housing that is growing my baby. My daughter.

My mind spins with all of the images swirling around.

Who will she look like?

Will I be a good father?

Will Nicole carry her to full term?

Can I protect her?

Can. I. Protect. Her? No. I can't. I couldn't protect Ivy. How can I protect my daughter?

STOP. If you continue, you're going to have another panic attack. Relax asshole. She isn't even born yet.

Breathe in. One, two, three, four. Breathe out. Four, three, two, one. *Listen.* Nicole's rhythmic breathing as she sleeps calms me. I concentrate and match her slow, shallow breaths to ground myself. I can do this. I can keep it together for her. For them.

The little sleep I got was restless. I spent most of the night listening to Nicole breathing. The steady rhythm of her chest rising and falling under my hand kept my panic from bubbling over. Working nights for the last month has trained my body to stay awake all night, and usually, the transition doesn't bother me, but I would have done anything to be able to sleep last night.

As I quietly slip out of bed, I make my way to the bathroom and turn on the shower to let the water heat up. The bags under my eyes show the lack of sleep my body had. Being exhausted doesn't help my medication work properly. If I have time today, I need to try to get a nap, both for my body and my mental health.

I quickly shower and get out, wrapping a towel around my waist. The mirror is foggy, and as I raise my hand to wipe away the steam, I remember the first time I showered with

Nicole. How I pinned her up against the counter and drew a smiley face in the corner of her mirror. Moving to the left, I draw a little smiley face on my mirror with the word Hi, and smile at the old memory and the thoughts of this new one. While she isn't in here now, I'll have to bend her over this counter sometime soon so she can see my handiwork.

Nicole is still sleeping when I reenter the room to find clothes. I grab what I need and quietly leave to get dressed in the guest bathroom. I know how much pregnant women need their sleep.

"Two minutes, girls." Java and Beans excitedly jump as I walk into the kitchen to make my coffee. Nicole hasn't realized, but I switched our coffee pods to half-caff. I was concerned about her caffeine intake and knew that was something small I could do. While the coffee brews, I get the dog's food and water bowls ready. I've never had animals because of my inconsistent job schedule, but I enjoy having them here. Nicole was right when she said even on her darkest days, they make her happy.

When my coffee is done, I release the beasts, and they run straight to the back door. I still need to call someone to install a dog door for them. I know they would love the freedom.

As I open the back door, I expect to be hit with a chill of cool air, but there's an unusually warm breeze this morning. Since I plan to grill, the weather may be mild enough to have an indoor/outdoor party. My back porch has a patio with a large wooden table under an awning that we can all fit around, but I assumed it would be too cold and we would eat inside. Checking my weather app shows me that being outside tonight will be possible. I can pull out the propane heaters from the shed in case of a chill.

Small hands snake around my waist from behind, and I feel her warm body press against mine.

"Good morning, Pumpkin. Did you sleep well?" I feel her hum on my back. The dogs must also hear it because they run towards us and bounce at our feet. I feel the chill she leaves behind when she lets me go to crouch down and pet them.

"Good morning, ladies." They dance excitedly around her, and I grab her shoulder and offer my hand when I see she's struggling to get back up. "Thank you. Maybe that wasn't my brightest idea." I hadn't realized my nerves were still frazzled at the end until I just pulled her into me.

Her arms around my waist as I lean in and take a kiss, feel as if they are holding me together. Our tongues tangle, and I taste the mint of her toothpaste, and I'm sure she can taste my coffee.

"Mmm. Caffeinate me, please."

"Coming right up, Pumpkin." I love taking care of her. Seeing her smile for something I've done for her can turn my entire day around. Her favorite coffee mug, which happens to be shaped like a pumpkin, is in the dishwasher, so I grab it and set it up to brew a fresh cup. Pancakes sound like a great breakfast choice, and I purchased a box mix of high-protein ones. Paired with some bacon or sausage and fresh fruit, it should be good for her numbers.

I'm mixing the pancake batter while sausage warms in a pan when I hear the back door open and the clicking of nails on the floors. Nicole kisses me on the cheek while looking over my shoulder.

"That looks and smells delicious." She steps towards her coffee and I step with her.

"Check your numbers before you touch that coffee." She sighs and smiles at me, picking up her monitor.

"So cruel to make me math before my caffeine." She sticks her tongue out towards me as she wipes the tip of her finger with an alcohol wipe. I pour the first circle of batter onto the electric griddle and listen to the sizzle. The smell of vanilla wafts into the air, and I hear Nicole moan at it.

"Pumpkin, between your moans and your tongue sticking out, you're going to get a very different breakfast if you keep it up." I hear the click of the needle and her quick intake of breath.

"That one hurt."

"Do you want me to kiss it all better?" I turn my head and bat my eyelashes at her.

"I want you to make my breakfast. Chop, chop. Or I guess flip, flip." She giggles, and I hear the monitor beep. "Ninety-four. See. Perfect." I hear her chanting 'coffee' over and over as she puts away her supplies and takes her creamer out of the refrigerator. I watch her open the spout, tilt the bottle over her pumpkin cup, and I stop her.

"Measure."

"I am. With my heart." I take the bottle from her hand and put it on the counter.

"With a measuring spoon."

"But—"

"Two tablespoons. It's in the drawer at your hip." Grumbling, she opens the drawer and pulls out the measuring spoons.

"One, twooooooo…" The creamer is slowly trickling over the sides of the spoon.

"Nicole." My tone has warning, but it's backed up with a

smile. We go through this every time she makes a coffee.

"Two."

"Uh, huh. I'm counting that as three for your records, and you get one less pancake. I hope you're happy with your choices." She encircles her hands around the mug and brings it to her nose, inhaling deeply.

"Very." The smile on her face would allow her to get away with murder, and I'd happily clean it up. She's so easy to love.

"Will you grab us plates, please? I doubled the batch so you can have easy breakfasts. I'll put the extras in the refrigerator and write how many you can have so you won't even have to think about it. Unless, of course, you continue to put half a bottle of creamer into your cup. Then we may need to reevaluate things."

"Hush your mouth about my creamer. It's my little luxury." A finger reaches around and boops my nose.

"Nothing little about that pour, you lush. Sit down, and I'll serve you."

"Oh, I like the sound of that." Like the dogs, she bounces around the counter and sits on a stool. Two pancakes, three sausages, and half a cup of strawberries adorn her plate as I slide it in front of her.

"Next time, if you don't want the sausage, you can add peanut butter to the pancakes." She smiles as I hand her a fork and knife and sit beside her.

This is nice. This is perfect. Making breakfast for the woman I love. Sitting and listening to her little moans as she enjoys the food I've made for her.

"Are we all set for the party tonight?"

"We are. I have to marinate the meat, and I'll do that after I clean up. The weather looks nice, so I'm going to text everyone to bring an extra layer, and we can try to have dinner outside."

"I'll clean, you marinate, and outside sounds great."

At five-thirty, the doorbell rings. I know who it will be before even opening the door. Spencer is perpetually early. Except, she doesn't usually ring the bell, so maybe I'm wrong.

"Webb. Thanks for having me." Axel walks in and slaps my back as he passes me.

"You're early."

"Thought I'd come help. Where's the beautiful mamma? There she is." When I walk into the kitchen, Axel has Nicole in a big bear hug.

"Don't squish my daughter, Axel." He laughs as he pulls away.

"Don't you look beautiful, Nicole." She does. She's wearing a navy long-sleeve dress that tapers in and flows over her baby bump. She's currently barefoot but has a pair of flats near the backdoor for when we go outside.

"You look handsome yourself." Axel is wearing dark jeans and a black button-up shirt rolled up at the sleeves. He steps back and spreads his arms out while doing a slow turn.

"A little better than the scrubs, right?"

"Absolutely. Let me take those for you." He has a bottle of wine in one hand and a six-pack of beer in the other. Nicole takes both and walks to the refrigerator.

"Thank you. I know you can't drink, but I was raised to never show up at someone's house empty-handed."

"Your mother taught you well."

"Grandmother, actually." I don't know much about Axel's story, but he's mentioned several times that his grandparents raised him. Nicole smiles shyly and places a soothing hand on his forearm.

"Even better. Now I understand where your manners come from." He smiles down at her, and they share a moment before he claps his hands together.

"Okay. I'm here. Use me for my culinary skills."

I snort a laugh. "Do you have any culinary skills?"

"I'll have you know that I can make a mean PB&J and can follow the directions on the back of a mac n cheese box to the letter. I am also an expert at ordering takeout."

"How are your knife skills? Justin wants to make roasted vegetables on the grill. Think you can cut some peppers?" Nicole is such a natural people person. She barely knows Axel, and you wouldn't know it with how welcoming she is.

"Knives huh? You know I'm a nurse, not a surgeon, right?"

"Don't be a dick, Axel."

"Hey, I'm just making sure she understands my skill set because I wouldn't want to get drawn and quartered for imperfect peppers."

"Don't worry. I made Justin put away all the torture devices before I moved in." She winks at him, pulls out the cutting board and a knife, and gets him set to cut.

Everyone shows up right around six. I haven't seen Annie in a while, and the size of her baby bump makes me pause, causing her to cry. I grab the steaks and chicken from the refrigerator and head outside, nodding for Cole to follow me on my way out. He grabs two beers and meets me by the grill.

"Cole, I'm so sorry. I had no intentions of upsetting her."

He claps a hand on my shoulder.

"Don't worry about it. Annie cried this morning because one of her muffins was smaller than the others." He leans closer so only I can hear. "We won't even talk about how inedible they were."

"She made them?"

"She made them."

"I thought Annie didn't cook?"

"Annie *doesn't* cook. But she's feeling like she needs to do more things around the house to be more maternal, and cooking is where she started."

"And I take it that's not going so well?"

"You're lucky we convinced her to bring a cheese tray. All she had to do was unwrap the cheeses and crackers. Give her a few minutes, and she'll either forget about you looking at her or find something else to obsess over. How's my sister?"

I look into the kitchen where Nicole's helping our arriving guests unwrap and set up food. "Wonderful as always."

"Eww." I turn my attention back to Cole.

"Eww? Eww, what?"

"You just looked at my sister like a love-sick puppy, and that made me think about her being pregnant, and you had to have sex together in order for her to be pregnant. So, eww. I don't want to think of my sister having sex."

"Well, good. I don't want you to think of your sister having sex either because then you'd be thinking of me having sex, and we aren't that kind of friends."

"No, but we are." Axel walks out the back door with a big smile on his face.

"We're barely friends, dick."

"Justin, you wound me." Axel slaps his hand to his chest as

if to cover a stab wound, and I roll my eyes.

"Axel, Cole. Cole, Axel. Cole is Nicole's sister. Axel is a nurse at the ED and took care of Nicole the other day." I wait and watch. And watch. I see the telltale sign of the lip twitch. "Don't fucking do it, Axel."

"I...I'm...I think I'm going to go grab a beer." He turns on his heels and walks back inside.

"You know we're both used to getting made fun of because of our matchy names?"

"Doesn't mean he has the right to do it. Besides, he's an asshole on the best days. He can be put in his place for a minute."

"Fair enough." We stand around the grill, drinking and flipping meat in silence. Cole's demeanor changes and I know what he's thinking.

"Just ask."

He sighs in relief. "How are you?"

"Handling things day by day. Your sister is in good hands. I promise."

"I know that, or I'd kick your ass." I shoot him a look, but I concede because he's right, and I'd allow it. "I'm just checking in with you. I'm not sure how, but if there's ever anything I can do to help, just let me know. That goes for Blake, too. I would say Annie, but she's more likely to kick your ass than me, so it's probably better you steer clear of her." We clink beer bottles and laugh.

"Webb!"

"Hey, Miller. Why so enthusiastic?" He heads towards us with a big, goofy smile.

"Steak and beer that I don't have to pay for. What's there not to be enthusiastic about?"

"Ever the interloper."

"I was invited, remember? And I like to consider myself an opportunist." He turns to Cole and extends his hand. "Hey man, I'm Miller. I work at the fire department with Justin. How do you have the unfortunate experience of knowing this asshole?" Cole takes his hand and smiles.

"Cole. I'm his baby mama's brother. And the baby daddy to the pregnant blonde inside. And also the boyfriend of the bouncy brunette." Miller's face lights up.

"Good deal, man. Impressive." They exchange smiles as I pull the first steaks off the grill.

"Miller drove us to the hospital in the ambulance."

"Thanks for helping out. I appreciate it." Cole offers him a smile and a nod of thanks.

"Any time." Cole finishes his beer and gestures, asking if anyone else needs another. Miller and I shake our heads, and he walks into the house.

"How you doing, Webb?"

"Is that going to be the question of the night?" He gives me a look that conveys he has no idea what I'm talking about. "Sorry. I'm good. Everything is good."

"Okay. Good." He rubs the back of his neck and looks into the house. "Is Spencer coming?" Ah, that explains the sudden unease.

"You got a thing for my partner, Miller?" His mouth opens and closes like a fish, and I chuckle. "Yeah, she's coming. I'm surprised she isn't here yet. She's always punctual." He nods and stares at the front door. "You're going to have some competition."

"Huh? What do you mean?"

"Axel in there also has a thing for my partner." His eyes

focus on Axel in the kitchen, laughing with Blake and Nicole as they make a salad.

"Axel? He's such a ladies man. What would he want with Spencer?" I pull the last of the meat off the grill and hand a plate to Miller.

"I'm going to pretend that was a jab at Axel and not my best friend." He begins to stutter and backtrack his words.

"What? Oh god. No. I mean. She's nothing like his type. That sounds worse." He groans. "Spencer doesn't seem like the one night stand kind of girl, and that's the only type of girl Axel knows. That's all that I meant." I laugh because I know what he meant from the start. It's always fun to see the guy get flustered.

"Let's eat."

We walk into the kitchen with our plates of chicken and steak. Miller raises his dish and boldly explains. "The men are here with the meat." There's a moment of silence before the room erupts into laughter. It takes him a moment to understand why everyone's laughing.

"Ha-ha, everyone. I meant the chicken and steak are finished."

"Sure you did, Miller." Spencer comes in from the foyer with a big smile and a paper bag in her hand and heads straight for Nicole. "These are for you. You don't have to share if you don't want to." Nicole accepts the bag, and when she opens it, her eyes light up.

38

Nicole

"Whatcha got there, Pumpkin?"

I clutch the bag to my chest. "Are they safe? The cheese?" Spencer nods.

"That's why I'm late. I confirmed all the ingredients and made the owner make them fresh for you." I can tell she isn't happy about being late, but I don't care. I lean over to Annie and open the bag, allowing her to peer in. Her eyes widen as I'm sure mine did.

"Don't share them. Unless of course, it's with me." Annie pushes the bag closed as wandering eyes try to glimpse inside.

"I like a little torture. You can all look, but no one gets to touch. Except Annie." I smirk at her as I pull the box of handmade cannolis from the bag. They are beautiful. The pastry looks light and fluffy. Some ends are adorned with chocolate chips and sprinkles; a few even have jelly. My mouth waters just looking at the deliciousness.

"Pumpkin, you can't eat all of those yourself. We'll have to look at the numbers."

"Don't kill my joy, Doc." He gives me a stern look, and

I know there will be an in-depth discussion about it later. "Who's ready to eat now that everyone is here?" There's a commotion of confirmation from our guests, and I direct everyone to grab a plate and fill it up.

The weather outside is as beautiful as we hoped, and with the addition of the gas heaters, it's perfectly toasty outside. I watch with rapt attention as Miller and Axel dance around Spencer. Evidently, they're both interested in her, and I'm not sure she has any idea. I stifle a giggle when she sits at the table, and they flank her.

"What's so funny?" Justin leans in and whispers in my ear, trying to follow my line of sight.

"Tweedle Dee and Tweedle Dum over there." He huffs a laugh at their ridiculousness. They're attempting to make small talk with Spencer, and she's having none of it.

"Looks like Spencer has options." Maybe.

"Or she could choose both." My eyes wander to my brother, sitting between Annie and Blake, lovingly conversing with both women.

"I can't imagine her with one of them, let alone both." I see Justin take out his phone and inspect everything on my plate. His fingers fly across the screen as he inputs all of my food into the app.

"Could I just enjoy one meal? Take a picture, and we can do this later." I look up and politely smile at our guests while quietly chastising Justin for ruining my fun.

"Do you want a cannoli later? If you do, we need to count these now. Wait. You didn't test before dinner." His chair scrapes across the cement patio and catches everyone's attention. Extending his hand, he waits for me to accept it, and if I didn't want to cause a scene, I would argue.

Our walk into the house is tense. We stop in the kitchen and he takes my monitor out of the cabinet.

"You're being ridiculous, Justin. One meal isn't going to harm my baby."

"Our." He rips open an alcohol pad and grabs at my hand to clean off a finger.

"What?"

"*Our.* She's our baby, not just yours. And you can't know that one overly carbohydrate-filled meal won't hurt her. You haven't even reconciled your numbers yet to know if the diet alone is working. You could need insulin if your sugars are too high." I don't even feel when the needle pricks my finger, and when the monitor beeps with its results, I don't even care.

"You're making a scene."

"I'm not. Half of the people out there are in the medical field, and the other half are or are soon to be family. No one will care if you're doing what's best for you and the baby."

"Our." I smirk at my smart-ass comment and his confusion.

"What?"

"It's *our* baby, not the baby. Remember? And if you want to be even more specific, it's our *daughter.*"

"Pumpkin." He sighs as my nickname rolls from his lips.

"Don't Pumpkin me. Am I allowed to go back to my friends and my meal, or are you going to carry me and feed me with an airplane fork?" He glances down at the monitor and then at the time on his watch.

"Let's go back and enjoy our meal. We'll check again in ninety minutes."

"I'm sure we will."

All eyes are on me as I take my seat at the table. Cole stands from his seat and crouches next to me.

"Everything okay, sis?" I can tell by the tone of Cole's voice that he's concerned.

"I'm fine. He's just worried for my health and the baby." He peers over his shoulder at Justin, who's still in the house.

"You don't have to stay here. You're always welcome at our house. You know that, right?" I turn in my chair to look at him.

"I promise I'm okay, little brother. I know I always have you. He's just a little overprotective sometimes." Cole stands and kisses me on the forehead when Justin returns to the patio.

The air between us is different when he takes his seat.

"I love you. Please don't be upset with me."

"It's fine." How many times can I say that word before I believe it?

"Hey, Annie? Have you all thought of any baby names yet? It's got to be hard having to do it for two." Miller asks such an innocent question, but based on Cole's groan and Blake's shifty eyes, it seems it's anything but.

"Well, Blake and Cole want matching names, but I don't." She looks between them, but they are looking anywhere but at her.

"Matching like Candy and Casey or Casey and Tracy?" Annie cringes at the name choices that Miller offered.

"Matching first letters," Blake answers. "We all agree on Ruby. That was my grandmother, and since I don't have a biological stake in these little ones, we thought it was a good compromise." Annie reaches over Cole and grabs Blake's hand.

"They are your babies too, *Mijn Diamant.*"

"I know, Baby. I don't mean anything negative by it."

Tears well in Annie's eyes. "We just can't agree on a boy's name. We need to decide soon, or he will be nameless. Baby Ruby and no-name brother." She's rambling, and Cole and Blake try their best to soothe her.

"Annie, the name Ruby is beautiful, and I'm sure you'll come up with the perfect name for her brother. There's still plenty of time." I try to reassure her, but it doesn't seem to work for me either.

"Have you thought of a name yet?" Blake attempts to turn the conversation away from them and onto us.

"Oh, well. Um, no, actually. We haven't even talked about it." Why haven't we talked about it?

"Do you have any ideas?" I don't but maybe Justin does. He looks pale as he stares off into space. I touch his shoulder, and he looks in my direction, but he's not actually looking at me. He's looking through me. Spencer stands and walks to us.

"Justin, let's clear some plates." His head turns to Spencer, and she smiles at him. Miller and Axel push back their chairs, saying they'll help, and Spencer looks at them sternly.

"Stay." Both men drop back to their seats, and as tense as this current situation is, I have to hold in a laugh. "Come on, Justin." Spencer grabs his upper arm and tugs until he responds to her and rises.

With worried eyes, they walk inside without any plates like she suggested. When they reach the door, Spencer looks at me and mouths, "I've got him."

There's a silence at the table; the clinking of silverware the only sound.

"He's a great guy, Nicole." Axel's face is full of genuine

hope. "He's been through some stuff. I don't know much, but I'd bet Spencer knows everything. He's really good with you." I give him a tight smile and nod.

I wish he would share more with me. Justin seems to shelter himself as if he doesn't think I can handle his past. I push my chair to stand, and Annie places her hand over mine.

"Give them a moment."

"Annie, I need him to talk to *me*. I can't keep tiptoeing around certain topics. Especially when I don't even know what those topics are. Blake asked him about a name for our daughter." My arms curl protectively around my bump, and my entire body deflates. "What kind of a future am I looking at if her father can't even say her name?"

"It's not like that—" This time I stand. I stand quickly and with enough force that the chair flies back with a loud crash.

"Then what is it like, Annie?" I can't contain my emotions any longer. "You know more about my boyfriend or baby daddy, or whatever he is, than I do. How is that fair to me?" I look down at my protruding belly and rub circles. I don't know if I'm talking to Annie or my daughter when I speak next because it comes out in barely a whisper. "How is that fair to you?"

Blake walks up to me and puts a hand over mine. "Why don't you come to our house for a few days? We can have lots of girl time."

"Running away isn't going to solve anything. I need Justin to talk to me. Confide in me. I need him to trust me as much as he trusts you, Annie. I understand I have a long way to go to be at Spencer's level. They have shared experiences. I get it. But I need to know. I need to be in his circle of trust. Half of this goddamn baby is his."

I've had enough. I'm not sure how much of my outburst is genuine and how much is hormone-filled. Either way, I've reached the end of my rope. I step back from Blake's touch and go in search of Justin. I hear the commotion of our guests behind me, and I can't care.

I follow Spencer's muffled voice down the hall towards our room. I'm confused by the sound of the shower. When I walk into the bedroom, it's empty. My eyes dart to the bathroom door, and when I reach it, I don't even bother to knock.

If I was a better person right now, the sight in front of me might have elicited different emotions. But I'm not. I'm angry. I'm sad. I'm frustrated, and I can't bring myself to care about anyone else except myself and the baby inside me that I will protect until my very last breath.

Spencer looks at me when I step inside the room.

"Nicole." I can't tell if she's surprised or not to see me. My name comes from her mouth without any emotion, and her head darts between Justin and me.

I look to the shower and see Justin sitting on the tile floor in only his boxers, clutching his legs. I can't see his face because it's buried in his knees, but I can see him rocking under the spray of the water.

My resolve wanes for only a moment when I realize I don't care. Our daughter's future comes first, above even our own emotions.

"I can't do this anymore, Justin. You have to talk to me." He doesn't move. Did he hear me? Maybe he didn't over the noise of the water. "Justin?"

Spencer stands straight from where she was leaning on the counter. "Nicole, he—"

"No! I've had it. I want answers. I *need* answers. I was perfectly accepting of raising this baby on my own, but he wants her. He wanted her. I don't know how he feels anymore. He never talks to me." I turn back to the shower and slam my hand on the glass. "Do you want her anymore? I don't care about me but I'd love for *our* daughter to have a father who cares. Do you care, Justin?" My only response is the sight of his shoulders shaking. Is he crying or shivering from the cold? Hell, he could be laughing for all I know because I get no response—nothing from him.

"Nicole, please listen to me. Please." Spencer takes a tentative step towards me. At this point, I'll listen to anyone who wants to give me insight into his feelings.

"What can you tell me that he won't, Spencer? He needs to be talking to me. How can we have a relationship if he won't let me in?"

"I wish it were that simple. He's been through a lot."

"I'm so tired of that excuse. We've all been through a lot, and we deal with it. He has to let me in."

"He's trying."

"Trying?" A frustrated laugh leaves me without my permission. I turn my focus on the broken man still unmoving on the shower floor. "I know about your sister, Justin. Annie told me she died. How fucked up is it that I had to hear about that from Annie."

"Nicole."

"Stop saying my name like I'm a petulant child, Spencer. He's a grown-ass man, and if he can't handle his own feelings, then how can I expect him to be able to handle my daughter? MY daughter, Justin, because you get the choice of walking away. I don't. I DON'T. I'll raise her on my own. You just

325

say the word, and it will be like she never existed to you."

"Get her out. Get her out of here, Spencer! GET HER OUT!" Justin screams so loud his voice turns horse and echos off the bathroom walls.

Spencer lightly pushes me backward, and I'm in such shock that I let her. She gently turns my shoulders, and we walk out of the bathroom together.

He told me to leave. He doesn't want to talk to me. He doesn't want me. He didn't fight for her. Our daughter. No. Mine. She's my daughter.

Cole appears at the bedroom door as we step out of the bathroom.

"Take her home, Cole."

"Fuck." I have no idea what I must look like, but Cole instantly reacts, wrapping an arm around my waist. "Blake," Cole yells for her over his shoulder. This can't be happening. We walk down the hall and see Blake coming towards us.

"What happened?" She swipes at my cheek, and I realize I'm crying. My body is on autopilot. Breathe in. Step. Breathe out. Step.

"Pack her a bag, please. We'll meet you in the car." Blake doesn't hesitate at his request.

"I can go to my apartment."

"No. You're coming home with us. We've got you, Nicole. I'll be right there." Blake steps around me, and I freeze.

"The dogs. I can't leave Java and Beans here. I need them. Candy loves them, too."

"I told you. We've got you, sweetie. I'll grab them with your things. Let Cole take care of you now." I dip my head once in acknowledgment, and we continue to the front door.

All of our other guests, our friends, are in the kitchen

cleaning up the last of our dinner party. I've never been so grateful to have people in my corner right now. Even if it's not the person I wish it were.

"I need my testing supplies."

Annie steps up next to me and rubs my arm. "Tell me where they are, and I'll get them for you." I give her directions on what I need as Cole and I put our jackets on.

"Thank you everyone for coming. I'm sorry the evening is being cut short. We'll...I will reschedule another dinner at a later time." Miller and Axel come over and hug me. Big manly bear hugs that squish some of my shattered pieces together.

Cole helps Annie put her coat on, and Blake meets us with my rolling suitcase. Miller grabs it from Blake.

"Axel and I are leaving too. Everything is cleaned and put away. I'll wheel this out for you."

"Thank you."

"Someone grab the cannolis." I turn to Annie, who has a big smile. "I've been dreaming about them since you showed me. No reason that tonight has to ruin our dessert."

Axel turns on his heel. "I'll grab the contraband." I laugh at the situation as tears roll down my cheeks. Cole pulls me into his chest, and his strong arms wrap around me.

"Shh. I've got you, big sis. We're going to take care of you." I know he will. He's always taken care of me. I'm the big sister. It's supposed to be my job to take care of him, but I feel too broken at the moment to do anything but let him.

Little nails scrape at my ankles when Blake brings Java and Beans over. I smile down to them, knowing that no matter what, they love me unconditionally.

My eyes wander down the hall once everyone gathers at

the door. I heard the shower turn off several minutes ago, but neither Spencer nor Justin have come out of the room.

"You ready sis?"

"No, but let's go." With Cole's hand on the small of my back, we leave Justin's house together.

39

Justin

"Have you thought of a name yet?" A name. For our daughter. The baby that's growing inside Nicole right now who will soon be an actual person.

"Oh, well. Um, no, actually. We haven't even talked about it." Nicole sounds concerned. We haven't talked about it. *Why* haven't we talked about it? We haven't picked out names or car seat brands. We haven't talked about a birth plan. Does she want to formula feed or breastfeed? Why haven't we talked about any of these things?

"Do you have any ideas?" Me? Is she asking me? About names? Ivy. Ivy is the only name I can think of right now. I can't name my daughter Ivy. I failed her. I can't fail my daughter.

"Justin, let's clear some plates." Spencer says my name, and I meet her eyes. I'm aware other things are happening around the table, but my mind is only focused on one thing. *Daughter.*

There's pressure on my arm where Spencer's hand is, and I realize she's trying to get me to stand. I'm always safe in

Spencer's hands so I get up, trusting whatever she's wanting me to do. We walk into the house, and she directs me to my bedroom.

"Talk to me, Justin." I open my mouth to respond, but there are no words. My chest begins to heave with the exertion of breathing. My fingers start to tingle, and I close my eyes.

5-4-3-2-1

"No you don't." Spencer shoves me into the bathroom. "You aren't having a panic attack on my watch. In you go." She opens the shower door and strips me to my boxers. I help as much as I can, but my concentration is on my breathing. Freezing water pelts my skin, and the shock stuns me enough that I'm able to take a deep breath. And another. I sink to the shower floor with the weight of my despair.

"Okay. Okay." Spencer understands me and turns on the hot water to warm me up. I wish I could say this is the first time I've had to take a cold shower to stave off a panic attack, but as the saying goes, "This ain't our first rodeo." It was Spencer who first threw me into a cold shower when I started a panic attack in my sleep. I had been dreaming about Ivy. All of my bad dreams are always about Ivy.

"Justin."

"Spencer. What's wrong with me?"

"You know what's wrong, and you know how to fix it. I think you know why this is happening. If I checked your meds right now, would they all be accounted for? Or will there be extra?"

"Fuck." *Fuck. Fuck. Fuck.* Drawing my legs up to my chest, I bury my head in my knees. She's right. I've done this to myself. I've been irresponsible with my meds. I've been worrying so much about Nicole's sugar levels and making sure she's eating the right foods at the right times that my health hasn't been my priority.

"You know you can't—"

"I know. I fucking know." Does she think I don't understand how vital my meds are?

"Well then—"

"I get it. I fucked up. Again. I fucked up again. She's too good for me, Spencer. I'm going to lose her. I need to get my shit together."

"Why haven't you talked to her?"

"I'm too broken. She'll leave me." Spencer's silence speaks volumes. Even my best friend doesn't think I'm good enough for the woman who's carrying my baby.

The bathroom door swings open, and I know it's Nicole without looking. She's yelling. She's angry, and I can't blame her. I am, too.

"I need answers."

"Do you want her anymore?"

Fuck. I want her more than anything. I want my daughter, but she doesn't deserve me. She deserves so much better than anything I can give her.

"I'll raise her on my own. You just say the word, and it will be like she never existed to you."

Hot tears stream down my cheeks, mixing with the punishing water beating on my back. My body shakes with adrenaline. With fear. With anger for my useless self.

"Get her out. Get her out of here, Spencer. GET HER OUT!" My throat is instantly sore from the force I put behind the last words. Every word she said was a piece of glass piercing my already battered heart.

I can hear muffled voices over the water and know Cole has

come to rescue Nicole from her asshole baby daddy. Thank fuck she has a support system to care for her. I hope they can be who she needs because it clearly isn't me.

I feel Spencer's presence when she comes back into the bathroom. "Who am I calling, Justin?"

"No one. Can you hand me a towel?" She reaches behind her and takes a dark green towel off the rack. Standing, I turn the water off and open the door, wrapping the terry cloth around my waist. "Thank you."

"That's not an option at this point, and you know it. You need your meds resituated."

"I'll take care of it." The last thing I need right now is a babysitter. I need to get my shit together, and having someone hover over me isn't going to help.

"Like I said, not an option anymore. Garret or Dr. Linnsy? You know what's going to happen if I make the call." Do I want that? Do I want to go to rehab again? Do I *need* to go? I know the fucking answer. It's been weeks of forgetting to take a pill here and there.

Defeated, I sigh and run my hands through my wet hair. "Okay. Yeah. Can you...Look, can you give me two days? Let me get my life organized before I disappear again."

"Two days?"

"Please. If I don't go willingly, I give you permission to drag my ass through the front doors. Let me call my staff and make sure there's room. If not, we can find somewhere else."

"Two days, Justin. That's all I'm giving you. Pack a bag because I'm not leaving you here alone. We're having a slumber party."

Laying on Spencer's couch in her guest room, staring at the dark ceiling, brings back the memories of doing exactly this. So many nights after my first stay at rehab, I imagined my future. Something that I hadn't allowed myself to do for so long before that. I always knew I had an expiration date that ran out sooner rather than later.

After rehab, I thought I had come to realize my self-worth. I lived every day, making people whole again. I helped them in their times of crisis. Split open heads on teenagers riding bikes or skateboards. Helping an elderly woman who fell from bed. A car accident like Annie's, leaving her with broken bones. Each moment would lead me to the next, where I could help someone else.

The sum of my whole was equivalent to how many people could fill up my helpfulness quota. The part of me that is a people pleaser.

Then came Nicole.

She's never needed me. This fun, sexy, independent woman rolled right over my shy, nerdy self. Then she ran me over with a bulldozer.

"I'll raise her on my own. You just say the word, and it will be like she never existed to you."

"I'll raise her on my own. You just say the word, and it will be like she never existed to you."

She can. She will. Maybe I should let her. Maybe they would both be better off without me in their lives to fuck things up.

"Fuck." Sitting up and swinging my legs off the couch, I bury my head in my hands. I don't know what to do, but I

333

know I need to start with the truth. Nicole deserves to know what my past was like. All the broken parts of me have been taped together with therapy and medications.

And my daughter. If I don't make it out of this cycle of self-deprecation, she deserves to know why. I need her to know that it wasn't about her. My decisions, whatever they may be, are all my own.

Standing from my makeshift bed, I cross the room and sit in the rolling chair. I find a pen and paper inside Spencer's desk and sit to write a note to Nicole and to my unborn daughter.

"Hello, sleepyhead. Was the couch too uncomfortable?" My head jolts up from the intrusion. Where am I? Looking around the room, I see I'm in Spencer's office. I must have fallen asleep. I look down and see the manila envelope on the desk, taunting my memory like an ominous khaki-colored bomb.

"Hi," I manage to croak out. My eyes feel swollen, and my throat is dry from the tears I shed last night.

"We have an hour before we have to leave. Anything else you need to get done before we go." I pick up the large envelope, ensuring it's sealed, and write Nicole's name on it.

"I need you to do a few things for me." She nods, and I continue. "I need to go no contact. Nicole is going to ask questions about where I've gone. I need you to not tell her."

"Are you sure that's for the best, Justin?" No, I'm not fucking sure.

"She deserves the best version of me. My daughter deserves even better. I have to do this alone to know that I can."

"Understood. What else?" Spencer raises her coffee cup in a silent gesture of offering, and I stand, following her to the kitchen with my letters. Inside the manila envelope is my confession to Nicole and a love letter of sorts to my daughter.

I make my coffee, glancing several times at the confessions held within the tiny blue lines that have no idea of the secrets they hold.

"Care to share? Do you want me to give that to her?" I spin around, almost spilling my coffee.

"No," I say all too quickly. "This isn't for Nicole. Well, it's for her, but not for her eyes at the moment. I need you to hold on to it for me until I ask you for it. Hopefully, I'll ask you to burn it one day soon, but just in case, can you please keep it safe for me."

"Of course. Did you decide how long you're going to stay?" Spencer pushes the start button on the microwave, and the thirty-second timer begins.

"A minimum of six weeks. I'll reassess after that. Six weeks is a day before Annie's scheduled c-section date and four weeks before Nicole's due date. It seems like an appropriate time." The microwave beeps and Spencer takes out a plate filled with eggs, pancakes, and sausage. She places it in front of me and hands me a fork and syrup.

"Eat."

"You didn't have to cook for me, Spence." She shrugs and sips her coffee.

"I know food is your love language. It felt like an appropriate way to support you." I take a forkful of eggs and greedily eat.

"I appreciate you more than you could possibly know. I talked to my lawyer and gave you temporary power of attorney while I'm…away. I've already signed it. You need to stop by his office and add your name, and he'll notarize it.

"Justin, is there more to this than you're telling me?" There's so much more.

"There's a lot more on the line this time. I have to do this for me because my life is more than just me now. I have a daughter that will be here in about two months."

"You can't do it for her or for Nicole. The decision has to be yours." I look at Spencer with all of the honesty I have.

"That's why I need you to be the bad guy for me. Nicole is going to come to you looking for answers when she can't reach me. I need to do this alone. I've already told the ward I want no visitors at any point in my stay. You are the only one allowed to contact me via Garret or Dr. Linnsy. But Spencer, unless it's an emergency, please don't reach out."

"That's really what you want?" She takes my empty plate away and washes it along with her cup in the sink.

"I want to know I can do this, and right now, I can't. As much as Nicole's words cut me, she wasn't wrong. She deserves all the best parts of me, and my mental health is in the worst place it's been since before we met."

"I'm proud of you. It takes a brave man to admit his faults. And Justin, a healthy you is all they need. But, you're enough for them, even at your worst." I don't feel proud of myself. I feel like a failure of a man. I finish my coffee and step to the sink to wash my cup. So many thoughts swirl in my head, and I place the mug in the drying rack once it's clean. My head dips to my chest, and I brace myself against the sink.

"Will you watch out for her while I'm gone? I know she's with her brother, and they will take good care of her, but I need to know there's someone on my side because I'm sure I'm not their favorite person right now."

"I'll take care of whatever you need. Nicole will be in

good hands. You know that." I turn to face her and nod my appreciation. I do know.

"I'll take a shower, and we can head out. I'm ready."

40

Nicole

It's been three days since Justin told me to leave. No. Let's not sugarcoat it. He kicked me out of his house. Did I deserve it? Probably for the things I said, but I don't regret any of it. I needed him to step up or step away. Except, I had no idea that he would choose to step away.

Sitting at Annie's kitchen counter, I stir my spoon in my cup of coffee sludge. I can't seem to force myself to eat. There's no pumpkin creamer. There's no nerdy paramedic taunting me with food and orgasms. All they have here is oat milk and powdered eggs. Annie's cook, Sarah, has made some beautiful-looking meals for me, but everything tastes bland.

"Want to go baby shopping?" No, I most definitely don't.

I turn, expecting to see Blake since she was the one who asked the question. Instead, I see Annie smiling brightly, looking adorable in a yellow maternity dress perfectly fitted to her beautiful round belly.

"Um, hi Annie." Blake pops up from the floor, and I'm shocked to see her bubbly attitude. "What were you doing down there?" Annie looks guilty.

"I can't see my feet. Blake was helping me put my shoes on." She rests her hands on her baby belly, and I'm in awe at how beautiful it looks. I feel frumpy, and she looks like she belongs on the cover of a maternity magazine.

"I don't mind helping, Baby." Blake kisses Annie on the cheek, and I look away. My emotions are still too raw, even for the simplest of affection. "So, baby shopping, Nicole?" Ugh. Back to that.

"I'm kind of tired today. I don't know?" I'm tired because I'm not eating right. *You know how to fix that, Nicole. Just eat. Track your numbers.*

"Come on, Nicole. You've moped since we brought you here. Come shopping with us." I want nothing more than to go shopping with them, but up until three days ago, I thought I'd be making a nursery at Justin's house.

Although he hadn't officially asked me to move in, I knew it was coming. We had talked about which room would be best for a nursery and what we needed to babyproof around the house. I guess now I need to turn the spare bedroom in my apartment into a nursery. I don't even know how I'm supposed to do everything baby-related while hiking up stairs or hoping and praying that the antique elevator works.

"Okay, let me see what I have to wear." Blake packed a good array of clothing for me, and I have no doubt I'll find something appropriate to put on.

When Blake and Annie asked me to go baby shopping, I was thinking of a big box store of some kind. Finding myself wandering the floors of several children's boutiques has my eyes nearly popping out of my head with the zeroes on these price tags. Why does a bib that will inevitably be covered in some kind of snot cost seventy-five dollars? It better be self-cleaning and save the damn sea turtles or something grand like that.

"You've barely even looked at anything. What's your vision for her nursery?" My shoulders fall as I think about Blake's question and answer honestly.

"One with her father in it."

"Oh, Nicole." Blake embraces me as best she can with my bump in the way. "I'm so sorry. I thought a day out would be good for you, but now I feel selfish. This is probably torture for you. I'll find Annie, and we can grab takeout somewhere and go home."

"No. I'm okay. I'm dealing with my own demons right now. The two of you wanted to shop. Let's stay. I'm sorry I'm not being any fun."

"Are you sure? I can totally go for some popcorn and a chick flick under some comfy blankets." I give her a warm smile.

"Can't we do both?" I don't want to be a killjoy for the baby shopping, but I also love her idea.

"We certainly can. Let's go find Annie and hurry her along. Otherwise, she'll buy the entire store." She grabs my hand to guide me, and I squeeze it.

"Can I ask two questions first?" She stops and looks at me.

"Of course."

"Have you heard from him? I would never ask you to give away anything, but he hasn't tried to contact me. I just want to make sure he's okay." She looks to the ground and takes my other hand.

"I wish I could say I have, but he isn't answering my texts. I was wondering the same thing, so I reached out yesterday. Let's give him a few more days to cool down, and we can reach out to Spencer if we don't hear anything."

"Okay." I don't like it, but she's probably thinking more rationally than me, so I'll accept her answer.

"You had a second question?" Huh? Oh yeah. I chuckle before I respond.

"Oh, um." I lean in closer to her ear so I can whisper. "Who the hell needs a bib worth seventy-five dollars?" We erupt into a fit of giggles at the pure absurdity of the price.

"What's so funny?" I spin my head to see Annie giving us a stern look.

"Nothing." The laughter can't be contained, and it feels nice to have a reprieve from my melancholy.

Watching movies and eating popcorn on the couch was as cathartic as I had hoped it would be. Cole joined the escapades, and the four of us laughed and joked around for hours. Candy, Java, and Beans were their adorable selves, all curled up together in a dog bed most of the evening, and when they weren't on the bed, they were trying to use us as pillows. I've never been so glad for an oversize sectional.

As the credits roll on our third movie of the evening, Annie yawns and tries to cover it with a blanket.

"Alright, baby mama, I think it's time to take Ruby and unnamed boy to bed." Cole's smile projects all of the love he has for Annie.

"Ruby and Toby? Ruby and Owen? Ruby and Remi?" Blake spouts out baby names, and Annie rolls her eyes.

"No. No. And definitely no. We've already talked about this. No double R names." Annie shifts towards the edge of the couch, and Cole jumps up to help her stand.

"I got you, Kitten." Annie glows at his nickname, and she rises into his arms.

"I'm ready for bed too, Pup." Blake stands on her toes and kisses Cole's cheek.

"I can't wait until I have to help you off the couch, Princess. Don't make me wait too long to put a baby in you." Blake giggles, and Annie groans.

"Make him wait, Little One. Make him wait." Cole kisses both women, and it's my turn to groan.

"Ugh. You all make me sick. Sounds like it's bedtime." I stand, and the room spins, causing me to sit back down.

"Nicole, are you okay?" Cole squats at my feet, looking me over for any issues.

"I got a little lightheaded. I must have stood up too quickly. I'm good." *Shit.* That's not random dizziness. I need to check my sugar levels. I'm either too low or too high. I relied way too much on Justin to make sure I was eating right and checking my sugar levels at the correct times.

"Let me help you up." Cole stands and offers me his hands. I rise slower this time, and the room stays in one place. "How are you now?"

"I'm better. I'm going to get some water from the kitchen and then head to bed. You should all go. I'll be fine."

"I can stay and make sure you get up the stairs."

"Don't be overbearing, Cole. I'm fine. Sometimes, pregnant women get dizzy. Annie?" I look at her with hopeful eyes that she's had even a single dizzy spell and will back me up with my half lie.

"It's happened a few times. The sudden blood rush from standing too quickly can make the room spin." I'm so happy I could kiss her.

"See, no big deal." Go to bed, Cole. Please go to bed. I need to check my sugar levels.

"Okay, big sis. We'll be just down the hall if you need us." He kisses the top of my head, and I hug Blake and Annie before they retreat upstairs.

I wait until the house is quiet, and I know they've reached their bedroom before I take my supplies out of the cabinet. I'm not looking forward to the needle prick since I've neglected to test since the night of the dinner.

At first, it felt like a good way to rebel from my situation I'm in, but the more testings I missed, the easier it was to forget to do it. Taking a deep breath, the pen needle clicks and as always, my shoulders jump at the sound. Collecting a few drops of blood for the test strip, I set the monitor up and wait. I know the number will be bad; I can tell by the way I feel.

While I wait for the dreaded number to appear, I make myself a glass of water. I've been lacking with my water intake as well. I've completely ignored my app because it's connected to Justin, and I wanted to be petty.

The monitor beeps, and I close my eyes, not wanting to see what it says. Unfortunately, ignoring the problem won't make it go away. Finding the strength to look, it reads two hundred eighty-seven.

Fuck.

I log the number into my phone, knowing Justin will see it.

Do I want him to call and yell at me for such a high number? Not necessarily. At this point, I want some communication. While I don't regret the things I said to him, I regret the circumstances that they were said in, and I'd like the chance to apologize.

Annie prepared the house with easy foods for me, so I know there are hard-boiled eggs in the refrigerator, hoping the protein will help regulate the high number. I decide to take my snack upstairs because I'm getting tired, so I wrap two eggs in a napkin, check to see if the dogs are still sleeping, and head to bed.

As I walk down the hallway, I hear a noise and freeze.

No. Please, no.

"Oh god. Right there."

No. No. Noooo.

I don't want to listen to my brother having sex again. Picking up my pace, I close the door behind me as soon as I reach my room. For a moment, I hear nothing, thankful that the barrier of the door has eliminated the sound.

"Fuck, Kitten. You feel fucking incredible."

Shower. I'll shower, and they should be done by the time I'm out.

Twenty minutes later, they're still going at it. This is absolute torture. Two of the three nights I've been here, I've heard them. I'm so happy that they have a healthy sex life, but I can't take much more of this.

The first night I was here, I heard them, and when I woke up in the middle of the night to use the bathroom, I heard them again. Or maybe still. I'm not sure and don't really want to think about my brother's stamina. At least I inhaled the eggs before the shower, and I feel better with the added protein. I shouldn't have eaten all that popcorn tonight.

You have got to be fucking kidding me. They're having sex again. It's six in the morning. Do they have any idea how loud they are?

Me: I hate to ask this, but I think I need to be rescued from this brothel.

Hopefully, a little humor will go a long way. It's early, and I'm surprised when I see the three bouncing dots.

Spencer: The brothel? I thought you were at Annie's house. What's wrong?
    Me: They have a very, VERY healthy sex life, and I need sleep. And to not hear my brother moaning.
    Spencer: What can I do for you?

Shit. I really didn't think this through. I expected more time to formulate my thoughts before she replied. Do I want to go back to my apartment? Some girl time? I know what I need. I need help.

Me: Is there any chance I could crash at your house for a bit? Besides the permanent trauma of hearing Cole moan out both Blake and Annie's names, I've been neglecting my monitoring and could really use some help.

Neglecting is an understatement. At my last appointment, my numbers were on the border of needing insulin, but Justin convinced the doctor that he could help me monitor my intake, and we would give it another two weeks to see if I could continue with diet alone.

Spencer: What time am I picking you up?

This is why she is Justin's best friend. With barely any hesitation, I admitted to needing help and she's coming to my rescue.

Me: Whatever time works with your schedule.
    Spencer: I'll be there at nine.

Now to tell my brother that I can't stay at his house anymore because he has too much sex. This should go over well.

The pitter-patter of feet makes me smile. They must have slept downstairs all night with Candy.

"Morning, ladies." Java and Beans bounce up the step stool and onto my bed, followed by a big dip of the mattress when Candy joins them. All three curl up around me, and I feel their warmth seeping through the blanket.

"You two like it here, don't you?" The guilt of knowing that I'm moving them again weighs heavy on me. I didn't even think to ask Spencer if I could bring them. Could I leave them here? *Should* I leave them here? Candy nudges my hand, urging me to pet her. Complying, I scratch her ear.

"Would you like it if they stayed here with you, Candy? Could you watch over them for a little while? I know how much you all like being together."

"Going somewhere, big sister?" Cole leans on the door frame, smiling at me.

"Yes. You know I love you, little brother, but your sex life is very...vocal. I'm gonna go stay at Spencer's house for a few days." He hangs his head in embarrassment or shame.

"I'm so sorry. Please don't say anything to the girls, they'll be so embarrassed. But I won't say I'm sorry for pleasing my women." He winks, and I toss a pillow at him, missing completely. The jostling stirs the dogs, and they all jump off the bed, bounding for Cole.

"Not sure how much you heard, but can they stay with you? I've moved them around so much, and I know they love it here with Candy." He walks into the room, careful not to trip over our four-legged friends, and sits beside me on the bed.

"You know they can. I'll do anything to help you. I don't want you to feel like you have to leave. Do you want to take the room downstairs instead? Unfortunately, as I'm sure you know, turning down my very hormonally pregnant... girlfriend, fiance, baby mama, isn't an option."

"Gee, thanks for that visual." I push his shoulder, and he barely budges. "By the way, what *is* your relationship status with them?"

He scoffs. "What day is it?"

"Is it that bad?"

"Nah. It's just complicated. I'd take them both to the courthouse right now if it was legal. Logic says I should marry Annie since she's about to have my kids, but I hate the thought of leaving Blake out. And I also want Blake to have my babies."

"Babies? How many kids do you plan to have?"

"All of them." His smile is wide and genuine, while his gaze is far off. He's imagining his future with them together as a family. While I love it for him, it makes the gaping hole in my heart larger.

"Have you heard from Justin?" I'm sure if he hasn't reached out to Blake or me, he hasn't spoken to Cole either, but I have to at least ask.

"No. And as far as I know, Annie and Blake haven't spoken to him either. I'm sorry, Nicole." I rest my head on his shoulder, and we sit in silence for a few minutes. "Do you need a ride to Spencer's?"

"No. She's coming to get me at nine. I should get my car and drive myself, but I haven't been feeling the greatest and probably shouldn't be driving." *Shit.* I didn't mean for that to slip out.

He moves out from under me and gives me a stern look. He already has the disappointed dad face down-pat, and I almost laugh at the ridiculousness of it.

"What's wrong?" I hate admitting my weaknesses to him, but I have to say them out loud because ignoring them is bad for our health.

"I guess I didn't realize how much I had become dependent on Justin. He marked all my meals with carb totals and how many servings I could have. It took the guessing game out of eating. I haven't been tracking my food intake since I've been here, and it's taking a toll. I asked Spencer for help."

"Nicole. Why didn't you say anything? We would have been happy to help you." He pulls me into him, wrapping his arms around my shoulder. Hugs from my little brother are always the best.

"Because I'm an independent woman, or I like to think I am. It seems I'm just a child that likes to whine and be spiteful." He hugs me tighter. "It's for the best. Spencer will whip me into shape."

"If that's what you need, I'll support you. I love you, big sister, and I want the best for you." I know he does.

"Love you too, little brother."

"Can I join in on the hug-fest?" I laugh into Cole's chest. Of course, Blake would want to join in. I'm sure Annie isn't far behind her.

"Bring it in, Blake." I open an arm, and she bounces next to me, joining in our embrace. A moment later, the bed dips again, and I know the fourth member of our party has arrived. When a small, cold, wet nose tickles my barefoot under the covers, I giggle, causing Candy to pounce on us.

"Candy, *Sitzen.*" That was not English, but whatever Annie said, Candy listens and jumps off the bed, sitting at attention. Java pokes her head out from the covers, and Candy whines, wanting to play. Cole puts Java and Beans on the floor, and the three dogs chase each other out of the room.

"Who wants breakfast?" As if my stomach can hear Cole, it growls in response. He places a hand on Annie's stomach and one on mine.

"Let's go feed these babies."

41

Nicole

At precisely nine a.m. Spencer rings the doorbell. Thanks to Cole, my bags are packed and ready by the front door. I open the door, and a small part of me hoped to see Justin standing next to her, but she's alone.

"Come on in." I step aside, but she doesn't move.

"I know you have questions, Nicole. I have some answers for you, but you aren't going to like all of them." Am I that obvious?

"Okay. Do you want to talk here?"

"I have Gage in the car. I thought I'd introduce him to your dogs before they come to our house."

"Gage?" Does she have a roommate?

"My German Shepherd. I know you have dachshunds. I thought it would be better to meet on more neutral territory." Dog. I had no idea she had an animal. She's never mentioned it before.

"Gage…is your dog. Okay. I wasn't planning to bring Java and Beans. I've moved them around a lot the past few weeks, and they love Candy, Annie's dog."

"Candy? A red Doberman?"

"Yeah. Didn't you meet her at the—oh, right. Cole mentioned they sent her to doggy daycare for the day of the party. How did you know what breed she is?"

"Do you need help getting the bags to the car? Hey, Spencer."

"Hi, Cole…Candy." Spencer reaches down and rubs the top of her head. Candy sniffs Spencer, her ears rotating back and forth. "Do you smell Gage? He's in the car." Spencer turns her attention to Cole. "Can I get him?"

Cole looks equally as confused as I just was. "Gage is Spencer's German Shepherd."

"Oh, you have a dog. Sure." Spencer turns to leave just as Java and Beans make it to the front door with their little legs. Spencer rounds the corner again with a beautiful dog walking perfectly obediently beside her.

Candy perks up next to us when she sees our new visitor. Spencer whispers something to Gage and unclips his leash. I can hear the pitter-patter of Java and Beans' lack of obedience and their eagerness to play. Spencer whispers again, and Gage walks gracefully towards us. I thought Candy behaved well, but Gage makes her look almost feral with his obedience.

He walks up to the doorway and stops, sitting in front of us.

"*Gehen.*" Gage jumps up and runs into the house, playing with the other three dogs like a puppy.

"Holy shit. That was…He's so well-behaved." Cole and I stare at them, playing for a few minutes.

"Who's this?" Annie stands at the bottom of the stairs, looking at the playful mayhem. "Do I know that dog?"

"He's mine. This is Gage." Spencer's tone radiates pride.

"Why do I know him?" Annie knows Gage?

"The dog park," Spencer says matter-of-factly.

Annie's gaze bounces between Cole and Gage with curiosity. I watch her mouth "dog park" several times. Her eyes light up like a light bulb turns on.

"Spencer. Dog park. *Your* name is Spencer."

"Correct. We've met several times, Annie. You're usually on your phone when you're there." Annie's hand comes up to her mouth, and her eyes glisten with tears. Cole rushes over, pulling her into his chest.

"Kitten, what's wrong?" Cole rubs her back as she cries into his chest.

"I'm a terrible person," she sobs. "I don't remember meeting Spencer, but I remember her dog. I'm so sorry, Spencer. This isn't like me. These baby hormones have fried my brain."

I can feel the beginnings of tears prickling the back of my eyes. Spencer looks at me, and I can see she's uneasy. She looks over my shoulder at the dogs still playing.

"Gage, *Kommen*." Gage immediately stops and comes to Spencer. Candy freezes and tilts her head. She understood the German command, but it wasn't her name or her human that used it. "It's your decision, Nicole. Your dogs are welcome at my house if you want to bring them."

I look down at my two babies, my original babies, and decide what to do. I hate being without them, but it's not about me. They deserve to stay in one place for a while.

"Cole, is it still okay if they stay?"

"Of course. Any time, big sister."

❤,❤

Spencer lives in a nice, established neighborhood. The trees lining the street are mature, and all the lawns are well-manicured. We pull into the driveway of a brick house with black shutters but pull to the back of the long road past a pool to a smaller bungalow.

I look behind me at the brick house and back to the light blue one in front of me. "Where are we?"

"My father lives in the house, and I live here. There are two bedrooms, but I typically use one as an office. I've put a twin-size mattress in there for you. It's all that would fit with the desk I have. It's small, but it's my home." I chuckle, and she gives me an accusatory look.

"What's so funny?"

"Sorry. It's not you. I was thinking that I once told Justin my apartment 'wasn't fancy, but it was home' and you reminded me of it." The sound of his name out of my mouth makes me pause.

"Let's get everything inside, and we can talk. We can go to the grocery store this afternoon and prepare easy meals for you. I'm not sure if my ways will be more or less strict than what you were used to, but I promise I will make sure you and your baby are safe."

"I know. That's what I'm hoping for. I'm floundering, Spencer." She opens her door, and Gage doesn't move. Not even when she pulls my suitcase out of the back seat, he sits and patiently waits until he's given permission.

"Gage, *Kommen*." Gage gracefully steps out of the back seat and walks next to Spencer.

"He's so well-behaved."

"He will be until we walk into the house. This is his home and his safe place. I don't require him to work when he's inside. He'll act more like you saw him at Annie's. I'll write down his basic commands for you."

"I recognized k-ko-men, I think. That means come, right? I've heard them say it to Candy." I'm sure I butchered that word. I know nothing about the German language.

"*Kommen*, correct. Gage has a more extensive vocabulary than Candy, but it's good you know the basics." Spencer unlocks two very serious-looking locks and opens the door. Once inside, she punches a code into an alarm pad. She seems very cautious, but I understand being a female and living alone.

"*Heimspiele*." Whatever she just said to Gage made his entire demeanor change. He's back to the playful puppy attitude I saw with the other dogs. "I told him home, play. The commands can also be used separately. I told him to play when we were at Annie's house, but he was still on alert. *Heimspiele* lets him know he can relax.

"So he's like a guard dog? Do I need to worry about my two, three, and four a.m. pee breaks?"

"Gage, *Kommen*." He trots over to us and sits next to Spencer. "Let me have your hand." She takes it and offers it to Gage to smell. "*Freund*. Nicole, *Freund*." He continues to sniff my hand and then back off. "*Spielen*."

"Who knew staying with you would earn me a high school diploma in German."

"I told him you were a friend. Coming from me, he will now protect you. Let's sit." Sitting means we're going to talk. I know I want answers, but I'm afraid. What if he's asked her to break up with me? Or are we already broken up? Oh god. Are we broken up? I haven't spoken to him in four days after he yelled at me to get out. That feels pretty permanent.

"Sit, Nicole. I can see you spiraling." I plop myself down on a comfy black suede couch, and she sits beside me. First things first.

"Is he okay, Spencer?"

"Physically, yes." Good. No, wait. That's a very specific answer.

"Physically. Not mentally?"

"No." She says nothing further. I can see this will be like twenty questions with yes or no answers. Be specific with your questions, Nicole.

"Where is he, Spencer? I'm worried I haven't heard from him."

"And you won't."

"What!" Gage's ears flip back at my piercing screech. "I won't? What does that mean."

"I'll tell you what he has allowed me to. Justin has voluntarily admitted himself to rehab."

"Rehab? Was he on drugs? Drinking? I never saw signs of either."

"You're spiraling again. He has no issues with either of those. He does however, have depression and anxiety, and they are extreme. Since your pregnancy, I've watched him gradually decline. He hasn't been consistent with his medication. What you saw the other day is a product of that."

"What does all that mean? Did he try to do something?"

"No." Her answer is out before I can even finish my question. "Has he told you how we met?" I shake my head, and she tells me about the details of Justin's suicide attempt. How a little girl saved him by rudely barging in and how she was his paramedic.

"I didn't have permission to tell you that story but it's my story as well so I don't feel as if I broke any rules."

"So he's in rehab, not because he's suicidal, but because he was mismanaging his meds?"

"Correct."

"Where is he, and why won't I hear from him?" I see the corner of her eye twitch, but her mask doesn't fall. "Spencer, this is your home. Please don't hide your true self for me." She stands and walks to the kitchen.

"Coffee, water?"

"Just answers, Spencer."

"He wants to do it alone. I'm under strict orders that he is not to be contacted unless it's an emergency."

"Even for me?"

"Yes."

"Even for you?" She nods.

"Yes. Unless there is an emergency."

"But why? I guess I can probably understand why me, but why you?" She comes back with two bottles of water and hands me one.

"He feels like he's failing you and her." Spencer looks at my stomach and back to my eyes. "He wants and needs to recover for his own reasons. He was doing everything in his life for you and her and nothing for him."

"I didn't ask for any of that. I swear I never meant—"

"I know." Spencer puts her hand on my knee. "I know. It's his personality. You didn't do anything to make it happen." We sit in silence, and she eventually moves her hand.

"Spencer, I can tell you're keeping things from me."

"Of course. Justin and I have many secrets between us." Her eyes flash to Gage lying at her feet.

"I won't ask you to share anything you can't, but I'd like to hear everything you can."

"I can tell you this is hard for him, and even when he gets out, he may not be ready to be a partner or a father." Why is it so easy for the father of a baby to walk away?

"Spencer...I don't want to do this alone. I never expected to do this at all, let alone as a single parent."

"Nicole, you will never be alone. You have your brother and his lovers. You have me, and I will consider this child as my niece if you allow it." Tears freely flow down my cheeks at her genuine words.

"C-Can I hug you? I understand if you're not comfortable." There's a moment of hesitation before she leans in and hugs me. I know this is a massive deal for her. My stress melts away little by little the longer we embrace. I feel a soft pressure on my leg and see Gage resting his head on me. Spencer pulls away and pets his head.

"He likes you, and he's a good judge of character." She stands and offers me her hand. "Let me show you to your room. I don't know how long you plan to stay, but you're welcome as long as you like. Please consider this your home."

I follow Spencer down the short hall, and I'm in awe of her minimalist style. It's the opposite of mine, but it's completely her. She opens a door for me, and just as described, there's a twin bed on one side and a desk and laptop on the other.

"Please make yourself at home. There isn't a dresser, but the closet is all yours for any clothes. Whenever you're ready, we can go to the store." She turns to leave, and I stop her, needing one more reassurance.

"Am I going to be okay?"

"I won't allow you not to be."

42

Spencer

Nicole has been at my house for two weeks. I find it pleasant to have another female around. I generally like to be alone, but she brings color into my world of black and white.

She's taking Justin's situation better than I would have thought. She's stronger than she realizes, and I hope she uses that strength to get through this bump in the road.

"How's Justin?" Miller looks at me with intense interest. He's been filling in Justin's shifts, and I'm thankful to have someone I know rather than a per diem person. I have nothing against temps, but Miller knows me, and I don't have to mask around him all the time. I'm thankful the chief took that into consideration.

"You know I don't know anything, Miller. He wanted no contact while he's away."

He scoffs. "Yeah, and I know you. There's no way you haven't heard from someone about how he's doing in the two weeks he's been locked up."

"He's not locked up." I side-eye him from the driver's seat

of the ambulance. He's also correct that I haven't strictly followed Justin's request. I've checked in with his doctors to see about his progress. That's the perk of the paperwork he had me sign.

"It's a process, and he's working through it." He nods.

"And, Nicole? How's she doing?"

"She's a trooper. Doing as well as can be expected. She keeps telling me it might be time to return to her apartment, but I know she doesn't want to be alone. I've offered to pick up her car, and she hasn't wanted to do that either. She's only seen a few clients, and Cole usually picks her up and brings her back."

"And her GD?"

"Wonderfully. While I commend Justin for making it easy for her, he didn't teach her how to balance her meals. She went to the doctor a few days ago, and he was happy with her numbers and can stay off insulin."

My phone buzzes in the center console with a new text message.

"Can you check that for me, Miller?"

"As long as you're sure there won't be a dick pic or anything on there?"

"Well you're with me, but if it's Axel I might worry."

"Why would Axel be sending you dick pics?"

"Why do you sound jealous, Miller? Just look at the text for me, please." He picks up the phone and looks at the sender.

"It's Nicole. Should I open it?" I nod and hear him whisper, "Oh shit." How bad could the text be? "Spencer, you might want to pull over and deal with this."

"What's wrong? Is Nicole okay?" Why would she text me if there was an issue?

"Um. She's writing in all caps, and the texts keep coming."

"Well, what is she saying?"

"She's freaking out. She's talking about guns and finding a letter from Justin. Suicide. Spencer, I really think you need to deal with this." *Shit.*

I look behind me, change lanes, and pull into a shopping center ahead.

"I'm going to put this down and let you deal with it. Shit, now she's calling." Miller holds the phone like it's going to explode in his hands. His eyes show fear and panic.

"It's just a phone, Miller. Relax." I pull into the parking lot and find a spot. Miller throws the phone at me and sighs.

"Nicole." I have to pull the phone away from my ear to dampen the screaming. Pushing the speaker button, I place the phone on the dashboard to try to listen.

"What the fuck is this Spencer? Why do you have so many guns? Did you know what this letter said? Who the fuck is Hannah? Was Justin cheating on me? Why aren't you answering any of my questions?" She yells in frustration, and I hear Gage whine in the background.

"Gage, *Ruhig.*" Telling Gage to calm down seems to have the same effect on Nicole because she pauses.

"What did you say to him? He's been pacing around me, but he just stopped."

"I told him to be calm, and I'm asking you the same thing. My shift ends in three hours. Can you stay calm until I get home, and we can discuss everything you just asked of me?"

"Spencer," she whines, and I hear a sob escape her. "Was he cheating on me? There's a note to me and a note to someone named Hannah."

"I don't know who Hannah is, but I do know Justin. He

360

has more integrity than any man I've ever known, and I can promise he was not cheating on you. Trust me, Nicole."

"But then who—"

"I know the envelope you found, but Justin had sealed it before he gave it to me. Only your name was on the outside. Can you hold on for a few more hours, and I can explain all of your other questions? Gage is great at cuddling. If you put *101 Dalmatians* on the TV, he'll curl up next to you and watch. Just pat the couch and use the command for sit."

She inhales a hiccuping sigh. "Okay. I'm not happy, but I understand you're at work. I'm sorry. I panicked. This is a lot."

"I know. I'll see you in three hours."

"Spencer?"

"Yes?" Her next words come out in a whisper as if she's afraid someone else in my empty house will hear her.

"Why do you have so many guns?" I see Miller look my way, probably wondering the same thing.

"Three hours, Nicole." She blows out a breath before agreeing and disconnecting the call.

"Care to share with *me* why you have so many guns? I know you're skilled in them, but I didn't take you for a weaponry girl."

"Miller, I'm a woman, not a girl. I don't know you well enough to tell you about my past, but I will tell you I'm prepared to never repeat it in the future."

"I respect that, and I hope one day I can be in your inner circle, Spencer." Why does a part of me hope that as well?

43

Nicole

"Gage, what should I have for lunch? It looks like your mom made us some chicken wraps. That sounds like a good idea, don't you think?" His ears tip back in response. I don't know why I bother talking to him. I know he only understands German.

Pulling the wraps out of the refrigerator, I take one and return the rest for later. I scour the door for the spicy mustard but only see yellow.

"Your mom seems like a spicy mustard kind of girl. I bet she just ran out and hasn't replaced it yet. Where would she keep the extra condiments?" As I place the wrap on a plate, I look around the kitchen, deciding where to search. I'll check the pantry first; it seems like the most logical place.

"Not in here. Where should I look next, Gage? Oh, I've seen dry goods in the cabinet under the island. Is it there?" When I open the door, I realize I'll have to get lower to the floor to see what's in there. With a heavy sigh, I bend my knees and sit uncomfortably.

"Do you know how to dial 9-1-1 if I get stuck down here?

What am I saying? Of course, you do. That was probably your first lesson." I scratch his ear before looking deeper inside. As I'm shifting things around, my hand bumps something on the top wall of the cabinet.

"What's that?" Bending impossibly further, I lean into the cabinet and almost bump my head in my haste to back out. "What the fuck. Was that a gun? Why does your mom have a gun hidden in the island cabinet?"

Okay, Nicole. Relax. Guns are legal, and I'm sure she has it for protection. Look at the dog she has; Gage isn't a typical house pet. He's probably a trained weapon himself.

"What other secrets is your mom hiding, Gage?" I'm a curious person by nature, and this just piqued my interest. Well, I might as well call a spade a spade. I'm a nosey bitch. I haven't had a reason to snoop because it didn't seem like there was much to look through, but now I know Spencer is tricky.

Standing up from the ground takes some maneuvering, but I make it upright. Gage follows me around the house as I search every cabinet and closet. With each hidden gun I find, my anxiety climbs. I find one in the pantry tucked away high in a corner and another under the bathroom cabinet, just like the kitchen. Her office, where I've been sleeping for the past two weeks, has one hidden like a mobster under the desk.

"Is your mom an undercover cop or something? This is starting to freak me out, Gage." A search of the living room finds yet another gun tucked away under the lip of the coffee table. The only room I haven't looked at yet is Spencer's. Everything in me tells me I shouldn't invade her privacy, but I'm already too far gone.

As I step into her room, Gage makes a sound I can only describe as disapproval. If he tries to stop me, I will. Someone needs to be my conscience, and it's clearly not me.

I check what I think would be the typical places to hide things: under her pillows or between the mattresses. Her nightstand has two drawers, and I can almost guarantee one of them has a gun and the other has what any typical female has in their nightstand drawer. Toys. The question is, which one is which, and do I want to possibly open the wrong one?

"Gage, blink once for the top drawer and twice for the bottom." He looks at me and cocks his head blinking once.

"Once is top. Good...but what does top mean? Did it mean open the top or don't open it? *Dammit*. Why didn't I decide what each blink meant before I asked you, Gage?"

"We'll go with the bottom drawer since the top is easier to reach in a rush." I pull it open ever so slightly, trying to see what's inside without seeing too much. I don't notice any cords or phallic-shaped objects, so I open it further. Laying on top is a manila envelope with my name on it. My finger scrolls across the familiar handwriting that I know intimately to be Justin's. His letters are boxy and always written in all capitals. Nicole. He wrote my name and not my nickname.

I sink onto the bed and pull the letter out. I chuckle as I see a gun under it, but the humor is short-lived, and I turn over the envelope to open it.

"What do you think I'll find in here, Gage? Should I be scared?" My fingers tremble as the adrenaline from my scavenger hunt wears off and the fear of what's inside creeps in.

Pinching the prongs, I lift open the flap and peer inside.

There are two envelopes. I immediately see the blocky PUMPKIN written on one and pull it out. The V-shaped fold slips out easily since it's only tucked in.

My Pumpkin,

If you're reading this, I'm not entirely sure what the circumstances are, and that scares the shit out of me. I owe you so much, and I had hoped that I would be reading this letter to you or burning it because I had already confessed everything that I needed to.

I owe you all of my truths through my trauma if we are going to develop our relationship into something solid and everlasting.

Tomorrow, I'm committing myself to a six-week rehabilitation program that I designed with my doctors. It's going to be hard work, and more than anything, it's going to be lonely.

So much of my life revolves around other people and what I can do to better their lives. I love you, and I love the daughter that you are growing, but if I don't take care of myself and learn to love myself first, I'll never be good enough for either of you.

If you're reading this, I hope it isn't because things got so difficult that Spencer gave this to you, but if you snooped and found it, you might want to run and hide from her.

Let me start at the beginning. I had a sister, and her name was Ivy. When she was five and I was seven, her life ended in my arms.

"Oh Justin." I read on about his sister's passing through blurry eyes and hiccuping sobs. How his father never treated him the same after that day because he could never forgive his son.

Now I understand where the name Ivy came from and why

he knows how to milk a cow.

I got kicked out onto the streets at the age of eighteen like the trash on garbage day. I wasn't allowed to see or say goodbye to my mother. I tried several times over the first year to call home, but no one ever answered the phone until one day, someone finally did. Unfortunately, they informed me it was a new-to-them phone number, and I realized I no longer had any connection to my parents.

I had no connection to anyone. My sister was dead, and my parents had abandoned me. They left me with my sister's life insurance money and threw me out into the world.

The year I was nineteen, I attempted to commit suicide for the first time. My juvenile mind thought that sleeping pills and shitty, cheap vodka would end my sorrows. It didn't. I got a three-day psychiatric hold in a hospital and a diagnosis of depression.

Selfishly, I decided I wanted to do it right next time and became an EMT. I tried to make my life better by helping others. As fulfilling as it was, I lost myself to helping everyone and not me.

A few years later, I found out from a neighbor that my mother had passed away, and my father had turned into a drunk with a failing farm. It didn't help my already plummeting mental health.

Then 9/11 happened. I know we haven't even talked about it, and you probably have no idea I was there, but I believe that's when the rapid decline started. The helper in me went to New York the first opportunity I could. The sheer devastation of what I saw is nothing I could ever put into words. I stayed for a week, helping with any task that I could. No one asked who I was or why I was there. Everyone was there to help. I was invisible but beneficial to whatever they needed me to do.

When I came back, I felt like my purpose was over. Nothing I did felt as substantial as what I did while I was in NYC. I worked as an EMT and still enjoyed what I did, but it was never enough.

My medication was constantly changing to help chase my demons away. Nothing ever quite fit to make me whole, and I got to a point where I couldn't take it anymore.

Nine years after my first attempt and lots of training and research, I was ready to end my life again. I had a plan and was ready. I had prepared to leave. I took the appropriate pills this time in just the right combination and drifted off to sleep and a final oblivion. Or so I thought. A nosy little girl who wouldn't take no for an answer saved me.

Oh my god. The pain he's gone through. I need to calm my breathing and crying or I won't be able to get through the rest of this. Patting the bed next to me, I tell Gage to sit. He pauses for a moment before jumping up and curling next to me. I run my hands down the soft fur on his back.

"I knew you understood English. Thank you for sitting with me, Gage." I take several minutes to compose myself before continuing to read. "Who saved you, Justin? Tell me about her."

Katy. Her name was Katy. She was a neighbor kid who liked coming over and watching me play the piano. She came over that day and wanted to play. I blew her off, but she returned a little while later, unaffected by my dismissal. She found me and screamed. Katy saved my life and brought me Spencer. She was the paramedic who came to my house.

I died twice in the hospital that night. Spencer never left my side. Ask her about it. I'm sure her version of the story is clearer than mine. You can show her this if she tells you it isn't her story to tell. It's just as much hers as mine.

Katy may have saved me, but Spencer brought me back to life, literally and figuratively. She never let me quit. She helped me train to be a paramedic. I slept in her guest room for weeks. I'll forever be grateful for Spencer.

I was content with the life I've lived for the last six years. Then you came along, and with a slap and a kiss, you rocked my world both for the good and the bad.

I lost myself in you. It's to no fault of your own, so please don't feel any guilt. I did it to myself, and I don't regret anything I've done for you. I regret neglecting myself and my body. I know the signs of my mental health declining, and I was ignoring them. Spencer tried to help and warn me, and I did what little I had to do to appease her, but it wasn't enough.

Please don't think for one moment that I don't want our daughter. I want her with every fiber of my being. I want to be her father, and I want to be your partner in whatever way you will have me.

My life is incomplete without my basic white bitch, Pumpkin. I have more to look forward to than living day by day. I have two beautiful girls that need me, and I love you both with all my heart. I love you, Pumpkin. I love you, Nicole Alivia McGrath.

Please know that I make every decision from now on with respect for myself and love for you. Times are hard right now, but I hope we will have a bright future.

I really wish that you aren't actually reading this. I don't know the outcome of what my six weeks will be. I don't know that I'll be ready to be who you deserve, but please know that every day, I'm trying to be him for you and for our daughter.

Please be patient with me. I love you.

XO Justin

I drop the letter and bury myself in Gage's fur. He sighs, and I think he can feel my anguish. When I shift on the bed, I hear a crinkle and remember there was another letter in the envelope. Using the back of my hand, I wipe my eyes and attempt to compose myself. I wonder if the other letter is for Spencer? It would make sense since I'm sure he feels terrible from what he mentions of her in my letter. He has so many people in his corner. I wish he would use us.

As I pull out the second letter, I'm shocked to see a name written that isn't Spencer's. It's a name that doesn't belong to anyone I know.

"What the fuck. Who's Hannah?" I begin to pace the room, wracking my brain of all the people I know. Could it be someone else he works with? One of his doctors? Maybe Spencer's real name is Hannah, and she goes by her middle name?

"Spencer." Gage jumps off the bed, hearing Spencer's name. "I'll call Spencer. Shit. She's working." I can text her, but what if she's on a call? Why the hell does everyone always keep secrets from me? I'm not a fragile flower. I won't break at the first big wind gust. This is fucking ridiculous. I need answers, and I need them now. Justin obviously can't give them to me, so his best friend is the next best thing. I stomp too loudly into the living room after grabbing my phone off the kitchen island.

Me: Spencer, I need to talk to you NOW.

Me: Or when you aren't busy.

Me: BUT SOONER RATHER THAN LATER.

Me: SPENCER I FOUND YOUR GUNS. WHY DO YOU HAVE SO MANY?

Me: I FOUND A LETTER FROM JUSTIN. SUICIDE!?!?

Me: THIS IS TOO FUCKING MUCH FOR ONE PERSON TO DEAL WITH.

I give up and call her. If she's busy, she won't answer. Just before the voicemail picks up, she answers.

"Nicole." I go off on a rant with Spencer making every attempt to appease me. Finally, she tempts me with a cuddly Gage and a *Disney* movie, and I relent. I can keep my crazy in check while she finishes her shift for the next three hours.

44

Spencer

What the crap has Justin gotten me into now? Nicole has so many questions that I don't know the answers to, but I'll help her navigate through this like I promised Justin I would.

"Are you going to be alright? Do you want me to come in with you?" I thought maybe Nicole would like some freedom after her realizations today. Justin gave me the keys before he left, so Miller drove me to his house, and we picked up Nicole's car.

"I have to do this alone, but I appreciate your offer. I'll see you in the morning. You'll be on time to pick me up, correct?" He raises two fingers in the air.

"I do solemnly promise I will be on time, Smithy."

"You don't even deserve the eye roll I want to give you." He gives me a megawatt smile and gets back in his car. When Miller found out I had a love of guns, we went to the shooting range together. He was impressed with my knowledge and shooting ability but was enamored when he saw my charcoal ruby-handled S&W J round boot. Now, he occasionally calls me Smithy. It could be a worse nickname, so I don't complain. Since he heard Nicole's call, he has even more knowledge of my collection.

As I unlock the door, I wonder what Nicole's emotional state will be. I've prepared myself the last several hours for tears or rage. I assume there will be no in-between. The door softly clicks behind me and locks, and I see a ball of fluff peek its head out over the arm of the couch. Nicole is lying under my fluffy black blanket that usually hangs over the couch and appears to be asleep.

Mild relief washes over me, knowing I have more time to prepare her barrage of questions I know are coming. I raise my palm in the air to Gage, signaling him to stay, and he rests his head on the arm of the couch.

My house looks like a tornado went off inside. Cabinets and doors are wide open. There's an uneaten chicken wrap on the counter and a cabinet door open on the island. That must have been the first gun she found. I clean up the mess, and assuming she hasn't eaten, I quietly prepare us a meal.

"Spencer?"

"I'm here." She shifts on the couch, and Gage comes to stand by me.

"What time is it? How long have I been asleep?" She wipes at her eyes and runs her hands through her unruly curls.

"I've been home for about two hours. I don't know when you fell asleep. I made dinner. Check your numbers, and we can eat."

"Yeah, okay." She slowly stands from the couch, and the blanket drops off her shoulders. As she bends to pick it up, she pauses. "Wait. You're home. We need to talk."

"Food first. I don't think you've eaten much today, and

you'll be better to talk to once you've eaten and your sugar levels are evened out." I can see on her face she wants to object but realizes I'm right. Sliding her supply pouch across the island, she approaches with a small smile.

"Thank you."

We eat in companionable silence. I made grilled chicken with potatoes and roasted carrots. I'm honestly shocked Nicole slept through the entire cooking process.

When her last bite is finished, she puts her napkin on the table and leans back in her seat. "I've been patient, and I'm about to explode if I don't get some answers."

"Where would you like to start?"

"The guns. I have a healthy respect for them, but I counted six that I found around the house. That seems excessive." I chuckle, and she looks at me like I'm crazy.

"If you only found six, you didn't look hard enough."

Her jaw drops. "There's more? This isn't a big house. How many more can there be?"

"It's better if you don't know." Nine guns are hidden in various places in my small pool house.

"Why?" Sighing heavily, I pick up our plates and walk to the kitchen. The dishes clank as they drop into the sink, and I turn the water on.

"It's a long story that I'd rather not tell. I was in a bad situation for many years, and I don't ever want to feel powerless again. My father is a retired police detective. All the guns are legally registered, and I am fully trained to fire all of them." I see her look out the window to the house at the front of the garage.

"You mentioned your dad lives up there. I've never seen him."

"He does, but he keeps to himself, and I keep to mine. We both value our privacy. What did the letter say from Justin?" I wash the dishes as she ponders what to say.

"He said so much. I don't even know where to begin. I think he told me everything. At least that's the impression I got." Good for him, and for her. It's about time he let her in. I just hope it's not too late.

"Do you need clarification on anything?"

"Why?"

"That's a loaded question, Nicole. Is there something specific you're asking about?"

"He told me you stayed with him in the hospital after he tried to end his life the second time." I can hear the crack in her voice and imagine her eyes welling with tears, but I don't turn from the sink. "Why did you stay with a total stranger? You helped him become a paramedic. You didn't owe him anything."

"I wish there was a better answer than it felt like something I needed just as much as he did." I place the last dish in the drying rack and finally turn around. "Shall we sit on the couch?" Nicole nods, and we sit with Gage between us, his head on her lap.

"I don't understand. Could you try to explain it more?"

"I saw a broken man, but not an irreparable one. Did he tell you in the letter the only words he spoke to me that night?" She shakes her head, and I try not to relive that memory. "He said, 'I'm not ready.'" Her breath hitches and she covers her face with her hands. I let her cry, knowing she's getting comfort from Gage.

"I had a time in my life when I had similar thoughts of killing myself. I was too afraid to go through with it, but

Justin wasn't afraid to change his mind and chose life. If I had a friend back then, someone to help me through the hardest time of my life, I might have gotten out of my situation sooner and have fewer mental scars."

Her tears flow freely now, but I know they come from a place of empathy.

"Do you..." she trails off. Pushing her shoulders back, she tries again. "Do you know who Hannah is?"

"I truly don't. I've never heard Justin mention anyone by that name before." Her face falls. What have you done, Justin? This almost makes me want to try and talk to him. She looks devastated, and I can't blame her. Hearing the importance of the things he wrote in her letter, I can only imagine what he wrote to Hannah. He didn't mention who the letter should go to in the event of...

"Do you want to open it?"

Her emotions war on her face. "I do, and I don't. Justin made it clear in his letter that he hoped I wouldn't read it. He wanted to tell me these things on his own terms. I feel guilty about snooping and seeing it when I shouldn't have." She looks up, directly into my eyes. "I am truly sorry for searching through your stuff. I never should have done that."

"Nicole, I told you to make yourself at home. This is your house, too. I probably should have warned you about the guns, and for that, I'm sorry." Silent tears fall down her cheeks as she rubs Gage's ear between her thumb and forefinger. "Was he good to you today? I've never seen him take to anyone as easily as you. Not even Justin." Gage nudges Nicole's belly as if giving a reason why he cares for her.

A smile tilts at the corner of her lip. "He's such a good boy. He really does like that movie." Nicole sighs heavily and attempts to dry her face with the back of her free hand.

"Is there anything else I can answer for you? I wish I could answer the question I know is weighing heaviest in your heart. I'm sure Justin has a reason why there's a letter in there addressed to someone neither of us knows. It's just over three weeks, and you can ask him yourself."

"I hope that's true. Justin said he might not be ready even when he gets out." Oh Justin. This poor woman deserves better than that.

"Nicole, you deserve answers, if for nothing else than to explain that letter to you. I'll make sure it happens."

45

Nicole

Home. It's such a relative term. What makes a home? The location? The atmosphere? The people in it? I've had many homes over the past several months, but none have felt as right as they did when I was at Justin's house with him and my puppies. I miss the normalcy of my life before Justin, and I know it's terrible to say because I wouldn't change anything that's happened since. But some days, I miss the struggle of deciding who gets the better meal, the dogs or me. How many appointments can I squeeze in this week because rent is due? What color will I paint my toenails next, or what panties will someone ask me to send them?

It's such a silly thing to miss. Who misses paying bills?

I was informed Justin took care of everything I could need before he went away when I called my landlord to pay rent. I was angry at first because he did it without asking, but I realized it was his way of showing he still cared even if he couldn't physically be here for me and the baby.

My apartment. My home. However, it feels like a

temporary home now. As much as I enjoyed and appreciated staying at Spencer's house, I needed to come back. There's a realistic possibility that I may be raising this baby on my own. I'm not Spencer's burden, despite all of her protests. I missed my puppers and I need to make a home for us and my daughter.

"Did you want to keep the bed in here?" Axel snaps me out of my daze and points to the queen-sized mattress in the spare room.

"Um. I suppose not. It doesn't leave much room for a crib or rocking chair. Maybe I should look into a comfortable couch or oversize chair."

When I told Spencer I needed to move back to my apartment, she insisted we plan a day to create a nursery for my daughter.

Julia? Casey? Valerie? Nothing seems right. I keep toying around with names in my head, but they all fall flat. I can't make this decision without Justin, no matter what our relationship ends up as. She's half of him.

This morning, Spencer, Axel, Cole, and Miller showed up at my door ready to work, and with more boxes filled with baby necessities than I could fathom was possible. I haven't bought anything for her yet, and I burst into tears seeing everything they had brought. Cole told me some was a present from Annie and Blake. Spencer informed me she used Justin's black card to purchase the rest. When I tried to protest, she assured me he would be upset with her if she hadn't used it.

The buzz around my apartment is full of energy while furniture gets built and swapped. I have music playing, beer in the fridge, and pizza on the counter.

Despite all the distractions, my mind keeps wandering to the thought that Justin gets out in three days, and I have no idea what that means for me. For us.

"Hey, big sis. The girls are almost here. Give us your last-minute instructions, and when you get back from your pedicure, we will have this nursery ready for my niece. If you're still looking for names, Colmina sounds great."

"I'm not even going to humor you on that one. I honestly don't care how the room gets set up. I'm grateful for you all, and I know it will look beautiful. And the thought of getting my feet rub trumps everything else right now." Cole kisses my forehead and rubs my belly.

"I've got you, big sis. I'll walk you outside."

"I want to marry whoever's idea this was." My legs have been massaged, wrapped in wax, lotioned, and heated with towels. I think I've melted into the seat.

"This was Blake's idea, but your brother might object to a marriage." Annie looks just as relaxed as I do but more radiant than is fair.

"Are you ready, Annie?" Her eyes are closed, and her hands rub circles over her bump absently.

"What choice do I have? They have their eviction date in three days." I can't help but laugh at her description of their birth.

Blake leans over and takes one of Annie's hands. "We're ready for Ruby and...Robert?"

"No double R names." Annie doesn't open her eyes as she protests Blake's baby name suggestion.

"You still haven't picked a name out for him yet?" I don't have a name for my little nugget either, so I shouldn't question them.

"Annie rejects everything we suggest, even if it's not an R name." There's a joking tone in Blake's voice as she ribs Annie.

"I'll know it when I hear it; if not, we'll decide when we see him."

Blake groans and flops back in her massage chair. "But how are we supposed to get cute, adorable monogrammed matching outfits if we don't know his name?"

"Darling, they will look just as adorable without monograms."

"But not *cute* and adorable. There's a difference." Annie sighs, and her belly rises and falls dramatically. She sucks in a breath and holds it before slowly releasing it.

"Annie, are you okay?"

"I'm fine. It's just Braxton Hicks contractions." She dismisses my question with a wave of a hand.

"Baby, are you still having those? How often are they coming?" Blake's face is riddled with concern.

"You sound as frantic as Cole. It's fine. I'm still four and a half weeks from my due date. They're just moving around a lot. There isn't much room in here." She rubs at her belly, and I can almost see it harden as she holds her breath again.

"Oh no. No, you don't. I'm calling the doctor. I don't care if it's *eight* weeks before your due date. I don't like the looks of that." I agree with Blake. At least we're almost done with our pedicures.

Me: Annie is having Braxton Hicks that seem to be coming

pretty regularly. Blake is calling the doctor.

Moments later, Annie's phone rings, and she shoots me a look before answering.

"You tattled on me to Cole?" I should have known he'd call her immediately. I mouth "sorry" while Annie tries to calm Cole down, and Blake talks to the doctor's office.

The anxiety in the air around us increases. Annie can't have a natural delivery because of the injuries she sustained to her hip in the car accident last year. From the sound of things, we're taking a trip to labor and delivery.

Not one but two beautiful babies lay in Annie's arms with Blake and Cole on either side of her, staring in awe. Her Braxton Hicks were actual contractions, and the babies made their debut a few days earlier than expected.

"They're beautiful guys. Did you decide on a name for baby boy?" I'm not sure what I said, but Annie burst into tears. "Oh my gosh. What did I say? I'm so sorry." Annie cries while Blake and Cole try not to laugh. I'm so confused.

"It just suits him. I saw him and knew his name." Annie kisses the baby's head with the little bow. "This is Ruby." She switches sides and kisses the other baby's head. "This is Rory."

"Ruby and Rory. Two R's." Now I understand the crying and laughing. "They're both beautiful names, Annie."

"Let it all out. All three of you. This is the one time I'm permitting you to laugh. I know I was adamant about no double letter names, and I'll admit when I'm wrong." The room glows with our laughter. Even Annie joins in.

It's a joyous occasion, but as I look at the pure love on my brother's face, I can't help feeling a tinge of sadness for myself.

46

Justin

Oه hour. Sixty minutes. Three thousand six hundred seconds. That's how much longer I have until I walk out of the building I've called home for the last six weeks. I've done the work. I detoxed from my previous medications and found a new regimen that works. I've attended the one-on-one and group therapy sessions. I'm a model patient on paper.

Do I feel better? That's debatable. I feel stable, and that's where I need to be with my medication. The rest is up to me to do myself.

Annie had her babies two days ago. Despite my no contact request, I got the message from Spencer through Garret, but I'm not mad about it. I'm happy for them and plan to find a time to visit as soon as I get my phone back.

I need to see Nicole. I want to see Nicole. But, despite my needs and wants, I don't feel ready. I do, however, feel like a complete asshole. I need to get my shit together before I miss the birth of my daughter.

"Are you all packed?" I look up to see Garret standing in

my doorway.

"You sure I can't stay another two weeks?"

He arches a brow at me. "Do you *want* to stay another two weeks?"

"No." I tilt my head towards the window. "It's just a big world out there that I can't control. Inside here, in this environment, I can."

"Justin, you have all of the coping skills that you need. Hell, you run group sessions here better than the counselors you saw. The only thing holding you back is you."

"I know. I'm always the problem."

"You're also the solution. That's what you need to focus on. Keep open lines of communication with those closest to you, and I'm always here if you need more."

"Thanks, Garret. Is Spencer here yet?"

"You know she is." I do. She's probably been here for a while.

I hesitate to ask the next question, but I need to be prepared. "Is she alone?"

"She is. Were you expecting her to be?" Was I? Did I want Nicole to be here?

"Honestly, I'm not sure. I have no idea what I'm returning to. I have to deal with Nicole's feelings eventually, but having more time to process them is ideal."

"I understand that. Let's not keep Spencer waiting. All of your discharge paperwork is at the desk, ready for you to sign." I sling my backpack over my shoulder, grab the handle of my rolling suitcase, and we leave the sterile-looking room.

"Third time's a charm."

"You got this, Justin."

When we reach the front desk, Spencer greets me with a

384

smile. Despite Garret saying Spencer was alone, I still look around the waiting room.

"She isn't here." I don't need to say anything for her to understand who I was looking for. Spencer leans in and hugs me. She feels like home as much as Nicole did in my arms. *Does.* As much as Nicole *does* in my arms. I will have her back as long as she allows me.

"Is she still with Cole?" Spencer chuckles, and I give her a look.

"She didn't last long there. Her brother and his girlfriends have a very active and loud sex life that she didn't want to be privy to on a regular basis."

"Oh god. I can only imagine. Did she go back to her apartment?" Poor Nicole. Having to hear her brother doing things a sibling doesn't want to think about was probably mildly traumatizing.

"Not right away. She spent a few weeks at my house. Nicole won over Gage. It was a sight to see."

"Gage?" Spencer's dog is impressive, but he gives his trust sparingly.

"He fell in love with her. But I have to warn you, she's been through a lot the past several weeks." She pauses, giving herself or me a moment before she continues. "She found your envelope and a bunch of my guns. But she read your letter you wrote to her." *Oh fuck.* "And we are both pretty curious who Hannah is."

"She didn't open Hannah's letter?"

"Why would she? Her first thought was you cheated on her. I can't blame her for jumping to that conclusion when she sees another woman's name on an envelope right next to the one addressed to her. Tell me I didn't make a liar out of myself by assuring Nicole you'd never cheat on her."

"Spencer, you know me." Does she think so little of me? Have I lost that much respect? "I have never and would never cheat on anyone, let alone Nicole. I love and respect that woman more than anything."

"Not more than yourself, Justin. Remember that." I turn to see Garret still standing at the desk behind me. "I didn't mean to eavesdrop, but you still need to sign the paperwork. You might own the place, but rules are rules, and I happen to know the boss is a stickler." He smiles and winks at me, and I return his gesture with an eye roll.

"Give me the papers, Garret." I quickly sign everything, and Spencer and I head towards the door.

"My house or yours?" She shoots me a look that I know says, "That's not even a real question."

"I added a twin bed in the office for Nicole, so you've been upgraded from the couch."

"Such a privilege. Thank you. How come you never added a bed for me in all the months I lived there?"

"You weren't pregnant, and I think I like her more. Gage definitely does." I throw my arm around her shoulder and laugh at her ribbing.

"I missed you, Spencer."

It's been a week since I left the rehab center. Most days, I'm on autopilot and perfectly okay with the monotony. Spencer and I work together; I help make people's lives better in that moment, and we go home. Rinse and repeat.

I pick up my phone and start a text to Nicole about a

hundred times a day but always delete it. Spencer has been talking to her, and she keeps telling Nicole I'm not ready. I'm doubting everything right now.

I struggled to start an IV yesterday, and Spencer had to take over. I miscounted the meds at the end of our shift the day prior. If I was working with anyone other than Spencer, I'd be in deep shit. She understands there's an adjustment period for reentering the real world after a stay in rehab.

"Justin, I think it's time to talk to Nicole." Me too.

"I'm not sure I'm ready, Spence. She deserves better than me. I want her to be happy."

"You make her happy. *You*. And she makes you happy. You can't wait until life isn't hard anymore to be happy. It's always going to be hard. Let yourself enjoy life. You're about to be half of a whole person."

"Well, aren't you a modern-day Socrates? Where did all of that come from?"

"It was yesterday's *Family Circus* comic." Spencer pulls into the Fire Department parking lot, and I sigh with relief. I'm exhausted. Working the night shift is something my body will never get used to.

"Looks like we have company." Standing around the open bay doors is a group of young freshmen.

"CPR day. Now I'm glad we were on nights and don't have to deal with this today." The local high school sends their freshman health class here to learn CPR every semester.

We pull the ambulance into the bay and quickly count the meds we used during our shift. We don't want to get roped into helping teach the angsty teens. They're always ungrateful.

When we're finished, we sneak around the front of the bay

in an attempt to avoid the crowd. We get lucky and make it into the locker rooms. I think we've made it without being noticed, but the chief calls me into his office.

"I'll meet you in the car, Spence." She nods, grabs her bag, and leaves the room.

"Hey Chief, you called?"

"How's it going, Webb? First week back. Things going well?"

"All good, Chief. All good." I'm not sure he looks convinced, but he nods towards his door, dismissing me. That was easy. I walk down the stairs of the Eagle's Nest without thinking and stumble into the group of teens learning how to check for a pulse on the necks of their dummies.

"Shit." As I hit the last step, I almost trip over one of the kids' Annie dolls but manage to do a funny spin and land on my ass.

"Damn, Jay. You alright?" One of the new recruits offers me his hand. I try not to look any of the kids in the eyes, already knowing they will have fun sharing the story of the dumb, old guy who tripped and fell on the stairs.

"Jay?" A young female voice says my name from the back of the group. I scan the crowd of kids, wondering where it came from. Finally, I see a face that looks vaguely familiar and stop. Dark hair and light brown eyes stare back at me from a girl wearing a red sweater and jeans.

She's all grown up now. Does she remember me? I'll never forget her.

"Mr. Jay?" Her hopeful eyes brim with tears.

"Katy." There's no question in my voice. This is the little girl that saved my life six years ago. I never saw her again after that day. My apartment was packed up and put into storage by Spencer.

"You're…alive." Oh god. She's thought this entire time that I was dead? How traumatizing must that have been for her?

"I'm so sorry, Katy. I didn't even think to have someone reach out to you." I find myself standing in front of her. My feet taking me across the room without my permission.

"Everything okay, Webb?" We must be making a scene.

"All good, cadette. I need to talk to this student for a minute." I touch Katy's shoulder and nod up the stairs that I just made a fool out of myself over. She follows me up the stairs, and we sit together on one of the couches in the Eagle's Nest.

Me: I'll grab another ride home. Gotta take care of something.

Spencer: I'll be up a while if you need a ride.

"How are you? How have you been? I feel like I'm seeing a ghost." I take her hand and cup it between mine. I don't care what it looks like to anyone around me. They have no idea what this young woman did for my life.

"I'm good, Katy. Wonderful actually. I'm about to have a daughter." Her face lights up and her eyes glance at my left hand before returning to my face. I smile and shake my head. "Not married yet, but I'm hopeful. How are you?"

"I'm good. School sucks. The usual." She shrugs one shoulder and gives me a small smile. Her eyes are still glazed over, but no tears have been shed. She says in a barely perceivable whisper, "You're here."

"I'm here…because of you. You saved me that day, Katy. You barged into my apartment unannounced, not taking no

389

for an answer, and you saved me."

She shakes her head. "All I did was scream. I was so scared, and I just screamed. Someone else called 9-1-1. I didn't do anything."

"You did *everything*. What made you come back? I sent you away and told you to come back the next day. You didn't even wait fifteen minutes." Finally, her tears fall, and I feel like I'm right behind her.

"You looked sad. I didn't often see you happy, but that day, I could tell you were really sad." She sighs and chews on her bottom lip. "When I first started showing up at your door after hearing your keyboard, you didn't question it. My mom would never even know I was missing. I just needed to escape her yelling and screaming at her boyfriend."

"I knew. I heard it too and wanted to provide you a safe place." Her mother would often get drunk and forget about Katy. The mac n cheese stocked in my pantry was always for her. Nothing soothes the soul better than a piano melody and some cheesy pasta, especially for a seven year old.

"You were so much more. I didn't realize until you were gone. Your apartment was cleaned out, and I never saw you again. I thought you were..."

"I am truly so sorry. I went to a rehabilitation center for three months. My mental health was terrible. My friend had everything packed up for me while I was away, and I stayed with her when I got out, and I guess I never looked back at my old life."

"I understand. I was just an annoying kid always knocking on your door."

"Not at all. When you would come by, and I could put a smile on your face, it would make my day so much better. I always appreciated you. Even at seven, you were wise beyond your years." Katy throws herself into my arms and hugs my neck. I return the hug and feel her back shudder with her crying.

"You were more of a dad than I ever had in the year you lived there. You cared about my feelings and my well-being. Your mac n cheese was the best I ever ate, and the funny songs we made up together still play in my head. You taught me how to survive."

"I did?" I never tried to do anything but give her some solace in her shitty situation. She was a good kid and never caused me any trouble. Singing with her was fun.

She pulls away and her light brown eyes stare me down.

"You did. I cried for two weeks straight after I saw you leave in the ambulance. And for months, I would close my eyes if I had to walk past your apartment. My mom started buying me boxes of mac n cheese because she realized that was the only thing that made me feel better. I learned how to make it for myself while standing on a kitchen chair." A chuckle escapes me as I imagine the adorable pigtailed girl standing on a chair, stirring a pot.

"You've always been the Angel on my shoulder, Katy. The look on your face when you screamed haunts my dreams. Sometimes, I wondered if I imagined it or if I was only remembering it because Spencer told me you screamed."

"Spencer?"

"The female paramedic that came to my rescue. We're friends now. You screamed, and she came. Seeing you now, I know I must have had a few moments of consciousness. You cared. You cared that I was lying there and you couldn't wake me. I felt like I had no one, but I had you. Thank you."

"You did." We both laugh and hug again. When we pull away this time, she looks sad. "This is going to sound really weird to say, but I love you. And not in the weird, icky schoolgirl crush way. In the father-daughter way. You really were the best one I ever had."

A father. She thought I was a good father at the lowest point in my life.

"All I did was make you some $.59 boxed noodles with powdered cheese. That's hardly father material."

"Mr. Jay—"

"Justin. My name is Justin." Her smile widens.

"Justin, you nurtured a seven year old kid that you didn't even have to give the time of day. If you treat your daughter with any amount of the love you showed me, I'd consider her a lucky girl."

Her statement makes my heart crack open. The raw vulnerability of her confession cuts deeply into the inadequacies of my impending fatherhood.

Tears stream down our faces, and I look around the room, realizing I'm surrounded by a firehouse full of men who probably wouldn't find this too manly.

"I'm sorry for all the crying, Katy. I know it's not macho for a guy to cry."

"You never used to care what other people's opinions of you were. You just cared. I hope that's still the case."

I huff a laugh. "So many damn smart women in my life." Her brows furrow as she tries to understand my statement. "I'm just an idiot. Would you mind if I gave you my phone number? I might need a babysitter in a couple of years." Her smile brightens at the topic change.

"I'd love that."

47

Nicole

Three days. Then, six weeks. Now, another week plus. How much patience is someone expected to be able to have? Mine is now nonexistent.

My due date is rapidly approaching, and Justin is still avoiding me. The letter, with an unknown woman's name on it, burns a hole in the side of my head despite being tucked in the back of a drawer in the bathroom.

"Girls, I'm done. I need answers, and only one person can give them to me." Grabbing my keys, I look down at my outfit. I never got the pregnancy glow; I got the whale glow. Just call me Olga the Orca.

My oversize T-shirt is accented by black leggings. I walk to the front door and slide my bare feet into the only shoes I can manage on my own, my rainbow checkered slip-ons. I complete my look with a hoodie, covering my huge belly, and plop my unruly curls on the top of my head with a scrunchie. Homeless prego-girl chique.

"I don't have to look hot to find out who my man's other woman is, right Beans?" Sighing, I stalk to the bathroom to grab the letter I want nothing to do with.

HANNAH, written in Justin's handwriting, stares back at me. I want to crush it, burn it, and shove it down the garbage disposal. A little paw scrapes my ankle, and I look down to see Java blinking up at me.

"I'm okay, little girl. Thanks for checking on me." I'd reach down to pet her, but I'm pretty sure I couldn't get back up.

"Let's do this, Nicole." I try giving myself a pep talk, but it's useless. My adrenaline courses through my body so hard, I drop my keys trying to lock the door. I drop them again when I make it to my car, but they can stay on the floor because I need to push the button to start it.

I head toward Spencer's house since she told me Justin is staying with her. They're on nights and should hopefully still be awake when I get there.

Pulling into the familiar driveway, I see Spencer and Justin's vehicles parked beside each other. They're both here.

I can do this.

I can do this.

My hand hovers over the letter sitting on the passenger seat. It taunts me with its block letters.

I'm getting answers right now.

When I approach the front door, I debate whether to knock or walk in. I hate that I have to think of that. For weeks, I walked in and out whenever I wanted, but he's here now. It doesn't feel right.

The door opens in front of me, and I look up in surprise. Spencer stares at me with a blank expression.

"How did—" She points to the doorbell camera, and I close my eyes. Duh.

"I need to talk to him, Spencer, and I'm not taking no for

an answer." I raise my hand with the half-crushed letter. "I need to know now."

She steps back to allow me to enter. As I walk in, her words crush me. "He's not here." I whip around, almost losing my balance. Spencer catches me by my forearms, steadying me.

"Sorry. My center of gravity is way off. What do you mean he isn't here? His truck is here."

"We carpooled to work, but he got stuck at the station and said he'd find his own way home."

"Oh." I can feel the adrenaline rushing out of me. He's not here. He could be here in five minutes or five hours. I walk over to the island and sit on a stool, resting my head in my hands. Spencer follows me into the kitchen and pulls things out of the refrigerator.

"What are you doing?"

"Cooking."

"Spencer." I sigh out her name because she's being intentionally aloof. "Let me be more specific. What are you cooking and why?"

"Vegetable omelets because I know you well enough to know that you were single-minded this morning and either didn't eat at all or didn't eat properly." Am I that easy to read? I had coffee and a few pieces of leftover bacon from the BLT I made yesterday.

I place my fisted hand on the counter and slowly release the tension in my fingers until the letter falls from my grip. Spencer snatches it without a word, and as much as I want to protest, I already feel some relief not having it staring at me.

"I can make you a decaf coffee if you'd like." She pauses from cutting the peppers and looks over her shoulder, waiting for a response. I bounce in my seat like a child and huff.

"Decaf is boring," I whine.

"Decaf tastes the same with all the flavoring you put in it."

"Yes, mother. I'll take a coffee."

"A decaf coffee."

"Ugh. A decaf coffee. Fine." I've missed our witty banter. Talking to my dogs that don't talk back doesn't quite have the same fulfillment. Spencer reaches into the cabinet above the coffee maker and pulls out a decaf pumpkin coffee pod. The next cabinet holds my favorite coffee mug, and with the push of a few buttons, the smell of pumpkin and cinnamon invades my senses.

"You know the way to my heart, Spencer." She pulls the vanilla almond milk from the fridge and slides it in front of me, along with my coffee cup. Her phone buzzes, and she responds to a text. When she returns to the refrigerator and grabs a few additional eggs, I know.

"Was that..."

"He'll be here in fifteen minutes. Whatever you have to say to each other can wait until after we all eat. Baby comes first right now. You're too close to your due date to mess with your sugar levels. Understood?"

"Yes, Mother," I mock again.

My stomach starts to flutter with nerves. I was ready to confront him when I got here, but all of my bravery is gone. I haven't seen him in almost two months. Pulling at the hem of my hoodie, I wonder what he'll think of how I look. I feel huge.

"You're beautiful, and he'll think the same. Stop fretting."

"It's so freaky when you do that, Spencer." She turns and

places a restaurant worthy omelet in front of me—my mouth waters at the sight.

"I have to understand people's mannerisms and facial expressions. I don't always understand their emotions from their tone of voice. It's a coping mechanism that serves me well in the medical field. People don't always say what they mean, but their body language will give them away."

"Well, you're terrible at picking up flirting," I mumble the comment more to myself, but of course, she hears me. My fork cuts into the egg perfection like melted butter. It's fluffy and full of veggies. My eyes roll back into my head at the first taste.

"What do you mean? Who's flirting?" I turn my head to my left as she sits beside me at the island.

"Seriously? You have two hunky men that fall all over you." Her brows furrow, and she looks down at her plate in concentration.

"Two?"

"Um, yeah. Have you not seen the way—" My head snaps to the front door at the sound of the lock clicking. He's here.

"Eat, Nicole. Remember. Food first." Food first. Baby first.

He must know I'm here. There's no way to miss my car in the driveway, but I'm sure Spencer warned him. I hear shuffling as he takes off his shoes. The jingling of his keys as he lays them in the dish on the entry table frazzles my nerves. His footsteps sound heavier than I'm used to.

Spencer stands and takes a plate out of the microwave that I didn't notice she put there. She places a third omelet to her left, putting herself in between us. Justin's footsteps stop just before he leaves the foyer and enters the main room where we'll be able to see each other.

What is he thinking? Is he deciding if he should leave? My body tries to stand, and Spencer puts her hand on my leg.

"Eat." That's the last thing I want to do right now. My body is vibrating with the need to see him. To look into his eyes and see if there's still a place in his heart for me. Because I'll know, I know this man's heart.

He finally enters the room, and I stare back at my plate, not wanting to give away how anxious I am to see him. Touch him. Be his everything.

No, Nicole. You need answers. Think about Hannah. Who the hell is Hannah? HANNAH. The letters that have haunted you for weeks without answers. That's why you're here.

"Justin, I'm going to tell you the same thing I told her. Eat first, talk after. She needs to feed that baby properly." I see him give her a curt nod out of the corner of my eye. He pauses to look at me before he sits. That two-second look was all it took to bang on the walls of my dwindling resolve.

Answers, Nicole. Answers.

The once delicious omelet now tastes like chalk in my mouth and helps fuel my need to be angry. His presence has taken away my desire to eat, and if I didn't have a general baseline of fear for Spencer, I'd stop trying to pretend and throw it away.

The last bite is the hardest to swallow, and I chase it with the last of my coffee. Standing, I take my plate and mug to the sink to wash. I hear Justin gasp when he gets the first glimpse of my belly. Despite the oversize hoodie, my roundness still protrudes.

Was his gasp a sign of disgust? Shock?

I scrub my dishes longer than I need to, wanting to prolong the inevitable. I wish Spencer wasn't so clean and washed things as she went. I could use something else to do. When Spencer steps next to me with her plate, I eagerly grab it, thankful for more to distract me. She places her hand on my shoulder with a squeeze and speaks only loud enough for me to hear.

"I'll be in my room if you need me. Do you want me to take Gage or leave him out here with you?" I'm floored by her offer.

"Here, please." She nods and walks off, telling him to stay. I hear the soft click of her door and feel Gage's heat on my legs.

I feel Justin's presence behind me before he says a word. His plate hovers over the sink, and I take it silently.

"Can I dry?" My head dips lower as I nod. My emotions war between anger, rage, need and love.

He dries the dishes and too quickly, there's nothing left to wash, and everything is put away. I turn, leaning on the sink, and cross my arms over my chest. I see Justin's hand move and hover towards my bump.

"May I?" I want to say no, but every fiber of my being yearns for his touch, even if it's just for our daughter, so I nod. The warmth of his hand, when it makes contact with my hoodie, feels like fire. His hand moves slowly back and forth, and I close my eyes.

Hesitantly, I reach for the hem of my hoodie and slowly lift it, along with my shirt. I expose my pregnancy belly to him in its entirety. I feel him shift, and a second-hand rubs soothingly along my bump.

"You're beautiful, Pumpkin." The nickname is both a balm and a knife to my heart. I've longed to hear it again, but it somehow feels tainted.

"Tell me who she is?" I have to get it out before I drown in him. "Who's Hannah," I whisper. It's hard to say the name, not knowing who she is to him. A small smile lifts his lips as he looks into my eyes.

"Did you open it? The letter to Hannah?"

"Of course not. I would never invade your privacy like that."

"Didn't you invade Spencer's by snooping to find them in the first place?" *Asshole.* Now he's almost laughing at me, and my blood boils. I thrust my hoodie down to cover myself, feeling too exposed for this conversation.

Sidestepping away from him, I walk to the couch and sit. Gage follows me, and I pat the couch. *"Sitzen."* He eagerly jumps up and relaxes, laying his head on my lap, nuzzled to my stomach.

"Spencer said he liked you better than me. I guess she wasn't lying."

"Who's Hannah, Justin? Why can't you just tell me?"

"Where's the letter?" I point to the corner of the kitchen counter where Spencer laid it when she took it from me. He walks over and picks it up, smoothing the wrinkles out that my fist made, and approaches me on the couch.

"Do you want me to read it or would you like to? Either way is fine with me." Why is he giving me this choice? I just want to know without all the theatrics. Our future relies on the contents of that letter—the identity of Hannah.

"I don't care what it says. Just tell me. *Please.*" The nonexistent patience that I arrived with is on its last thread.

"Okay." He sits on the couch opposite Gage. I've never been so happy to have a dog as a buffer. "You read my letter, right?"

"Yeah."

"Good." He glides his hand down Gage's back, collecting his thoughts. "When my parents, my father, kicked me out at eighteen, I wasn't allowed to say goodbye to my mother. I was devastated. Everything I had known in life was ripped away from me."

"What does this have to do with who Han—"

"Please. Listen, and I'll explain." His voice is full of emotion.

"I was given a suitcase and a check and told not to return. I was barely an adult and only knew of a life on the farm. Ivy was my best friend, and the years after her death were never the same as when she was here. My father never allowed my mother to show me any affection. I was traumatized. I thought my mother didn't love me. I never saw it as her obeying my father until much later." His gaze lands on his hands in his lap, and he plays with his cuticles before continuing.

"I went to a hotel nearby, having no idea what to do. I showed the clerk the check, and he showed me mercy for one night, as long as I went to the bank the next day and paid for the room. That night, as I stared at the ceiling and reflected on my life, I thought it was over. I had nothing. I decided to take a shower and sleep." He pauses and looks at me. "Do you remember when you asked me if I had any name ideas?"

"Yes." He nods.

"When I opened the suitcase to see what the only possessions I now owned on the earth were, I came across something hard amongst the clothes." Justin sighs, getting lost in the memory. "Hannah."

"Hannah?" What does she have to do with his suitcase? Was that his mother's name?

"It could have only been my mother. Her last effort to show me she still loved me. She gave me Hannah."

"Justin, I don't understand."

"Wrapped up in my suitcase was my sister's favorite doll—her Hannah. I never saw it after she was gone. I guess my mother kept it safe somewhere. My father had gotten rid of all Ivy's other things, claiming it was too hard to look at and reminded him his daughter wasn't here. But my mother had Hannah all those years and gave her to me."

"So Hannah is…"

"Hannah was my sister's favorite doll, her prized possession. I wrote that letter to 'Hannah' because I thought maybe we could name our daughter after her. I wrote the letter as if I was speaking to her. I had no intention of you seeing them. I wrote them for myself." I feel like such a fool. I'm a damn fucking fool. How could I ever think there was another woman in Justin's life? This passionate, selfless man was thinking of her the entire time.

"Why haven't you contacted me since you've been back?" He sighs heavily.

"That's a harder question, and I figured out the answer this morning. I was planning to come see you today, but you seemed to have gotten here first."

"What happened today?"

48

Justin

"What happened today?" Everything happened today.

"I've stayed away because I still didn't feel worthy of you."

"Justin, I've never thought that. You've always been enough. You *are* enough."

"Nicole, I couldn't give you what you deserved. I didn't feel like I could be a father to our daughter. I...I saw Katy today." Her head tilts as she waits for me to explain who Katy is. I'm not surprised the name didn't stick out in her mind. "Katy was the little girl that came into my apartment the last time I tried to end my life."

Nicole's hand flies to her mouth, and she gasps. Tears that she's been holding back now stream down her cheeks.

"Do you mind if Spencer comes in for this part of the conversation?" Her eyes flash to her bedroom door, and she nods. I stand and knock. Spencer answers with hesitation, only cracking the door.

"Yes?"

"Will you join us? I want to tell both of you something."
She looks past me to Nicole, who nods her approval. Spencer
sits in an armchair and faces us.

"I was telling Nicole why I stayed at the station this
morning. One of the freshmen recognized me. Spencer,
it was Katy." There's no question on Spencer's face. She
knows who Katy is.

"Katy was there? For the CPR class?"

"Yeah. She…God, I don't even know how to explain what
her words meant to me. She told me I was the best father she's
ever had." I can't help but chuckle at my initial reaction. "Of
course I thought she was ridiculous at first, but the more she
explained what I did for her, the more I believed it. Nicole, I
was worried I couldn't be a father to our daughter, but I was
a father to someone without even trying. I can do this. I can
be a father to her."

"To, Hannah?" Her tone is cautious as she tests out the
name.

"What?" I stare at her. Is she serious? Is she considering
using Hannah to name our baby girl?

"Hannah. I like it. It's beautiful."

"Sorry to break up the mood, but I'd still like to know who
Hannah is." Spencer's eyes dart between the two of us with
questions. I'm still in shock, so Nicole answers.

"Hannah was the name of his sister Ivy's favorite doll that
Justin's mom gave him when his father kicked him out. She
snuck it into his suitcase. He wants to name our daughter
Hannah, and I like it. I think I love it, actually."

"Pumpkin, are we naming our daughter Hannah?" Her
hands surround her belly, and she nods. I join her in her
crying and sit next to her on the couch.

"Are you two ready to kiss and make up because I'd like my house back." I know Spencer is joking. She loves having a purpose. I heard the disappointment in her voice when she said Nicole went back to her apartment. But I'm more than ready to kiss and make up.

"What do you think, Pumpkin? I know we aren't all sorted out, but I'd like to spend time together. Are the puppers at your house?"

"They are. She has a nursery there too. Hannah's nursery." Her face beams using our daughter's name. Hannah. It feels right to be able to honor my sister in this special way.

Standing from the couch, I offer my hand to Nicole, and she accepts. Her hand in mine feels like a puzzle piece clicking together—two halves of a whole reuniting.

When she rises from the couch, I pull her into me. Her belly smushes between us, causing an interesting barrier. Nicole giggles, and it's music to my ears.

"I'm a little bigger than the last time you saw us." Her words, meant as a joke, only make me feel guilty about what I missed. Seeing the change in my demeanor she places a hand on my cheek.

"Please don't ever feel guilty or apologize for putting your mental health first. I wish you would have told me you were struggling. I should have seen it. I've been trained to see it, and for that, *I'm* sorry." She has nothing to apologize for. I should have remembered that she has a psychology background, and we could have worked through it together.

"I promise to communicate better."

"You better. Garret will have your head if you end up back there again."

"No comments from the peanut gallery, Spencer."

405

"You're still in my living room, Justin."

"Wanna get out of here, Pumpkin?" Nicole enthusiastically nods her head.

I turn to face Spencer and kiss her forehead. She scowls at me before smiling. I mouth "Thank you" and she nods.

"Don't mess up this time, Justin."

"Wouldn't dream of it, Spence."

The ride to her apartment was quiet. We took Nicole's car, but I drove. She admitted it's hard to comfortably reach the steering wheel around her belly. I took a chance, laced my fingers with her on the center console, and she accepted them.

My body is on fire from the simple touch as they stay together while we walk up to her apartment.

"Hey, Doc?" My smile instantly reaches my ears. She used my nickname. She's waiting for me to respond, so I squeeze her hand. "I know you're working nights and haven't slept yet. I'm more than happy to cuddle and let you sleep. You don't need to stay up for me or anything." She's an angel thinking about me.

"That's what I was planning. I'll take Java and Beans out for you, and then we can lay down. How does that sound?"

"Perfect. I have to check my numbers anyway."

I lean down closer to her ear, taking a chance. "Good girl." I hear the word "fuck" hiss pass her lips, making me smile. She's still affected by me, and that's all I need to know.

Once inside, I quickly take Java and Beans out to use the bathroom, thinking of everything my mind wants to do to

Nicole. My body yearns to touch and be close to her, and I want nothing more, but my mind can fuck off and wait.

I didn't ask her about her gestational diabetes because that was the beginning of our end before rehab, but I was excited to hear she was still taking it seriously. I know Spencer made our omelets, but she ate it, and I got a notification telling me she logged her food. In fact, when I got my phone back, I saw all of the progress she made over those months. She got the hang of her GD, and I couldn't be more proud.

When I return to the apartment, it's quiet. I put Java and Beans back behind the gate in the kitchen and see that Nicole has filled their bowls already. Walking down the familiar hallways seems as natural as it does foreign. It feels different. The open guest room door tells me why. I stop and look inside—a crib, glider, and changing table line the walls. A small bookshelf sits in the corner, and there are teddy bears in the bedding design and decorations around the room.

"It's not fancy, but it's home." Small hands wrap around my midsection, and I feel her turn to the side to accommodate her bump. I wrap my arms around her and feel the warmth of her embrace.

"It's perfect." I spin in her arms to face her. She's wearing only a sports bra and loose shorts that hang low on her hips under her belly. She sees me looking her up and down and smiles.

"Everything else feels like I'm strangling while I sleep."

"I'm not complaining at all." I nod to the room behind us. "I'd like to have one at my house too."

"I'd like to only have one at one house." *Oh.* My shoulders fall. I made a giant leap, assuming she would also want to have a nursery at my house. She laughs, and I'm confused by her huge smile.

"Not like that, Doc. We still have some things to discuss, but your house was always the ultimate plan. This was set up because you weren't around, and everyone said I needed to be prepared."

"So you want to *only* have one nursery, and you want that to be at my house? That would mean you'd have to spend a lot of time at my house." She nods with a small smile. "Like probably every day." Her smile grows. "And night. Like every day and night. All the time." Her smile reaches ear to ear.

"But let's make that a tomorrow problem. Come on. You need sleep, and this pregnant lady can always nap." She pulls me across the hall, and other than the addition of a bassinet in the corner, everything looks the same.

Nicole crawls into bed, and I take a moment to stare at her ass while I take my clothes off.

"Boxers okay?" I don't want to assume anything.

"Um, do you see how I'm dressed?" I take another look and see how full her breasts have gotten. She looks fucking stunning. "So, yeah. Boxers are perfectly acceptable. Show me what you have on, then hurry and come cuddle me." My pants hit the floor, and I set my glasses on the nightstand before removing my shirt. She watches every move I make. She giggles when she sees my dino boxers, and I shrug.

With hungry eyes matching hers, I crawl into bed and lay down facing her. She places a hand on my cheek, and I place one on her belly.

"Hi." She beams at me.

"Hi."

"I'm going to turn around. It will probably be easier to cuddle. I didn't want you to think I was giving you my back for a negative reason."

"Never." She turns, and I soak in her creamy complexion. Her hair is in her silk bonnet that I've come to love. From the back, you can't even tell she's pregnant. Inching closer, I glide my hand over her hip and around to her bump. I'm amazed at how firm it is.

"When is your next appointment?" She nestles back into my chest, getting comfortable in my arms.

"It's tomorrow. Would you like to come?"

"I'd love nothing more." I lean up and kiss her bare shoulder. She hums in appreciation.

"I missed you, Doc." I run my hand along the curve of her bump, feeling the soft skin under me.

"I missed both my girls."

I wake up to the smell of tomato sauce and garlic and a loud "Shit," exclaimed from across the apartment. The bed beside me is empty, and the sheets are cool, letting me know Nicole has been up for a while. Squinting at the clock, I see it's only a little after six, and I still have several hours before work.

I hear another low string of curses and decide I should rescue Nicole from whatever kitchen disaster she's found herself in. I put my jeans on, forgo the shirt, and quietly head to the kitchen.

The sight before me is comical and stunning. Nicole stands in a neutral-colored t-shirt style dress and bare feet. The dress flows beautifully over her baby bump, but it's covered in red splotches.

Strayed across the counter and lower cabinets are splatters of tomato sauce. A snicker escapes me, and Nicole jumps and turns around.

"I'm sorry. Did I wake you?" She looks at the mess behind her. "This is a disaster. Look at me." She pulls out her dress, looking at the stains.

"What happened?" I walk towards her and grab the paper towels to help clean up.

"I thought I'd make us dinner, or at least something for you to take to work, depending on how long you slept. I was adding minced garlic to the sauce, and the jar fell out of my hand and into the pot, causing all this." Her hands gesture wildly to the massacred kitchen. "I'm sure I've ruined the sauce. I was following a recipe so it had less sugar and—"

I silence her with a finger to her lips. "I'm sure it's not ruined. Let's clean this up, and we can figure it out together." Her head nods under my hand.

We work together to clean up the tomato mess and decide the sauce still tastes great. Nicole strains the gluten free pasta while I clean the cooking dishes.

I'm washing the last pot when I feel a delicate finger trail down my bare spine. I brace my hands on the edge of the sink and drop my head forward, feeling the desire her touch leaves. Feather-like fingers dance across my shoulder blades, and I can't contain the moan that rumbles through my chest. Tiny kisses begin to pepper my back, and I feel my cock stirring awake.

"What are you doing, Pumpkin?" Whatever it is you're thinking, keep fucking doing it. Please.

"Thanking you for your help with the clean up." Every touch of her lips or hands on me sends electric shocks to my dick. I shift on my feet, trying to alleviate any of the pressure in my pants. I inhale a shuttered breath when her hands trace the waste of my jeans to the front.

"Pumpkin, I need you to think about what you're doing. I don't and have never had any willpower when it comes to you." I feel her smile on my back between kisses.

"I know." Her sing-songy words test my resolve.

"So you're aware that I want to turn around right now and say fuck dinner and take you to bed?"

"I know," she repeats.

I growl and spin in her arms, capturing her cheeks in my hands. I bend down, hovering my lips a hair's breadth away.

Her chest heaves under me, and I can tell she wants this as much as I do.

"Pumpkin, I haven't had you in over two months, and once our daughter, Hannah, gets here, it will be at least another two before I can have you again. Do you understand how wild that makes me feel right now?" She nods. My eyes dart between hers, looking for any doubt that she doesn't want this. I find none.

"What do you want, Nicole?"

Without hesitation, she stares me in the eyes. "You."

My lips crash to hers, and she kisses me as ferociously as I do her. I've missed her taste—the softness of her lips. I slide my hands into her hair and deepen our kiss.

"Hey, Doc?"

"Yeah?"

"Say 'fuck dinner.'"

"Fuck. Dinner."

49

Nicole

His taste is intoxicating. His hands on my cheeks, in my hair. I've missed him so much.

"Fuck. Dinner." Those words are magic to my ears. I feel him leaning down, knowing he will try to pick me up.

"Nope. We'll topple over. We will walk to the bedroom like civilized people." His eyes narrow and a predatory look washes over his face.

"You better run, Pumpkin, or I'm taking you right here in the kitchen." A hand reaches down and lightly swats at my ass cheek. "Hurry."

I take off with a giggle, and he stalks after me. Plopping onto the side of the bed, I anxiously wait for him to come into the room. He doesn't keep me waiting. Justin's jeans are already undone and fall to the floor when he reaches the door.

"I was hoping you'd be naked."

"Make it happen, Doc." I stand and raise my hands above my head. The dress easily slides up and off, leaving me in a tan bra and black boyshorts.

"You're fucking stunning. Your body makes me feral knowing I did this to you." His hands stroke reverent circles over my bump. I run my hands through his hair. It's longer now on top. Enough to grab, and I do. He moans when I pull his head back to look at him.

"Keep the length. I like it." He smiles slyly.

"I have another length that I know you'll like." He wiggled his eyebrows at me, and I swat his forehead.

"That was completely cheesy."

"I have something else that's completely cheesy." There are a few seconds of silence until we both burst into laughter.

Our lips meet again, exploring. Remembering all the other times we kissed.

"I love you, Justin." He pulls away, his face full of shock.

"Say it again."

I smile and grab his cheeks. "I love you."

"Fuck." Any restraint he had left is gone. He crawls onto the bed, dragging me to the top until we rest side by side, facing each other. He kisses across my shoulder and chest until it's evident his need takes over, and he pushes me on my back.

"I'm not a rag doll you can throw around at your whim." His mouth sweeps hungrily over my shoulder, sucking and nipping.

"I disagree." He sucks my nipple in over my bra, and I hiss at the sensation. Justin's kisses turn tender as he peppers what feels like every inch of my belly. All the while whispering I love yous to Hannah and his promises for her future.

Continuing lower, his fingers dip into the side of my panties, and I freeze, sitting up.

"Wait." He stops and sits up on his knees.

"I'm sorry. We don't have to do this if you're not ready. I didn't mean to assume."

"No. I want this. I want this so fucking bad. I just..." Why am I embarrassed? I'm a grown fucking woman, this shouldn't be embarrassing.

I took a shower when I woke up and shaved my legs over and over until they were smooth. It was a huge chore. But I couldn't...

"Pumpkin, talk to me." He looks at me with concern.

"You've been gone for almost two months. This belly keeps getting bigger. Some...maintenance has been a struggle."

"Okay." He stretches out the word, trying to make sense of my random sentences.

"My...my...ladygardenisovergrown." The words rush out of me in one long string of letters. Justin grabs my hand and looks into my eyes.

"Can you try that again a little slower?"

I groan. "My lady garden is overgrown. I haven't...no I *can't* see to shave it. It probably looks like a chia pet." Justin's body visibly convulses as he tries to contain his laughter. Grabbing a pillow behind me, I swat him with it.

"It's not funny. Don't laugh at me." His laugh spills over, and I join him. He collapses next to me, and we laugh and giggle until we can't breathe.

"I love you, Pumpkin."

I kiss the end of his nose. "I love you, Doc. Did I kill the mood with my wild garden?"

"Not even the slightest. Let me help you."

"Help. Me." The words have never sounded more foreign put together.

"Let me shave you."

"Um, yeah no." The thought of anyone coming near me with a razor sounds terrifying.

"Do you trust me?"

"That's a low blow. Trusting you and *trusting you* are two very different things."

"Trust me, Pumpkin." He kisses my shoulder. "Trust me." My collarbone. "Trust. Me." He dips his tongue into the hollow at the base of my neck and my back arches. Damn him and his skillful tongue. His hand slides over my belly from top to bottom until it reaches the top of my panties. The tip of his finger sneaks under the elastic, and I grab his hand.

"It's overgrown. There's nothing sexy about it."

"Everything about you is sexy. Let me see what I'm working with, and trust me enough to take care of you."

"Uugh! You're so frustrating. You know you're going to get your way, you damn sweet talker."

"I know." He bounces off the bed and stands. Grabbing my hand, he helps me up and pulls me to the bathroom. He's like a kid in a candy store, knowing he got his way.

"Strip."

"Really? You go from playful to seductive to *trust me*, and now all I get is 'strip.' Bad form, Doc."

Suddenly, I'm pushed up against the wall next to the shower. Every possible inch of him, connecting with me, and pinning me in place. Normally, this feels seductive, but he's compressing my diaphragm, making it even more difficult to breathe. He must see my distress and steps back.

"Shit. I'm sorry." I grab the front of his boxers with one hand and shove the other into them, firmly grabbing his cock.

415

His mouth pops open, and he looks at my hands. "Okay. Not sorry."

I stroke him, causing a bead of pre-cum to leak from his tip and a guttural groan to rumble in his chest.

"Fuuuuck."

"Don't be sorry. We just need to adjust." Justin's hand blindly reaches back, and I hear the water of the shower turn on.

"What are you doing?" I punctuate my question with another hard stroke.

"Goddamn, Pumpkin. Are you trying to kill me? It'll be easier to shave in the shower. Ohhh." I love the literal power that I have in my hands. Each stroke elicits a new moan.

"I want this cock in my mouth so bad, but if I get on my knees, I'm not getting back up." His attempt at a laugh is cut short by another moan as I continue to stroke him. His arms fly up and lean against the wall on either side of my head. Justin's forehead dips to rest on mine, and I breathe in his scent. He smells clean, like fresh laundry that's hung outside to dry in the sun.

"Please stop." There's no conviction in his words. "Fuck, Pumpkin. I don't want to come all over your hand. You're killing me. Please." I love his whining but I show mercy and release him, and he groans at the loss of my touch. I can't help the wicked smile tattooed on my face. "You're the devil. *Please* get naked and get in the shower."

Raising my pointer finger, I boop him on the nose. "Only because you asked so nicely. And as long as you promise not to laugh at my shrubbery."

Teeth poke out as he bites his bottom lip. "How can you expect me not to laugh when you keep comparing it to foliage?"

"Try harder." I unclasp my bra, and his objections stop. While he's distracted, I remove my panties and step into the shower. Justin wipes his hands over his face before groaning and letting his boxers fall to the floor.

When he steps in, there's a noticeable difference in the size of the space with my belly. Justin wastes no time and drops to his knees. I don't have time to protest when I feel his hands running up my inner thigh.

"Put your foot on the ledge so I can see what I'm working with." I want to object, but I know there's no point. This is going to happen. Justin is going to shave me.

"Don't judge me. What I didn't mention is that I tried and failed. Miserably. I can't see down there, but I can only imagine how bad it looks."

"Shh. An artist needs to concentrate on his work." I groan. There's nothing more to do or say. His hand gently wraps around my ankle and lifts with light pressure. Justin guides it to the ledge of the tub and makes sure I'm steady before letting go.

"How bad is it?" I can barely see him around my bump, but he isn't moving much. My body jolts to life when his fingers pull my lips apart, and his hot tongue caresses my core. I brace myself on the wall and his shoulder. With one swipe of his tongue, my knees threaten to buckle.

"I've missed you so fucking much, Doc."

"She…You still taste the same. Just extra seasoning." I smack the top of his head as he chuckles at his dumb joke.

"Am I really about to let you shave me?" I ask the question for myself, but Justin answers.

"Yes, you are. Will you hand me the shaving cream?" His

hand reaches across and picks up the razor, waiting for me to hand him the can. I stretch behind me and pull it from the hanging rack.

This is intimacy. An act that feels monumental in our relationship. Do I trust him? Of course I do, with my life and the life of our daughter.

The can hisses as he squirts the foaming gel into his hand. He gently lathers it into my pubic area until he's satisfied I'm covered. Nerves cause my eyes to close, which almost makes it worse. I've taken away one sense, and it heightens the rest.

The first swipe of the razor is delicate. There's no pain. No scraping or hair pulling. It's perfect. He cleans the razor off under the water stream and swipes again. He continues shaving me, adjusting my body how he needs it. It's become a sensual act between us. Almost like a dance...with moaning. I can't help the noises that escape through my lips. I don't want to.

It's not long before Justin stands and smiles at me. I feel his adept fingers glide through my now bare folds and swirls around my clit.

"You're all better. No more overgrown lady garden, Pumpkin."

"Shut up and make me orgasm." My mind is crazed with lust. Justin spins me around and places my hands on the wall in front of me. Large hands cup my belly before sliding downward. I open my legs to accommodate his fingers, and he purrs in my ear.

"You're already so wet for me. Did that turn you on? My hands on your pussy but not touching you where you yearn for it the most?" He knows me so well, my body even better. The relenting circles made by his fingers bring me closer and closer to the edge. My fingers begin to tingle as my orgasm starts to crest.

I add my forehead to the wall alongside my hands for stability as my orgasm rips through me. Justin is relentless with his finger speed and depth. He doesn't skip a beat, not even slowing until he knows I'm done.

"I *need* to be inside you. Let's get out." I've never turned the water off so quickly. I take two towels off the rack and hand one back to him.

As I step out and look at the fogged-up mirror, a smile crosses my face. I haven't seen it in months. I don't usually take long, steamy showers, so the complete mirror doesn't usually fog over. Down in the corner is the smiley face Justin drew the first time he was here with the word hi. I smile at the fond memory while I dry off.

A sharp sting stretches across my hip, and I see Justin has snapped me with a towel. I rub the offending wound and wait for the lingering pain, but it doesn't come. Instead, desire pools low in my stomach.

"Hmm. You liked that." Turning to face him, I glide my hands up his bare chest and smirk.

"You know I like my spankings…and more. We still have so much to explore." His chest vibrates under my hands as he growls.

"There's so much I want to do to you right now, but I think we should start with a punishment."

"Punishment, huh? What's my crime, Doc?"

"Doubting me for a second that I would ever cheat on you." I open my mouth to speak, and he stops me. "Don't. I don't want your guilt. I want your submission. Get on the bed now and get on your hands and knees." *Fuck. Yes.*

With more pep in my step than should be present with my impending punishment, I rush to the bed and crawl into the middle.

"Fuck you're a sight to see, Pumpkin. God damn, you're gorgeous." I can't help but preen at his attention and praise.

"Mark me, Justin. I want to feel your handprints for days. Sink your fingers so far into my hips you leave bruises while you fill me with your come. I've missed you so fucking much." I think his brain malfunctions at my confession. He's staring at me, eyes slightly squinted, soaking in my words.

"Holy fuck, Pumpkin. Marry me." I giggle at his words. I have no doubt he's serious, and I would say yes, but not now. Right now, I want to feel dirty and used.

"Doc, either spank me, fuck me, or both. You said you needed to be inside me. Well, I need you everywhere on me. Own me, Justin."

He wakes from his trance, and a hand slides through my lips, testing my wetness. He doesn't have to worry. I'm ready.

"Do you remember our safeword?"

"Banana."

"That's a good girl. Use it if you need it."

"I won't."

"I hope not."

Just like I wanted, he grips my hips and thrusts into me fast and deep. His fingers are sure to leave bruises, but the feel of him inside me right now cancels any other thought in my mind.

A few hard thrusts and he pulls out slowly. The air almost hisses with the movement of his hand before it crashes down onto my left ass cheek. He gives me a matching pair before returning to his deep thrusts.

420

"Yes. Harder." I don't know if I'm asking for his hand or his thrusts to be harder, but he somehow knows and does both. The sound of our hips slapping together fills the room. My chest lays on the bed, ass in the air, giving Justin a deep angle to fuck me. His hands smack and soothe. Hips pump and thrust. Moans of pleasure and pain and pleasurable pain hang heavy in the air. We create a symphony with our lust and desire.

I've lost count of how many times he's smacked my ass. Every feeling is so intense I'm caught off guard when a soul-shattering orgasm takes my breath away.

The room fills with cursing, and my orgasm pulls Justin's from him.

"Fucking shit. Your pussy is milking my cock. Take it all, Pumpkin." His words are deliciously erotic. When he finally pulls out, I immediately feel the emptiness. He rolls to my side, and I follow, facing him. I shift, already feeling the soreness from where his fingers gripped my hips.

"Was I too rough?"

"God, no. You were amazing. I asked you to be rougher, and you listened." I brush my fingers over his chest. "You need to leave soon, don't you? It's a little before ten."

"I do. I wish I didn't have to, though."

I trace my finger along his jawline. "You don't technically *have* to. But Spencer would have your head and then mine."

"I happen to like your head. I'd hate for you to lose it." I push his chest, but he doesn't budge. "Go to work."

"Are you getting rid of me already? I'm wounded."

"Oh shush. Rub some cream on my ass before you leave me."

"With pleasure."

50

Justin

Keep *the line of communication open. Always.*
That was the line that we focused on the most in
therapy for the six weeks I was there. Nicole and I
talked. I communicated. Her anger stemmed from the letter,
and that was dealt with.

The feel of her under me, around me again, was heaven.

"I take it you did more than just kiss and make up?" Spencer
snaps me out of my daydream.

"We worked out our issues." My cheeks hurt with the
amount of smiling I've done tonight. I know I'll smile later
while eating the spaghetti I brought from home.

I rubbed arnica cream on Nicole's ass before I left. She
had two very clear handprints that will most likely form into
bruises. I'm proud of my trophies.

"Other than the baby's name, did you happen to talk about
the future?"

"We didn't. We just took the time to reconnect." My phone
buzzes in my pocket, and I check it, seeing Nicole is calling.

"Hey, Pumpkin."

422

"How do you know when your water breaks?" All the air leaves my lungs and I sit up straight in the passenger seat of the ambulance.

"Why are you asking? Do you think it's happened?"

She laughs, but it has a nervous undertone. "If I was confident, I wouldn't have to ask."

"Are you having contractions? Are you in any pain?"

"Justin, is everything okay?" I wave Spencer's question off with my hand.

"Mostly just Braxton Hicks." I cup my hand over the speaker and tell Spencer to head to Nicole's apartment. She must hear me and lets out a deep sigh.

"You don't need to come here. I'm fine."

"Why are you asking about your water breaking?" I can tell she's hesitant to answer my question.

"Well, I was coming back inside from taking the dogs out after you left. I decided to use the stairs to go back up, and I felt Hannah do a big shift. It took my breath away. Then she was sitting on my bladder, and I really had to pee but didn't quite make it back to the apartment. And now it kind of feels like I can't control my bladder."

"Hey, Pumpkin?"

"Yeah?"

"It's baby time. Are your bags packed?" *Shit.* I don't have a bag packed. We never got around to talking about any of this. I don't know her birth needs and wants. It always felt like we had plenty of time, and then we didn't.

"I have a bag in the nursery, but how do you know it's time? I've read that bladder issues late in pregnancy can be a real problem."

"Nicole. Pumpkin, trust me. We'll be there in ten minutes.

423

I have to call work and make arrangements. It never hurts to get checked out anyway. Call your doctor."

"The dogs? What if we get stuck at the hospital?"

"We can make arrangements for Java and Beans."

"I'll take them," Spencer offers. "Gage enjoyed them that day at Annie's house." What? When?

"When were you at Annie's house with Gage? Nevermind. Did you hear Spencer, Pumpkin? She'll take care of the dogs for us."

"Okay. I'll see you in ten." We hang up, and my mind feels like it's misfiring. All of my doubts try to push themselves to the surface, but I'm stronger than them now. I always have been. Seeing Katy helped me realize that. Her words gave me the last push I needed to trust in myself as much as everyone trusts me. That doesn't mean I'm not nervous.

I call the chief and let him know what's going on. He's going to call in another crew and give Spencer and me the night off.

"Spencer, will you—"

"I'll go to your house and pack you a bag once I get the ambulance returned and the dogs settled." We're like a well-oiled machine, as usual. "Are you ready?"

A chuckle bubbles up my chest. "Do I have a choice? But yeah. Yeah, I am. I'm ready to be a dad. I have a great example of how not to be one. I'm ready to meet Hannah."

We pull up to Nicole's apartment, and she's ready at her door, waiting for us. I pull her face into mine and kiss her passionately. She's wearing another T-shirt dress. This time, it's a navy blue color. They must be comfortable.

"How are you feeling?"

"Silly. I swear I've just lost control of my bladder, and

you're being ridiculous."

"You can never be too careful. What did the doctor say?" I pick up her bag from its spot inside the door and grab the leashes off the wall, handing them to Spencer.

"I spoke to his receptionist. She's going to call ahead to the Emergency Department and let them know I'm coming to get checked. We'll go from there."

"Good." I thread my hands through her hair and kiss her forehead. "I have a question. Do you want me in the room with you? We haven't discussed it, and I don't want to assume."

She looks panicked and sounds it when words start rapidly tumbling out of her. "What? Of course I want you in there. Don't you want to see the birth of your daughter? Do you not want to be in there with me? You don't have to be if you don't want to. Oh god. I'm sorry. I just assumed you'd want to—" I silence her mild panic with a kiss.

"I want to. I absolutely want to. I want to support you through your contractions, and I want to cut our daughter's cord. I especially can't wait to hear all the mean names you call me as you're dealing with the birth." I watch her eyes exaggeratedly roll back into her head.

"Okay." She sighs with relief.

"Let's go have a baby."

"Let's go meet our daughter." She smiles sweetly with adoration in her eyes.

"Let's go meet our daughter," I agree.

"You're brave and fierce, and you've got this."

"Why did I want to be brave? 'I don't need drugs. I'm a strong independent woman.'" She mocks her former self from two hours ago.

"Think of what this pain will bring us. She's almost here. Today will be Hannah's birthday."

The Emergency Department confirmed Nicole's water broke, and the monitors showed she was indeed having actual contractions, not Braxton Hicks.

I chuckle, remembering how mortified Nicole was when we first got back to the exam room.

"Nicole, come on back." Axel beams at us as we follow him to our room. I was glad to read the text back from Axel letting me know he was working tonight. He had us back and in an exam room before we finished filling out paperwork at the front desk.

"Thank you for making this quick, Axel. I feel ridiculous. I'm not feeling any contractions, and I think we'll be laughing about this once we realize I can't hold my bladder anymore. Silly girl." She pokes her stomach, mockingly chastising our daughter.

We follow Axel to an exam room, and he motions to the gown on the bed.

"Here's where I get to tell you to strip, and it's not for my sexual pleasure." He winks at me, and if I wasn't in a euphoric mood, I'd probably punch him for his comment. "I'll give you a few minutes to change, and I'll come back to take your vitals. Your doctor called ahead and said he'd be here in the next thirty minutes, but we can administer the test to see if you're leaking amniotic fluid before he gets here." He smiles and closes the door behind him.

Nicole pulls her dress over her head, beginning to change, and when she turns to pick up the gown, I see them.

"Oh shit."

426

"What's wrong?"

"Nothing is wrong per se. I did exactly as you asked of me earlier and...well... you're very much 'marked'."

"No. Oh god, no. I didn't even think of it. We have to leave. I'm probably not in labor anyway." She reduces her voice to a whisper and continues. "I can't let these professional people see me with these bruises. What do they even look like?" She begins to spin in a circle as she attempts to see what her ass and upper thighs look like.

"Justin, help me. Take a picture so I can see how bad it is." I'm biting my lips, trying not to laugh at this situation, but I'm not doing the greatest job. She glares at me with eyes I know will stop our kids in their tracks in years to come. Kids? Plural? "Justin," she hisses.

"Okay, hold still." I pull my phone out of my pocket and snap a quick picture. I take a second to admire it before she snatches it out of my hand.

"Perv."

"Hey, I took a picture, so it'll last longer. That's how the saying goes, right?" I wink, and she huffs.

"Holy shit." Her eyes widen at the bruises and marks I left just a few hours ago.

"Okay, but also, ho-ly shit, right. You look beautiful."

"Justin, I can't let the doctors see my bruised and battered ass." Every word from her mouth is whisper-shouted.

"And thighs."

"Ugh! You're impossible."

"Knock, knock. Everyone descent?"Axel peeks his head in the door, and Nicole hides behind me.

"We have a little problem," Nicole starts.

"Come on in, Axel."

427

"Justin."

"Everything alright?"Axel looks between us, his head tilted in confusion.

"Nicole is nervous because we had rough sex today, and she has a few bruises." Nicole's hand grips my arm and squeezes. Through gritted teeth, she says, "Stop it," and I can't contain my laughter.

"We aren't strangers to a few bruises around here."

"There's also handprints." I know Axel didn't hear her because I barely did, and she's standing right behind me.

"What?"

"There's..." She looks around the room, making sure no one else can hear, despite it just being the three of us behind a closed door. "Handprints."

"Oh." Axel's head slowly nods, and a smile creeps across his face. When he raises his fist for me to bump, I feel Nicole's nails dig into my arm when we connect.

"Axel," she warns. "If you make one more joke out of this, I'll run my hand through your hair and ruin your curls." To anyone else, that would sound like an absolutely ridiculous threat, but after hearing them talk about their hair care routines, I know it's a valid one for Axel.

Axel raises his hands in surrender, not wanting to anger the pregnant hairdresser anymore. "Can I see so that I can mark it in the chart and we don't have any issues?"

"Show him the picture." She hides her face in my back.

I turn so I'm facing her. "Pumpkin, unfortunately, even though we're friends, he'll need to actually see the marks. Code of ethics trumps friendship in most cases." She's not happy, but I lean over and grab the dressing gown. "These don't cover much of your ass anyway."

"Har-har." I hold up the standard ugly blue patterned wrap

gown, and she slips her arms in. I help her tie the back, giving her some sense of modesty.

"Nicole, would you feel more comfortable with a female nurse? I could get one."

"No. It's okay. You aren't seeing much more than if I was in a bikini." I step aside so her back is exposed. Axel looks at me and winks after seeing my handiwork. Luckily, Nicole can't see since her back is to us.

"Hey Nicole, if he did this much damage from your escapades tonight, I can guarantee that's why you're having a baby today."

"What is so funny?" I shake my head and quickly wipe the expression off my face, giving her my full attention.

"Annie had it so easy. Show up, get meds in a needle, get cut open, and bam...babies."

"Hey, mama?" The nurse at Nicole's feet calls up to her. "Your friend with the c-section may not have felt any pain at the time, but I promise it wasn't easier. Once your little girl is out, you'll be able to hold her and love her, and you'll forget every moment of pain you're feeling right now."

Nicole has been pushing for four hours, and she's exhausted. Despite her protest, I haven't stopped praising her, and I mean every word of it. She's never looked more beautiful to me than she is right now. Her hair is a mess of curls piled high on top of her head. Tendrils have fallen and matted to her forehead. Her cheeks are flushed from her exertion, and a sheen of sweat is across her chest.

Using a cool, damp cloth, I wipe her forehead and rest mine against hers. "You're about to bring our baby girl into the world and make me the happiest man alive. You can do this, Pumpkin. One ten-count at a time. Are you ready?" She nods.

"Here comes another one, mama. Ready and push. Ten, nine, eight, seven, six. Wanna see Dad?" The nurse smiles up at me as she continues to count. Nicole grabs my arm, eyes wide as I try to look.

"Relax. Keep pushing. I'm a professional, remember?"

"Two, one. Great Job. I think the next contraction will do it. Let me grab the doctor." The nurse picks up the phone and makes the call.

"Are you ready? I'm so proud of you. She's almost here."

"Don't watch. What if I poop? What if I poop on the baby?" I love her panic. I run soothing fingers across her cheek.

"For one, that's not how gravity works, but also, I don't care. I want to watch our daughter being born. Poop or not, I'm not afraid." She flops back onto the bed.

"There will be no more secrets between us anymore."

"Nope. And if you need me to help you change your mesh undies after she's here, I'll gladly help with that, too." She props herself back up again.

"Mesh what?" Nicole looks horrified.

"Did Annie not tell you about the fancy lingerie they give you? You'll love it. Just wait." She opens her mouth to respond, but we're interrupted by the doctor. He pulls on a pair of gloves and sits on the stool between Nicole's legs.

"Alright, let's wish this girl a happy birthday, Mom and Dad."

Nicole does incredibly well over the next several pushes, and our beautiful baby girl is born and placed on her chest. I get to cut the cord, and although this isn't the first cord I've ever cut, it never felt as paramount as this one.

"You did it, Pumpkin. She's beautiful." I kiss her forehead and, lift the tiny blue and pink striped hat, and kiss Hannah's, too. The room has finally settled after all of Hannah's measurements and checkups were done, and we're alone— our brand new family of three.

"She's perfect." Nicole runs a delicate finger over her tiny cheek.

"Pumpkin, I'd love nothing more than if my two favorite girls would come home with me when they get sprung from this place." She smiles sweetly and speaks to Hannah.

"What do you think, baby girl? Do you want to go live with Daddy?" *Holy shit. Daddy. I'm a daddy.* It's such an obvious title. I have a child; therefore, I'm their daddy. But that specific word, daddy, hasn't crossed my mind. Father, yeah. Even when the doctor called me dad, it didn't evoke this visceral feeling of pride and ownership.

Hannah is mine, and I'm her daddy.

I have a daughter. She's mine to love and to protect.

51

Nicole

Six months later

"Blake, everything looks beautiful." Their house is decorated in black and gold everywhere you look. Balloons, streamers, and tablecloths surround the inside and outside of the house, with a huge banner reading "HALFWAY TO ONE" as the room's focal point.

Annie insists we celebrate every milestone, and Hannah has become an extension of their celebrations. Of course, their half-birthday would be a big one. Our babies are only two weeks apart and relatively follow the same timelines for now. When they started solid foods last month, she threw a party with everything pureed. Needless to say, I left that party hungry. When all three babies finally rolled over for the first time, she had rolls imported from around the world, and we had more carbs than we knew what to do with.

I'll never be upset to see others love on my daughter. Our daughter. Our Hannah. Warm arms wrap around me from behind, and gentle kisses pepper my neck.

"Your brother is an awesome uncle." He's sitting on their gray sectional, bouncing Hannah on his leg, and she's squealing with laughter.

"Yeah, well, his sister is an awesome aunt." I look down at a sleeping Rory in my arms. His lips pout into an adorable heart shape, and he sighs in his sleep.

"That she is." Justin rubs a thumb over Rory's tiny shoulder. "We need one of these."

"We have one right over there." I look back to see Cole now blowing raspberries on Hanna's tummy. Justin pulls my attention and kisses me tenderly while I rock a sleeping baby in my arms. "Yes, but we don't have one with parts like his."

"Parts like…Oh. You want a little boy." He nods into my shoulder.

"Don't you think Hannah would like a sibling?"

"Don't you think Hannah's Mommy would like an engagement ring?" It's been our running tease for a while. Hannah has Justin's last name. There was never any doubt in my mind that she would.

Justin will ask me to do something, and I'll tell him I can't because it sounds like a wife chore. I'll ask him for a favor, and he'll tell me to call my other boyfriend because he's trying to upgrade to husband. It's become fun and flirty and the start of several role playing scenes in the bedroom.

"Done."

I have to think of what I said for him to answer that way. Baby brain is a real thing. He flags down Annie and gestures for her to come take Rory.

"I'm okay; I can hold him." He ignores me, and when Annie approaches, she takes the sleeping bundle from my arms with a wide smile.

I notice movement out of the corner of my eye and see Justin down on one knee.

Oh. Done. I get it now. I basically just told him I wanted a ring, and here he is proposing. He opens a small black box with a ring with a large blue circular sapphire surrounded by diamonds.

He listened. I told him I wanted a non-traditional engagement ring and thought a sapphire would look beautiful. And I was right.

"Nicole Alivia McGrath. I'm ready to ask you my daily question." I chuckle and shake my head at him. "Will you join Hannah and me and become a Webb? I could make some grand speech and get all mushy, but that's not what you want to hear. I tell you every day how incredible you are and how much I love you. So, I'll cut to the chase. Will you marry me, Pumpkin?"

"Without a doubt, yes." He stands and pulls me in for a deep, long, passionate kiss. It seems to go on forever when we hear a throat clear. We pull away to see Cole standing beside us, holding a smiling Hannah.

"I thought she might want to celebrate with you?" I take our daughter from my brother's arms and mold her between Justin and me.

"I love you, Pumpkin."

"I love you, Doc. It might be nice to make another one of these again soon."

Justin

I beam at my daughter and my new fiancé, thinking how I could have missed this moment in my life. None of this would have been possible if, almost seven years ago, a little girl I fed powdered mac n cheese to and made up silly songs on a piano with, hadn't been persistent and walked into my apartment unannounced.

Aspire to Inspire; Before you Expire
THE END

Epilogue

It's coffee day. One day a month, I volunteer to bring everyone on shift a cup of coffee. Because it makes me less awkward when my co-workers can associate me with a normal mundane task. When I hand them a cup of coffee, I hide behind my mask and put on my "work smile." They forget that I don't understand sarcasm as well as my peers or that I might answer a question they haven't voiced because I noticed their micro expressions. Something I've perfected over the years to help me with social cues.

The Hippie Bean is a little shop that personifies its name. It always smells like patchouli with an undertone of coffee. Rainbow tapestries drape along the walls, and I have to avoid staring at them, or they make my mind feel fuzzy with the overload of colors.

The owner, Flower, opens early to complete my order so I can make it to work on time. She knows how much I hate being late. Flower slipped and broke her leg in the store about two years ago and I was one of the paramedics who came to help her. She took one look at me and proclaimed we were kindred spirits.

The doorbell dings, and I glance at my watch before looking over my shoulder. It's still fifteen minutes before opening. No one should be coming in yet.

My eyes connect with a rugged-looking man wearing a

cowboy hat and boots in the middle of Chicago. It's not something you see every day yet he doesn't look out of place. His brown beard shows hints of red and I can see dark auburn hair peeking out under his hat.

"Thanks for waiting, asshole." The doorbell dings again, and my brain tickles. That voice. Why do I know that voice?

"You're too slow, dickhead." The man in the cowboy hat has a slight drawl to his words. It's subtle and probably not noticeable to the untrained ear, but I pick up on those things.

"Boys, behave." Flower startles me with her reprimand as she stacks the last of my coffees into a large box.

"Sorry, Miss Flower." That. Voice. It's deep and rich and so familiar. It's paired with dark green eyes framed by thick black lashes and hair that reminds me of the color of cinnamon.

"I'm just finishing up with Spencer, and I'll go grab your pastries from the back." The bearded man tips his hat at me and then Flower. "Oh, don't leave yet, Spencer. I want to give you some pastries as well."

"That's not necessary, Flower." She's gone before I've finished my sentence.

"There's no use arguing, darling. Just let her spoil you." Cowboy hat offers his hand to me. "Name's Tucker. I'd like it if you let me help you take this out to your vehicle." He nods to the box of coffees on the counter as I shake his hand.

Handshaking is a societal norm and something that I've perfected. Similar to my ability to handle the ambulance sirens when I drive, I can control a handshake's firmness and general length, which makes touching strangers acceptable. You can also tell a lot about someone's character by their handshake—Tucker's handshake is firm and confident, just how his personality seems to be.

"I can take care of it, but thank you." I offer a small smile in thanks. Sometimes my tone is too flat and a smile eases my words.

"No use arguing with me either." Tucker winks and reaches for the box. Once again, the doorbell dings. I freeze. I'm the only one facing the door as the masked man dressed all in black pointing a gun stalks in.

"Nobody move! I just want the money." Tucker stops with his hands inches away from my coffee box, and his friend's entire demeanor changes.

"Alright, boys, I have all of your—Ahhhh!" Flower drops her box of pastries and screams as the masked man steps closer, pointing the gun at her. Tucker wraps his arm around my waist and slowly pulls me behind him.

"I just want the money," the man repeats to Flower. With her hands in the air, she takes tentative steps toward the cash register. Tucker and his friend have a silent conversation, and I hope they aren't planning to do anything irrational. I'm calm on the outside, but my heart is racing like the Indy 500.

Flower opens the register with trembling hands and passes over all of the money. The masked man takes it and walks backward with his head on a swivel, watching all of us. When he passes Tucker's friend, he spins on his heels to walk out while shoving the money and gun into his pockets.

As if it was slow playing on a movie screen, Tucker's friend whips around and tackles the masked man to the ground in a bear hug.

"Lincoln, be careful." Tucker sees the gun fall out of the masked man's pocket and rushes over to...Lincoln? I focus my attention on the two men rolling around when I hear

Flower talking on the phone. She must be talking to the police.

"Yes, Officer Reed has him tackled to the floor. Please hurry." *Officer Reed?* Lincoln Reed. It can't be.

"Miss Flower, do you have any zip ties?" Lincoln's baritone voice booms with exertion from the floor. He's sitting on the thief's back holding both his hands in one of his, and the other hand is holding...a gun? A quick look shows me it's not the gun that the thief had because that's kicked in the corner. Where was Lincoln hiding a gun?

"Are you okay, Little Miss?" Tucker's hands rub up and down my arms. I watch and wait for the feeling of unease to wash over me, but it doesn't come.

Sirens outside catch my attention, and two uniformed police officers run through the door. They take over for Lincoln and handcuff the thief, bringing him to his feet and escorting him out the door.

I close my eyes, take a deep breath and count backward from five, attempting to refocus myself. There's too much unknown going on around me, and I need to concentrate on one thing. Opening my eyes I can feel them bouncing around the room, attempting to find anything to help my brain regroup.

"Hey. It's Spencer, right?" Tucker grabs my cheeks with his large hands, and once again, I wait for the itchy feeling I usually get when someone touches me. Why doesn't this man elicit the same reactions that everyone else does? Justin is the only other person I've ever felt this instant connection with, that someone's touch didn't bother me. "Little Miss, talk to me. Please."

I look deep into Tucker's eyes. They're blue. I couldn't see them until now because they were hidden by his hat. They're as blue as the color of glass. I can focus on his eyes. My father collects blue glass. Something familiar to focus on.

I grab his wrists to further solidify my connection—to ground me. Tucker's thumbs slowly glide over my cheek, and suddenly, my eyes are closed, and warm lips feather across mine. He's holding his breath, and I realize I am too. I can't tell who got us to this position, him or me. I don't remember moving, but the light brush of his lips turns searing, and my hands fist into his t-shirt.

Tucker's tongue sweeps over my lower lip, asking permission to enter, and I part mine. As our tongues tangle together, I feel his fingertips massage the nape of my neck. I imagine if my hair wasn't in Dutch braids, he'd be running his hand through it, and the thought of that doesn't make me uncomfortable.

"Spencer, are you o—Oh. Okay." I pull away at the sound of Justin's voice. What was I doing? I look down at my hand and release Tucker's shirt.

"Justin, what are you doing here?" My focus hasn't left Tucker's face as I talk to my partner, Justin.

"I-I have to go. Thank you for…" I'm at a loss of words from the smile that radiated on Tucker's face.

"You're welcome. And Spencer,"—He reaches into his back pocket and pulls a card out of his wallet.—"I'm the owner of Midnight Moonshine. If you'd ever like to come by, it's on the house." He leans close to my ear. "That kiss was fucking incredible, Little Miss. Thank you."

Tucker walks towards the door, and Justin steps up beside me. I watch Tucker clap a hand on Lincoln's shoulder as they walk outside to talk to the officers and Flower.

440

"What the hell was that, Spence? I heard the call come on the radio and knew you'd be here getting everyone's coffees. I got here as quickly as possible to find you playing tonsil hockey with...Who the hell was he?" Justin plucks the business card from my hand.

"No way. Do you know who that is? That's Tucker Bennett. He owns Midnight Moonshine, according to his card. And you just had your tongue down his throat. I'm proud of you, friend." Now I understand the cowboy hat and boots. But...

"Do you know who he was with? Officer Lincoln Reed, I believe."

"Linc? You know him. Lincoln is one of our dispatchers." Dispatcher. It's him. The voice I recognized. The one that makes my stomach flutter whenever I hear it on the radio.

"Of course. Why don't you take the box of coffee and bring it back to the station? The police might want to talk to me, and I don't want to leave my car here. Let Chief know I'll be at the station as soon as I can."

"I'll make sure to let Miller know, too. He was freaking out a bit." *Crap*.

"Justin, what the hell did I just do?"

About the Author

Casiddie is a single mom to five amazing children who are her biggest cheerleaders. Casiddie enjoys writing contemporary romance but hopes to dive into more darker subjects in the near future.

You can connect with me on:

 https://www.facebook.com/casiddiewilliams

 https://www.tiktok.com/@casiddiewilliams_author

Also by Casiddie Williams

Welcome to my little corner. I hope you've enjoyed reading about Justin and Nicole. Justin's book is the second in a three book series. Spencer and her men (yes MEN) are next!

Hazel is the first in a four book series. Dellah and Wynnie's stories are available now and Elliot's will be the final book.

All my works can be found in KU.

If you enjoyed this, or any of my novels, I'd love you forever if you'd leave a review on the platform of your choosing. <3

Hazel's Harem

A new job opportunity brings curvaceous, single mom Hazel Gibson, back to her hometown where she finds her hands full with a little more than just her 12 year old daughter.

When two gorgeous men offer her a six week proposition to be with both of them together, no strings attached, Hazel decides you only live once, and why choose if you don't have to?

But life has a habit of throwing Hazel curve balls, and she finds herself having to make some major life decisions to protect her family. Curve ball #1: When you're already juggling two men, what's one more?

This is a why choose MMFM novel suitable for 18+

Annie You're Okay

Danika "Annie" Poulsen is a grumpy Billionaire and Dominatrix who has everything she could ever want out of life at the age of 34. A thriving software company, a gorgeous submissive girlfriend, and a trouble-making Doberman complete her life.

Blake Rogers is a 29 year old bubbly secretary who is willing to submit and give her body and pleasure over to her billionaire girlfriend.

Together, they're happy in their relationship and their roles within it until they meet a man who shakes up everything they know about themselves and each other.

Cole McGrath is starting over in a new town at 22. A dog walker with an Alpha personality and a side of Golden Retriever mixed in, it wasn't part of his plan to meet two beautiful women and rock their worlds in more ways than one.

When tragedy strikes and their lives and relationships are tested, will they be able to repair their shattered pieces?

Will they be okay?

This is an FFM poly novel suitable for ages 18+

445

Made in the USA
Middletown, DE
26 April 2025

74680210R00272